ODD THOMAS

Dean Koont
Pennsylvania.
number one b
wife Gerda anc
California.

ALSO BY DEAN KOONTZ

The Face

By The Light of the Moon	*The Vision*
One Door Away From Heaven	*The Face of Fear*
From the Corner of His Eye	*Night Chills*
False Memory	*Shattered*
Seize the Night	*The Voice of the Night*
Fear Nothing	*The Servants of Twilight*
Mr. Murder	*The House of Thunder*
Dragon Tears	*The Key to Midnight*
Hideaway	*The Eyes of Darkness*
Cold Fire	*Shadowfires*
The Bad Place	*Winter Moon*
Midnight	*The Door to December*
Lightning	*Dark Rivers of the Heart*
Watchers	*Icebound*
Strangers	*Strange Highways*
Twilight Eyes	*Intensity*
Darkfall	*Sole Survivor*
Phantoms	*Ticktock*
Whispers	*The Funhouse*
The Mask	*Demon Seed*

ODD THOMAS

DEAN KOONTZ

HarperCollins*Publishers*

HarperCollins*Publishers*
77–85 Fulham Palace Road
Hammersmith, London W6 8JB

www.harpercollins.co.uk

This paperback edition 2004
1

First published in Great Britain by
HarperCollins*Publishers* 2004

A catalogue record for this book
is available from the British Library

ISBN 978-0-00-785185-0

Typeset in Trump Mediaeval by
Palimpsest Book Production Limited,
Polmont, Stirlingshire

Printed and bound in Great Britain by
Clays Ltd, St Ives plc

To the Old Girls:
Mary Crowe, Gerda Koontz,
Vicky Page, and Jana Prais.
We'll get together. We'll
nosh. We'll tipple. We'll
dish, dish, dish.

Hope requires the contender
Who sees no virtue in surrender.
From the cradle to the bier,
The heart must persevere.
—*The Book of Counted Joys*

ODD THOMAS

CHAPTER 1

MY NAME IS ODD THOMAS, THOUGH IN this age when fame is the altar at which most people worship, I am not sure why you should care who I am or that I exist.

I am not a celebrity. I am not the child of a celebrity. I have never been married to, never been abused by, and never provided a kidney for transplantation into any celebrity. Furthermore, I have no desire to be a celebrity.

In fact I am such a nonentity by the standards of our culture that *People* magazine not only will never feature a piece about me but might also reject my attempts to subscribe to their publication on the grounds that the black-hole gravity of my noncelebrity is powerful enough to suck their entire enterprise into oblivion.

I am twenty years old. To a world-wise adult, I am little more than a child. To any child, however, I'm old enough to be distrusted, to be excluded forever from the magical community of the short and beardless.

Consequently, a demographics expert might conclude that my sole audience is other young men and women currently adrift between their twentieth and twenty-first birthdays.

In truth, I have nothing to say to that narrow audience. In my experience, I don't care about most of the things that other twenty-year-old Americans care about. Except survival, of course.

I lead an unusual life.

By this I do not mean that my life is better than yours. I'm sure that your life is filled with as much happiness, charm, wonder, and abiding fear as anyone could wish. Like me, you are human, after all, and we know what a joy and terror that is.

I mean only that my life is not typical. Peculiar things happen to me that don't happen to other people with regularity, if ever.

For example, I would never have written this memoir if I had not been commanded to do so by a four-hundred-pound man with six fingers on his left hand.

His name is P. Oswald Boone. Everyone calls him Little Ozzie because his father, Big Ozzie, is still alive.

Little Ozzie has a cat named Terrible Chester. He loves that cat. In fact, if Terrible Chester were to use up his ninth life under the wheels of a Peterbilt, I am afraid that Little Ozzie's big heart would not survive the loss.

Personally, I do not have great affection for Terrible Chester because, for one thing, he has on several occasions peed on my shoes.

His reason for doing so, as explained by Ozzie, seems credible, but I am not convinced of his truthfulness. I mean to say that I am suspicious of Terrible Chester's veracity, not Ozzie's.

Besides, I simply cannot fully trust a cat who claims to be fifty-eight years old. Although photographic evidence exists to support this claim, I persist in believing that it's bogus.

For reasons that will become obvious, this manuscript cannot be published during my lifetime, and my effort will not be repaid with royalties while I'm alive. Little Ozzie suggests that I should leave my literary estate to the loving maintenance of Terrible Chester, who, according to him, will outlive all of us.

I will choose another charity. One that has not peed on me.

Anyway, I'm not writing this for money. I am writing it to save my sanity and to discover if I can convince myself that my life has purpose and meaning enough to justify continued existence.

Don't worry: These ramblings will not be insufferably gloomy. P. Oswald Boone has sternly instructed me to keep the tone light.

"If you don't keep it light," Ozzie said, "I'll sit my four-hundred-pound ass on you, and that's not the way you want to die."

Ozzie is bragging. His ass, while grand enough, probably weighs no more than a hundred and fifty pounds. The other two hundred and fifty are distributed across the rest of his suffering skeleton.

When at first I proved unable to keep the tone light, Ozzie suggested that I be an unreliable narrator. "It worked for Agatha Christie in *The Murder of Roger Ackroyd*," he said.

In that first-person mystery novel, the nice-guy narrator turns out to be the murderer of Roger Ackroyd, a fact he conceals from the reader until the end.

Understand, I am not a murderer. I have done nothing evil that I am concealing from you. My unreliability as a narrator has to do largely with the tense of certain verbs.

Don't worry about it. You'll know the truth soon enough.

Anyway, I'm getting ahead of my story. Little Ozzie and Terrible Chester do not enter the picture until after the cow explodes.

This story began on a Tuesday.

For you, that is the day after Monday. For me, it is a day that, like the other six, brims with the potential for mystery, adventure, and terror.

You should not take this to mean that my life is romantic and magical. Too much mystery is merely an annoyance. Too much adventure is exhausting. And a little terror goes a long way.

Without the help of an alarm clock, I woke that Tuesday morning at five, from a dream about dead bowling-alley employees.

I never set the alarm because my internal clock is so reliable. If I wish to wake promptly at five, then before going to bed I tell myself three times that I must be awake sharply at 4:45.

While reliable, my internal alarm clock for some reason runs fifteen minutes slow. I learned this years ago and have adjusted to the problem.

The dream about the dead bowling-alley employees has troubled my sleep once or twice a month for three years. The details are not yet specific enough to act upon. I will have to wait and hope that clarification doesn't come to me too late.

So I woke at five, sat up in bed, and said, "Spare me that I may serve," which is the morning prayer that my Granny Sugars taught me to say when I was little.

Pearl Sugars was my mother's mother. If she had been my father's mother, my name would be Odd Sugars, further complicating my life.

Granny Sugars believed in bargaining with God. She called Him "that old rug merchant."

Before every poker game, she promised God to

spread His holy word or to share her good fortune with orphans in return for a few unbeatable hands. Throughout her life, winnings from card games remained a significant source of income.

Being a hard-drinking woman with numerous interests in addition to poker, Granny Sugars didn't always spend as much time spreading God's word as she promised Him that she would. She believed that God expected to be conned more often than not and that He would be a good sport about it.

You can con God and get away with it, Granny said, if you do so with charm and wit. If you live your life with imagination and verve, God will play along just to see what outrageously entertaining thing you'll do next.

He'll also cut you some slack if you're astonishingly stupid in an amusing fashion. Granny claimed that this explains why uncountable millions of breathtakingly stupid people get along just fine in life.

Of course, in the process, you must never do harm to others in any serious way, or you'll cease to amuse Him. Then payment comes due for the promises you didn't keep.

In spite of drinking lumberjacks under the table, regularly winning at poker with stone-hearted psychopaths who didn't like to lose, driving fast cars with utter contempt for the laws of physics (but never while intoxicated), and eating a diet rich in pork fat, Granny Sugars died peacefully in her sleep at the age of seventy- two. They found her with a nearly empty snifter of brandy on the nightstand, a book by her favorite novelist turned to the last page, and a smile on her face.

Judging by all available evidence, Granny and God understood each other pretty well.

Pleased to be alive that Tuesday morning, on the dark side of the dawn, I switched on my nightstand lamp and surveyed the chamber that served as my bedroom, living room, kitchen, and dining room. I never get out of bed until I know who, if anyone, is waiting for me.

If visitors either benign or malevolent had spent part of the night watching me sleep, they had not lingered for a breakfast chat. Sometimes simply getting from bed to bathroom can take the charm out of a new day.

Only Elvis was there, wearing the lei of orchids, smiling, and pointing one finger at me as if it were a cocked gun.

Although I enjoy living above this particular two-car garage, and though I find my quarters cozy, *Architectural Digest* will not be seeking an exclusive photo layout. If one of their glamour scouts saw my place, he'd probably note, with disdain, that the second word in the magazine's name is not, after all, *Indigestion*.

The life-size cardboard figure of Elvis, part of a theater-lobby display promoting *Blue Hawaii*, was where I'd left it. Occasionally, it moves—or is moved—during the night.

I showered with peach-scented soap and peach shampoo, which were given to me by Stormy Llewellyn. Her real first name is Bronwen, but she thinks that makes her sound like an elf.

My real name actually is Odd.

According to my mother, this is an uncorrected birth-certificate error. Sometimes she says they intended to name me Todd. Other times she says it was Dobb, after a Czechoslovakian uncle.

My father insists that they always intended to name

me Odd, although he won't tell me why. He notes that I don't have a Czechoslovakian uncle.

My mother vigorously asserts the existence of the uncle, though she refuses to explain why I've never met either him or her sister, Cymry, to whom he is supposedly married.

Although my father acknowledges the existence of Cymry, he is adamant that she has never married. He says that she is a freak, but what he means by this I don't know, for he will say no more.

My mother becomes infuriated at the suggestion that her sister is any kind of freak. She calls Cymry a gift from God but otherwise remains uncommunicative on the subject.

I find it easier to live with the name Odd than to contest it. By the time I was old enough to realize that it was an unusual name, I had grown comfortable with it.

Stormy Llewellyn and I are more than friends. We believe that we are soul mates.

For one thing, we have a card from a carnival fortune-telling machine that says we're destined to be together forever.

We also have matching birthmarks.

Cards and birthmarks aside, I love her intensely. I would throw myself off a high cliff for her if she asked me to jump. I would, of course, need to understand the reasoning behind her request.

Fortunately for me, Stormy is not the kind of person to ask such a thing lightly. She expects nothing of others that she herself would not do. In treacherous currents, she is kept steady by a moral anchor the size of a ship.

She once brooded for an entire day about whether to keep fifty cents that she found in the change-return slot of a pay phone. At last she mailed it to the telephone company.

Returning to the cliff for a moment, I don't mean to imply that I'm afraid of Death. I'm just not ready to go out on a date with him.

Smelling like a peach, as Stormy likes me, not afraid of Death, having eaten a blueberry muffin, saying goodbye to Elvis with the words "Taking care of business" in a lousy imitation of his voice, I set off for work at the Pico Mundo Grille.

Although the dawn had just broken, it had already flash-fried into a hard yellow yolk on the eastern horizon.

The town of Pico Mundo is in that part of southern California where you can never forget that in spite of all the water imported by the state aqueduct system, the true condition of the territory is desert. In March we bake. In August, which this was, we broil.

The ocean lay so far to the west that it was no more real to us than the Sea of Tranquility, that vast dark plain on the face of the moon.

Occasionally, when excavating for a new subdivision of tract homes on the outskirts of town, developers had struck rich veins of seashells in their deeper diggings. Once upon an ancient age, waves lapped these shores.

If you put one of those shells to your ear, you will not hear the surf breaking but only a dry mournful wind, as if the shell has forgotten its origins.

At the foot of the exterior steps that led down from my small apartment, in the early sun, Penny Kallisto waited like a shell on a shore. She wore red sneakers, white shorts, and a sleeveless white blouse.

Ordinarily, Penny had none of that preadolescent despair to which some kids prove so susceptible these days. She was an ebullient twelve-year-old, outgoing and quick to laugh.

This morning, however, she looked solemn. Her blue eyes darkened as does the sea under the passage of a cloud.

I glanced toward the house, fifty feet away, where my landlady, Rosalia Sanchez, would be expecting me at any minute to confirm that she had not disappeared during the night. The sight of herself in a mirror was never sufficient to put her fear to rest.

Without a word, Penny turned away from the stairs. She walked toward the front of the property.

Like a pair of looms, using sunshine and their own silhouettes, two enormous California live oaks wove veils of gold and midnight-purple, which they flung across the driveway.

Penny appeared to shimmer and to darkle as she passed through this intricate lace of light and shade. A black mantilla of shadow dimmed the luster of her blond hair, its elaborate pattern changing as she moved.

Afraid of losing her, I hurried down the last of the steps and followed the girl. Mrs. Sanchez would have to wait, and worry.

Penny led me past the house, off the driveway, to a birdbath on the front lawn. Around the base of the pedestal that supported the basin, Rosalia Sanchez had arranged a collection of dozens of the seashells, all shapes and sizes, that had been scooped from the hills of Pico Mundo.

Penny stooped, selected a specimen about the size of an orange, stood once more, and held it out to me.

The architecture resembled that of a conch. The rough exterior was brown and white, the polished interior shone pearly pink.

Cupping her right hand as though she still held the shell, Penny brought it to her ear. She cocked her head to listen, thus indicating what she wanted me to do.

When I put the shell to my ear, I did not hear the sea. Neither did I hear the melancholy desert wind that I mentioned previously.

Instead, from the shell came the rough breathing of a beast. The urgent rhythm of a cruel need, the grunt of mad desire.

Here in the summer desert, winter found my blood.

When she saw from my expression that I had heard what she wished me to hear, Penny crossed the lawn to the public sidewalk. She stood at the curb, gazing toward the west end of Marigold Lane.

I dropped the shell, went to her side, and waited with her.

Evil was coming. I wondered whose face it would be wearing.

Old Indian laurels line this street. Their great gnarled surface roots have in places cracked and buckled the concrete walkway.

Not a whisper of air moved through the trees. The morning lay as uncannily still as dawn on Judgment Day one breath before the sky would crack open.

Like Mrs. Sanchez's place, most houses in this neighborhood are Victorian in style, with varying degrees of gingerbread. When Pico Mundo was founded, in 1900, many residents were immigrants from the East Coast, and they preferred architectures better suited to that distant colder, damper shore.

Perhaps they thought they could bring to this valley only those things they loved, leaving behind all ugliness.

We are not, however, a species that can choose the baggage with which it must travel. In spite of our best intentions, we always find that we have brought along a suitcase or two of darkness, and misery.

For half a minute, the only movement was that of a hawk gliding high above, glimpsed between laurel branches.

The hawk and I were hunters this morning.

Penny Kallisto must have sensed my fear. She took my right hand in her left.

I was grateful for this kindness. Her grip proved firm, and her hand did not feel cold. I drew courage from her strong spirit.

Because the car was idling in gear, rolling at just a few miles per hour, I didn't hear anything until it turned the corner. When I recognized the vehicle, I knew a sadness equal to my fear.

This 1968 Pontiac Firebird 400 had been restored with loving care. The two-door, midnight-blue convertible appeared to glide toward us with all tires a fraction of an inch off the pavement, shimmering like a mirage in the morning heat.

Harlo Landerson and I had been in the same high-school class. During his junior and senior years, Harlo rebuilt this car from the axles up, until it looked as cherry as it had in the autumn of '67, when it had first stood on a showroom floor.

Self-effacing, somewhat shy, Harlo had not labored on the car with the hope either that it would be a babe magnet or that those who had thought of him as tepid would suddenly think he was cool enough to freeze the mercury in a thermometer. He'd had no social ambitions. He had suffered no illusions about his chances of ever rising above the lower ranks of the high-school caste system.

With a 335-horsepower V-8 engine, the Firebird could sprint from zero to sixty miles per hour in under eight seconds. Yet Harlo wasn't a street racer; he took no special pride in having wheels of fury.

He devoted much time, labor, and money to the Firebird because the beauty of its design and function enchanted him. This was a labor of the heart, a passion almost spiritual in its purity and intensity.

I sometimes thought the Pontiac figured so large in Harlo's life because he had no one to whom he could give the love that he lavished on the car. His mom died when he was six. His dad was a mean drunk.

A car can't return the love you give it. But if you're lonely enough, maybe the sparkle of the chrome, the luster of the paint, and the purr of the engine can be mistaken for affection.

Harlo and I hadn't been buddies, just friendly. I liked the guy. He was quiet, but quiet was better than the boast and bluster with which many kids jockeyed for social position in high school.

With Penny Kallisto still at my side, I raised my left hand and waved at Harlo.

Since high school, he'd worked hard. Nine to five, he unloaded trucks at Super Food and moved stock from storeroom to shelves.

Before that, beginning at 4:00 A.M., he dropped hundreds of newspapers at homes on the east side of Pico Mundo. Once each week, he also delivered to *every* house a plastic bag full of advertising flyers and discount-coupon books.

This morning, he distributed only newspapers, tossing them with a snap of the wrist, as though they were boomerangs. Each folded and bagged copy of the Tuesday edition of the *Maravilla County Times* spun through the air and landed with a soft *thwop* on a driveway or a front walk, precisely where the subscriber preferred to have it.

Harlo was working the far side of the street. When he reached the house opposite me, he braked the coasting Pontiac to a stop.

Penny and I crossed to the car, and Harlo said, "Good mornin', Odd. How're you this fine day?"

"Bleak," I replied. "Sad. Confused."

He frowned with concern. "What's wrong? Anything I can do?"

"Something you've already done," I said.

Letting go of Penny's hand, I leaned into the Firebird from the passenger's side, switched off the engine, and plucked the key from the ignition.

Startled, Harlo grabbed for the keys but missed. "Hey, Odd, no foolin' around, okay? I have a tight schedule."

I never heard Penny's voice, but in the rich yet silent language of the soul, she must have spoken to me.

What I said to Harlo Landerson was the essence of what the girl revealed: "You have her blood in your pocket."

An innocent man would have been baffled by my statement. Harlo stared at me, his eyes suddenly owlish not with wisdom but with fear.

"On that night," I said, "you took with you three small squares of white felt."

One hand still on the wheel, Harlo looked away from me, through the windshield, as if willing the Pontiac to move.

"After using the girl, you collected some of her virgin blood with the squares of felt."

Harlo shivered. His face flushed red, perhaps with shame.

Anguish thickened my voice. "They dried stiff and dark, brittle like crackers."

His shivers swelled into violent tremors.

"You carry one of them with you at all times." My voice shook with emotion. "You like to smell it. Oh, God, Harlo. Sometimes you put it between your teeth. And bite on it."

He threw open the driver's door and fled.

I'm not the law. I'm not vigilante justice. I'm not vengeance personified. I don't really know what I am, or why.

In moments like these, however, I can't restrain myself from action. A kind of madness comes over me, and I can no more turn away from what must be done than I can wish this fallen world back into a state of grace.

As Harlo burst from the Pontiac, I looked down at Penny Kallisto and saw the ligature marks on her throat, which had not been visible when she had first appeared to me. The depth to which the garroting cloth had scored her flesh revealed the singular fury with which he had strangled her to death.

Pity tore at me, and I went after Harlo Landerson, for whom I had no pity whatsoever.

CHAPTER 2

BLACKTOP TO CONCRETE, CONCRETE TO grass, alongside the house that lay across the street from Mrs. Sanchez's place, through the rear yard, to a wrought-iron fence and over, then across a narrow alleyway, up a slumpstone wall, Harlo Landerson ran and clambered and flung himself.

I wondered where he might be going. He couldn't outrun either me or justice, and he certainly couldn't outrun who he was.

Beyond the slumpstone wall lay a backyard, a swimming pool. Dappled with morning light and tree shadows, the water glimmered in shades of blue from sapphire to turquoise, as might a trove of jewels left by long-dead pirates who had sailed a sea since vanished.

On the farther side of the pool, behind a sliding glass door, a young woman stood in pajamas, holding a mug of whatever brew gave her the courage to face the day.

When he spotted this startled observer, Harlo changed direction toward her. Maybe he thought he needed a shield, a hostage. Whatever, he wasn't looking for coffee.

I closed on him, snared his shirt, hooked him off

his feet. The two of us plunged into the deep end of the pool.

Having banked a summer's worth of desert heat, the water wasn't cold. Thousands of bubbles like shimmering showers of silver coins flipped across my eyes, rang against my ears.

Thrashing, we touched bottom, and on the way up, he kicked, he flailed. With elbow or knee, or foot, he struck my throat.

Although the impeding water robbed the blow of most of its force, I gasped, swallowed, choked on the taste of chlorine flavored with tanning oil. Losing my grip on Harlo, I tumbled in slomo through undulant curtains of green light, blue shadow, and broke the surface into spangles of sunshine.

I was in the middle of the pool, and Harlo was at the edge. He grabbed the coping and jacked himself onto the concrete deck.

Coughing, venting atomized water from both nostrils, I splashed noisily after him. As a swimmer, I have less potential for Olympic competition than for drowning.

On a particularly dispiriting night when I was sixteen, I found myself chained to a pair of dead men and dumped off a boat in Malo Suerte Lake. Ever since then, I've had an aversion to aquatic sports.

That man-made lake lies beyond the city limits of Pico Mundo. Malo Suerte means "bad luck."

Constructed during the Great Depression as a project of the Works Progress Administration, the lake originally had been named after an obscure politician. Although they have a thousand stories about its treacherous waters, nobody around these parts can quite pin down when or why the place was officially renamed Malo Suerte.

All records relating to the lake burned in the courthouse fire of 1954, when a man named Mel Gibson protested the seizure of his property for nonpayment of taxes. Mr. Gibson's protest took the form of self-immolation.

He wasn't related to the Australian actor with the same name who would decades later become a movie star. Indeed, by all reports, he was neither talented nor physically attractive.

Now, because I hadn't been burdened on this occasion by a pair of men too dead to swim for themselves, I reached the edge of the pool in a few swift strokes. I levered myself out of the water.

Having arrived at the sliding door, Harlo Landerson found it locked.

The pajamaed woman had disappeared.

As I scrambled to my feet and started to move, Harlo backed away from the door far enough to get momentum. Then he ran at it, leading with his left shoulder, his head tucked down.

I winced in expectation of gouting blood, severed limbs, a head guillotined by a blade of glass.

Of course the safety pane shattered into cascades of tiny, gummy pieces. Harlo crashed into the house with all his limbs intact and his head still attached to his neck.

Glass crunched and clinked under my shoes when I entered in his wake. I smelled something burning.

We were in a family room. All the furniture was oriented toward a big-screen TV as large as a pair of refrigerators.

The gigantic head of the female host of the *Today* show was terrifying in such magnified detail. In these dimensions, her perky smile had the warmth of a barracuda's grin. Her twinkly eyes, here the size of lemons, seemed to glitter maniacally.

In this open floor plan, the family room flowed into the kitchen with only a breakfast bar intervening.

The woman had chosen to make a stand in the kitchen. She gripped a telephone in one hand and a butcher knife in the other.

Harlo stood at the threshold between rooms, trying to decide if a twentysomething housewife in too-cute, sailor-suit pajamas would really have the nerve to gut him alive.

She brandished the knife as she shouted into the phone. "He's inside, he's right *here*!"

Past her, on a far counter, smoke poured from a toaster. Some kind of pop-up pastry had failed to pop. It smelled like strawberries and smoldering rubber. The lady was having a bad morning.

Harlo threw a bar stool at me and ran out of the family room, toward the front of the house.

Ducking the stool, I said, "Ma'am, I'm sorry about the mess," and I went looking for Penny's killer.

Behind me, the woman screamed, *"Stevie, lock your door! Stevie, lock your door!"*

By the time I reached the foot of the open stairs in the foyer, Harlo had climbed to the landing.

I saw why he had been drawn upward instead of fleeing the house: At the second floor stood a wide-eyed little boy, about five years old, wearing only undershorts. Holding a blue teddy bear by one of its feet, the kid looked as vulnerable as a puppy stranded in the middle of a busy freeway.

Prime hostage material.

"Stevie, lock your door!"

Dropping the blue bear, the kid bolted for his room.

Harlo charged up the second flight of stairs.

Sneezing out the tickle of chlorine and the tang of burning strawberry jam, dripping, squishing, I ascended with somewhat less heroic flair than John Wayne in *Sands of Iwo Jima.*

I was more scared than my quarry because I had something to lose, not least of all Stormy Llewellyn and our future together that the fortune-telling machine had seemed to promise. If I encountered a husband with a handgun, he'd shoot me as unhesitatingly as he would Harlo.

Overhead, a door slammed hard. Stevie had done as his mother instructed.

If he'd had a pot of boiling lead, in the tradition of Quasimodo, Harlo Landerson would have poured it on me. Instead came a sideboard that evidently had stood in the second-floor hall, opposite the head of the stairs.

Surprised to discover that I had the agility and the balance of a monkey, albeit a wet monkey, I scrambled off the stairs, onto the railing. The deadfall rocked past step by step, drawers gaping open and snapping shut repeatedly, as if the furniture were possessed by the spirit of a crocodile.

Off the railing, up the stairs, I reached the second-floor hall as Harlo began to break down the kid's bedroom door.

Aware that I was coming, he kicked harder. Wood splintered with a dry crack, and the door flew inward.

Harlo flew with it, as if he'd been sucked out of the hall by an energy vortex.

Rushing across the threshold, pushing aside the rebounding door, I saw the boy trying to wriggle under the bed. Harlo had seized him by the left foot.

I snatched a smiling panda-bear lamp off the red nightstand and smashed it over Harlo's head. A ceramic carnage of perky black ears, fractured white face, black paws, and chunks of white belly exploded across the room.

In a world where biological systems and the laws of physics functioned with the absolute dependability that scientists claim for them, Harlo would have dropped stone-cold unconscious as surely as the lamp shattered. Unfortunately, this isn't such a world.

As love empowers some frantic mothers to find the superhuman strength to lift overturned cars to free their trapped children, so depravity gave Harlo the will to endure a panda pounding without significant effect. He let go of Stevie and rounded on me.

Although his eyes lacked elliptical pupils, they reminded me of the eyes of a snake, keen with venomous intent, and though his bared teeth included no hooked or dramatically elongated canines, the rage of a rabid jackal gleamed in his silent snarl.

This wasn't the person whom I had known in high school so few years ago, not the shy kid who found magic and meaning in the patient restoration of a Pontiac Firebird.

Here was a diseased and twisted bramble of a soul, thorny and cankerous, which perhaps until recently had been imprisoned in a deep turning of Harlo's mental labyrinth. It had broken down the bars of its cell and climbed up through the castle keep, deposing the man who had been Harlo; and now it ruled.

Released, Stevie squirmed all the way under his bed, but no bed offered shelter to me, and I had no blankets to pull over my head.

I can't pretend that I remember the next minute with clarity. We struck at each other when we saw an opening. We grabbed anything that might serve as a weapon, swung it, flung it. A flurry of blows staggered both of us into a clinch, and I felt his hot breath on my face, a spray of spittle, and heard his teeth snapping,

snapping at my right ear, as panic pressed upon him the tactics of a beast.

I broke the clinch, shoved him away with an elbow under the chin and with a knee that missed the crotch for which it was intended.

Sirens arose in the distance just as Stevie's mom appeared at the open door, butcher knife glinting and ready: two cavalries, one in pajamas, the other in the blue-and-black uniform of the Pico Mundo Police Department.

Harlo couldn't get past both me and the armed woman. He couldn't reach Stevie, his longed-for shield, under the bed. If he threw open a window and climbed onto the front-porch roof, he would be fleeing directly into the arms of the arriving cops.

As the sirens swelled louder, nearer, Harlo backed into a corner where he stood gasping, shuddering. Wringing his hands, his face gray with anguish, he looked at the floor, the walls, the ceiling, not in the manner of a trapped man assessing the dimensions of his cage, but with bewilderment, as though he could not recall how he had come to be in this place and predicament.

Unlike the beasts of the wild, the many cruel varieties of human monsters, when at last cornered, seldom fight with greater ferocity. Instead, they reveal the cowardice at the core of their brutality.

Harlo's wringing hands twisted free of each other and covered his face. Through the chinks in that ten-fingered armor, I could see his eyes twitching with bright terror.

Back jammed into the corner, he slid down the junction of walls and sat on the floor with his legs splayed in front of him, hiding behind his hands as though they were a mask of invisibility that would allow him to escape the attention of justice.

The sirens reached a peak of volume half a block away, and then subsided from squeal to growl to waning groan in front of the house.

The day had dawned less than an hour ago, and I had spent every minute of the morning living up to my name.

CHAPTER 3

THE DEAD DON'T TALK. I DON'T KNOW why. Harlo Landerson had been taken away by the authorities. In his wallet they had found two Polaroids of Penny Kallisto. In the first, she was naked and alive. In the second, she was dead.

Stevie was downstairs, in his mother's arms.

Wyatt Porter, chief of the Pico Mundo Police Department, had asked me to wait in Stevie's room. I sat on the edge of the boy's unmade bed.

I had not been alone long when Penny Kallisto walked through a wall and sat beside me. The ligature marks were gone from her neck. She looked as though she had never been strangled, had never died.

As before, she remained mute.

I tend to believe in the traditional architecture of life and the afterlife. This world is a journey of discovery and purification. The next world consists of two destinations: One is a palace for the spirit and an endless kingdom of wonder, while the other is cold and dark and unthinkable.

Call me simple-minded. Others do.

Stormy Llewellyn, a woman of unconventional views, believes instead that our passage through this world is intended to toughen us for the next life. She says that our honesty, integrity, courage, and determined resistance to evil are evaluated at the end of our days here, and that if we come up to muster, we will be conscripted into an army of souls engaged in some great mission in the next world. Those who fail the test simply cease to exist.

In short, Stormy sees this life as boot camp. She calls the next life "service."

I sure hope she's wrong, because one of the implications of her cosmology is that the many terrors we know here are an inoculation against worse in the world to come.

Stormy says that whatever's expected of us in the next life will be worth enduring, partly for the sheer adventure of it but primarily because the reward for service comes in our third life.

Personally, I'd prefer to receive my reward one life sooner than she foresees.

Stormy, however, is into delayed gratification. If on Monday she thirsts for a root-beer float, she'll wait until Tuesday or Wednesday to treat herself to one. She insists that the wait makes the float taste better.

My point of view is this: If you like root-beer floats so much, have one on Monday, another on Tuesday, and a third on Wednesday.

According to Stormy, if I live by this philosophy too long, I'm going to be one of those eight-hundred-pound men who, when they fall ill, must be extracted from their homes by construction crews and cranes.

"If you want to suffer the humiliation of being hauled to the hospital on a flatbed truck," she once said, "don't expect me to sit on your great bloated gut like Jiminy Cricket on the brow of the whale, singing 'When You Wish Upon a Star.'"

I'm reasonably sure that in Disney's *Pinocchio*,

Jiminy Cricket never sits on the brow of the whale. In fact I'm not convinced that he himself encounters the whale.

If I were to make this observation to Stormy, however, she would favor me with one of those wry looks that means *Are you hopelessly stupid or just being pissy?* This is a look to be avoided if not dreaded.

As I waited there on the edge of the boy's bed, even thinking about Stormy couldn't lift my spirits. Indeed, if the grinning images of Scooby-Doo, imprinted on the sheets, didn't cheer me, perhaps nothing could.

I kept thinking about Harlo losing his mother at six, about how his life might have been a memorial to her, about how instead he had shamed her memory.

And I thought about Penny, of course: her life brought to such an early end, the terrible loss to her family, the enduring pain that had changed their lives forever.

Penny put her left hand in my right and squeezed reassuringly.

Her hand felt as real as that of a living child, as firm, as warm. I didn't understand how she could be this real to me and yet walk through walls, this real to me and yet invisible to others.

I wept a little. Sometimes I do. I'm not embarrassed by tears. At times like this, tears exorcise emotions that would otherwise haunt me and, by their haunting, embitter me.

Even as my vision blurred at the first shimmer of tears not yet spent, Penny clasped my hand in both of hers. She smiled, and winked as if to say, *It's all right, Odd Thomas. Get it out, be rid of it.*

The dead are sensitive to the living. They have walked this path ahead of us and know our fears, our failings, our desperate hopes, and how much we cherish what cannot last. They pity us, I think, and no doubt they should.

When my tears dried, Penny rose to her feet, smiled again, and with one hand smoothed the hair back from my brow. *Good-bye,* this gesture seemed to say. *Thank you, and good-bye.*

She walked across the room, through the wall, into the August morning one story above the front yard—or into another realm even brighter than a Pico Mundo summer.

A moment later, Wyatt Porter appeared in the bedroom doorway.

Our chief of police is a big man, but he isn't threatening in appearance. With basset eyes and bloodhound jowls, his face has been affected by Earth's gravity more than has the rest of him. I've seen him move fast and decisively, but in action and in repose he seems to carry a great weight on his beefy, rounded shoulders.

Over the years, as the low hills encircling our town have been sculpted into neighborhoods of tract houses, swelling our population, and as the meanness of an ever crueler world has crept into the last havens of civility, like Pico Mundo, perhaps Chief Porter has seen too much of human treachery. Perhaps the weight he carries is a load of memories that he would prefer to shed, but can't.

"So here we are again," he said, entering the room.

"Here we are," I agreed.

"Busted patio door, busted furniture."

"Didn't bust most of it myself. Except the lamp."

"But you created the situation that led to it."

"Yes, sir."

"Why didn't you come to me, give me a chance to figure a way Harlo could entrap himself?"

We had worked together in that fashion in the past.

"My feeling," I said, "was that he needed to be confronted right away, that maybe he was going to do it again real soon."

"Your feeling."

"Yes, sir. That's what I think Penny wanted to convey. There was a quiet urgency about her."

"Penny Kallisto."

"Yes, sir."

The chief sighed. He settled upon the only chair in the room: a child-size, purple upholstered number on which Barney the dinosaur's torso and head served as the back support. He appeared to be sitting in Barney's lap. "Son, you sure complicate my life."

"*They* complicate your life, sir, and mine much more than yours," I said, meaning the dead.

"True enough. If I were you, I'd have gone crazy years ago."

"I've considered it," I admitted.

"Now listen, Odd, I want to find a way to keep you out of the courtroom on this one, if it comes to that."

"I want to find a way, too."

Few people know any of my strange secrets. Only Stormy Llewellyn knows all of them.

I want anonymity, a simple and quiet life, or at least as simple as the spirits will allow.

The chief said, "I think he's going to give us a confession in the presence of his attorney. There may be no trial. But if there is, we'll say that he opened his wallet to pay some bet he'd made with you, maybe on a baseball game, and the Polaroids of Penny fell out."

"I can sell that," I assured him.

"I'll speak with Horton Barks. He'll minimize your involvement when he writes it up."

Horton Barks was the publisher of the *Maravilla*

County Times. Twenty years ago in the Oregon woods, while hiking, he'd had dinner with Big Foot—if you can call some trail mix and canned sausages *dinner*.

In truth, I don't know for a fact that Horton had dinner with Big Foot, but that's what he claims. Given my daily experiences, I'm in no position to doubt Horton or anyone else who has a story to tell about an encounter with anything from aliens to leprechauns.

"You all right?" Chief Porter asked.

"Pretty much. But I sure hate being late for work. This is the busiest time at the Grille."

"You called in?"

"Yeah." I held up my little cell phone, which had been clipped to my belt when I went into the pool. "Still works."

"I'll probably stop in later, have a pile of home fries and a mess of eggs."

"Breakfast all day," I said, which has been a solemn promise of the Pico Mundo Grille since 1946.

Chief Porter shifted from one butt cheek to the other, causing Barney to groan. "Son, you figure to be a short-order cook forever?"

"No, sir. I've been thinking about a career change to tires."

"Tires?"

"Maybe sales first, then installation. They've always got job openings out at Tire World."

"Why tires?"

I shrugged. "People need them. And it's something I don't know, something new to learn. I'd like to see what that life's like, the tire life."

We sat there half a minute or so, neither of us saying anything. Then he asked, "And that's the only thing you see on the horizon? Tires, I mean."

"Swimming-pool maintenance looks intriguing.

With all these new communities going in around us, there's a new pool about every day."

Chief Porter nodded thoughtfully.

"And it must be nice working in a bowling alley," I said. "All the new people coming and going, the excitement of competition."

"What would you do in a bowling alley?"

"For one thing, take care of the rental shoes. They need to be irradiated or something between uses. And polished. You have to check the laces regularly."

The chief nodded, and the purple Barney chair squeaked more like a mouse than like a dinosaur.

My clothes had nearly dried, but they were badly wrinkled. I checked my watch. "I better get moving. I'm going to have to change before I can go to the Grille."

We both rose to our feet.

The Barney chair collapsed.

Looking at the purple ruins, Chief Porter said, "That could have happened when you were fighting Harlo."

"Could have," I said.

"Insurance will cover it with the rest."

"There's always insurance," I agreed.

We went downstairs, where Stevie was sitting on a stool in the kitchen, happily eating a lemon cupcake.

"I'm sorry, but I broke your bedroom chair," Chief Porter told him, for the chief is not a liar.

"That's just a stupid old Barney chair, anyway," the boy said. "I outgrew that stupid old Barney stuff *weeks* ago."

With a broom and a dustpan, Stevie's mom was sweeping up the broken glass.

Chief Porter told her about the chair, and she was inclined to dismiss it as unimportant, but he secured from her a promise that she would look up the original cost and let him know the figure.

He offered me a ride home, but I said, "Quickest for me is just to go back the way I came."

I left the house through the hole where the glass door had been, walked around the pool instead of splashing through it, climbed the slumpstone wall, crossed the narrow alleyway, climbed the wrought-iron fence, walked the lawn around another house, crossed Marigold Lane, and returned to my apartment above the garage.

CHAPTER 4

I SEE DEAD PEOPLE. BUT THEN, BY GOD, I *DO* something about it.

This proactive strategy is rewarding but dangerous. Some days it results in an unusual amount of laundry.

After I changed into clean jeans and a fresh white T-shirt, I went around to Mrs. Sanchez's back porch to confirm for her that she was visible, which I did every morning. Through the screen door, I saw her sitting at the kitchen table.

I knocked, and she said, "Can you hear me?"

"Yes, ma'am," I said. "I hear you just fine."

"Who do you hear?"

"You. Rosalia Sanchez."

"Come in then, Odd Thomas," she said.

Her kitchen smelled like chiles and corn flour, fried eggs and jack cheese. I'm a terrific short-order cook, but Rosalia Sanchez is a natural-born chef.

Everything in her kitchen is old and well worn but scrupulously clean. Antiques are more valuable when time and wear have laid a warm patina on them. Mrs. Sanchez's kitchen is as beautiful as the finest antique, with the priceless patina of a life's work and of cooking done with pleasure and with love.

I sat across the table from her.

Her hands were clasped tightly around a coffee mug to keep them from shaking. "You're late this morning, Odd Thomas."

Invariably she uses both names. I sometimes suspect she thinks Odd is not a name but a royal title, like *Prince* or *Duke*, and that protocol absolutely requires that it be used by commoners when they address me.

Perhaps she thinks that I am the son of a deposed king, reduced to tattered circumstances but nonetheless deserving of respect.

I said, "Late, yes, I'm sorry. It's been a strange morning."

She doesn't know about my special relationship with the deceased. She's got enough problems without having to worry about dead people making pilgrimages to her garage.

"Can you see what I'm wearing?" she asked worriedly.

"Pale yellow slacks. A dark yellow and brown blouse."

She turned sly. "Do you like the butterfly barrette in my hair, Odd Thomas?"

"There's no barrette. You're holding your hair back with a yellow ribbon. It looks nice that way."

As a young woman, Rosalia Sanchez must have been remarkably beautiful. At sixty-three, having added a few pounds, having acquired the seams and crinkles of seasoning experience, she possessed the deeper beauty of the beatified: the sweet humility and the tenderness that time can teach, the appealing glow of care and character that, in their last years on this earth, no doubt marked the faces of those who were later canonized as saints.

"When you didn't come at the usual time," she said,

"I thought you'd been here but couldn't see me. And I thought I couldn't see you anymore, either, that when I became invisible to you, you also became invisible to me."

"Just late," I assured her.

"It would be terrible to be invisible."

"Yeah, but I wouldn't have to shave as often."

When discussing invisibility, Mrs. Sanchez refused to be amused. Her saintly face found a frown of disapproval.

"When I've worried about becoming invisible, I've always thought I'd be able to see other people, they just wouldn't be able to see or hear me."

"In those old Invisible Man movies," I said, "you could see his breath when he went out in really cold weather."

"But if other people become invisible to me when I'm invisible to them," she continued, "then it's like I'm the last person in the world, all of it empty except for me wandering around alone."

She shuddered. Clasped in her hands, the coffee mug knocked against the table.

When Mrs. Sanchez talks about invisibility, she's talking about death, but I'm not sure she realizes this.

If the true first year of the new millennium, 2001, had not been good for the world in general, it had been bleak for Rosalia Sanchez in particular, beginning with the loss of her husband, Herman, on a night in April. She had gone to sleep next to the man whom she had loved for more than forty years—and awakened beside a cold cadaver. For Herman, death had come as gently as it ever does, in sleep, but for Rosalia, the shock of waking with the dead had been traumatic.

Later that year, still mourning her husband, she had not gone with her three sisters and their families on a long-planned vacation to New England. On the morning of September 11, she awakened to the news that their return flight out of Boston had been hijacked and used as a guided missile in one of the most infamous acts in history.

Although Rosalia had wanted children, God had given her none. Herman, her sisters, her nieces, her nephews had been the center of her life. She lost them all while sleeping.

Sometime between that September and that Christmas, Rosalia had gone a little crazy with grief. Quietly crazy, because she had lived her entire life quietly and knew no other way to be.

In her gentle madness, she would not acknowledge that they were dead. They had merely become invisible to her. Nature in a quirky mood had resorted to a rare phenomenon that might at any moment be reversed, like a magnetic field, making all her lost loved ones visible to her again.

The details of all the disappearances of ships and planes in the Bermuda Triangle were known to Rosalia Sanchez. She'd read every book that she could find on the subject.

She knew about the inexplicable, apparently overnight vanishment of hundreds of thousands of Mayans from the cities of Copan, Piedras Negras, and Palenque in A.D. 610.

If you allowed Rosalia to bend your ear, she would nearly break it off in an earnest discussion of historical disappearances. For instance, I know more than I care to know and immeasurably more than I *need* to know about the evaporation, to a man, of a division of three thousand Chinese soldiers near Nanking, in 1939.

"Well," I said, "at least you're visible this morning.

You've got another whole day of visibility to look forward to, and that's a blessing."

Rosalia's biggest fear is that on the same day when her loved ones are made visible again, she herself will vanish.

Though she longs for their return, she dreads the consequences.

She crossed herself, looked around her homey kitchen, and at last smiled. "I could bake something."

"You could bake *anything*," I said.

"What would you like me to bake for you, Odd Thomas?"

"Surprise me." I consulted my watch. "I better get to work."

She accompanied me to the door and gave me a good-bye hug. "You are a good boy, Odd Thomas."

"You remind me of my Granny Sugars," I said, "except you don't play poker, drink whiskey, or drive fast cars."

"That's sweet," she said. "You know, I thought the world and all of Pearl Sugars. She was so feminine but also . . ."

"Kick-ass," I suggested.

"Exactly. At the church's strawberry festival one year, there was this rowdy man, mean on drugs or drink. Pearl put him down with just two punches."

"She had a terrific left hook."

"Of course, first she kicked him in that special tender place. But I think she could have handled him with the punches alone. I've sometimes wished I could be more like her."

From Mrs. Sanchez's house, I walked the six blocks to the Pico Mundo Grille, which is in the heart of downtown Pico Mundo.

Every minute that it advanced from sunrise, the

morning became hotter. The gods of the Mojave don't know the meaning of the word *moderation*.

Long morning shadows grew shorter before my eyes, retreating from steadily warming lawns, from broiling blacktop, from concrete sidewalks as suitable for the frying of eggs as the griddle that I would soon be attending.

The air lacked the energy to move. Trees hung limp. Birds either retreated to leafy roosts or flew higher than they had at dawn, far up where thinner air held the heat less tenaciously.

In this wilted stillness, between Mrs. Sanchez's house and the Grille, I saw three shadows moving. All were independent of a source, for they were not ordinary shadows.

When I was much younger, I called these entities *shades*. But that is just another word for ghosts, and they are not ghosts like Penny Kallisto.

I don't believe they ever passed through this world in human form or knew this life as we know it. I suspect they don't belong here, that a realm of eternal darkness is their intended home.

Their shape is liquid. Their substance is no greater than that of shadows. Their movement is soundless. Their intentions, though mysterious, are not benign.

Often they slink like cats, though cats as big as men. At times they run semi-erect like dream creatures that are half man, half dog.

I do not see them often. When they appear, their presence always signifies oncoming trouble of a greater than usual intensity and a darker than usual dimension.

They are not shades to me now. I call them *bodachs*.

Bodach is a word that I heard a visiting six-year-old English boy use to describe these creatures when, in my company, he glimpsed a pack of them roaming a Pico Mundo twilight. A bodach is a small, vile, and supposedly mythical beast of the British Isles, who comes down chimneys to carry off naughty children.

I don't believe these spirits that I see are actually bodachs. I don't think the English boy believed so, either. The word popped into his mind only because he had no better name for them. Neither do I.

He was the only person I have ever known who shared my special sight. Minutes after he spoke the word *bodach* in my presence, he was crushed to death between a runaway truck and a concrete-block wall.

By the time I reached the Grille, the three bodachs had joined in a pack. They ran far ahead of me, shimmered around a corner, and disappeared, as though they had been nothing more than heat imps, mere tricks of the desert air and the grueling sun.

Fat chance.

Some days, I find it difficult to concentrate on being the best short-order cook that I can be. This morning, I would need more than the usual discipline to focus my mind on my work and to ensure that the omelets, home fries, burgers, and bacon melts that came off my griddle were equal to my reputation.

CHAPTER 5

"EGGS—WRECK 'EM AND STRETCH 'EM," said Helen Arches. "One Porky sitting, hash browns, cardiac shingles."

She clipped the ticket to the order rail, snatched up a fresh pot of coffee, and went to offer refills to her customers.

Helen has been an excellent waitress for forty-two years, since she was eighteen. After so much good work, her ankles have stiffened and her feet have flattened, so when she walks, her shoes slap the floor with each step.

This soft *flap-flap-flap* is one of the fundamental rhythms of the beautiful music of the Pico Mundo Grille, along with the sizzle and sputter of things cooking, the clink of flatware, and the clatter of dishes. The conversation of customers and employees provides the melody.

We were busy that Tuesday morning. All the booths were occupied, as were two-thirds of the stools at the counter.

I like being busy. The short-order station is the center stage of the restaurant, in full view, and I draw fans as surely as does any actor on the Broadway boards.

Being a short-order cook on a slow shift must be

akin to being a symphony conductor without either musicians or an audience. You stand poised for action in an apron instead of a tuxedo, holding a spatula rather than a baton, longing to interpret the art not of composers but of chickens.

The egg is art, sure enough. Given a choice between Beethoven and a pair of eggs fried in butter, a hungry man will invariably choose the eggs—or in fact the chicken—and will find his spirits lifted at least as much as they might be by a requiem, rhapsody, or sonata.

Anyone can crack a shell and spill the essence into pan, pot, or pipkin, but few can turn out omelets as flavorful, scrambled eggs as fluffy, and sunnysides as sunny as mine.

This is not pride talking. Well, yes it is, but this is the pride of accomplishment, rather than vanity or boastfulness.

I was not born with the artistry of a gifted hash-slinger. I learned by study and practice, under the tutelage of Terri Stambaugh, who owns the Pico Mundo Grille.

When others saw in me no promise, Terri believed in my potential and gave me a chance. I strive to repay her faith with cheeseburgers of exemplary quality and pancakes almost light enough to float off the plate.

She isn't merely my employer but also my culinary mentor, my surrogate mother, and my friend.

In addition, she is my primary authority on Elvis Presley. If you cite any day in the life of the King of Rock-'n'-Roll, Terri will without hesitation tell you where he was on that date and what he was doing.

I, on the other hand, am more familiar with his activities since his death.

Without referencing Helen's ticket on the rail, I

stretched an order of eggs, which means that I added a third egg to our usual serving of two. Then I wrecked 'em: scrambled them.

A "Porky sitting" is fried ham. A pig sits on its ham. It lies on its abdomen, which is the source of bacon, so "one Porky lying" would have called for a rasher with the eggs.

"Cardiac shingles" is an order of toast with extra butter.

Hash browns are merely hash browns. Not every word we speak during the day is diner lingo, just as not every short-order cook sees dead people.

I saw only the living in the Pico Mundo Grille during that Tuesday shift. You can always spot the dead in a diner because the dead don't eat.

Toward the end of the breakfast rush, Chief Wyatt Porter came in. He sat alone in a booth.

As usual, he washed down a tablet of Pepcid AC with a glass of low-fat moo juice before he ordered the mess of eggs and the home fries that he'd mentioned earlier. His complexion was as milky gray as carbolic-acid solution.

The chief smiled thinly at me and nodded. I raised my spatula in reply.

Although eventually I might trade hash-slinging for tire sales, I'll never contemplate a career in law enforcement. It's stomach-corroding work, and thankless.

Besides, I'm spooked by guns.

Half the booths and all but two of the counter stools had been vacated by the time a bodach came into the diner.

Their kind don't appear to be able to walk through walls as do the dead like Penny Kallisto. Instead they slip through any crevice or crack, or keyhole.

This one seeped through the thread-thin gap

between the glass door and the metal jamb. Like an undulant ribbon of smoke, as insubstantial as fumes but not translucent, ink-black, the bodach entered.

Standing rather than slinking on all fours, fluid in shape and without discernible features, yet suggestive of something half man and half canine, this unwanted customer slouched silently from the front to the back of the diner, unseen by all but me.

It seemed to turn its head toward each of our patrons as it glided along the aisle between the counter stools and the booths, hesitating in a few instances, as though certain people were of greater interest to it than were others. Although it possessed no discernible facial features, a portion of its silhouette appeared headlike, with a suggestion of a dog's muzzle.

Eventually this creature returned from the back of the diner and stood on the public side of the counter, eyeless but surely watching me as I worked at the short-order station.

Pretending to be unaware of my observer, I focused more intently on the grille and griddle than was necessary now that the breakfast rush had largely passed. From time to time, when I looked up, I never glanced at the bodach but at the customers, at Helen serving with her signature *slap-slap-slap*, at our other waitress—sweet Bertie Orbic, round in name and fact—at the big windows and the well-baked street beyond, where jacaranda trees cast shadows too lacy to cool and where heat snakes were charmed off the blacktop not by flute music but by the silent sizzle of the sun.

As on this occasion, bodachs sometimes take a special interest in me. I don't know why.

I don't think they realize that I am aware of them. If they knew that I can see their kind, I might be in danger.

Considering that bodachs seem to have no more substance than do shadows, I'm not sure how they could harm me. I'm in no hurry to find out.

The current specimen, apparently fascinated by the rituals of short-order cookery, lost interest in me only when a customer of peculiar demeanor entered the restaurant.

In a desert summer that had toasted every resident of Pico Mundo, this newcomer remained as pale as bread dough. Across his skull spread short, sour-yellow hair furrier than a yeasty mold.

He sat at the counter, not far from the short-order station. Turning his stool left and right, left and right, as might a fidgety child, he gazed at the griddle, at the milkshake mixers and the soft-drink dispensers, appearing to be slightly bewildered and amused.

Having lost interest in me, the bodach crowded the new arrival and focused intently on him. If this inky entity's head was in fact a head, then its head cocked left, cocked right, as though it were puzzling over the smiley man. If the snout-shaped portion was in fact a snout, then the shade sniffed with wolfish interest.

From the service side of the counter, Bertie Orbic greeted the newcomer. "Honey, what can I do you for?"

Managing to smile and talk at the same time, he spoke so softly that I couldn't hear what he said. Bertie looked surprised, but then she began to scribble on her order pad.

Magnified by round, wire-framed lenses, the customer's eyes disturbed me. His smoky gray gaze floated across me as a shadow across a woodland pool, registering no more awareness of me than the shadow has of the water.

The soft features of his wan face brought to mind

pale mushrooms that I once glimpsed in a dark dank corner of a basement, and mealy puffballs clustered in moist mounds of forest mast.

Busy with his mess of eggs, Chief Porter appeared to be no more aware of Fungus Man than he was of the observing bodach. Evidently, his intuition did not tell him that this new customer warranted special attention or concern.

I, however, found Fungus Man worrisome—in part but not entirely because the bodach remained fascinated by him.

Although, in a sense, I commune with the dead, I don't also have premonitions—except sometimes while fast asleep and dreaming. Awake, I am as vulnerable to mortal surprises as anyone is. My death might be delivered through the barrel of a terrorist's gun or by a falling stone cornice in an earthquake, and I would not suspect the danger until I heard the crack of the fatal shot or felt the earth leap violently beneath my feet.

My wariness of this man came from suspicion based not on reason, either, but on crude instinct. Anyone who smiled this relentlessly was a simpleton—or a deceiver with something to hide.

Those smoke-gray eyes appeared to be bemused and no more than half-focused, but I saw no stupidity in them. Indeed, I thought that I detected a cunningly veiled watchfulness, like that of a stone-still snake feigning prestrike indifference to a juicy mouse.

Clipping the ticket to the rail, Bertie Orbic relayed his order: "Two cows, make 'em cry, give 'em blankets, and mate 'em with pigs."

Two hamburgers with onions, cheese, and bacon.

In her sweet clear voice, which sounds like it belongs in a ten-year-old girl destined for a scholarship to

Juilliard, she continued: "Double spuds twice in Hell."

Two orders of French fries made extra crispy.

She said: "Burn two British, send 'em to Philly for fish."

Two English muffins with cream cheese and lox.

She wasn't finished: "Clean up the kitchen, plus midnight whistleberries with zeppelins."

An order of hash, and an order of black beans with sausages.

I said, "Should I fire this or wait till his friends join him?"

"Fire it," Bertie replied. "This is for one. A skinny boy like you wouldn't understand."

"What's he want first?"

"Whatever you want to make."

Fungus Man smiled dreamily at a salt shaker, which he turned around and around on the counter in front of him, as if the white crystalline contents fascinated and mystified him.

Although the guy didn't have a buffed physique that would qualify him as a spokesman for a health club, he wasn't fat, just gently rounded in his mushroom way. If his every meal was this elaborate, he must have the metabolism of a Tasmanian devil on methamphetamine.

I toasted and finished the muffins first, while Bertie prepared both a chocolate milkshake and a vanilla Coke. Our star eater was also a two-fisted drinker.

By the time I followed the muffins with the hash and sausages, a second bodach had appeared. This one and the first moved through the diner with an air of agitation, back and forth, here and there, always returning to the smiley gourmand, who remained oblivious of them.

When the bacon cheeseburgers and the well-done

fries were ready, I slapped one hand against the bell that rested beside the griddle, to alert Bertie that the order was up. She served it hot, kissing plate to counter without a rattle, as she always does.

Three bodachs had gathered at the front window, persistent shadows that remained impervious to the wilting power of the desert sun, peering in at us as though we were on exhibit.

Months often pass during which I encounter none of their kind. The running pack that I'd seen earlier in the street and now this convocation suggested that Pico Mundo was in for hard times.

Bodachs are associated with death much the way that bees seek the nectar of flowers. They seem to sip of it.

Ordinary death, however, does not draw a single bodach, let alone a swarm of them. I've never seen one of these beasts hovering at the bedside of a terminal cancer patient or in the vicinity of someone about to suffer a fatal heart attack.

Violence attracts them. And terror. They seem to know when it's coming. They gather like tourists waiting for the predictable eruption of a reliable geyser in Yellowstone Park.

I never saw one of them shadowing Harlo Landerson in the days before he murdered Penny Kallisto. I doubt that any bodachs were in attendance when he raped and throttled the girl.

For Penny, death had come with terrible pain and intolerable fear; surely each of us prays—or merely hopes, depending on his certainty of God—that his death will not be as brutal as hers. To bodachs, however, a quiet strangulation apparently isn't sufficiently exciting to bestir them from whatever lairs they inhabit in whatever strange realm is their true home.

Their appetite is for operatic terror. The violence they crave is of the most extreme variety: multiple untimely deaths spiced with protracted horror, served with cruelty as thick as bad gravy.

When I was nine years old, a drug-whacked teenager named Gary Tolliver sedated his family—little brother, little sister, mother, father—by doctoring a pot of homemade chicken soup. He shackled them while they were unconscious, waited for them to wake, and then spent a weekend torturing them before he killed them with a power drill.

During the week preceding these atrocities, I had twice crossed Tolliver's path. On the first occasion, he'd been followed closely by three eager bodachs. On the second occasion: not three but fourteen.

I have no doubt that those inky forms roamed the Tolliver house throughout that bloody weekend, invisible to the victims and to the killer alike, slinking from room to room as the scene of the action shifted. Observing. Feeding.

Two years later, a moving van, driven by a drunk, sheered off the gasoline pumps at a busy service station out on Green Moon Road, triggering an explosion and fire that killed seven. That morning, I had seen a dozen bodachs lingering there like misplaced shadows in the early sun.

Nature's wrath draws them as well. They were seething over the ruins of the Buena Vista Nursing Home after the earthquake eighteen months ago, and did not leave until the last injured survivor had been extracted from the rubble.

If I had passed by Buena Vista prior to the quake, surely I would have seen them gathering. Perhaps I could have saved some lives.

When I was a child, I first thought that these shades

might be malevolent spirits who fostered evil in those people around whom they swarmed. I've since discovered that many human beings need no supernatural mentoring to commit acts of savagery; some people are devils in their own right, their telltale horns having grown inward to facilitate their disguise.

I've come to believe that bodachs don't foster terror, after all, but take sustenance from it in some fashion. I think of them as psychic vampires, similar to but even scarier than the hosts of daytime-TV talk shows that feature emotionally disturbed and self-destructive guests who are encouraged to bare their damaged souls.

Attended now by four bodachs inside the Pico Mundo Grille and also watched by others at the windows, Fungus Man washed down the final bites of his burgers and fries with the last of his milkshake and vanilla Coke. He left a generous tip for Bertie, paid his check at the cashier's station, and departed the diner with his slinking entourage of slithery shadows.

Through dazzles of sunlight, through shimmering curtains of heat rising from the baked blacktop, I watched him cross the street. The bodachs at his sides and in his wake were difficult to count as they swarmed over one another, but I would have bet a week's wages that they numbered no fewer than twenty.

CHAPTER 6

ALTHOUGH HER EYES ARE NEITHER golden nor heavenly blue, Terri Stambaugh has the vision of an angel, for she sees through you and knows your truest heart, but loves you anyway, in spite of all the ways that you are fallen from a state of grace.

She's forty-one, therefore old enough to be my mother. She is not, however, *eccentric enough* to be my mother. Not by half.

Terri inherited the Grille from her folks and runs it to the high standard that they established. She's a fair boss and a hard worker.

Her only offbeat quality is her obsession with Elvis and all things Elvisian.

Because she enjoyed having her encyclopedic knowledge tested, I said, "Nineteen sixty-three."

"Okay."

"May."

"What day?"

I picked one at random: "The twenty-ninth."

"That was a Wednesday," Terri said.

The lunch rush had passed. My workday had ended at two o'clock. We were in a booth at the back of the Grille, waiting for a second-shift waitress, Viola Peabody, to bring our lunch.

I had been relieved at the short-order station by Poke Barnet. Thirty-some years older than I am, lean and sinewy, Poke has a Mojave-cured face and gunfighter eyes. He is as silent as a Gila monster sunning on a rock, as self-contained as any cactus.

If Poke had lived a previous life in the Old West, he had more likely been a marshal with a lightning-quick draw, or even one of the Dalton gang, rather than a chuck-wagon cook. With or without past-life experience, however, he was a good man at grill and griddle.

"On Wednesday, May 29, 1963," Terri said, "Priscilla graduated from Immaculate Conception High School in Memphis."

"Priscilla Presley?"

"She was Priscilla Beaulieu back then. During the graduation ceremony, Elvis waited in a car outside the school."

"He wasn't invited?"

"Sure he was. But his presence in the auditorium would have been a major disruption."

"When were they married?"

"Too easy. May 1, 1967, shortly before noon, in a suite in the Aladdin Hotel, Las Vegas."

Terri was fifteen when Elvis died. He wasn't a heart-throb in those days. By then he had become a bloated caricature of himself in embroidered, rhinestone-spangled jumpsuits more appropriate for Liberace than for the bluesy singer with a hard rhythm edge who had first hit the top of the charts in 1956, with "Heartbreak Hotel."

Terri hadn't yet been born in 1956. Her fascination with Presley had not begun until sixteen years after his death.

The origins of this obsession are in part mysterious

to her. One reason Elvis mattered, she said, was that in his prime, pop music had still been politically innocent, therefore deeply life-affirming, therefore relevant. By the time he died, most pop songs had become, usually without the conscious intention of those who wrote and sang them, anthems endorsing the values of fascism, which remains the case to this day.

I suspect that Terri is obsessed with Elvis partly because, on an unconscious level, she has been aware that he has moved among us here in Pico Mundo at least since my childhood, perhaps ever since his death, a truth that I revealed to her only a year ago. I suspect she is a latent medium, that she may sense his spiritual presence, and that as a consequence she is powerfully drawn to the study of his life and career.

I have no idea why the King of Rock-'n'-Roll has not moved on to the Other Side but continues, after so many years, to haunt this world. After all, Buddy Holly hasn't hung around; he's gotten on with death in the proper fashion.

And why does Elvis linger in Pico Mundo instead of in Memphis or Vegas?

According to Terri, who knows everything there is to know about all the days of Elvis's busy forty-two years, he never visited our town when he was alive. In all the literature of the paranormal, no mention is made of such a geographically dislocated haunting.

We were puzzling over this mystery, not for the first time, when Viola Peabody brought our late lunch. Viola is as black as Bertie Orbic is round, as thin as Helen Arches is flat-footed.

Depositing our plates on the table, Viola said, "Odd, will you read me?"

More than a few folks in Pico Mundo think that I'm some sort of psychic: perhaps a clairvoyant, a thaumaturge, seer, soothsayer, *something*. Only a handful know that I see the restless dead. The others have whittled an image of me with the distorting knives of rumor until I am a different piece of scrimshaw to each of them.

"I've told you, Viola, I'm not a palmist or a head-bump reader. And tea leaves aren't anything to me but garbage."

"So read my face," she said. "Tell me—do you see what I saw in a dream last night?"

Viola was usually a cheerful person, even though her husband, Rafael, had traded up to a waitress at a fancy steak house over in Arroyo City, thereafter providing neither counsel nor support for their two children. On this occasion, however, Viola appeared solemn as never before, and worried.

I told her, "The *last* thing I can read is faces."

Every human face is more enigmatic than the time-worn expression on the famous Sphinx out there in the sands of Egypt.

"In my dream," Viola said, "I saw myself, and my face was . . . broken, dead. I had a hole in my forehead."

"Maybe it was a dream about why you married Rafael."

"Not funny," Terri admonished me.

"I think maybe I'd been shot," Viola said.

"Honey," Terri comforted her, "when's the last time you had a dream come true?"

"I guess never," Viola said.

"Then I wouldn't worry about this one."

"Best I can remember," Viola said, "I've never before seen myself face-on in a dream."

Even in my nightmares, which sometimes *do* come true, I've never glimpsed my face, either.

"I had a hole in my forehead," she repeated, "and my face was . . . spooky, all out of kilter."

A high-powered round of significant caliber, upon puncturing the forehead, would release tremendous energy that might distort the structure of the entire skull, resulting in a subtle but disturbing new arrangement of the features.

"My right eye," Viola added, "was bloodshot and seemed to . . . to swell half out of the socket."

In our dreams, we are not detached observers, as are the characters who dream in movies. These internal dramas are usually seen strictly from the dreamer's point of view. In nightmares, we can't look into our own eyes except by indirection, perhaps because we fear discovering that therein lie the worst monsters plaguing us.

Viola's face, sweet as milk chocolate, was now distorted by a beseeching expression. "Tell me the truth, Odd. Do you see death in me?"

I didn't say to her that death lies dormant in each of us and will bloom in time.

Although not one small detail of Viola's future, whether grim or bright, had been revealed to me, the delicious aroma of my untouched cheeseburger induced me to lie in order to get on with lunch: "You'll live a long happy life and pass away in your sleep, of old age."

"Really?"

Smiling and nodding, I was unashamed of this deception. For one thing, it might be true. I see no real harm in giving people hope. Besides, I had not sought to be her oracle.

In a better mood than she'd arrived, Viola departed, returning to the paying customers.

Picking up my cheeseburger, I said to Terri, "October 23, 1958."

"Elvis was in the army then," she said, hesitating only to chew a bite of her grilled-cheese sandwich. "He was stationed in Germany."

"That's not very specific."

"The evening of the twenty-third, he went into Frankfurt to attend a Bill Haley concert."

"You could be making this up."

"You know I'm not." Her crisp dill pickle crunched audibly when she bit it. "Backstage, he met Haley and a Swedish rock-'n'-roll star named Little Gerhard."

"Little Gerhard? That can't be true."

"Inspired, I guess, by Little Richard. I don't know for sure. I never heard Little Gerhard sing. Is Viola going to be shot in the head?"

"I don't know." Juicy and cooked medium-well, the meat in the cheeseburger had been enhanced with a perfect pinch of seasoned salt. Poke was a contender. "Like you said, dreams are just dreams."

"She's had things hard. She doesn't need this."

"Shot in the head? Who *does* need it?"

"Will you look after her?" Terri asked.

"How would I do that?"

"Put out your psychic feelers. Maybe you can stop the thing before it happens."

"I don't have psychic feelers."

"Then ask one of your dead friends. They sometimes know things that are going to happen, don't they?"

"They're generally not friends. Just passing acquaintances. Anyway, they're helpful only when they want to be helpful."

"If I was dead, I'd help you," Terri assured me.

"You're sweet. I almost wish you were dead." I put down the cheeseburger and licked my fingers. "If somebody in Pico Mundo is going to start shooting people, it'll be Fungus Man."

"Who's he?"

"Sat at the counter a while ago. Ordered enough food for three people. Ate like a ravenous swine."

"That's my kind of customer. But I didn't see him."

"You were in the kitchen. He was pale, soft, with all rounded edges, like something that would grow in Hannibal Lecter's cellar."

"He put off bad vibes?"

"By the time he left, Fungus Man had an entourage of bodachs."

Terri stiffened and looked warily around the restaurant. "Any of them here now?"

"Nope. The worst thing on the premises at the moment is Bob Sphincter."

The real name of the pinchpenny in question was Spinker, but he earned the secret name we gave him. Regardless of the total of his bill, he always tipped a quarter.

Bob Sphincter fancied himself to be two and a half times more generous than John D. Rockefeller, the oil billionaire. According to legend, even in the elegant restaurants of Manhattan, Rockefeller had routinely tipped a dime.

Of course in John D's day, which included the Great Depression, a dime would purchase a newspaper and lunch at an Automat. Currently, a quarter will get you just a newspaper, and you won't want to read anything in it unless you're a sadist, a masochist, or a suicidally lonely wretch desperate to find true love in the personal ads.

Terri said, "Maybe this Fungus Man was just passing through town, and he hit the highway as soon as he cleaned his plate."

"Got a hunch he's still hanging around."

"You gonna check him out?"

"If I can find him."

"You need to borrow my car?" she asked.

"Maybe for a couple hours."

I walk to and from work. For longer trips, I have a bicycle. In special cases, I use Stormy Llewellyn's car, or Terri's.

So many things are beyond my control: the endless dead with all their requests, the bodachs, the prophetic dreams. I'd probably long ago have gone seven kinds of crazy, one for each day of the week, if I didn't simplify my life in every area where I *do* have some control. These are my defensive strategies: no car, no life insurance, no more clothes than I absolutely need—mostly T-shirts, chinos, and jeans—no vacations to exotic places, no grand ambitions.

Terri slid her car keys across the table.

"Thanks," I said.

"Just don't haul any dead people around in it. Okay?"

"The dead don't need a ride. They can appear when they want, where they want. They walk through air. They fly."

"All I'm saying is, if you tell me some dead person was sitting in my car, I'll waste a whole day scrubbing the upholstery. It creeps me out."

"What if it's Elvis?"

"That's different." She finished her dill pickle. "How was Rosalia this morning?" she asked, meaning Rosalia Sanchez, my landlady.

"Visible," I said.

"Good for her."

CHAPTER 7

GREEN MOON MALL STANDS ALONG GREEN Moon Road, between old-town Pico Mundo and its modern western neighborhoods. The huge structure, with walls the color of sand, had been designed to suggest humble adobe construction, as though it were a home built by a family of gigantic Native Americans averaging forty feet in height.

In spite of this curious attempt at environmentally harmonious but deeply illogical architecture, patrons of the mall can still be Starbucked, Gapped, Donna Karaned, and Crate & Barreled as easily in Pico Mundo as in Los Angeles, Chicago, New York, or Miami.

In a corner of the vast parking lot, remote from the mall, stands Tire World. Here the architecture is more playful.

The single-story building supports a tower crowned by a giant globe. This model of Earth, rotating lazily, seems to represent a world of peace and innocence lost when the snake entered Eden.

Like Saturn, this planet sports a ring, not of ice crystals and rocks and dust but of rubber. Encircling the globe is a tire that both rotates and oscillates.

Five service bays ensure that customers will not

wait long to have new tires installed. The technicians wear crisp uniforms. They are polite. They smile easily. They seem happy.

Car batteries can be purchased here, as well, and oil changes are offered. Tires, however, remain the soul of the operation.

The showroom is saturated with the enchanting scent of rubber waiting for the road.

That Tuesday afternoon, I wandered the aisles for ten or fifteen minutes, undisturbed. Some employees said hello to me, but none tried to sell me anything.

I visit from time to time, and they know that I am interested in the tire life.

The owner of Tire World is Mr. Joseph Mangione. He is the father of Anthony Mangione, who was a friend of mine in high school.

Anthony attends UCLA. He hopes to have a career in medicine.

Mr. Mangione is proud that his boy will be a doctor, but he is disappointed, as well, that Anthony has no interest in the family business. He would welcome me to the payroll and would no doubt treat me as a surrogate son.

Here, tires are available for cars, SUVs, trucks, motorcycles. The sizes and degrees of quality are many; but once the inventory is memorized, no stress would be associated with any job at Tire World.

That Tuesday, I had no intention of resigning my spatula at the Pico Mundo Grille anytime soon, although short-order cooking can be stressful when the tables are full, tickets are backed up on the order rail, and your head is buzzing with diner lingo. On those days that also feature an unusual number of encounters with the dead, in addition to a bustling breakfast and lunch trade, my stomach sours and I know that I am courting not merely burnout but also early-onset gastrointestinal reflux disease.

At times like that, the tire life seems to be a refuge almost as serene as a monastery.

However, even Mr. Mangione's rubber-scented corner of paradise was haunted. One ghost stubbornly inhabited the showroom.

Tom Jedd, a well-regarded local stonemason, had died eight months previous. His car careened off Panorama Road after midnight, broke through rotted guardrails, tumbled down a rocky hundred-foot embankment, and sank in Malo Suerte Lake.

Three fishermen had been in a boat, sixty yards offshore, when Tom went swimming in his PT Cruiser. They called the cops on a cell phone, but emergency-rescue services arrived too late to save him.

Tom's left arm had been severed in the crash. The county coroner declared himself undecided as to whether Tom had bled to death or drowned first.

Since then, the poor guy had been moping around Tire World. I didn't know why. His accident had not been caused by a defective tire.

He'd been drinking at a roadhouse called Country Cousin. The autopsy cited a blood-alcohol level of 1.18, well over the legal limit. He either lost control of the vehicle due to inebriation or he fell asleep at the wheel.

Each time I visited the showroom to stroll the aisles and mull a career change, Tom realized that I saw him, and he acknowledged me with a look or a nod. Once he even winked at me, conspiratorially.

He had not, however, made any attempt to communicate either his purpose or his needs. He was a reticent ghost.

Some days I wish more of them were like him.

He had died in a parrot-patterned Hawaiian shirt, khaki shorts, and white sneakers worn without socks. He always appeared in those clothes when he roamed Tire World.

Sometimes he was dry, but at other times he appeared to be soaked, as if he'd just walked out of Malo Suerte Lake. Usually he had both arms, but occasionally his left arm was missing.

You can tell a lot about a dead person's state of mind by the condition in which he manifests. When dry, Tom Jedd seemed to be resigned to his fate if not fully at peace with it. When wet, he looked angry or distressed, or sullen.

On this occasion, he was dry. His hair had been combed. He appeared to be relaxed.

Tom had both arms this time, but the left wasn't attached to his shoulder. He carried his left arm in his right hand, casually, as though it were a golf club, gripping it by the biceps.

This grotesque behavior did not include gore. Fortunately, I had never seen him bloody, perhaps because he was squeamish or because he remained in denial that he had bled to death.

Twice, when he knew that I was looking, he used his severed arm as a back scratcher. He clawed between his shoulder blades with the stiff fingers of that detached limb.

As a rule, ghosts are serious about their condition and solemn in their demeanor. They belong on the Other Side but are stuck here, for whatever reasons, and they are impatient to move on.

Once in a while, however, I encounter a spirit with his sense of humor intact. For my amusement, Tom even conspired to pick his nose with the forefinger of his severed arm.

I prefer ghosts to be somber. There's something about a walking dead man trying to get a laugh that chills me, perhaps because it suggests that even postmortem we have a pathetic need to be liked—as well as the sad capacity to humiliate ourselves.

If Tom Jedd had been in less of a jokey mood, I might have lingered longer at Tire World. His shtick disturbed me, as did his twinkly-eyed smile.

As I walked to Terri's Mustang, Tom stood at a showroom window, vigorously and clownishly waving good-bye with his severed arm.

I drove across sun-scorched acres of parking lot and found a space for the Mustang near the main entrance to the mall, where workmen were hanging a banner announcing the big annual summer sale that would run Wednesday through Sunday.

Inside this cavernous retail mecca, most of the stores appeared to be only moderately busy, but the Burke & Bailey's ice-cream parlor drew a crowd.

Stormy Llewellyn has worked at Burke & Bailey's since she was sixteen. At twenty, she's the manager. Her plan is to own a shop of her own by the time she's twenty-four.

If she had gone into astronaut training after high school, she would have a lemonade stand on the moon by now.

According to her, she's not ambitious, just easily bored and in need of stimulation. I have frequently offered to stimulate her.

She says she's talking about *mental* stimulation.

I tell her that, in case she hasn't noticed, I do have a brain.

She says there's definitely no brain in my one-eyed snake and that what might be in my *big* head is still open to debate.

"Why do you think I sometimes call you Pooh?" she once asked.

"Because I'm cuddly?"

"Because Pooh's head is full of stuffin'."

Our life together isn't always a New Wave Abbott & Costello routine. Sometimes she's Rocky and I'm Bullwinkle.

I went to the counter in Burke & Bailey's and said, "I need something hot and sweet."

"We specialize in cold," Stormy said. "Go sit out there in the promenade and be good. I'll bring you something."

Although busy, the parlor offered a few empty tables; however, Stormy prefers not to chat on the premises. She is an object of fascination for some of the other employees, and she doesn't want to give them fuel for gossip.

I understand precisely how they feel about her. She's an object of fascination for me, too.

Therefore I stepped out of Burke & Bailey's, into the public promenade, and sat with the fish.

Retail sales and theater have joined forces in America: Movies are full of product placements, and malls are designed with drama in mind. At one end of Green Moon Mall, a forty-foot waterfall tumbled down a cliff of man-made rocks. From the falls, a stream coursed the length of the building, over a series of diminishing rapids.

At the end of a compulsive-shopping spree, if you realized that you had bankrupted yourself in Nordstroms, you could fling yourself into this water feature and drown.

Outside Burke & Bailey's, the stream ended in a tropical pond surrounded by palm trees and lush ferns. Great care had been taken to make this vignette look real. Faint recorded bird calls echoed hauntingly through the greenery.

Except for the lack of enormous insects, suffocating humidity, malaria victims groaning in death throes, poisonous vipers as thick as mosquitoes, and rabid jungle cats madly devouring their own feet, you would have sworn you were in the Amazon rainforest.

In the pond swam brightly colored koi. Many were large enough to serve as a hearty dinner. According to the mall publicity, some of these exotic fish were valued as high as four thousand dollars each; tasty or not, they weren't within everyone's grocery budget.

I sat on a bench with my back to the koi, unimpressed by their flashy fins and precious scales.

In five minutes, Stormy came out of Burke & Bailey's with two cones of ice cream. I enjoyed watching her walk toward me.

Her uniform included pink shoes, white socks, a hot-pink skirt, a matching pink-and-white blouse, and a perky pink cap. With her Mediterranean complexion, jet-black hair, and mysterious dark eyes, she looked like a sultry espionage agent who had gone undercover as a hospital candy striper.

Sensing my thoughts, as usual, she sat beside me on the bench and said, "When I have my own shop, the employees won't have to wear stupid uniforms."

"I think you look adorable."

"I look like a goth Gidget."

Stormy gave one of the cones to me, and for a minute or two we sat in silence, watching shoppers stroll past, enjoying our ice cream.

"Under the hamburger and bacon grease," she said, "I can still smell the peach shampoo."

"I'm an olfactory delight."

"Maybe one day when I have my own shop, we can work together and smell the same."

"The ice-cream business doesn't move me. I love to fry."

"I guess it's true," she said.

"What?"

"Opposites attract."

"Is this the new flavor came in last week?" I asked.

"Yeah."

"Cherry chocolate coconut chunk?"

"Coconut cherry chocolate chunk," she corrected. "You've got to get the proper adjective in front of *chunk* or you're screwed."

"I didn't realize the grammar of the ice-cream industry was so rigid."

"Describe it your way, and some weasel customers will eat the whole thing and then ask for their money back because there weren't chunks of coconut in it. And don't ever call me adorable again. Puppies are adorable."

"As you were coming toward me, I thought you looked sultry."

"The smart thing for you would be to stay away from adjectives altogether."

"Good ice cream," I said. "Is this the first taste you've had?"

"Everyone's been raving about it. But I didn't want to rush the experience."

"Delayed gratification."

"Yeah, it makes everything sweeter."

"Wait too long, and what was sweet and creamy can turn sour."

"Move over Socrates. Odd Thomas takes the podium."

I know when the thin ice under me has begun to

crack. I changed the subject. "Sitting with my back to all those koi creeps me out."

"You think they're up to something?" she asked.

"They're too flashy for fish. I don't trust them."

She glanced over her shoulder, at the pond, then turned her attention once more to the ice cream. "They're just fornicating."

"How can you tell?"

"The only thing fish ever do is eat, excrete, and fornicate."

"The good life."

"They excrete in the same water where they eat, and they eat in the semen-clouded water where they fornicate. Fish are disgusting."

"I never thought so until now," I said.

"How'd you get out here?"

"Terri's Mustang."

"You been missing me?"

"Always. But I'm looking for someone." I told her about Fungus Man. "This is where my instinct brought me."

When someone isn't where I expect to find him, neither at home nor at work, then sometimes I cruise around on my bicycle or in a borrowed car, turning randomly from street to street. Usually in less than half an hour, I cross paths with the one I seek. I need a face or a name for focus, but then I'm better than a bloodhound.

This is a talent for which I have no name. Stormy calls it "psychic magnetism."

"And here he comes now," I said, referring to Fungus Man, who ambled along the promenade, following the descending rapids toward the tropical koi pond.

Stormy didn't have to ask me to point the guy out

to her. Among the other shoppers, he was as obvious as a duck in a dog parade.

Although I had nearly finished the ice cream without being chilled, I shivered at the sight of this strange man. He trod the travertine promenade, but my teeth chattered as if he had just walked across my grave.

CHAPTER 8

PALE, PUFFY, HIS WATERY GRAY GAZE floating over store windows, looking almost as bemused as an Alzheimer's patient who has wandered out of his care facility into a world he no longer recognizes, Fungus Man carried stuffed shopping bags from two department stores.

"What's that yellow thing on his head?" Stormy asked.

"Hair."

"I think it's a crocheted yarmulke."

"No, it's hair."

Fungus Man went into Burke & Bailey's.

"Are the bodachs still with him?" Stormy asked.

"Not as many as before. Just three."

"And they're in my store with him?"

"Yeah. They all went inside."

"This is bad for business," she said ominously.

"Why? None of your customers can see them."

"How could slinky, slithering evil spirits be *good* for business?" she countered. "Wait here."

I sat with the fornicating koi at my back and the unfinished ice cream in my right hand. I had lost my appetite.

Through the windows of Burke & Bailey's, I could

see Fungus Man at the counter. He studied the flavor menu, then placed an order.

Stormy herself didn't serve him but hovered nearby, behind the counter, on some pretense.

I didn't like her being in there with him. I sensed that she was in danger.

Although experience has taught me to trust my feelings, I did not go inside to stand guard near her. She had asked me to wait on the bench. I had no intention of crossing her. Like most men, I find it mortifying to be ass-kicked by a woman who doesn't even weigh 110 pounds *after* Thanksgiving dinner.

If I'd had a lamp and a genie and one wish, I would have wished myself back to Tire World, to the serenity of that showroom with its aisles of soothingly round rubber forms.

I thought of poor Tom Jedd, waving good-bye with his severed arm, and I decided to finish my ice cream, after all. None of us ever knows when he's approaching the end of his road. Maybe this was the last scoop of coconut cherry chocolate chunk that I'd ever have a chance to eat.

As I finished the final bite, Stormy returned and sat beside me again. "He's ordered takeout. One quart of maple walnut and one quart of mandarin-orange chocolate."

"Are the flavors significant?"

"That's for you to decide. I'm just reporting in. He's sure one megaweird son of a bitch. I wish you'd just forget about him."

"You know I can't."

"You have a messiah complex, got to save the world."

"I don't have a messiah complex. I just have . . . this gift. It wouldn't have been given to me if I wasn't supposed to use it."

"Maybe it's not a gift. Maybe it's a curse."

"It's a gift." Tapping my head, I said, "I've still got the box it came in."

Fungus Man stepped out of Burke & Bailey's. In addition to the two department-store bundles, he carried a quilted, insulated bag that contained the ice cream.

He looked right, looked left, and right again, as though not certain from which direction he had arrived here. His vague smile, which seemed to be as permanent as a tattoo, widened briefly, and he nodded as though in cheerful agreement with something that he'd said to himself.

When Fungus Man began to move, heading upstream toward the waterfall, two bodachs accompanied him. For the moment, the third remained in Burke & Bailey's.

Rising from the bench, I said, "I'll see you for dinner, Goth Gidget."

"Try to show up alive," she said. "Because, remember, *I* can't see the dead."

I left her there, all pink and white and sultry, in the palmy tropics with the scent of amorous koi, and I followed the human mushroom to the main entrance of the mall and then out into sunshine almost sharp enough to peel the corneas off my eyes.

The griddle-hot blacktop seemed but one degree cooler than the molten tar pits that had sucked down dinosaurs in distant millennia. The air flash-dried my lips and brought to me that summer scent of desert towns that is a melange of superheated silica, cactus pollen, mesquite resin, the salts of long-dead seas, and exhaust fumes suspended in the motionless dry air like faint nebulae of mineral particles spiraling through rock crystal.

Fungus Man's dusty Ford Explorer stood in the row behind mine and four spaces farther west. If my psychic magnetism had been any stronger, we would have been parked bumper to bumper.

He opened the tailgate of the SUV and put in the shopping bags. He had brought a Styrofoam cooler to protect the ice cream, and he snugged both quarts in that insulated hamper.

Earlier, I had forgotten to prop the reflective sun barrier against the windshield in the Mustang. It was folded and tucked between the passenger's seat and the console. Consequently, the steering wheel had grown too hot to touch.

I started the engine, turned on the air conditioner, and used my rearview and side mirrors to monitor Fungus Man.

Fortunately, his movements were nearly as slow and methodical as the growth of mildew. By the time he backed out of his parking space, I was able to follow him without leaving scraps of blistered skin on the steering wheel.

We had not yet reached the street when I realized that none of the bodachs had accompanied the smiley man when he'd left the mall. None were currently in the Explorer with him, and none loped after it, either.

Earlier, he had departed the Grille with an entourage of at least twenty, which had shrunk to three when he arrived at Burke & Bailey's. The bodachs are usually devout in their attendance to any man who will be the source of terrible violence, and they do not desert him until the last drop of blood has been spilled.

I wondered if Fungus Man was, after all, the evil incarnation of Death that I had taken him to be.

The lake of blacktop glistened with so much stored heat that it appeared to have no more surface tension than water, and yet the Explorer cruised across it without leaving wake or wimple.

Even in the absence of bodachs, I continued to trail my quarry. My shift at the Grille was done. The rest of the afternoon as well as the evening lay ahead. No one is more restless than a short-order cook at loose ends.

CHAPTER 9

CAMP'S END IS NOT A TOWN IN ITSELF BUT a neighborhood of Pico Mundo that is the living memory of hard times even when the rest of our community is experiencing an economic boom. More lawns are dead than not, and some are gravel. Most of the small houses need new stucco, fresh paint, and a truce with termites.

Shacks were built here in the late 1800s, when prospectors with more dreams than common sense were drawn to the area by silver and rumors of silver. They discovered rich veins of the latter.

Over time, as the prospectors became legend and could not be found anymore in the flesh, the weathered shacks were replaced by cottages, shingled bungalows, and casitas with barrel-tile roofs.

In Camp's End, however, renovation turned to ruin faster than elsewhere. Generation after generation, the neighborhood retained its essential character, an air not so much of defeat as of weary patience: the sag, the peel, the rust, the bleak and blanched but never quite hopeless spirit of a precinct in purgatory.

Hard luck seemed to seep out of the ground itself, as though the devil's rooms in Hades were directly beneath these streets, his sleeping loft so near the surface that his fetid breath, expelled with every snore, percolated through the soil.

Fungus Man's destination was a pale-yellow stucco casita with a faded blue front door. The carport leaned precipitously, as if the weight of sunshine alone might collapse it.

I parked across the street from the house, in front of an empty lot full of parched jimson weed and brambles as intricately woven as a dreamcatcher. They had caught only crumpled papers, empty beer cans, and what appeared to be a tattered pair of men's boxer shorts.

As I put down the car windows and switched off the engine, I watched Fungus Man carry his ice cream and other packages into the house. He entered by a side door in the carport shadows.

Summer afternoons in Pico Mundo are long and blistering, with little hope of wind and none of rain. Although my wristwatch and the car clock agreed on 4:48, hours of searing sunshine remained ahead.

The morning weather forecast had called for a high of 110 degrees, by no means a record for the Mojave. I suspected that this prediction had been exceeded.

When cool-climate relatives and friends are astonished to hear such temperatures, Pico Mundians put a chamber-of-commerce spin on our meteorology, noting that the humidity is a mere fifteen or twenty percent. Our average summer day, they insist, isn't like a sweltering steam bath but like a refreshing sauna.

Even in the shade of a huge old Indian laurel with roots no doubt deep enough to tap the Styx, I couldn't pretend that I was being coddled in a sauna. I felt like a child who had wandered into the gingerbread house of a Black Forest witch and had been popped into her oven with the control at SLOW BAKE.

Occasionally a car passed, but no pedestrians appeared.

No children were at play. No homeowner ventured forth to putter in a withered garden.

One dog slumped past, head low, tongue lolling, as if it were stubbornly tracking the mirage of a cat.

Soon my body provided the humidity that the air lacked, until I sat in a puddle of sweat.

I could have started the Mustang and switched on the air conditioning, but I didn't want to waste Terri's gasoline or overheat the engine. Besides, as any desert denizen knows, repeated heating and cooling may temper some metals, but it softens the human mind.

After forty minutes, Fungus Man reappeared. He locked the side door of the house, which suggested that no one remained at home, and got behind the wheel of his dust-shrouded Explorer.

I slid down in my seat, below the window, listening as the SUV drove past and left a trail of sound that dwindled into silence.

Crossing to the pale-yellow house, I didn't worry unduly about being watched from any of the sun-silvered windows along the street. Living in Camp's End inspired alienation rather than the community spirit needed to form a Neighborhood Watch committee.

Instead of going to the blue front door and making a greater spectacle of myself, I sought the shadows of the carport and knocked on the side door that Fungus Man had used. No one answered.

If the door had featured a deadbolt lock, I would have had to force a window. Confronted by a mere latch bolt, I was confident that, like other young Americans, I had been so well educated by TV cop dramas that I could slip easily into the house.

To simplify my life, I keep no bank accounts and

pay only cash; therefore, I have no credit cards. California had thoughtfully issued to me a laminated driver's license stiff enough to loid the lock.

As I'd anticipated, the kitchen wasn't a shrine either to Martha Stewart decor or to cleanliness. The place couldn't be fairly called a pig stye, either; it was just plagued by a general disarray, with here and there an offering of crumbs to ants if they wished to visit.

A faint but unpleasant smell laced the well-cooled air. I could not identify the source, and at first I thought that it must be the singular fragrance of Fungus Man, for he appeared to be one who would issue strange and noxious odors if not also deadly spoors.

I didn't know what I sought here, but I expected to recognize it when I saw it. Something had drawn the bodachs to this man, and I had followed in their wake with the hope of discovering a clue to the reason for their interest.

After I circled the kitchen, trying but failing to find meaning in a mug half filled with cold coffee, in a browning banana peel left on a cutting board, in the unwashed dishes in the sink, and in the ordinary contents of drawers and cupboards, I realized that the air was not just cool but inexplicably chilly. For the most part, the sweat on my exposed skin had dried. On the nape of my neck, it felt as though it had turned to ice.

The pervasive chill was inexplicable because even in the Mojave, where air conditioning was essential, a house as old and as humble as this rarely had central cooling. Window-mounted units, each serving a single chamber, were a viable alternative to the costly retrofitting of a dwelling that didn't merit the expense.

The kitchen had no such window units.

Often in a home like this, the residents held the

heat at bay only at night and only in the bedroom. Sleep might otherwise be difficult. Even in this small house, however, an air conditioner in the bedroom would not be able to cool the entire structure. Certainly it could not have made an icebox of the kitchen.

Besides, window-mounted units were noisy: the chug and hum of the compressor, the rattle of the fan. I heard none of that here.

As I stood, head cocked, listening, the house waited in silence. On consideration, I suddenly found this stillness to be unnatural.

My shoes should have teased noise from the cracked linoleum, from floorboards loosened by time, heat, and shrinking aridity. Yet when I moved, I had the stealth of a cat on pillows.

In retrospect, I realized that the drawers and the cupboard doors had opened and closed with only the softest whisper, as though constructed with frictionless slides and hinges.

When I moved toward the open doorway between the kitchen and the next room, the cold air seemed to thicken, further muffling the transmission of sound.

The sparsely furnished living room proved to be as dreary and as marked by disorder as the kitchen. Old battered paperbacks, no doubt purchased at a used-book store, and magazines littered the floor, the couch, the coffee table.

The magazines were what you might expect. Photos of nude women were featured between articles about extreme sports, fast cars, and pathetic seduction techniques, all surrounded by ads for virility herbs and for devices guaranteed to increase the size of the average man's favorite body part, by which I do not mean his brain.

My favorite body part is my heart because it is the only thing I have to give Stormy Llewellyn. Furthermore, the beat of it, when I wake each morning, is my first best evidence that I have not, during the night, joined the community of the stubbornly lingering dead.

The paperbacks surprised me. They were romance novels. Judging by the cover illustrations, these were of the more chaste variety, in which bosoms seldom heaved and bodices were not often lustily ripped open. They were stories less concerned with sex than with love, and they were a peculiar counterpoint to the magazines full of women fondling their breasts, spreading their legs, and licking their lips lasciviously.

When I picked up one of the books and thumbed through it, the riffling pages made no noise.

By this point, I seemed to be able to hear no sounds except those that had an internal origin: the thud of my heart, the rush of blood in my ears.

I should have fled right then. The eerie muffling effect of the malign atmosphere in the house ought to have alarmed me.

Because my days are characterized as much by strange experiences as by the aroma of meat smoke and the sizzle of fat on the griddle, I don't alarm easily. Furthermore, I admit to a tendency, sometimes regrettable, to surrender always to my curiosity.

Riffling the soundless pages of the romance novel, I thought that perhaps Fungus Man did not live here alone. These books might have been the preferred reading material of his companion.

This possibility turned out not to be supported by the evidence in his bedroom. The closet contained only his clothes. The unmade bed, the scatter of yesterday's underwear and socks, and a half-eaten raisin Danish on a paper plate, on the nightstand, argued against the civilizing presence of a woman.

An air conditioner, mounted in the window, wasn't running. No breeze blew from its vents.

The faint foul smell first detected in the kitchen grew stronger here, reminiscent of the malodor of a shorting electrical cord, but not quite that, with a hint of ammonia and a trace of coal dust and a whiff of nutmeg, but not quite any of those things, either.

The short hallway that served the bedroom also led to the bath. The mirror needed to be cleaned. On the counter, the toothpaste tube had not been capped. A small wastebasket overflowed with used Kleenex and other trash.

Across the hall from Fungus Man's bedroom stood another door. I assumed it led either to a closet or to a second bedroom.

At that threshold, the air grew so chilled that I could see my breath, a pale plume.

Icy against my palm, the doorknob turned. Beyond lay a vortex of silence that sucked the last sound out of my ears, leaving me for the moment deaf even to the labor of my heart.

The black room waited.

CHAPTER 10

DURING MY TWENTY YEARS, I HAVE BEEN in many dark places, some lacking light and others devoid of hope. In my experience, none had been darker than that strange room in the home of Fungus Man.

Either this chamber had no windows or all the windows had been boarded over and caulked against every prying blade of sunshine. No lamps glowed. In this profound gloom, had there been a digital clock with an LED readout, the faint radiance of its numerals would have seemed like a blazing beacon.

At the threshold, I squinted into such absolute blackness that I seemed to be peering not into a room at all but into dead space in a far region of the universe where the ancient stars were burnt-out cinders. The bone-brittling cold, deeper here than elsewhere in the house, and the oppressive silence argued as well that this was some bleak way station in the interstellar vacuum.

More peculiar than anything else: The hallway light failed to penetrate even a fraction of an inch into the realm beyond the door. The demarcation of light and utter lightlessness was as sharp as a painted line at the inner edge of the threshold, up the jamb, and across the header. The perfect gloom did not merely resist the intrusion of light but foiled it entirely.

This seemed to be a wall of blackest obsidian, though obsidian that lacked polish and glimmer.

I am not fearless. Toss me in a cage with a hungry tiger, and if I should escape, I will need a bath and clean pants as surely as will the next guy.

My unique path through life has led me, however, to fear known threats but seldom the unknown, while most people fear both.

Fire scares me, yes, and earthquakes, and venomous snakes. People scare me more than anything, for I know too well the savagery of which humankind is capable.

To me, however, the most daunting mysteries of existence—death and what lies beyond—have no fright factor because I deal with the dead each day. Besides, I have faith that where I am ultimately going is not to mere oblivion.

In spooky movies, do you rail at the beleaguered characters to get the hell out of the haunted house, to get smart and *leave*? They poke into rooms with a history of bloody murder, into attics hung with cobwebs and shadows, into cellars acrawl with cockroaches and cacodemons, and when they are chopped-stabbed-gutted-beheaded-burned with the flamboyance necessary to satisfy Hollywood's most psychotic directors, we gasp and shudder, and then we say, "Idiot," for by their stupidity they have earned their fate.

I'm not stupid, but I am one of those who will never flee the haunted place. The special gift of paranormal sight, with which I was born, impels me to explore, and I can no more resist the demands of my talent than a musical prodigy can resist the magnetic pull of a piano; I am no more deterred by the mortal risks than is a fighter pilot eager to take flight into war-torn skies.

This is part of the reason why Stormy occasionally wonders if my gift might be instead a curse.

On the brink of unblemished blackness, I raised my right hand as if I were taking an oath—and pressed my palm to the apparent barrier before me. Although this darkness could fend off light, it offered no resistance whatsoever to the pressure that I applied. My hand disappeared into the tarry gloom.

By "disappeared," I mean that I could perceive not even the vaguest impression of my wiggling fingers beyond the surface of this wall of blackness. My wrist ended as abruptly as that of an amputee.

I must admit that my heart raced, though I felt no pain, and that I exhaled with relief—and without sound—when I withdrew my hand and saw that all my digits were intact. I felt as though I had survived an illusion performed by those self-proclaimed bad boys of magic, Penn and Teller.

When I stepped across the threshold, however, holding fast to the door casing with one hand, I entered not an illusion but a real place that seemed more unreal than any dream. The blackness ahead remained uncannily pure; the cold was unrelenting; and the silence cloyed as effectively as congealed blood in the ears of a head-shot dead man.

Although from the far side of the doorway I had been unable to discern one scintilla of this room, I could look out from within it and see the hallway in normal light, unobstructed. This view shed no more illumination into the room than would have a painting of a sunny landscape.

I half expected to find that Fungus Man had returned and that he was staring at the only part of me now visible from out there: my hooked fingers desperately clutching the casing. Fortunately, I was still alone.

Having discovered that I could see the exit to the hall and therefore could find my way out, I let go of the doorway. I eased entirely into this lightless chamber and, turning away from the sight of the hall, became at once as blind as I was deaf.

Without either sound or vision, I quickly grew disoriented. I felt for a light switch, found it, flicked it up and down and up again without effect.

I grew aware of a small red light that I was certain hadn't been there a moment earlier: the murderous red of a sullen and bloody eye, though it was not an eye.

My sense of spatial reality and my ability to gauge distance with accuracy abandoned me, for the tiny beacon seemed to be miles from my position, like the mast light of a ship far away on a night sea. This small house, of course, could not contain such a vastness as I imagined lay before me.

When I let go of the useless light switch, I felt as unnervingly buoyant as a hapless drunkard inflated by the fumes of alcohol. My feet seemed not quite to touch the floor as I determinedly approached the red light.

Wishing that I'd had a second scoop of coconut cherry chocolate chunk while I'd had the chance, I took six steps, ten, twenty. The beacon didn't increase in size and seemed in fact to recede from me at precisely the speed at which I approached it.

I stopped, turned, and peered back at the door. Although I had made no progress toward the light, I had traveled what appeared to be approximately forty feet.

Of more interest than the distance covered was the figure now silhouetted in the open door. Not Fungus Man. Backlit by the hallway light stood . . . me.

Although the mysteries of the universe do not greatly frighten me, I've not lost my capacity for astonishment, amazement, and awe. Now, across the keyboard of my mind played arpeggios of those three sentiments.

Convinced that this wasn't a mirror effect and that I was in fact gazing at another me, I nevertheless tested my certainty by waving. The other Odd Thomas didn't return my wave, as a reflection would have done.

Because I stood submerged in this swampish blackness, he could not see me, and so I tried to shout to him. In my throat, I felt the quiver of strummed vocal chords, but if sound was produced, I could not hear it. Most likely he, too, was deaf to that cry.

As tentatively as I had done, this second Odd Thomas reached into the palpable dark with one questing hand, marveling as I had done at the illusion of amputation.

This timid intrusion seemed to disturb a delicate equilibrium, and abruptly the black room shifted like the pivot mountings of a gyroscope, while the red light at the center remained fixed. Flung by forces beyond my control, much as a surfer might be tossed from his board in the collapsing barrel of a mammoth wave, I was magically churned out of that weird chamber and—

—into the drab living room.

I found myself not tumbled in a heap, as I might have expected to be, but standing approximately where I had stood earlier. I picked up one of the paperback romance novels. As before, the pages made no noise, and I could hear only those sounds of internal origin, such as my heart beating.

Glancing at my wristwatch, I convinced myself that this was, indeed, *earlier*. I had not merely been magically transported from the black room to the living room but also had been cast a few minutes backward in time.

Since I had a moment ago seen myself peering into the blackness from the hall doorway, I could assume that by the grace of some anomaly in the laws of physics, *two* of me now existed simultaneously in this house. There were the me here with a Nora Roberts novel in my hands and the other me in some nearby room.

At the start, I warned you that I lead an unusual life.

A great deal of phenomenal experience has fostered in me a flexibility of the mind and imagination that some might call madness. This flexibility allowed me to adjust to these events and accept the reality of time travel more quickly than you would have done, which does not reflect badly on you, considering that *you* would have been wise enough to get the hell out of the house.

I didn't flee. Neither did I at once retrace my original route to Fungus Man's bedroom—with its scatter of underwear and socks, the half-eaten raisin Danish on the nightstand—or to his bathroom.

Instead, I put down the romance novel and stood quite still, carefully thinking through the possible ramifications of encountering the *other* Odd Thomas, responsibly calculating the safest and most rational course of action.

Okay, that's bullshit. I could *worry* about the ramifications, but I didn't have either *enough* phenomenal experience or the brain power to imagine all of them, let alone to figure out the best way to extract myself from this bizarre situation.

I'm less skilled at extracting myself from trouble than I am at plunging into it.

At the living-room archway, I cautiously peeked into the hallway and spotted the other me standing at the open door of the black room. This must have been the earlier me that had not yet crossed that threshold.

If all sound had not by now been entirely suppressed within the house, I would have been able to call out to that other Odd Thomas. I'm not sure that would have been prudent, and I'm grateful that the circumstances prevented me from hailing him.

If I had been able to speak to him, I'm not certain what I would have said. *How's it hanging?*

Were I to walk up to him and give him a narcissistic hug, the paradox of two Odd Thomases might at once be resolved. One of us might disappear. Or perhaps both of us would explode.

Big-browed physicists tell us that two objects cannot under any circumstances occupy the same place at the same time. They warn that any effort to put two objects in the same place at the same time will have catastrophic consequences.

When you think about it, a lot of fundamental physics is the solemn statement of the absurdly obvious. Any drunk who has tried to put his car where a lamppost stands is a self-educated physicist.

Assuming that two of me could not coexist without calamity, not charmed by the prospect of exploding, I remained in the archway, watching, until the other Odd Thomas stepped across the threshold into the black room.

You no doubt suppose that upon his departure the time paradox had been resolved and that the crisis described by those doomsaying scientists was at an end, but your optimism is a result of the fact that you are happy in your world of the five standard senses. You are not, as I am, compelled to action by a paranormal talent that you do not understand and cannot fully control.

Lucky you.

As soon as that Odd Thomas stepped for the first time across the threshold into the lightless chamber, I walked directly to the door that he'd left open behind him. I could not see him, of course, out there in the mysteries of the black room, but I assumed that soon he would turn, look back, and see me—an event that in my experience had already come to pass.

When I judged that he'd spotted the sullen red light and had progressed about twenty paces toward it, when he'd had time to look back and see me standing here, I checked my wristwatch to establish the beginning of this episode, reached into the blackness with my right hand, just to be sure nothing felt different about that strange realm, and then I crossed the threshold once more.

CHAPTER 11

MY GREATEST CONCERN, ASIDE FROM exploding and aside from being late for dinner with Stormy, was that I might find myself caught in a time loop, doomed to follow myself repeatedly through Fungus Man's house and through the door into the black room, over and over for all of eternity.

I'm not sure that such a thing as a time loop is possible. The average physicist might laugh smugly at my concern and charge me with ignorance. This was *my* crisis, however, and I felt free to speculate without restraint.

Rest assured that no time loop became established: The remainder of my story will not consist of endless repetitions of the events immediately heretofore described—although there are reasons that I wish it did.

Less hesitant on my second visit to the black room, I strode more boldly, yet with that same queasy-making buoyancy, toward the crimson beacon at the center of the chamber. This mysterious lamp seemed to shed a more ominous light than it had previously, though as before it did not relieve the gloom.

Twice I glanced back toward the open door to the hallway but didn't see myself on either occasion.

Nevertheless, I experienced that sudden gyroscopic spin, as before, and I was again churned out of that strange chamber—

—this time into the hot July afternoon, where I found myself walking out of the shadows under the carport, into sunshine that stabbed like fistfuls of golden needles at my eyes.

I halted, squinted against the glare, and retreated to the gloom.

The profound silence that reigned in the house did not extend beyond those walls. A dog barked lazily in the distance. An old Pontiac with a knocking engine and a squealing fan belt passed in the street.

Certain that I had spent no more than a minute in the black room, I consulted my wristwatch again. Apparently I had been not only cast out of the house but also five or six minutes into the future.

Out in the half-burnt yard and in the bristling weeds along the chain-link fence between this property and the next, cicadas buzzed, buzzed, as though the sunlit portion of the world were plagued by myriad short circuits.

Many questions arose in my mind. None of them concerned either the benefits of a career in tires or the financial strategy by which a twenty-year-old short-order cook might best begin to prepare for his retirement at sixty-five.

I wondered if a man living behind a perpetual half-wit smile, a man incapable of keeping a neat house, a man conflicted enough to split his reading time between skin magazines and romance novels, could be a closet supergenius who, with electronic components from Radio Shack, would be able to transform one room of his humble home into a time machine. Year by year, weird experience has squeezed all but a few drops of skepticism from me, but the supergenius explanation didn't satisfy.

I wondered if Fungus Man was really a man at all—or something new to the neighborhood.

I wondered how long he had lived here, who he pretended to be, and what the hell his intentions were.

I wondered if the black room might be not a time machine but something even stranger than that. The time-related occurrences might be nothing more than side effects of its primary function.

I wondered how long I was going to stand in the shade of the sagging carport, brooding about the situation instead of *doing something*.

The door between the carport and the kitchen, through which I had initially entered the house, had automatically locked behind me when I had first gone inside. Again I popped the latch bolt with my laminated driver's license, pleased to know that finally I was getting something back for the state income taxes that I had paid.

In the kitchen, the browning banana peel continued to shrivel on the cutting board. No time-traveling housemaid had attended to the dirty dishes in the sink.

Softcore pornography and romance novels still littered the living room, but when I had crossed halfway to the hallway arch, I stopped abruptly, struck by what had changed.

I could hear normally. My footsteps had crackled the ancient linoleum in the kitchen, and the swinging door to the living room had squeaked on unoiled hinges. That vortex of silence no longer sucked all sound out of the house.

The air, which had been freezing, was now merely cool. And getting warmer.

The singular foul odor that smelled like not-exactly-burning-electrical-cord blended with not-exactly-ammonia-coal-dust-nutmeg had grown far more pungent than before but no easier to identify.

Ordinary instinct, rather than any sixth sense, told me not to proceed to the black room. In fact, I felt an urgent need to retreat from the nearby hallway arch.

I returned to the kitchen and hid behind the swinging door, holding it open two inches to see from whom, if anyone, I had fled.

Only seconds after I had reached concealment, bodachs swarmed out of the hallway into the living room.

CHAPTER 12

A GROUP OF BODACHS ON THE MOVE sometimes brings to mind a pack of stalking wolves. On other occasions they remind me of a pride of slinking cats.

Pouring through the hallway arch into the living room, this particular swarm had an unnerving insectile quality. They exhibited the cautiously questing yet liquid-swift progress of a colony of cockroaches.

They came in roachlike numbers, too. Twenty, thirty, forty: They quivered into the room as silent and as black as shadows but, unlike shadows, they were untethered from any entities that might have cast them.

To the ill-fitted front door, to the poorly caulked living-room windows, they streamed as if they were billows of soot drawn by a draft. Through crack and chink, they fled the house, into the sun-drenched afternoon of Camp's End.

Still they swarmed out of the hallway: fifty, sixty, seventy, and more. I had never before encountered so many bodachs at one time.

Although, from my position in the kitchen, I couldn't see around the living-room archway and down the hall, I knew where the intruders must have entered the house. They had not arisen spontaneously from among the gray dust balls and the moldering socks under Fungus Man's unmade bed. Nor had they manifested out of a boogeyman-infested closet, out of a bathroom faucet, from the toilet bowl. They had arrived in the house by way of the black room.

They seemed eager to leave this place behind them and to explore Pico Mundo—until one of them separated from the churning swarm. It abruptly halted in the center of the living room.

In the kitchen, I considered that no available cutlery, no toxic household cleanser, no weapon known to me would wound this beast that had no substance. I held my breath.

The bodach stood so hunched that its hands, if they were hands, dangled at its knees. Turning its lowered head from side to side, it scanned the carpet for the spoor of its prey.

No troll, crouched in the darkness beneath its bridge, relishing the scent of a child's blood, had ever looked more malevolent.

At the gap between jamb and door, my left eye felt pinched, as though my curiosity had become the serrated jaws of a vise that held me immobile even when it seemed wise to exit at a sprint.

As others of its kind continued to roil and ripple past it, my nemesis rose from its crouch. The shoulders straightened. The head lifted, turned slowly left, then right.

I regretted using peach-scented shampoo, and suddenly I could smell the meaty essence that the greasy smoke from the griddle had deposited upon my skin and hair. A short-order cook, just off work, makes easy tracking for lions and worse.

The all but featureless, ink-black bodach had the

suggestion of a snout but no visible nostrils, no apparent ears, and if it had eyes, I could not discern them. Yet it searched the living room for the source of whatever scent or sound had snared its attention.

The creature appeared to focus on the door to the kitchen. As eyeless as Samson in Gaza, it nevertheless detected me.

I had studied the story of Samson in some detail, for he was a classic example of the suffering and the dark fate that can befall those who are . . . gifted.

Standing very erect now, taller than me, the bodach was an imposing figure in spite of its insubstantiality. Its bold poise and a quality of arrogance in the lift of its head suggested that I was to it as the mouse is to the panther, that it had the power to strike me dead in an instant.

Pent-up breath swelled in my lungs.

The urge to flee became almost overpowering, but I remained frozen for fear that if the bodach had not for certain seen me, then even the small movement of the swinging door would bring it at a run.

Grim expectation made seconds seem like minutes—and then to my surprise, the phantom slumped into a crouch once more and loped away with the others. With the suppleness of black silk ribbon, it slipped between window sash and sill, into sunlight.

I blew out my sour breath and sucked sweet air, watching as a final score of bodachs spilled through the hallway arch.

When these last foul spirits had departed for the Mojave heat, I returned to the living room. Cautiously.

At least a hundred of them had passed through this room. More likely, there had been half again that many.

In spite of all that traffic, not one page of any magazine or romance novel had been ruffled. Their passage had left no slightest impression in the nap of the carpet.

At one of the front windows, I peered out at the blighted lawn and the sun-scorched street. As far as I could determine, none of the recently departed pack lingered in the neighborhood.

The unnatural chill in this small house had gone the way of the bodachs. The desert day penetrated the thin walls until every surface in the living room seemed to be as radiant as the coils of an electric heater.

During their passage, that tumult of purposeful shadows had left no stain on the hallway walls. No trace of the burning-electrical-cord smell remained, either.

For the third time, I stepped up to that doorway.

The black room was gone.

CHAPTER 13

BEYOND THE THRESHOLD LAY AN ORDINARY chamber, not infinite in its dimensions, as it had seemed earlier, measuring no more than twelve by fourteen feet.

A single window looked out through the branches of a lacy melaleuca that screened much of the sunlight. Nevertheless, I could see well enough to determine that no source existed for a sullen red light either in the center of this humble space or in any corner.

The mysterious power that had transformed and controlled this room—casting me minutes back, and then forward, in time—was no longer in evidence.

Apparently, this served as Fungus Man's study. A bank of four-drawer filing cabinets, an office chair, and a gray metal desk with a laminated imitation-wood-grain top were the only furnishings.

Side by side on the wall opposite the desk hung three black- and-white, poster-size photographs that appeared to have been printed on a draftsman's digital plotter. They were head shots, portraits of men—one with feverish eyes and a gleeful smile, the other two glowering in the gloom.

All three were familiar, but I could at first put a name to only the one with the smile: Charles Manson, the vicious manipulator whose fantasies of revolution and race war had exposed a cancer at the core of the flower-power generation and had led to the demise of the Age of Aquarius. He had carved a swastika on his forehead.

Whoever the other two might be, they didn't have the look of either Vegas comics or famous philosophers.

Perhaps my imagination, as much as the melaleuca-filtered sunlight, imparted a faint silvery luminescence to each man's intense gaze. This glow reminded me of the milky radiance that informs the hungry glare of animate corpses in movies about the living dead.

In part to alter the quality of those eyes, I switched on the overhead light.

The dust and disorder that characterized the rest of the house were not in evidence here. When he crossed this threshold, Fungus Man left his slovenliness behind and became a paragon of neatness.

The file cabinets proved to contain meticulously kept folders filled with articles clipped from publications and downloaded from the Internet. Drawer after drawer contained dossiers on serial killers and mass murderers.

The subjects ranged from Victorian England's Jack the Ripper to Osama bin Laden, for whom Hell had prepared a special suite of fiery rooms. Ted Bundy, Jeffrey Dahmer. Charles Whitman, the sniper who killed sixteen in Austin, Texas, in 1966. John Wayne Gacy: He liked to dress up as a clown at children's parties, had his picture taken at a political event with First Lady Rosalyn Carter, and buried numerous dismembered bodies in his backyard and under his house.

A particularly thick file had been assembled for Ed Gein, who had been the inspiration for both Norman

Bates in *Pyscho* and Hannibal Lecter in *The Silence of the Lambs*. Gein had enjoyed eating soup from a human skull and had fashioned a fancy belt from the nipples of his victims.

The unknown dangers of the black room had not daunted me, but here was a known evil, entirely comprehensible. Cabinet by cabinet, my chest tightened with dread and my hands trembled, until I slammed shut a file drawer and resolved to open no more of them.

Memory freshened by what I'd seen in those folders, I could now put names to the poster-size photographs that flanked Charles Manson.

A portrait of Timothy McVeigh hung to the right of Manson. McVeigh had been convicted and executed for the bombing of the federal building in Oklahoma City, where 168 people were killed in 1995.

To the left hung Mohammed Atta, who had flown an airliner into one of the World Trade Center towers, killing thousands. I had seen no evidence that Fungus Man sympathized with the cause of radical Islamic fascists. As with Manson and McVeigh, he apparently admired Atta for the terrorist's cruel vision, brutal actions, and accomplishments in the service of evil.

This room was less of a study than it was a shrine.

Having seen enough, too much, I wanted to get out of the house. I yearned to return to Tire World, breathe the scent of rubber ready for the road, and think about what to do next.

Instead, I sat in the office chair. I am not squeamish, but I cringed slightly when I put my hands on the arms of the chair where his hands might have rested.

On the desk were a computer, a printer, a brass lamp, and a day-date calendar. Not a speck of dust or lint could be seen on any surface.

From this perch, I surveyed the study, trying to understand how it could have become the black room and then could have reverted to this ordinary space again.

No residual St. Elmo's fire of supernatural energy glimmered along the metal edges of the file cabinets. No otherworldly presences revealed themselves.

For a while, this room had been transformed into . . . a portal, a doorway between Pico Mundo and somewhere far stranger, by which I do not mean Los Angeles or even Bakersfield. Perhaps for a while this house had been a train station between our world and Hell, if Hell exists.

Or if I had reached the bloody red light at the center of that otherwise perfect darkness, perhaps I would have found myself on a planet in a remote arm of the galaxy, where bodachs ruled. Lacking a boarding pass, I had instead been flung into the living room and the past, then into the carport and the future.

Of course I examined the possibility that what I had seen could have been mere delusion. I might be as crazy as a laboratory rat that has been fed a diet of psychosis-inducing toxins and forced to watch TV "reality" shows that explore in detail the daily lives of washed-up supermodels and aging rock stars.

From time to time, I do consider that I might be mad. Like any self-respecting lunatic, however, I am always quick to dismiss any doubts about my sanity.

I saw no reason to search the study for a hidden switch that might convert it again into the black room. Logic suggested that the formidable power needed to open that mysterious doorway had been projected not from here but from the other side, wherever that might be.

Most likely Fungus Man was unaware that his sanctum served not merely as a catalogued repository for his homicidal fantasies but also as a terminal admitting bodachs to a holiday of blood. Without my sixth sense, perhaps he could sit here, happily working on one of his grisly files, and not be conscious of the ominous transformation of the room or of the arriving hordes of demonic entities.

From nearby came a *tick-tick-tick*, a bone-on-bone rattle that brought to mind Halloween images of ambulatory skeletons, and then a brief scuttling sound.

I rose from the chair and listened, alert.

Tickless seconds passed. A rattle-free half minute.

A rat, perhaps, had stirred in the walls or attic, made sick and restless by the heat.

I sat once more and opened the desk drawers one by one.

In addition to pencils, pens, paper clips, a stapler, scissors, and other mundane items, I found two recent bank statements and a checkbook. All three were addressed to Robert Thomas Robertson at this house in Camp's End.

Good-bye, Fungus Man; hello, Bob.

Bob Robertson didn't have the necessary malevolent ring for the name of a would-be mass murderer. It sounded more like a jovial car salesman.

The four-page statement from Bank of America reported upon a savings account, two six-month certificates of deposit, a money-market account, and a stock-trading account. The combined value of all Robertson's assets at Bank of America amounted to $786,542.10.

I scanned the figure three times, certain that I must be misreading the placement of the comma and the decimal point.

The four-page statement from Wells Fargo Bank, accounting for investments in its care, showed a combined value of $463,125.43.

Robertson's handwriting was sloppy, but he faithfully kept a running balance in his checkbook. The current available resources in this account totaled $198,648.21.

That a man with liquid assets of nearly one and a half million dollars should make his home in a shabby, sweltering casita in Camp's End seemed downright perverse.

If I had this much green at my command, I might continue to cook short-order now and then purely for the artistic satisfaction, but never for a living. The tire life might not in the least appeal to me any longer.

Perhaps Robertson required few luxuries because he found all the pleasure he needed in ceaseless bloody fantasies that gouted through his imagination.

A sudden frenzied flapping-rattling almost brought me up from the chair again, but then a sharp and repeated *skreek* identified the source as crows pecking out their turf on the roof. They come out early on summer mornings, before the heat is insufferable, spend the afternoon in leafy bowers, and venture out again when the gradually retreating sun begins to lose some of its blistering power.

I am not afraid of crows.

In the checkbook register, I pored back through three months of entries but found only the usual payments to utilities, credit-card companies, and the like. The sole oddity was that Robertson had also written a surprising number of checks to *cash*.

During the past month alone, he had withdrawn a total of $32,000 in $2,000 and $4,000 increments. For the past two months, the total reached $58,000.

Even with his prodigious appetite, he couldn't eat that much Burke & Bailey's ice cream.

Evidently he had expensive tastes, after all. And

whatever indulgence he allowed himself, it was one that he couldn't purchase openly with checks or credit cards.

Returning the financial statements to the desk drawer, I began to sense that I had stayed too long in this place.

I assumed that the engine noise of the Explorer pulling into the carport would alert me to Robertson's return and that I would be able to slip out of the front as he entered by the side door. If for any reason he parked in the street or came home on foot, however, I might find myself trapped before I discovered that he had arrived.

McVeigh, Manson, and Mohammed Atta seemed to watch me. How easily I could imagine that genuine awareness informed the intense eyes in those photographs and that they glinted now with wicked expectation.

Lingering a moment longer, I turned backward through the small, square day-date pages on the desk calendar, searching for notations of appointments or other reminders that Robertson might have written during recent weeks. All the note lines were blank.

I returned to the current date—Tuesday, August 14—and then flipped forward, into the future. The page for August 15 was missing. Nothing had been written in the calendar after that date for as far as I cared to look.

Leaving everything as I had found it, I rose from the desk and went to the door. I switched off the overhead light.

Golden sunshine, trimmed into flame shapes by the intervening bladelike leaves of the melaleuca, made a false fire on the sheer curtains, without greatly illuminating the room, and the emboldened shadows seemed to gather more heavily around the portraits of the three killers than elsewhere.

A thought occurred to me—which happens more often than some people might suppose and certainly more often than I would prefer—whereupon I switched the light on again and went to the bank of file cabinets. In the drawer labeled *R*, I checked to see if, among these dossiers of butchers and lunatics, Fungus Man kept a file on himself.

I found one. The tab declared: ROBERTSON, ROBERT THOMAS.

How convenient it would have been if this folder had contained newspaper clippings concerning unsolved murders as well as highly incriminating items related to those killings. I could have memorized the file, replaced it, and reported my findings to Wyatt Porter.

With that information, Chief Porter could have figured a way to entrap Robertson. We could have put the creep behind bars before he had a chance to commit whatever crimes he might be currently contemplating.

The file, however, contained but a single item: the page that was missing from the desk calendar. Wednesday, August 15.

Robertson had written nothing on the note lines. Apparently, in his mind, the date itself was significant enough to include as the first item in the file.

I consulted my wristwatch. In six hours and four minutes, August 14 and August 15 would meet at the midnight divide.

And after that, what would happen? Something. Something . . . not good.

Returning to the living room, to the stained furniture and the dust and the litter of publications, I was struck once more by the sharp contrast between the well-cleaned and well-ordered study and the rest of the residence.

Out here, engrossed sometimes in raunchy magazines and sometimes in romances innocent enough to be read by ministers' wives, evidently oblivious of forgotten banana peels and empty coffee mugs and dirty socks long overdue for laundering, Robertson seemed to be unfocused, adrift. This was a man of half-formed clay, his identity in doubt.

By contrast, the Robertson who spent time in the study, creating and tending to those hundreds of files, surfing websites dealing with serial killers and mass murderers, knew precisely who he was—or at least who he wished to be.

CHAPTER 14

I LEFT AS I HAD ENTERED, BY THE SIDE DOOR connecting the kitchen and the carport, but I didn't immediately return to the Mustang that I had borrowed from Terri Stambaugh. Instead, I went behind the house to have a close look at the backyard.

The front lawn had been half dead, but the grass here in back had withered away long ago. The well-baked dirt had not received a drop of water since the last rain in late February, five and a half hot months ago.

If a man were in the habit of burying his victims, dismembered or not, in the backyard, a la John Wayne Gacy, he would keep the soil receptive to a shovel. This hardpan would break the point of a pick and send any midnight gravedigger in search of a jackhammer.

Fenced with open chain-link on which grew no vines or other screening vegetation, the backyard offered no privacy to a murderer with an inconvenient corpse on his hands. If they were of a ghoulish disposition, the neighbors could open a keg of beer, set up lawn chairs, and watch the interment for entertainment.

Supposing that Robertson was an actual serial killer instead of merely a wannabe, he had planted his garden elsewhere. I suspected, however, that the file he had created for himself was complete as of this date and that his debut performance would be tomorrow.

Watching from the edge of the barrel-tile roof, a crow cracked its orange beak and shrieked, as though it suspected that I had come to poach whatever crispy beetles and other sparse fare it fed upon in this parched territory.

I thought of Poe's dire raven, perched above the parlor door, maddeningly repeating one word—*nevermore, nevermore*.

Standing there, gazing up, I didn't realize that the crow was an omen, or that Poe's famous verse would, in fact, serve as the key to unlock its meaning. Had I understood then that this shrill crow was my raven, I would have acted much differently in the hours that followed; and Pico Mundo would still be a place of hope.

Failing to understand the importance of the crow, I returned to the Mustang, where I found Elvis sitting in the passenger's seat. He wore boat shoes, khaki slacks, and a Hawaiian shirt.

All other ghosts of my acquaintance have been limited in their wardrobes to the clothes that they were wearing when they perished.

For instance, Mr. Callaway, my high-school English teacher, died on his way to a costume party, dressed as the Cowardly Lion from *The Wizard of Oz*. Because he had been a man of some refinement, born with dignity and poise, I found it depressing, in the months following his death, to encounter him around town in his cheap velour costume, his whiskers drooping, his tail dragging the ground after him. I was much relieved when at last he let go of this world and moved on.

In death as in life, Elvis Presley makes his own

rules. He seems to be able to conjure any costume that he wore on a stage or in the movies, as well as the clothes that he wore when not performing. His attire is different from one manifestation to the next.

I have read that after downing an imprudent number of sleeping pills and depressants, he died in his underwear or maybe in his pajamas. Some say that he was found in a bathrobe as well, but some say not. He has never yet appeared to me in quite such casual dress.

For certain, he died in his bathroom at Graceland, unshaven and facedown in a puddle of vomit. This is in the coroner's report.

Happily, he always greets me clean-shaven and without a beard of upchuck.

On this occasion, when I sat behind the steering wheel and closed the car door, he smiled and nodded. His smile had an unusual melancholy quality.

He reached out and patted me on the arm, clearly expressing sympathy, if not pity. This puzzled and somewhat troubled me, for I had suffered nothing that would warrant such an expression of commiseration.

Here in the aftermath of August 15, I still cannot say how much Elvis knew then of the terrible events that were about to unfold. I suspect he foresaw all of it.

Like other ghosts, Elvis does not speak. Nor sing.

He dances sometimes if he's in a rhythmic mood. He's got some cool moves, but he's no Gene Kelly.

I started the car and punched up some random-play music on the CD box. Terri keeps the six-disc magazine stocked with the best work of her idol.

When "Suspicious Minds" came from the speakers, Elvis seemed to be pleased. With his fingertips, he tapped the rhythm on the dashboard as I drove out of Camp's End.

By the time we reached Chief Wyatt Porter's house in a better neighborhood, we were listening to "Mama Liked the Roses," from *Elvis's Christmas Album*, and the King of Rock and Roll had succumbed to quiet tears.

I prefer not to see him like this. The hard-driving rocker who sang "Blue Suede Shoes" wears a cocky smile and even a sneer better than he does tears.

Karla Porter, Wyatt's wife, answered the door. Willowy, lovely, with eyes as green as lotus petals, she unfailingly projects an aura of serenity and quiet optimism that is in contrast with her husband's doleful face and mournful eyes.

I suspect Karla is the reason that Wyatt's job has not worn him down to total ruin. Each of us needs a source of inspiration in his life, a cause for hope, and Karla is Wyatt's.

"Oddie," she said, "what a pleasure to see you. Come in, come in. Wyatt is out back, getting ready to destroy some perfectly good steaks on the barbecue. We're having a few people to dinner, we've got plenty extra, so I hope you'll stay."

As she led me through the house, unaware that Elvis accompanied us in a "Heartbreak Hotel" mood, I said, "Thank you, ma'am, that's very gracious of you, but I've got another engagement. I just stopped by to have a quick word with the chief."

"He'll be delighted to see you," she assured me. "He always is."

In the backyard, she turned me over to Wyatt, who was wearing an apron bearing the words BURNT AND GREASY GOES BETTER WITH BEER.

"Odd," Chief Porter said, "I hope you've not come here to ruin my evening."

"That's not my intention, sir."

The chief was tending to two grills—the first fired by gas for vegetables and ears of corn, the second by charcoal for the steaks.

With the sun still more than two hours above the horizon, a day of desert sunshine stored in the patio concrete, and visible waves of heat pouring off both barbecues, he should have been making enough salt water to reconstitute the long-dead sea of Pico Mundo. He was, however, as dry as the star of an antiperspirant commercial.

Over the years, I have seen Chief Porter sweat only twice. On the first occasion, a thoroughly nasty man was aiming a spear gun at the chief's crotch from a distance of just two feet, and the second occasion was much more unnerving than that.

Checking out the bowls of potato salad, corn chips, and fresh fruit salad on the picnic table, Elvis seemed to lose interest when he realized that no deep-fried banana-and-peanut-butter sandwiches would be provided. He wandered off to the swimming pool.

After I declined a bottle of Corona, the chief and I sat in lawn chairs, and he said, "You been communing with the dead again?"

"Yes, sir, off and on all day. But this isn't so much about who's dead as who might be soon."

I told him about Fungus Man at the restaurant and later at Green Moon Mall.

"I saw him at the Grille," the chief said, "but he didn't strike me as suspicious, just . . . unfortunate."

"Yes, sir, but you didn't have the advantage of being able to see his fan club." I described the disturbing size of Fungus Man's bodach entourage.

When I recounted my visit to the small house in Camp's End, I pretended, rather ludicrously, that the side door had been standing open and that I had gone inside under the impression that someone might be in trouble. This relieved the chief of the need to conspire with me, after the fact, in the crime of breaking and entering.

"I'm not a high-wire artist," he reminded me.

"No, sir."

"You expect me to walk a dangerously narrow line sometimes."

"I have great respect for your balance, sir."

"Son, that sounds perilously like bullshit."

"There's some bullshit in it, sir, but it's mostly sincerity."

Telling him what I found in the house, I omitted any mention of the black room and the traveling swarm. Even a man as sympathetic and open-minded as Wyatt Porter will become a skeptic if you force too much exotic detail upon him.

When I finished my story, the chief said, "What's got your attention, son?"

"Sir?"

"You keep looking over toward the pool."

"It's Elvis," I explained. "He's behaving strangely."

"Elvis Presley is here? Now? At my house?"

"He's walking on the water, back and forth, and gesticulating."

"Gesticulating?"

"Not rudely, sir, and not at us. He looks like he's arguing with himself. Sometimes I worry about him."

Karla Porter reappeared, this time with their first two dinner guests in tow.

Bern Eckles, in his late twenties, was a recent addition to the Pico Mundo Police Department. He had been on the force just two months.

Lysette Rains, who specialized in false fingernails, was the assistant manager at the thriving beauty shop that Karla owned on Olive Street, around the corner and two blocks from where I worked at the Grille.

These two had not arrived as a couple, but I could see that the chief and Karla were engaged in some matchmaking.

Because he didn't know—and never would—about my sixth sense, Officer Eckles couldn't figure out what to make of me, and he had not yet decided whether he liked me. He couldn't understand why the chief always made time for me even on the busiest of days.

After the new arrivals had been served drinks, the chief asked Eckles to come to his study for a few minutes. "I'll get on the computer to the DMV while you make some phone calls for me. We need to work up a quick profile on this odd duck from Camp's End."

On his way into the house with the chief, Bern Eckles twice looked over his shoulder at me, frowning. Maybe he thought that in his absence I would try to make time with Lysette Rains.

When Karla returned to the kitchen, where she was working on the dessert, Lysette sat in the chair that the chief had occupied. With both hands, she held a glass of Coke spiked with orange vodka, from which she took tiny sips, licking her lips after each.

"How does that taste?" I wondered.

"Sort of like cleaning fluid with sugar. But sometimes I have a low energy level, and the caffeine helps."

She was wearing yellow shorts and a frilly yellow blouse. She looked like a lemon cupcake with fancy icing.

"How's your mother these days, Odd?"

"Still colorful."

"I would expect so. And your dad?"

"He's about to get rich quick."

"What with this time?"

"Selling real estate on the moon."

"How does that work?"

"You pay fifteen bucks, you get a deed to one square foot of the moon."

"Your father doesn't own the moon," Lysette said with the faintest note of disapproval.

She is a sweet person and reluctant to give offense even at evidence of flagrant fraud.

"No, he doesn't," I agreed. "But he realized that nobody else owned it, either, so he sent a letter to the United Nations, staking claim to it. The next day he started peddling moon property. I hear you've been made assistant manager of the shop."

"It's quite a responsibility. Especially 'cause I've also moved up in my specialty."

"You're not doing fingernails anymore?"

"Yes, I am. But I was just a nail technician, and now I'm a certified nail *artist*."

"Congratulations. That's really something."

Her shy smile of pride made me love her. "It's not so much to some people, but it's a thrill to me."

Elvis returned from the swimming pool and sat in a lawn chair opposite us. He was weeping again. Through his tears, he smiled at Lysette—or at her cleavage. Even in death he likes the ladies.

"Are you and Bronwen still an item?" Lysette asked.

"Forever. We have matching birthmarks."

"I'd forgotten about that."

"She prefers to be called Stormy."

"Who wouldn't?" Lysette said.

"How about you and Officer Eckles?"

"Oh, we just met. He seems nice."

"'Nice.'" I winced. "The poor guy's already struck out with you, hasn't he?"

"Two years ago, he would've, yeah. But lately, I'm thinking nice would be enough. You know?"

"There's a lot worse than nice out there."

"For sure," she agreed. "It takes a while to realize what a lonely world it is, and when you do . . . then the future looks kinda scary."

Already in a delicate emotional condition, Elvis was wrecked by Lysette's observation. The rillets of tears on his checks became twin floods, and he buried his face in his hands.

Lysette and I chatted for a while, and Elvis sobbed without making a sound, and eventually four more guests showed up.

Karla was circulating with a tray of cheese dumplings that gave new weight to the word *hors d'oeuvre*, when the chief returned with Officer Eckles. He drew me aside and walked with me to the far end of the pool, so we could talk in private.

He said, "Robertson moved into town five months ago. Paid in full for that house in Camp's End, no mortgage."

"Where's he get his money?"

"Inherited. Bonnie Chan says he moved here from San Diego after his mother's death. He was still living with his mother at thirty-four."

Bonnie Chan, a Realtor famous in Pico Mundo for her flamboyant hats, had evidently sold the residence to Robertson.

"As far as I can see at this point," the chief said, "he's got a clean record. He's never even had a speeding ticket."

"You might look into how the mother died."

"I've already put out some inquiries about that. But right now I don't have any handle to pick him up."

"All those files on all those killers."

"Even if I had a legitimate way of knowing he keeps them, it's just a sick hobby or maybe book research. There's nothing illegal about it."

"Suspicious, though."

He shrugged. "If being suspicious was enough, we'd all be in jail. You first."

"But you're gonna keep a watch on him?" I asked.

"Only because you've never been wrong. I'll park somebody over there this evening, pin a tail on this Mr. Robertson."

"I wish you could do more," I said.

"Son, this is the United States of America. Some would say it's unconstitutional to try to prevent psychopaths from fulfilling their potential."

Sometimes the chief can amuse me with that kind of cynical-cop patter. This wasn't one of those occasions.

I said, "This one's really bad, sir. This guy, when I picture his face in my mind . . . I get spiders down the spine."

"We're watching him, son. Can't do more than that. Can't just go to Camp's End and shoot him." The chief gave me a peculiar look and added, "Neither can you."

"Guns scare me," I assured him.

The chief looked over toward the swimming pool and said, "He still walking the water?"

"No, sir. He's standing next to Lysette, looking down her blouse and crying."

"That's nothing to cry about," the chief said, and winked.

"The crying has nothing to do with Lysette. He's just in a mood today."

"What about? Elvis never struck me as weepy."

"People change when they die. It's traumatic. He's like this from time to time, but I don't know for sure what the trouble is. He doesn't try to explain himself to me."

Clearly, the chief was dismayed by the image of Presley weeping. "Is there anything I can do for him?"

"That's thoughtful of you, sir, but I don't see what anyone can really do. From what I've observed on other occasions, my sense of it is . . . he misses his mother, Gladys, and wants to be with her."

"As I recall, he was especially fond of his mama, wasn't he?"

"He adored her," I said.

"Isn't she dead, too?"

"Much longer than he's been, yes."

"Then they're together again, aren't they?"

"Not as long as he's reluctant to let go of this world. She's over there in the light, and he's stuck here."

"Why won't he move on?"

"Sometimes they have important unfinished business here."

"Like little Penny Kallisto this morning, leading you to Harlo Landerson."

"Yes, sir. And sometimes they just love this world so much they don't want to leave it."

The chief nodded. "This world sure was good to him."

"If it's unfinished business, he's had more than twenty-six years to take care of it," I noted.

The chief squinted toward Lysette Rains, trying to see some smallest evidence of her spirit companion—a wisp of ectoplasm, a vague distortion of the air, a quiver of mystical radiance. "He made some great music."

"Yes, he did."

"You tell him he's always welcome here."

"I will, sir. That's kind of you."

"Are you sure you can't stay for dinner?"

"Thank you, sir, but I've got a date."

"With Stormy, I'm sure."

"Yes, sir. My destiny."

"You're a smooth operator, Odd. She must love to hear you say that—'my destiny.'"

"*I* love to hear me say it."

The chief put his arm around my shoulders and walked me to the gate at the north side of the house. "Best thing that can happen to a man is a good woman."

"Stormy is beyond just good."

"I'm happy for you, son." He lifted the latch and opened the gate for me. "Don't you worry about this Bob Robertson. We'll dog him, but so he doesn't suspect we're watching. He tries to make a wrong move, we'll be all over him."

"I'll worry just the same, sir. He's a very bad man."

When I got to the Mustang, Elvis was already sitting in the passenger's seat.

The dead don't need to walk where they want to go—or ride in a car, for that matter. When they choose to walk or cruise the streets, they're motivated by nostalgia.

From the poolside party to the Mustang, he had changed out of the clothes from *Blue Hawaii*. Now he was wearing black slacks, a dressy tweed sport coat, white shirt, black tie, and black pocket handkerchief, an outfit from (as Terri Stambaugh later told me) *It Happened at the World's Fair*.

Driving away from the Porter house, we listened to "Stuck on You," as infectious a tune as ever the King recorded.

Elvis rapped out the rhythm on his knees and bobbed his head, but the tears kept flowing.

CHAPTER 15

IN DOWNTOWN PICO MUNDO, AS WE WERE passing a church, Elvis indicated that he wanted me to pull to the curb.

When I stopped the car, he held out his right hand to me. His grip was as real and warm as Penny Kallisto's.

Instead of shaking my hand, he clasped it in both of his. Maybe he was simply thanking me, but it seemed like more than that.

He appeared to be worried about me. He gently squeezed my hand, staring intensely at me with evident concern, and then squeezed my hand again.

"It's all right," I said, although I had no idea whether that was in any way an adequate response.

He got out of the car without opening the door—just phased through it—and walked up the steps of the church. I watched until he passed through the heavy oak doors and out of sight.

My dinner date with Stormy wasn't until eight o'clock, so I had time to kill.

Keep busy, Granny Sugars used to say, *even if with poker, fighting, and fast cars, because idleness will get you in worse trouble.*

Even lacking Grandma's advice, I couldn't just have

gone to my rendezvous point with Stormy and waited for her. With nothing else to occupy my mind, I'd dwell on Bob Robertson and his demonic files.

Cruising away from the church, I phoned P. Oswald Boone, he of the four hundred pounds and the six-fingered left hand.

Little Ozzie answered on the second ring. "Odd, my beautiful cow exploded."

"Exploded?"

"Boom," said Little Ozzie. "One minute all is right with the world, and the next minute your fabulous cow is blown to bits."

"When did this happen? I haven't heard anything about it."

"Exactly two hours and twenty-six minutes ago. The police have been here and gone, and I believe that even they, with all their experience of criminal savagery, were shocked by this."

"I just saw Chief Porter, and he didn't mention it."

"After they left here, the responding officers no doubt needed a stiff drink or two before writing their report."

"How're you doing?" I asked.

"I'm not bereft, because that would be a morally offensive overreaction, but I *am* sad."

"I know how much you loved that cow."

"I loved that cow," he confirmed.

"I was thinking of coming over for a visit, but maybe this isn't the best time."

"This is the perfect time, dear Odd. Nothing is worse than being alone on the evening of the day when one's cow has exploded."

"I'll be there in a few minutes," I promised.

Little Ozzie lives in Jack Flats, which fifty years ago was called Jack Rabbit Flats, an area west and downhill from the historical district. I have no idea where the rabbit went.

When the picturesque downtown commercial district began to be a tourist draw in the late 1940s, it was given a series of quaintness injections to increase its appeal. The less photogenic enterprises—muffler shops, tire stores, gun shops—were squeezed to the Flats.

Then twenty years ago, glittering new commercial centers arose along Green Moon Road and Joshua Tree Highway. They drained customers from the shabbier businesses in the Flats.

Gradually during the past fifteen years, Jack Flats has been gentrified. Old commercial and industrial buildings were bulldozed. Homes, townhomes, and upscale apartments took their place.

The first to settle in the neighborhood when few could see its future, Little Ozzie purchased a one-acre parcel on which had stood a long-out-of-business restaurant. There he built his dream home.

This two-story, Craftsman-style residence has an elevator, wide doorways, and steel-reinforced floors. Ozzie constructed it both to accommodate his proportions and to withstand the punishment that he might inflict upon it if eventually he becomes, as Stormy fears, one of those men for whom the attending mortician requires a crane and a flatbed truck.

When I parked in front of the now cowless house, I was more shocked by the carnage than I had expected to be.

Standing under one of the Indian laurels that cast long shadows in the westering sun, I stared in dismay at the giant carcass. All things of this earth eventually pass away, but sudden and premature departures are nonetheless disturbing.

The four legs, chunks of the blasted head, and slabs of the body were scattered across the front lawn, shrubbery, and walkway. In a particularly macabre touch, the inverted udder had landed on one of the gateposts in the picket fence, and the teats pointed skyward.

This black-and-white Holstein cow, approximately the size of an SUV, had previously stood atop two twenty-foot-tall steel poles, neither of which had been damaged in the explosion. The only thing left on that high perch was the cow's butt, which had shifted position until it faced the street, as if mooning passersby.

Under the plastic Holstein had once hung a sign for the steak-house restaurant that had previously occupied the property. When he built his home, Little Ozzie had not preserved the sign, only the giant plastic bovine.

To Ozzie, the cow wasn't merely the largest lawn ornament in the world. It was art.

Of the many books that he has written, four have been about art, so he ought to know what he's talking about. In fact, because he is Pico Mundo's most famous resident (living, anyway) and perhaps its most respected, and because he was building a home in the Flats when everyone else expected it to remain a blighted zone in perpetuity, only Little Ozzie could have argued successfully before the city building department to keep the cow, as sculpture.

As the Flats became more upscale, some of his neighbors—not most, but a highly vocal minority—objected to the giant cow on aesthetic grounds. Perhaps one of them had resorted to violence.

By the time that I navigated through the jagged shards of cow art and climbed the front porch steps, before I could ring the bell, Ozzie opened the wide door, hoved across the threshold, and greeted me. "Is this not pathetic, Odd, what some ill-educated fool has done? I take solace in reminding myself that 'art is long and critics are the insects of a day.'"

"Shakespeare?" I asked.

"No. Randall Jarrell. A wonderful poet, now all but forgotten because modern universities teach nothing but self-esteem and toe-sucking."

"I'll clean this up for you, sir."

"You will not!" Ozzie declared. "Let them look at the ruin for a week, a month, these 'venomous serpents who delight in hissing.'"

"Shakespeare?"

"No, no. W. B. Daniel, writing on critics. I'll have the debris picked up eventually, but the ass of that fine cow will remain up there, my answer to these bomb-toting philistines."

"So it was a bomb?"

"A very small one, affixed to the sculpture during the night, with a timer that allowed these 'serpents who feed on filth and venom' to be far from the crime when the blast came. That's not Shakespeare, either. Voltaire writing on critics."

"Sir, I'm a little worried about you," I said.

"Don't be concerned, lad. These cowards have barely sufficient courage to sneak up on a plastic cow in the dead of night, but they don't have the spine to confront a fat man with forearms as thick as mine."

"I'm not talking about them. I'm referring to your blood pressure."

With a dismissive wave of one of his formidable arms, Little Ozzie said, "If you carried my bulk, your blood rich with cholesterol molecules the size of miniature marshmallows, you'd understand that a little righteous outrage from time to time is the only thing that keeps your arteries from clogging shut altogether. Righteous outrage and fine red wine. Come in, come in. I'll open a bottle, and we'll toast the destruction of all critics, 'this wretched race of hungry alligators.'"

"Shakespeare?" I asked.

"For Heaven's sake, Odd, the Bard of Avon wasn't the only writer ever to put pen to paper."

"But if I just stick with him," I said, following Ozzie into the house, "I'll get one of these right sooner or later."

"Was it with such pathetic tricks that you slid through high school?"

"Yes, sir."

Ozzie invited me to make myself comfortable in his living room while he fetched the Robert Mondavi Cabernet Sauvignon, and thus I found myself alone with Terrible Chester.

This cat is not fat, but he is big and fearless. I once saw him stand off an aggressive German shepherd sheerly with attitude.

I suspect that even a pit bull, gone bad and in a murdering mood, would have turned away as the shepherd did, and would have gone in search of easier prey. Like crocodiles.

Terrible Chester is the color of a rubescent pumpkin, with black markings. Judging by the black-and-orange patterns on his face, you might think he was the satanic familiar of that old rock group, Kiss.

Perched on a deep windowsill, gazing out at the front yard, he pretended for a full minute to be unaware that company had arrived.

Being ignored was fine with me. The shoes I wore had never been peed on, and I hoped to keep them that way.

Finally turning his head, he regarded me apprais-ingly, with contempt so thick that I expected to hear it drizzle to the floor with a spattering sound. Then he shifted his attention once more to the window.

The exploded Holstein seemed to fascinate him and to put him in a somber, contemplative mood. Perhaps he had used up eight of his lives and felt a chill of mortality.

The furniture in Ozzie's living room is custom, oversized, and built for comfort. A Persian carpet in dark jewel tones, Honduras mahogany woodwork, and shelves upon shelves of books create a cozy ambience.

In spite of the danger to my shoes, I quickly relaxed and experienced less of a sense of impending doom than at any time since finding Penny Kallisto waiting at the foot of my apartment steps earlier in the day.

Within half a minute, Terrible Chester put me on edge again with his threatening, angry hiss. All cats have this talent, of course, but Chester rivals both rattlesnakes and cobras for the intensity and the menace of his hiss.

Something outside had so disturbed him that he rose to his feet on the windowsill, arched his back, and bristled his hackles.

Although clearly I was not the cause of his agita-tion, I slid to the edge of my armchair, poised for flight.

Chester hissed again, then clawed the glass. The *skreeeek* of his nails on the window made the fluid quiver in the hollows of my spine.

Suddenly I wondered if the cow-demolition squad had returned in daylight to bring down the stubborn bovine butt.

When Chester raked the glass again, I got to my feet. I eased toward the window with caution, not because I feared that a Molotov cocktail would crash through it but because I didn't want the vexated cat to misunderstand my motives.

Outside, at the picket fence, facing the house, stood the Fungus Man, Bob Robertson.

CHAPTER 16

MY FIRST INSTINCT WAS TO DUCK BACK from the window. If Fungus Man was already following me, however, he must somehow suspect that earlier I had been in his house in Camp's End. My furtive behavior would serve to confirm my guilt.

I remained near the window, but I was grateful that Terrible Chester stood between me and Robertson. I also found it gratifying that the cat's apparent intense dislike of the man, even at such a distance as this, confirmed my distrust of him.

Until this moment, I would never have assumed that Terrible Chester and I would agree on any issue or have anything in common other than our affection for Little Ozzie.

For the first time in my experience, Robertson wore no smile, dreamy or otherwise. Standing in sunshine that the weight of the day had condensed from white glare into honey-gold, backdropped by the forms and shadows of the laurels, he looked as grim as the giant photo of Timothy McVeigh on his study wall.

From behind me, Ozzie said, "'Oh, God, that men should put an enemy in their mouths, to steal away their brains.'"

Turning, I found him with a tray on which he offered

two glasses of wine and a small plate of cubed cheese surrounded by thin white crackers.

Thanking him, I took one of the glasses and glanced outside.

Bob Robertson was not where he had been.

Risking a dangerous misunderstanding with Terrible Chester, I stepped closer to the window, looking north and south along the street.

"Well?" Ozzie asked impatiently.

Robertson had gone, and quickly, as if with an urgent purpose.

As spooked as I had been to see this strange man at the picket fence, I was still more disturbed to have lost sight of him. If he wanted to follow me, I would submit to being tailed because then I would know where he was and, knowing, would rest easier.

"'Oh, God, that men should put an enemy in their mouths, to steal away their brains,'" Ozzie repeated.

Turning from the window, I saw that he had put down the tray and stood now with his glass raised as if making a toast.

Struggling to recover my composure, I said, "Some days are so difficult that if we didn't let wine steal our wits, how would we sleep?"

"Lad, I'm not asking you to debate the statement, merely to identify its source."

Still rattled by Robertson, I said, "Sir?"

With some exasperation, Ozzie said, "*Shakespeare!* I stack the quiz to ensure you a passing grade, and still you fail. That was Cassio speaking in Act 2, Scene 3 of *Othello.*"

"I was . . . distracted."

Indicating the window, where Chester no longer appeared to be agitated and had once more settled into a furry pile on the deep sill, Ozzie said, "The destruction that barbarians leave behind has a grim fascination, doesn't it? We're reminded how thin is the veneer of civilization."

"Sorry to disappoint you, sir, but my thoughts weren't running that deep. I just . . . I thought I saw someone I knew passing by."

Raising the wineglass in his five-fingered hand, Ozzie said, "To the damnation of all miscreants."

"That's pretty strong, sir—damnation."

"Don't spoil my fun, lad. Just drink."

Drinking, I glanced at the window again. Then I returned to the armchair where I had been seated before the cat hissed so alarmingly.

Ozzie settled down, as well, but his chair made a noisier issue of it than mine did.

I looked around at the books, at the wonderful reproductions of Tiffany lamps, but the room didn't exert its usual calming influence. I could almost hear my wristwatch ticking off the seconds toward midnight and August 15.

"You've come here with a burden," Ozzie said, "and since I don't see a hostess gift, I assume the weight you carry is some trouble or other."

I told him everything about Bob Robertson. Although I'd withheld the story of the black room from Chief Porter, I shared it with Ozzie because he has an imagination big enough to encompass anything.

In addition to his nonfiction books, he has written two highly successful series of mystery novels.

The first, as you might expect, is about a fat detective of incomparable brilliance who solves crimes while tossing off hilarious bon mots. He relies on his beautiful and highly athletic wife (who utterly adores him) to undertake all the investigative footwork and to perform all the derring-do.

Those books, Ozzie says, are based on certain hormone-drenched adolescent fantasies that preoccupied him throughout his teenage years. And still linger.

The second series involves a female detective who remains a likable heroine in spite of numerous neuroses and bulimia. This character had been conceived over a five-hour dinner during which Ozzie and his editor made less use of their forks than they made of their wineglasses.

Challenging Ozzie's assertion that a fictional detective could have *any* personal problems or habits, however unpleasant, and still be a hit with the public as long as the author had the skill to make the character sympathetic, the editor had said, "No one could make a large audience want to read about a detective who stuck a finger down her throat and threw up after every meal."

The first novel featuring such a detective won an Edgar Award, the mystery genre's equivalent of an Oscar. The tenth book in the series had been recently published to greater sales than any of the previous nine.

In solemn tones that fail to disguise his impish glee, Ozzie says that no novels in the history of literature have featured so much vomiting to the delight of so many readers.

Ozzie's success doesn't in the least surprise me. He likes people and he *listens* to them, and that love of humanity shines out of his pages.

When I finished telling him about Robertson, the black room, and the file cabinets packed with thick case histories of homicidal maniacs, he said, "Odd, I wish you would get a gun."

"Guns scare me," I reminded him.

"Your *life* scares *me*. I'm certain Wyatt Porter would issue you a permit to carry a concealed weapon."

"Then I'd have to wear a sports jacket."

"You could switch to Hawaiian shirts, carry the gun in a belt holster in the small of your back."

I frowned. "Hawaiian shirts are just not me."

"Oh, yes," he said with undisguised sarcasm, "your T-shirts and jeans are such a unique fashion statement."

"Sometimes I wear chinos."

"The depth of your wardrobe dazzles the mind. Ralph Lauren weeps."

I shrugged. "I am who I am."

"If I purchase a suitable weapon for you and personally instruct you in its use—"

"Thank you, sir, for your concern, but for sure I'd shoot off both my feet, and the next thing I knew, you'd be writing a series about a footless private investigator."

"It's already been done." He sipped his wine. "Everything's already been done. Only once in a generation does anything as fresh as a vomiting detective come along."

"There's still chronic diarrhea."

He grimaced. "I'm afraid you haven't the knack to be a popular mystery novelist. What have you been writing lately?"

"This and that."

"Assuming 'this' refers to grocery-shopping lists and 'that' refers to mash notes to Stormy Llewellyn, what *else* have you been writing?"

"Nothing," I admitted.

When I was sixteen, P. Oswald Boone, then a mere 350 pounds, agreed to judge a writing contest at our high school, from which he himself had graduated some years earlier. My English teacher required each of her students to submit an entry to the contest.

Because my Granny Sugars had only recently died and because I'd been missing her, I wrote a piece about her. Unfortunately, it won first prize, making of me a minor celebrity in high school, though I preferred to keep a low profile.

For my memories of Granny, I received three hundred dollars and a plaque. I spent the money on an inexpensive but quite listenable music system.

The plaque and the music system were later smashed to bits by an angry poltergeist.

The only long-term consequence of that writing contest had been my friendship with Little Ozzie, for which I was grateful, although for five years he had harassed me to write, write, write. He said that such a talent was a gift and that I had a moral obligation to use it.

"Two gifts are one too many," I told him now. "If I had to deal with the dead and also write something worthwhile, I'd either go stark raving mad or shoot myself in the head with that gun you want to give me."

Impatient with my excuses, he said, "Writing isn't a source of pain. It's psychic chemotherapy. It reduces your psychological tumors and *relieves* your pain."

I didn't doubt either that this was true for him or that he had enough pain to require a lifetime of psychic chemotherapy.

Although Big Ozzie was still alive, Little Ozzie saw his father only once or twice a year. On each occasion, he required two weeks to recover his emotional equilibrium and trademark good humor.

His mother was alive, too. Little Ozzie hadn't spoken to her in twenty years.

Big Ozzie currently weighed, at a guess, only fifty pounds less than his son. Consequently, most people assumed that Little Ozzie had inherited his obesity.

Little Ozzie, however, refused to portray himself as a victim of his genetics. He said that at the heart of him was a weakness of will that resulted in his immensity.

Over the years, he sometimes implied and I frequently inferred that his parents had broken a part of his heart that resulted in this mortal weakness of will. He never spoke of his difficult childhood, however, and refused to describe what he had endured. He just wrote mystery novel after mystery novel . . .

He didn't speak of his folks with bitterness. Instead, he spoke of them hardly at all and avoided them as best he could—and wrote book after book about art, music, food, and wine . . .

"Writing," I told him now, "can't relieve my pain as much as it's relieved by the sight of Stormy . . . or by the taste of coconut cherry chocolate chunk ice cream, for that matter."

"I have no Stormy in my life," he replied, "but I can understand the ice cream." He finished his wine. "What are you going to do about this Bob Robertson?"

I shrugged.

Ozzie pressed me: "You've got to do something if he knows that you were in his house this afternoon and already he's following you around."

"All I can do is be careful. And wait for Chief Porter to get something on him. Anyway, maybe he wasn't actually following me. Maybe he heard about your exploding cow and stopped by to gawk at the ruins."

"Odd, I would be indescribably disappointed if, having not yet employed your writing gift to any useful purpose, you wound up dead tomorrow."

"Just think how *I'd* feel."

"I might wish that you'd grow wiser faster, get a

gun and write a book, but I won't wish anyone's life away for him. 'How swift are the feet of the days of the years of youth.'"

Giving attribution to the quote, I said, "Mark Twain."

"Excellent! Perhaps you aren't a willfully ignorant young fool, after all."

"You used that quote once before," I admitted. "That's how I know it."

"But at least you remembered! I believe this reveals in you a desire, even if unconscious, to give up the griddle and make yourself a man of literature."

"I expect I'll switch to tires first."

He sighed. "You're a tribulation sometimes." He rang his empty wineglass with one fingernail. "I should've brought the bottle."

"Sit still. I'll get it," I said, for I could fetch the Cabernet from the kitchen in the time that he would require merely to lever himself up from his armchair.

The ten-foot-wide hallway served as a gallery for fine art, and opening off both sides of it were rooms rich with still more art and books.

At the end of the hall lay the kitchen.

On a black-granite counter stood the bottle, uncorked to let the wine breathe.

Although the front rooms had been comfortably air-conditioned, the kitchen proved to be surprisingly warm. Entering, I thought for an instant that all four ovens must be filled with baking treats.

Then I saw that the back door stood open. The desert evening, still broiling in the stubborn summer sun, had sucked the coolness from the kitchen.

When I stepped to the door to close it, I saw Bob Robertson in the backyard, as pale and fungoid as ever he had looked.

CHAPTER 17

ROBERTSON STOOD FACING THE HOUSE, AS though waiting for me to see him. Then he turned and walked toward the back of the property.

For too long, I hesitated in the doorway, uncertain what I should do.

I assumed that one of his neighbors might have recognized me and might have told him that earlier I'd been snooping around during his absence. But the swiftness with which he'd tracked me down and had begun to tail me was disconcerting.

My paralysis broke with the realization that I had endangered Ozzie, had led this psychopath to his house. I left the kitchen, crossed the porch, descended the steps to a patio, stepped onto the lawn, and went after Robertson.

Ozzie's house sits at the front of his one-acre lot, and most of the property is given over to lawn and to trees that screen him from his neighbors. In the back half of the acre, the trees grow thicker than at the front, and stand close enough to qualify as a small woods.

Into this copse of laurel, podocarpus, and California pepper, Robertson strode—and disappeared from view.

The westward-dawdling sun slanted between the trees where it could find narrow gaps, but for the most part the layered branches successfully resisted it. Cooler than the sun-baked lawn, these greenery-scented shadows were nevertheless warm, and they pressed against me in stifling folds.

No less than the cloying shadows, the trunks of the many trees offered concealment. My quarry made good use of them.

I tacked quickly but warily through the woods, north to south, then south to north, first in silence, then calling his name—"Mr. Robertson?"—but he didn't answer.

The few intruding flares of sunlight inhibited rather than assisted the search. They illuminated little but were just numerous enough to prevent my eyes from adjusting well to the gloom.

Afraid of leaving the woods unsearched and therefore giving Robertson a chance to creep in behind me, I took too long to get to the gate in the back fence. I found it closed, but it was held by a gravity latch that would have engaged automatically when it fell shut behind him.

The gate opened into a picturesque brick-paved alleyway, flanked by back fences and garages, shaded here and there by queen palms and willowy pepper trees. Neither Bob Robertson nor anyone else was afoot as far as I could see in either direction.

Returning through the woodlet, I half expected him to lunge at me, not gone after all but waiting to catch me with my guard down. If Robertson was hiding in that grove, he must have recognized that I remained alert, for he didn't risk an assault.

When I reached the back porch, I stopped, turned, and studied the pocket forest. Birds flew from those branches, not as if chased out by anything, but only as if taking a last flight before sunset.

In the kitchen again, I closed the door. I engaged the deadbolt lock. And the security chain.

I peered through the windowpanes in the upper half of the door. Peaceful, the woods. And still.

When I returned to the living room with the bottle of Cabernet, half the cheese had disappeared from the canape plate, and Little Ozzie was still ensconced in his commodious chair, where he himself had once said that he looked as cozy as the Toad King on his throne.

"Dear Odd, I was beginning to think you'd stepped through a wardrobe into Narnia."

I told him about Robertson.

"You mean," Ozzie said, "that he was *here*, in my house?"

"Yes, I think so," I said as I refilled his wineglass.

"Doing what?"

"Probably standing in the hall, just beyond that archway, listening to us talk."

"That's damn bold."

Setting the bottle on a coaster beside his glass, striving hard to repress the palsy of fear that would have trembled my hands, I said, "No more bold than I was when I slipped into his house to poke through his drawers."

"I suppose not. But then you're on the side of the gods, and this bastard sounds like a giant albino cockroach on a day pass from Hell."

Terrible Chester had moved from the windowsill to my chair. He raised his head to challenge me for possession of the seat. His eyes are as green as those of a scheming demon.

"If I were you," Ozzie advised, "I would sit elsewhere." He indicated the bottle of wine. "Won't you have a second glass?"

"Haven't quite finished my first," I said, "and I've

really got to be going. Stormy Llewellyn, dinner—all of that. But don't get up."

"Don't tell me not to get up," he grumped as he began the process of disengaging his bulk from armchair cushions that, like the hungry jaws of an exotic flesh-eating plant, had closed with considerable suction around his thighs and buttocks.

"Sir, it's really not necessary."

"Don't tell me what's necessary, you presumptuous pup. What's necessary is whatever I wish to do, regardless of how unnecessary it might seem."

Sometimes when he gets up after having been seated for a while, his complexion reddens with the effort, and at other times he goes sheet-white. I'm frightened to think that such a simple thing as rising from a chair should tax him so much.

Fortunately, his face neither flushed nor paled this time. Perhaps fortified by the wine and burdened by only half a plate of cheese, he was on his feet markedly faster than a desert tortoise extracting itself from a dry slough of treacherous sand.

"Now that you're up," I said, "I think you should lock the door behind me. And keep all the doors locked till this thing is resolved. Don't answer the bell unless you can see who rang it."

"I'm not afraid of him," Ozzie declared. "My well-padded vital organs are hard to reach with either blade or bullet. And I know a few things about self-defense."

"He's dangerous, sir. He might have controlled himself so far, but when he cracks, he'll be so vicious that he'll make the evening news from Paris to Japan. *I'm* scared of him."

Ozzie dismissed my concern with a wave of his six-fingered hand. "Unlike you, I've got a gun. More than one."

"Start keeping them handy. I'm so sorry to have drawn him here."

"Nonsense. He was just something stuck to your shoe that you didn't know was there."

Each time that I leave this house after a visit, Ozzie hugs me as a father hugs a beloved son, as neither of us was ever hugged by his father.

And every time, I am surprised that he seems so fragile in spite of his formidable bulk. It's as if I can feel a shockingly thin Ozzie within the mantles of fat, an Ozzie who is being steadily crushed by the layers that life has troweled upon him.

Standing at the open front door, he said, "Give Stormy a kiss for me."

"I will."

"And bring her around to bear witness to my beautiful exploded cow and the villainy it represents."

"She'll be appalled. She'll need wine. We'll bring a bottle."

"No need. I have a full cellar."

I waited on the porch until he closed the door and until I heard the deadbolt being engaged.

As I negotiated the cow-strewn front walk and then rounded the Mustang to the driver's door, I surveyed the quiet street. Neither Robertson nor his dusty Ford Explorer was to be seen.

In the car, when I switched on the engine, I suddenly expected to be blown up like the Holstein. I was too jumpy.

I followed a twisty route from Jack Flats to St. Bartholomew's Catholic Church in the historical district, giving a tail plenty of opportunities to reveal himself. All the traffic behind me seemed to be innocent of the intent to pursue. Yet I felt watched.

CHAPTER 18

PICO MUNDO IS NOT A SKYSCRAPER TOWN. The recent construction of a five-story apartment building made longtime residents dizzy with an unwanted sense of metropolitan crowding and led to editorials in the *Maravilla County Times* that used phrases like "high-rise blight," and worried about a future of "heartless canyons of bleak design, in which people are reduced to the status of drones in a hive, and into which the sun never fully reaches."

The Mojave sun is not a timid little Boston sun or even a don't-worry-be-happy Caribbean sun. The Mojave sun is a fierce, aggressive beast that isn't going to be intimidated by the shadows of five-story apartment buildings.

Counting its tower and the spire that sits atop the tower, St. Bartholomew's Church is by far the tallest structure in Pico Mundo. Sometimes at twilight, under the barrel-tile roofs, the white stucco walls glow like the panes in a storm lantern.

With half an hour remaining before sunset on this Tuesday in August, the western sky blazed orange, steadily deepening toward red, as though the sun were wounded and bleeding in its retreat. The white walls of the church took color from the heavens, and appeared to be full of holy fire.

Stormy waited for me in front of St. Bart's. She sat on the top step, beside a picnic hamper.

She had traded her pink-and-white Burke & Bailey's uniform for sandals, white slacks, and a turquoise blouse. She had been cute then; she was ravishing now.

With her raven hair and jet-black eyes, she might have been the bride of a pharaoh, swept forward in time from ancient Egypt. In her eyes are mysteries to rival those of the Sphinx and those of all the pyramids that ever were or ever will be excavated from the sands of the Sahara.

As if reading my mind, she said, "You left your hormone spigot running. Crank it shut, griddle boy. This is a church."

I snatched up the picnic hamper and, as she rose to her feet, I kissed her on the cheek.

"On the other hand, that was a little too chaste," she said.

"Because that was a kiss from Little Ozzie."

"He's sweet. I heard they blew up his cow."

"It's a slaughterhouse, plastic Holstein splattered everywhere you look."

"What's next—hit squads shooting lawn gnomes to pieces?"

"The world is mad," I agreed.

We entered St. Bart's through the main door. The narthex is a softly lighted and welcoming space, paneled in cherry wood stained dark with ruby high-lights.

Instead of proceeding into the nave, we turned immediately to the right and stepped up to a locked door. Stormy produced a key and let us into the bottom of the bell tower.

Father Sean Llewellyn, rector of St. Bart's, is Stormy's uncle. He knows she loves the tower, and he indulges her with a key.

When the door fell quietly shut behind us, the sweet fragrance of incense faded, and a faint musty smell arose.

The tower stairs were dark. Unerringly, I found her lips for a quick but sweeter kiss than the first, before she switched on the light.

"Bad boy."

"Good lips."

"Somehow it's too strange . . . getting tongue in church."

"Technically, we're not in the *church*," I said.

"And I suppose technically that wasn't tongue."

"I'm sure there's a more correct medical term for it."

"There's a medical term for *you*," she said.

"What's that?" I wondered as, carrying the hamper, I followed her up the spiral staircase.

"Priapic."

"What's it mean?"

"Perpetually horny."

"You wouldn't want a doctor to cure *that*, would you?"

"Don't need a doctor. Folk medicine offers a reliable cure."

"Yeah? Like what?"

"A swift, hard blow to the source of the problem."

I winced and said, "You are no Florence Nightingale. I'm going to start wearing a cup."

At the top of the spiral stairs, a door opened to the belfry.

A carillon of three bronze bells, all large but of different sizes, hung from the ceiling in the center of this lofty space. A six-foot-wide catwalk encircled them.

The bells had rung for vespers at seven and would not ring again until morning Mass.

Three sides of the belfry were open above a waist-high wall, presenting splendid views of Pico Mundo, the Maravilla Valley, and the hills beyond. We stationed ourselves at the west side, the better to enjoy the sunset.

From the hamper, Stormy produced a Tupperware container filled with shelled walnuts that she had deep-fried and seasoned lightly with both salt and sugar. She fed me one. Delicious—both the walnut and being fed by Stormy.

I opened a bottle of good Merlot and poured while she held the wineglasses.

This was why earlier I had not finished the glass of Cabernet: As much as I love Little Ozzie, I would rather drink with Stormy.

We don't eat in this perch every evening, only two or three times a month, when Stormy needs to be high above the world. And closer to Heaven.

"To Ozzie," Stormy said, raising her glass in a toast. "With the hope that one day there'll be an end to all his losses."

I didn't ask what she meant by that because I thought perhaps I knew. By the affliction of his weight, there is much in life that Ozzie has been denied and may never experience.

Citrus-orange near the western horizon, blood-orange across the ascending vault, the sky darkened to purple directly overhead. In the east, the first stars of the night would soon begin to appear.

"The sky's so clear," Stormy said. "We'll be able to see Cassiopeia tonight."

She referred to a northern constellation named after a figure of classic mythology, but Cassiopeia was also the name of Stormy's mother, who had died when Stormy was seven years old. Her father had perished in the same plane crash.

With no family but her uncle, the priest, she had been placed for adoption. When in three months the adoption failed for good reason, she made it explicitly clear that she didn't want new parents, only the return of those whom she had loved and lost.

Until the age of seventeen, when she graduated from high school, she was raised in an orphanage. Thereafter, until she was eighteen, she had lived under the legal guardianship of her uncle.

For the niece of a priest, Stormy has a strange relationship with God. There is anger in it—always a little, sometimes a lot.

"What about Fungus Man?" she asked.

"Terrible Chester doesn't like him."

"Terrible Chester doesn't like anyone."

"I think Chester's even afraid of him."

"Now that *is* news."

"He's a hand grenade with the pin already pulled."

"Terrible Chester?"

"No. Fungus Man. Real name's Bob Robertson. The hair on his back was standing straight up like I've never seen it."

"Bob Robertson has a lot of hair on his back?"

"No. Terrible Chester. Even when he scared off that huge German shepherd, he didn't raise his hackles like he did today."

"Loop me in, odd one. How did Bob Robertson and Terrible Chester happen to be in the same place?"

"Since I broke into his house, I think maybe he's been following me around."

Even as I spoke the word *following*, my attention was drawn to movement in the graveyard.

Immediately west of St. Bart's is a cemetery very much in the old style: not bronze plaques set in granite flush with the grass, as in most modern graveyards, but vertical headstones and monuments. An iron fence with spearpoint pickets surrounds those three acres. Although a few California live oaks, more than a century old, shade portions of the burial ground, most of the green aisles are open to the sun.

In the fiery glow of that Tuesday twilight, the grass appeared to have a bronze undertone, the shadows were as black as char, the polished surfaces of the granite markers mirrored the scarlet sky—and Robertson stood as still as any headstone in the churchyard, not under the cover of a tree but out where he could be easily seen.

Having set her wineglass on the parapet, Stormy crouched at the hamper. "I've got some cheese that's perfect with this wine."

If Robertson had been standing with his head bowed, studying the engraving on a memorial, I would still have been disturbed to see him here. But this was worse. He had not come to pay his respects to the dead, not for *any* reason as innocent as that.

With his head tipped back, with his eyes fixed on me where I stood at the belfry parapet, the singular intensity of his interest all but crackled from him like arcing electricity.

Past the oaks and beyond the iron fence, I could see parts of two streets that intersected at the northwest corner of the cemetery. As far as I could tell, no marked or unmarked police vehicle was parked along either avenue.

Chief Porter had promised to assign a man at once

to watch the house in Camp's End. If Robertson hadn't been home yet, however, that officer could not have established surveillance.

"You want crackers with the cheese?" Stormy asked.

Crimson had seeped down the summer sky, closer to the horizon, staining the western swathe of bright orange until it narrowed to a swatch. The air itself seemed to be stained red, and the shadows of trees and tombstones, already soot-black, grew even blacker.

Robertson had arrived with nightfall.

I set my wineglass beside Stormy's. "We've got a problem."

"Crackers aren't a problem," Stormy said, "just a choice."

A sudden loud flapping-fluttering startled me.

Turning to see three pigeons swooping into the belfry and to their roost in the rafters above the bells, I bumped into Stormy as she rose with two small containers. Crackers and wedges of cheese spilled across the catwalk.

"Oddie, what a mess!" She stooped, set the containers aside, and began to gather the crackers and cheese.

Down on the darkening grass, Robertson had thus far stood with his arms at his sides, a slump-shoulder hulk. Aware that I was as fixated on him as he was on me, he now raised his right arm almost as if in a Nazi salute.

"Are you going to help me here," Stormy asked, "or are you going to be a typical man?"

Initially I thought he might be shaking his fist at me, but in spite of the poor—and rapidly fading—light, I soon saw that the gesture was even less polite than it had seemed at first. His middle finger was extended, and he thrust it toward me with short, angry jabs.

"Robertson's here," I told her.

"Who?"

"Fungus Man."

Suddenly he was on the move, walking between the headstones, toward the church.

"We better forget dinner," I said, drawing Stormy to her feet with the intention of hustling her out of the belfry. "Let's get down from here."

Resisting me, she turned to the parapet. "I don't let anyone intimidate me."

"Oh, I do. If they're crazy enough."

"Where is he? I don't see him."

Leaning out, peering down, I couldn't see him either. Apparently he had reached the front or the back of the church and had turned a corner.

"The door at the bottom of the steps," I said, "did it lock behind us automatically when we came into the tower?"

"I don't know. I don't think so."

I didn't like the idea of being trapped at the top of the tower, even though we could shout for help and surely be heard. The belfry door had no lock, and I doubted that the two of us could hold it shut against him if, in a rage, he was determined to open it.

Grabbing her by the hand, pulling to impress on her the need for urgency, I hurried along the catwalk, stepping over the cheese and crackers, around the bells. "Let's get out of here."

"The hamper, our dinner—"

"Leave it. We'll get it later, tomorrow."

We had left the lights on in the tower. But the spiral stairs were enclosed, and I couldn't see all the way to the bottom, only as far as the continuously curving walls allowed.

Below, all was quiet.

"Hurry," I urged Stormy, and without using the handrail, I preceded her down those steep steps, setting a pace too fast to be safe.

CHAPTER 19

DOWN, DOWN, AROUND AND DOWN, I LED and she followed, striking too much noise from the Mexican-tile steps, unable to hear Robertson if he was climbing to meet us.

At the halfway point I wondered if this haste might be an overreaction. Then I remembered his upraised fist, the extended finger, the glowering photos in his study.

I plunged even faster, around and around, unable to block from my mind the image of him waiting below with a butcher knife on which I might impale myself before I could stop.

When we reached the bottom without encountering him, we found the lower door unlocked. I opened it cautiously.

Contrary to my expectations, he wasn't waiting for us in the softly lighted narthex.

Descending the tower stairs, I had let go of Stormy's hand. Now I seized it again to keep her close to me.

When I opened the centermost of three front doors, I saw Robertson climbing the church steps from the sidewalk. Although not racing toward me, he approached with the grim implacability of a tank crossing a battlefield.

In the apocalyptic crimson light, I could see that his creepy but previously reliable smile had deserted him. His pale-gray eyes borrowed a bloody cast from the sunset, and his face wrenched into a knot of murderous wrath.

Terri's Mustang waited at the curb. I wouldn't be able to reach it without going through Robertson.

I will fight when I have to, against opponents who dwarf me if I must. But I turn to physical conflict neither as a first resort nor as a matter of misguided principle.

I'm not vain, but I like my face just the way it is. I prefer that it not be stomped.

Robertson was bigger than me, but soft. Had his anger been that of an ordinary man, perhaps pumped up by one beer too many, I might have confronted him and would have been confident of taking him down.

He was a lunatic, however, an object of fascination to bodachs, and an idolizer of mass murderers and serial killers. I had to assume that he carried a gun, a knife, and that in the middle of a fight, he might begin to bite like a dog.

Perhaps Stormy would have tried to kick his ass—such a response is not alien to her—but I didn't give her that option. Turning from the entrance, I held fast to her hand and encouraged her through one of the doors between the narthex and the nave.

In the deserted church, low pathlights marked the center aisle. The enormous crucifix behind the altar glowed in a soft spotlight directed on it from above. Flames flickered in ruby-colored glasses on the votive-candle racks.

Those points of light and the fading red sunset behind the stained-glass windows in the western wall failed to press back the congregation of shadows that filled the pews and the side aisles.

We hurried down the center aisle, expecting Robertson to slam with charging-bull fury through one of the doors from the narthex. Having heard nothing by the time we reached the communion railing, we paused and looked back.

As far as I could tell, Robertson had not arrived. If he had entered the nave, surely he would have come directly after us, along the center aisle.

Although logic argued against my hunch and no evidence supported it, I suspected that he was with us. The prickled skin on my arms suggested that I should speak in a honk, have webbed feet, and be covered with feathers.

Stormy's instinct was in sync with mine. Surveying the geometric shadows of pews, aisles, and colonnades, she whispered, "He's closer than you think. He's very close."

I pushed open the low gate in the communion railing. We passed through, moving in all but absolute silence now, not wanting to mask any sounds of Robertson's approach.

As we passed the choir enclosure and ascended the ambulatory toward the high altar, I glanced back less and proceeded with greater caution. Inexplicably, in opposition to my head, my heart said danger lay in front of us.

Our stalker couldn't have slipped around us unseen. Besides, there was no reason for him to have done so instead of assaulting us directly.

Nevertheless, with every step I took, the tension increased in the cords of muscle at the back of my neck, until they felt as tight as key-wound clock springs.

From the corner of my eye, I glimpsed movement

past the altar, twitched toward it, and drew Stormy closer to my side. Her hand clutched mine tighter than before.

The crucified bronze Christ moved, as if metal miraculously had become flesh, as if He would pull loose from the cross and step down to resume the earthly mantle of messiah.

A large scallop-winged moth flew away from the hot lens of the overhead spotlight. The illusion of movement—which the insect's exaggerated, fluttering shadow had imparted to the bronze figure—was at once dispelled.

Stormy's tower-door key would also unlock the door at the back of the sanctuary. Beyond waited the sacristy, in which the priest readied himself before every Mass.

I glanced back at the sanctuary, the nave. Silence. Stillness but for the moth's shadow play.

After using and returning Stormy's key, I pushed the paneled door inward with some trepidation.

This particular fear had no rational basis whatsoever. Robertson wasn't a magician able to appear by legerdemain inside a locked room.

Nevertheless, my heart played knock-and-rattle with my ribs.

When I felt for the light switch, my hand was *not* pinned to the wall by either a stiletto or a hatchet. The overhead light revealed a small, plain room but no large psychopath with yellow yeast-mold hair.

To the left stood the *prie-dieu*, where the priest knelt to offer his private devotions before saying Mass. To the right were cabinets containing the sacred vessels and the vestments, and a vesting bench.

Stormy closed the sanctuary door behind us and with a thumb-turn engaged the deadbolt.

We quickly crossed the room to the outer sacristy door. I knew that beyond lay the east churchyard, the one without tombstones, and a flagstone path leading to the rectory where her uncle lived.

This door also was locked.

From within the sacristy, the lock could be released without a key. I gripped the thumb-turn . . . but hesitated.

Perhaps we had not heard or seen Robertson enter the nave from the narthex for the simple reason that he'd never come into the front of the church after I had glimpsed him ascending the steps.

And perhaps, anticipating that we would try to flee from the back of the church, he had circled the building to wait for us outside the sacristy. This might explain why I had sensed that we were moving *toward* danger rather than away from it.

"What's wrong?" Stormy asked.

I shushed her—a fatal mistake in any circumstances but these—and listened at the crack between the door and the jamb. The thinnest breath of a warm draft tickled my ear, but with it came no sounds from outside.

I waited. I listened. I grew increasingly uneasy.

Stepping away from the outer door, I whispered to Stormy, "Let's go back the way we came."

We returned to the door between the sacristy and the sanctuary, which she had locked behind us. But I hesitated again with my fingers on the deadbolt release.

Putting my ear against the crack between *this* door and jamb, I listened to the church beyond. No teasing draft spiraled down my auditory canal, but no telltale stealthy sounds came to me, either.

Both sacristy doors had been locked from the inside.

To get at us, Robertson would need a key, which he didn't possess.

"We're not going to wait here till morning Mass," Stormy said, as though she could scroll through my thoughts as easily as through a document on her computer.

My cell phone was clipped to my belt. I could have used it to call Chief Porter and explain the situation to him.

The possibility existed, however, that Bob Robertson had been overcome by second thoughts about the wisdom of assaulting me in such a public place as the church, even though at this moment there were no worshipers or witnesses present. Having reined in his rampant anger, he might have gone away.

If the chief dispatched a patrol car to St. Bart's or if he came himself, only to find no smiley psychopath, my credibility would take a hit. Over the years, I had banked enough good will with Wyatt Porter to afford to make a withdrawal or two from my account, but I was reluctant to do so.

It is human nature to want to believe in the wizardry of the magician—but also to turn against him and to scorn him the moment that he commits the slightest error that reveals his trickery. Those in the audience are embarrassed to have been so easily astonished, and they blame the performer for their gullibility.

Although I employ no sleight of hand, though what I offer is truth glimpsed by supernatural means, I am aware not only of the magician's vulnerability but also of the danger of being the boy who cried wolf—or in this case, the boy who cried Fungus Man.

Most people desperately desire to believe that they are part of a great mystery, that Creation is a work of grace and glory, not merely the result of random forces colliding. Yet each time that they are given but one reason to doubt, a worm in the apple of the heart makes them turn away from a thousand proofs of the miraculous, whereupon they have a drunkard's thirst for cynicism, and they feed upon despair as a starving man upon a loaf of bread.

As a miracle worker of sorts, I walk a wire, too high to make one misstep and survive.

Chief Porter is a good man, but he is human. He would be slow to turn against me, but if he was made to feel foolish and gullible more than once, that turn would surely occur.

I could have used my cell phone to call Stormy's uncle, Father Sean, in the rectory. He would come to our aid without delay and without too many awkward questions.

Robertson, however, was a human monster, not one of supernatural origin. If he was lurking in the churchyard, he would not be deterred from violence by the sight of a Roman collar or by the brandishing of a crucifix.

Having put Stormy in jeopardy, I shrank at once from the idea of endangering her uncle, as well.

Two sacristy doors. The outer led to the churchyard. The inner led to the sanctuary.

Having heard nothing at either exit, I had to rely on intuition. I chose the door to the sanctuary.

Apparently the bouncing ball of Stormy's intuition hadn't yet rattled to a stop on any number. She put her hand atop mine as I took hold of the lock.

Our eyes met for a moment. Then we turned our heads to stare at the outer door.

This was an instance when the card that we had drawn from that carnival fortune-telling machine and our matching birthmarks seemed indisputably to be meaningful.

Without exchanging a word, we arrived at a plan that we both understood. I remained at the door to the sanctuary. Stormy returned to the churchyard door.

If when I unlocked my door, Robertson lunged for me, Stormy would throw open the outer door and bolt from the sanctuary, shouting for help. I would attempt to follow her—and stay alive.

CHAPTER 20

THAT MOMENT IN THE SACRISTY DISTILLED the essence of my entire existence: always between two doors, between a life with the living and a life with the dead, between transcendence and terror.

Across the room, Stormy nodded.

On the *prie-dieu*, a small book of prayers waited for a kneeling priest.

No doubt bottles of sacramental wine were stored in one of the cabinets. I could have used a little spiritual fortification.

I leaned hard against the sanctuary door to brace it. When I disengaged the lock, the bolt made a thin sound reminiscent of a razor sharpening against a strop.

Had Robertson been poised to burst in upon me, he ought to have reacted to the deadbolt retracting from the striker plate in the door frame. Of course he might be less of a hothead and more cunning than he had appeared to be when he'd stood in the graveyard, flipping us the finger.

Perhaps he suspected that I was wedging the door shut with my body and that I would snap the lock in place the instant that he tried to shove into the sacristy. Insane as he might be, he would nonetheless have some intuition of his own.

The Bob Robertson who left his kitchen strewn with dirty dishes, banana peels, and crumbs was too sloppy to be a wise strategist. The Robertson who kept the neat study and maintained the meticulous files in those cabinets of dread was, however, a different man from the one whose living room had featured drifts of sleazy magazines and well-read paperback romances.

I couldn't know *which* Bob Robertson might be, at this moment, beyond the door.

When I glanced at Stormy, she made a gesture that meant either "get on with it" or "up yours."

Leaning against the door with undiminished purpose, I turned the knob all the way to the left. It squeaked. I would have been amazed if it hadn't.

I shifted my weight and let the door ease open half an inch . . . an inch . . . and all the way.

If Robertson waited at either entrance to the sacristy, he was outside in the churchyard. Standing in the ruddy reduction of the last red light, he must have looked like something that belonged under a granite headstone.

Stormy stepped away from her station. Together we quickly returned to the sanctuary from which we had been so eager to flee only two minutes ago.

The moth danced across the light, and again Christ seemed to twist upon the cross.

The lingering incense smelled not sweet, as before, but had a new astringency, and the votive flames throbbed with the urgency of arterial aneurysms about to burst.

Down the ambulatory, past the choir enclosure, through the gate in the communion railing, I half expected Robertson to spring at us from unlikely cover. He had grown into such a menacing figure in my mind that I would not have been surprised if he had dropped upon us from the vaulted ceiling, suddenly having sprouted wings, a furious dark angel with death upon his breath.

We were in the main aisle when a great crash and shattering of glass shook away the churchly silence behind us. We spun, we looked, but saw no wreckage.

The sacristy had been windowless, and there'd been no glass in the door to the churchyard. Nevertheless, that chamber, which we'd just left, seemed to be the source of these sounds of destruction. They rose again, louder than before.

I heard what might have been the vesting bench slamming against the vestment closets, heard wine bottles smashing, heard the silver chalice and other sacred vessels ricocheting off walls and cabinets with a reverberant metallic clatter.

In our haste to escape, we had left the light on in that room. Now, through the open door, secondhand movement was visible: a farrago of leaping shadows and flares of shimmery light.

I didn't know what was happening, and I didn't intend to return to the sacristy for a look. Holding Stormy's hand again, I ran with her along the center aisle, the length of the nave, and through a door into the narthex.

Out of the church, down the steps, we fled into a twilight that had nearly bled to death, had little red left to give, and had begun to pull purple shrouds over the streets of Pico Mundo.

For a moment I couldn't fit the trembling key in the Mustang's ignition. Stormy urged me to hurry, as if hurrying weren't already my intention, and finally the key mated as it should, and the engine roared to life.

Leaving a significant offering of rubber in front of

St. Bart's, we traveled a block and a half on smoking tires, so fast that we almost seemed to have teleported, before I had the breath to say, "Call the chief."

She had a cell phone of her own, and she entered Wyatt Porter's home number as I gave it to her. She waited as it rang, said, "Chief, it's Stormy," listened, and said, "Yeah, it does sound like a weather report, doesn't it. Odd needs to speak to you."

I took the phone and blurted, "Sir, if you send a car to St. Bart's real quick, you might catch that Robertson guy trashing the sacristy, maybe more than the sacristy, maybe the whole church."

He put me on HOLD and made a call on another line.

Three blocks from St. Bartholomew's, I pulled the Mustang off the street, into a Mexican fast-food franchise.

"Dinner?" I asked Stormy.

"After all that in the church?"

I shrugged. "The entire rest of our lives will be after all that in the church. Personally, I intend to eat again, and the sooner the better."

"It's not going to be the equal of my tower feast."

"What could be?"

"I *am* starved."

Holding the phone to my ear and driving with one hand as if that were still legal, I swung the Mustang into the line of vehicles waiting to get to the drive-up service window.

When Chief Porter came back, he said, "Why is he vandalizing St. Bart's?"

"Don't have a clue, sir. He tried to trap me and Stormy in the church belfry—"

"What were you doing in the belfry?"

"Having a picnic, sir."

"I suppose that makes sense to you."

"Yes, sir. It's nice. We have dinner up there a couple times a month."

"Son, I don't ever want to catch you having dinner on the courthouse flagpole."

"Maybe just hors d'oeuvres, sir, but never dinner."

"If you want to come by here, we can still feed you two from the barbecue. Bring Elvis."

"I left him at the Baptist church, sir. I'm with Stormy—in line to have some tacos, but thanks just the same."

"Tell me about Robertson. I have a man watching his house in Camp's End, but he hasn't gone home yet."

I said, "He was down in the graveyard, saw us up in the belfry. He gave us the rude number one with lots of emphasis and then came after us."

"You think he knows you were in his house?" the chief asked.

"If he hasn't been home since I was there, I don't see how he could know, but he must. Excuse me a second, sir."

We had reached the menu board.

"Swordfish tacos with extra salsa, fried corn fritters, and a large Coke, please," I told the sombrero-wearing donkey that holds the order microphone in its mouth. I looked at Stormy. She nodded. "Make that two of everything."

"Are you at Mexicali Rose?" the chief asked.

"Yes, sir."

"They have fantastic churros. You should try some."

I took his advice and placed a double order with the donkey, which, as before, thanked me in the voice of a teenage girl.

As the line of cars crept forward, I said, "When we

gave Robertson the slip in the church, he must've been angry. But why he decided to take it out on the building, I don't know."

"Two cars are on the way to St. Bart's, no sirens. They might even be there now. But vandalism—that doesn't measure up to the horrors you said he's going to commit."

"No, sir. Not close. And there's less than three hours till August fifteenth."

"If we can park his butt in jail overnight for vandalism, we'll have an excuse to poke around in his life. Maybe that'll give us a chance to figure out the bigger thing he's up to."

After wishing the chief luck, I pressed END and returned the phone to Stormy.

I checked my watch. Midnight—and August 15—seemed like a tsunami, building height and power, racing toward us with silent but deadly force.

CHAPTER 21

WAITING TO HEAR FROM THE CHIEF THAT they had nailed Robertson in the act of vandalism, Stormy and I ate dinner in the Mexicali Rose parking lot, with the windows of the Mustang rolled down, hoping to catch a breeze. The food was tasty, but the hot night air smelled of exhaust fumes.

"So you broke into Fungus Man's house," Stormy said.

"Didn't smash any glass. Just used my driver's license."

"Does he keep severed heads in his refrigerator?"

"I didn't open his refrigerator."

"Where else would you expect to find severed heads?"

"I wasn't looking for any."

She said, "That creepy smile of his, those weird gray eyes . . . *First* thing I'd look for is a collection of knickknacks with ears. These tacos are fabulous."

I agreed. "And I like all the colors in the salsa. Yellow and green chiles, the red of the chopped tomatoes, the little purple flecks of onion . . . sort of looks like confetti. You should do it this way when you make salsa."

"What—you were bitten by Martha Stewart, now

you're a walking-dead lifestyle guru? So tell me what you found if you didn't find heads?"

I told her about the black room.

Licking corn-fritter crumbs off her elegant fingers, she said, "Listen to me, odd one."

"I'm all ears."

"They're big, but they're not all of you. Open them wide now and hear this: Don't go in that black room again."

"It doesn't exist anymore."

"Don't even go looking for it, hoping it'll come back."

"That never even crossed my mind."

"Yes, it did," she said.

"Yes, it did," I admitted. "I mean, I'd like to understand it—what it is, how it works."

To emphasize her objection, she poked a corn fritter in my direction. "It's the gate to Hell, and you're not meant for that neighborhood."

"I don't think it's the gate to Hell."

"Then what is it?"

"I don't know."

"It's the gate to Hell. If you go looking for it, and you find it, and you wind up in Hell, I'm not going to go down there looking for you and pull your ass out of the fire."

"Your warning is duly noted."

"It's hard enough being married to a guy who sees dead people and goes chasing after them every day, and just *too* hard if he goes on some quest to find the gate to Hell."

"I don't go chasing after them," I said, "and since when are we married?"

"We will be," she said, and finished her final fritter.

On more than one occasion, I have asked her to

marry me. Though we both agree that we are soul mates and that we will be together forever, she has always shied from my proposals with something like, *I love you madly, desperately, Oddie, so madly that I would cut off my right hand for you, if that made any sense as a proof of love. But as for this marriage thing—let's put a pin in it.*

Understandably, dribbles of swordfish taco fell out of my mouth when I heard that we were going to be taking vows. I plucked those morsels off my T-shirt and ate them, buying time to think furiously, before I said, "So . . . you mean you're accepting my proposal?"

"Silly, I accepted it ages ago." Of my look of bewilderment, she said, "Oh, not with a conventional 'Yes, darling, I'm yours,' but I accepted in so many words."

"I didn't interpret 'put a pin in it' as meaning *yes*."

Brushing swordfish crumbs off my shirt, she said, "You have to learn to listen with more than your ears."

"What orifice do you suggest I listen with?"

"Don't be crude. It doesn't become you. I mean, sometimes you have to listen with your heart."

"I've listened with my heart for so long I've periodically had to swab earwax out of my aortal valve."

"Churros?" she asked, opening a white pastry bag and at once filling the car with a delicious, cinnamony, doughnutlike aroma.

I said, "How can you think about dessert at a time like this?"

"You mean at *dinner* time?"

"I mean at talking-about-getting-married time." My heart raced as if I were chasing someone or being chased, but with luck that part of the day was over. "Listen, Stormy, if you really mean it, then I will do something big to improve my financial situation. I'll give up the short-order job at the Grille, and I don't just mean for tires. Something bigger."

Her look of amused speculation was so heavy that the weight of it tilted her head. Cocking one eye at me, she said, "And from your perspective, what could be bigger than tires?"

I gave it some thought. "Shoes."

"What kind of shoes?"

"All kinds. Retail shoe sales."

She looked dubious. "That's bigger than tires?"

"Sure. How often do you buy tires? Not even once a year. And you need only one set of tires per vehicle. But people need more than one pair of shoes. They need all types. Brown dress shoes, black dress shoes, running shoes, sandals—"

"Not you. All you have is three pairs of the same sneakers."

"Yes, but I'm not like other people."

"Not in the least," she agreed.

"Another thing to consider," I said, "is that not every man, woman and child has a car, but everyone has feet. Or nearly everyone. A family of five might have two cars, but they have *ten* feet."

"There are so many reasons to love you, Oddie, but this is maybe my favorite thing about you."

Stormy no longer tilted her head or cocked one eye. She stared at me directly. Her eyes were galactic: as deep as the darkness between any two stars in the sky. Her expression had softened with affection. She seemed sincere and genuinely touched by something that I said, and this perception was supported by the fact that she had still not taken a churro out of the bag.

Unfortunately, I must have been listening with only my ears, because I didn't know what she meant. "Your favorite thing about me? You mean . . . my analysis of shoe retailing?"

"You're as smart as anyone I've ever known . . . and yet so simple. It's a lovely combination. Brains and innocence. Wisdom and naivete. Sharp wit and genuine sweetness."

"That's your favorite thing about me?"

"At the moment, yes."

"Well, gee, it's not something I can work on."

"Work on?"

"Things you like about me, I want to do them even better. Say instead you liked my grooming or my taste in clothes, or my pancakes. I'm always improving my pancakes, just ask Terri—they're light and fluffy yet full of taste. But I don't know how to be smart and simple at the same time better than I am now. In fact, I'm not even sure I know what you mean."

"Good. It's nothing you should think about. It's nothing you can work on. It's just who you are. Anyway, when I marry you, it won't be for money."

She offered a churro to me.

Considering how fast my heart was racing and my mind was spinning, the last thing that I needed was sugar, but I took the pastry.

We ate in silence for a minute, and then I said, "So this marriage—when do you think we should order the cake?"

"Soon. I can't wait much longer."

With relief and delight, I said, "Too much delayed gratification can be a bad thing."

She grinned. "You see what's happening here?"

"I guess I'm just looking with my eyes. What should I see?"

"What's happening is—I want a second churro, and

I'm going to have it now instead of next Thursday."

"You're a wild woman, Stormy Llewellyn."

"You don't know the half of it."

This had been a bad day, what with Harlo Landerson and Fungus Man and the black room and the bodachs everywhere and Elvis in tears. Yet as I sat with Stormy, eating churros, for the moment all was right with the world.

The moment didn't last long. My cell phone rang, and I wasn't surprised to hear Chief Porter's voice.

"Son, the sacristy at St. Bart's gives new meaning to the word *trashed*. Someone went purely berserk in there."

"Robertson."

"I'm sure you're right. You always are. It was probably him. But he was gone by the time my men reached the church. You haven't seen him again?"

"We're sort of hiding out here but . . . no, not a sign of him." I surveyed the parking lot, the continuous traffic coming in and out of Mexicali Rose's drive-up service lane, and the street beyond, looking for Bob Robertson's dusty Ford Explorer.

The chief said, "We've had a watch on his house for a few hours, but now we're actively looking for him."

"I might give psychic magnetism a chance," I said, referring to my ability to locate just about anyone by cruising at random for half an hour.

"Is that wise, son? I mean, with Stormy being in the car?"

"I'll take her home first."

Stormy quashed that idea: "Like hell you will, Mulder."

"I heard that," said Chief Porter.

"He heard that," I told Stormy.

"What do I care?" she said.

Chief Porter seemed tickled: "She calls you Mulder, like on *The X-Files*?"

"Not often, sir. Only when she thinks I'm being paternalistic."

"Do you ever call her Scully?"

"Only when I'm in the mood to be bruised."

"You ruined that show for me," the chief said.

"How'd I do that, sir?"

"You made all that weird stuff too real. I didn't find the supernatural to be entertaining anymore."

"Me neither," I assured him.

By the time Chief Porter and I finished talking, Stormy had gathered all our dinner wrappings and containers, and had stuffed them into one bag. When we left Mexicali Rose, she dropped them in a trash can that was stationed along the exit lane.

As I turned left into the street, she said, "Let's stop by my place first, so I can get my pistol."

"That's a home-defense gun. You're not licensed to carry."

"I'm not licensed to breathe, either, but I do it anyway."

"No gun," I insisted. "We'll just cruise and see what happens."

"Why're you afraid of guns?"

"They go bang."

"And why is that a question you always avoid answering?"

"I don't always avoid answering it."

"Why're you afraid of guns?" she persisted.

"I was probably shot to death in a past life."

"You don't believe in reincarnation."

"I don't believe in taxes, either, but I pay them."

"Why are you afraid of guns?"

"Maybe because I've had a prophetic dream in which I was shot."

"Have you had a prophetic dream in which you were shot?"

"No."

She can be relentless. "Why're you afraid of guns?"

I can be stupid. As soon as I spoke, I regretted my words: "Why're you afraid of sex?"

From the suddenly icy and distant perch of the passenger's seat, she gave me a long, hard, marrow-freezing look.

For a moment I tried to pretend that I didn't realize the impact that my words had on her. I tried to focus on the street ahead as if I were nothing if not always a responsible driver.

I have no talent for pretense. Sooner than later, I looked at her, felt terrible, and said, "I'm so sorry."

"I'm not afraid of sex," she said.

"I know. I'm sorry. I'm an idiot."

"I just want to be sure—"

I tried to hush her.

She persisted: "I just want to be sure the reason why you're in love with me has less to do with *that* than with other things."

"It does," I assured her, feeling small and mean. "A thousand other things. You know that."

"When we're together, I want it to be right and clean and beautiful."

"So do I. And it will be, Stormy. When the time is right. We have plenty of time."

Stopping for a red traffic light, I held out my right hand to her. I was relieved when she took it, touched when she held it so tightly.

The light changed to green. I drove with only one hand on the wheel.

After a while, in a voice soft with emotion, she said, "I'm sorry, Oddie. That was my fault."

"It wasn't your fault. I'm an idiot."

"I pushed you into a corner about why you're afraid of guns, and when I kept pushing, you pushed back."

That was the truth, but the truth didn't make me feel any better about what I'd done.

Six months after the deaths of her mother and father, when Stormy was seven and a half years old and still Bronwen, she was adopted by a childless, well-to-do couple in Beverly Hills. They lived on a fine estate. The future looked bright.

One night during her second week with her new family, her adoptive father came to her room and woke her. He exposed himself to her and touched her in ways that frightened and humiliated her.

Still grieving her birth parents, afraid, desperately lonely, confused, ashamed, she endured this man's sick advances for three months. Finally, she reported him to a social worker who was making a follow-up house call for the adoption agency.

Thereafter, she lived in St. Bart's Orphanage, untouched, until her high-school graduation.

She and I became an item when we were juniors. We have been together—and each other's best friend—for more than four years.

In spite of all that we had been to each other and all that we hoped to achieve together in the years to come, I had been able to hurt her—*Why're you afraid of sex?*—when she pushed me too hard about my fear of guns.

A cynic once said that the most identifying trait of humanity is our ability to be inhumane to one another.

I am an optimist about our species. I assume God is, too, for otherwise He would have scrubbed us off the planet a long time ago and would have started over.

Yet I can't entirely dismiss that cynic's sour assessment. I harbor a capacity for inhumanity, glimpsed in my cruel retort to the person I love most in all the world.

We sailed the blacktop rivers for a while, not finding Fungus Man, but slowly finding our way back to each other.

In time she said, "I love you, Oddie."

My voice was thick when I replied. "I love you more than life."

"We'll be okay," she said.

"We *are* okay."

"We're weird and screwed-up, but we're okay," she agreed.

"If someone invented a thermometer that measured weirdness, it would melt under my tongue. But you—you're cool."

"So you deny me weirdness but agree that I'm screwed-up."

"I see your problem. Certain kinds of weirdness can be hip, but screwed-upness never is."

"Exactly."

"It wasn't gentlemanly of me to deny you your weirdness."

"Apology accepted."

We cruised for a while, using the car as a dowser uses his rod to seek water, until I found myself pulling into the parking lot of Green Moon Lanes. This is a bowling alley half a mile from the mall where earlier in the day I had visited Stormy at the ice-cream shop.

She knows about the recurring dream that has disturbed my sleep once or twice a month for the past three years. It features dead bowling-alley employees:

gut-shot, limbs shattered, faces hideously disfigured not by a few bullets but by *barrages*.

"He's here?" Stormy asked.

"I don't know."

"Is it coming true now, tonight—the dream?"

"I don't think so. I don't know. Maybe."

The fish tacos were swimming the acidic currents of my stomach, churning a bitter backwash into my throat.

My palms were damp. And cold. I blotted them on my jeans.

I almost wanted to drive back to Stormy's place and get her gun.

CHAPTER 22

THE BOWLING-CENTER PARKING LOT WAS two-thirds full. I circled, searching for Robertson's Explorer, but I couldn't find it.

Finally I parked and switched off the engine.

Stormy opened the passenger's door, and I said, "Wait."

"Don't make me call you Mulder," she warned.

Staring at the green and blue neon letters that spelled out GREEN MOON LANES, I hoped to get a sense of whether the slaughter I had foreseen was imminent or still some distance in the future. The neon failed to speak to my sixth sense.

The architect for the bowling center had designed it with a responsible awareness of the expense involved in air-conditioning a large building in the Mojave. The squat structure, which featured low ceilings inside, thwarted heat transfer by using a minimum of glass. Pale beige stucco walls reflected the sun during the day and cooled quickly with the coming of night.

In the past this building had not seemed ominous; its character impressed me only because of the efficiency of design, for it had the clean lines and the plain facade of most modern buildings in the desert. Now it reminded me of a munitions bunker, and I sensed that a tremendous explosion might soon occur within its walls. Munitions bunker, crematorium, tomb . . .

"The employees here wear black slacks and blue cotton shirts with white collars," I told Stormy.

"So?"

"In my dream, the victims all wear tan slacks and green polo shirts."

Still in her seat but with one leg out of the Mustang, one foot on the blacktop, she said, "Then this isn't the place. There's some other reason you cruised here. It's safe to go inside, see if we can figure out why we're here."

"Over at Fiesta Bowl," I said, referring to the only other bowling center in Pico Mundo and surrounding environs, "they wear gray slacks and black shirts with their names stitched in white on the breast pockets."

"Then your dream must be about something that's going to happen outside Pico Mundo."

"That's never been the case before."

I have lived my entire life in the relative peace of Pico Mundo and the territory immediately encircling it. I have not even seen the farther reaches of Maravilla County, of which our town is the county seat.

If I were to live to be eighty, which is unlikely and which is a prospect that I view with despondency if not despair, I might one day venture into the open countryside and even as far as one of the smaller towns in the county. But perhaps not.

I don't desire a change of scenery or exotic experiences. My heart yearns for familiarity, stability, the comfort of home—and my sanity depends upon it.

In a city the size of Los Angeles, with so many people crammed atop one another, violence occurs daily, hourly. The number of bloody encounters in a single year might be greater than those in the entire history of Pico Mundo.

The aggressive whirl of Los Angeles traffic produces death as surely as a bakery produces muffins. Earthquakes, apartment-house fires, terrorist incidents . . .

I can only imagine how many lingering dead people haunt the streets of that metropolis or any other. In such a place, with so many of the deceased turning to me for justice or consolation, or just for silent companionship, I would no doubt quickly seek escape in autism or suicide.

Not yet either dead or autistic, however, I had to face the challenge of Green Moon Lanes.

"All right," I said, able to summon resignation if not bravado, "let's go in and have a look around."

With nightfall, the blacktop pavement returned the heat that it had borrowed from the sun during the day, and with the heat came a faint tarry smell.

So low and large that it seemed to be falling toward us, the moon had risen in the east: a dire yellow countenance, the vague cratered sockets of its timeless blind gaze.

Perhaps because Granny Sugars had been seriously superstitious about yellow moons and believed that they were an omen of bad cards in poker, I surrendered to an irrational urge to escape from the sight of that leprous and jaundiced celestial face. Taking Stormy's hand, I hurried her toward the front doors of the bowling center.

Bowling is one of the oldest sports in the world and in one form or another was played as early as 5,200 B.C.

In the United States alone, over 130,000 lanes await action in more than 7,000 bowling centers.

Total annual bowling revenues in America are approaching five billion dollars.

With the hope of clarifying my recurring dream and understanding the meaning of it, I had researched bowling. I knew a thousand facts about the subject, none of them particularly interesting.

I also rented shoes and played eight or ten games. I am no good at the sport.

Watching me play, Stormy had once said that if I were to become a regular bowler, I would spend far more time in the gutter than would the average alcoholic hobo.

Over sixty million people in the United States go bowling at least once each year. Nine million of them are diehards who belong to bowling leagues and regularly compete in amateur tournaments.

When Stormy and I entered Green Moon Lanes that Tuesday night, a significant percentage of those millions were rolling balls down polished lanes toward more spares than splits, but more splits than strikes. They were laughing, cheering one another, eating nachos, eating chili-cheese fries, drinking beer, and having such a good time that it was difficult to imagine Death choosing this place to harvest a sudden crop of souls.

Difficult but not impossible.

I must have been pale, because Stormy said, "Are you all right?"

"Yeah. Okay. I'm good."

The low thunder of rolling balls and the clatter of tenpins had never previously struck me as fearsome sounds; but this irregular series of rumbles and crashes strummed my nerves.

"What now?" Stormy asked.

"Good question. No answer."

"You want to just wander around, scope the scene, see if you get any bad vibes?"

I nodded. "Yeah. Scope the scene. Bad vibes."

We didn't wander far before I saw something that made my mouth go dry. "Oh, my God."

The guy behind the shoe-rental counter had not come to work in the usual black slacks and blue cotton shirt with white collar. He wore tan slacks and a green polo shirt, like the dead people in my bowling dream.

Stormy turned, surveying the long busy room, and pointed toward two additional employees. "They've all gotten new uniforms."

Like every nightmare, this one of mine was vivid and yet not rich in detail, more surreal than real, not specific as to place or time or circumstances. The faces of the murder victims were twisted in agony, distorted by terror and shadow and strange light, and when I woke, I could never describe them well.

Except for one young woman. She would be shot in the chest and throat, but her face would remain remarkably untouched by violence. She would have shaggy blond hair, green eyes, and a small beauty mark on her upper lip, near the left corner of her mouth.

As Stormy and I proceeded farther into Green Moon Lanes, I saw the blonde from the dream. She stood behind the bar, drawing draft beer from one of the taps.

CHAPTER 23

STORMY AND I SAT AT A TABLE IN THE BAR alcove, but we didn't order drinks. I was already half drunk with fear.

I wanted to get her out of the bowling alley. She didn't want to leave.

"We've got to deal with this situation," she insisted.

The only way that I could deal with it was to phone Chief Wyatt Porter and tell him, with little explanation, that when Bob Robertson had his coming-out party to celebrate his status as a full-fledged murderous psychopath, the site of his debutante ball was likely to be Green Moon Lanes.

For a man tired from a day of hard work, bloated with barbecue and beer, and ready for bed, the chief responded with admirable quickness and clarity of mind. "How late are they open?"

Phone to my right ear, finger in my left ear to block the alley noise, I said, "I think until midnight, sir."

"A little more than two hours. I'll dispatch an officer right now, have him stand security, be on the lookout for Robertson. But, son, you said this might go down August fifteenth—tomorrow, not today."

"That's the date on the calendar page in his file. I'm not sure what it means. I won't be certain it couldn't happen today until today is over and he hasn't shot anyone."

"Any of these things you call bodachs there?"

"No, sir. But they could show up when he does."

"He hasn't returned home to Camp's End yet," the chief said, "so he's out and about. How were the churros?"

"Delicious," I told him.

"After the barbecue, we had a difficult choice between mud pie and homemade peach pie. I thought it through carefully and had some of both."

"If ever I had a glimpse of Heaven, sir, it was a slice of Mrs. Porter's peach pie."

"I'd have married her for the peach pie alone, but fortunately she was smart and beautiful, too."

We said good-bye. I clipped the cell phone to my belt and told Stormy we needed to get out of there.

She shook her head. "Wait. If the blond bartender isn't here, the shooting won't happen." She kept her voice low, leaning close to be heard over the clash and clatter of bowlers bowling. "So somehow we get her to leave."

"No. A premonition in a dream isn't in every detail a picture of *exactly* what will happen. She could be home safe, and the shooter could show up here anyway."

"But at least *she* will have been saved. One less victim."

"Except that somebody else who *wouldn't* have died might be shot in her place. Like the bartender who replaces her. Or me. Or you."

"*Might* be."

"Yes, *might* be, but how can I save one if there's a likelihood that it means condemning another?"

Three or four bowling balls slammed into pin setups

in quick succession. The racket sounded a little like automatic gunfire, and though I knew it *wasn't* gunfire, I twitched anyway.

I said, "I've got no right to decide that someone else should die in her place."

Prophetic dreams—and the complex moral choices they present—come to me only rarely. I'm grateful for that.

"Besides," I said, "what's her reaction going to be if I walk over to the bar and tell her she's going to be shot to death if she doesn't get out of here."

"She'll think you're eccentric or dangerous, but she might go."

"She won't. She'll stay there. She won't want to jeopardize her job. She won't want to appear fearful, because that makes her look weak, and these days women don't want to seem weak any more than men do. Later she might ask someone to walk with her to her car, but that's all."

Stormy stared at the blonde behind the bar while I surveyed the room for any bodachs that might precede the executioner. Nobody here but us humans.

"She's so pretty, so full of life," Stormy said, meaning the bartender. "So much personality, such an infectious laugh."

"She seems more alive to you because you know she might be fated to die young."

"It just seems wrong to walk out and leave her there," Stormy said, "without warning her, without giving her a *chance*."

"The best way to give her a chance, to give *all* the potential victims a chance, is to stop Robertson before he does anything."

"What's the likelihood you'll stop him?"

"Better than if he'd never come into the Grille this

morning and I'd never gotten a look at him with his bodach entourage."

"But you can't be sure you'll stop him."

"Nothing's for sure in this world."

Searching my eyes, she thought about what I'd said, and then reminded me: "Except us."

"Except us." I pushed my chair away from the table. "Let's go."

Still staring at the blonde, Stormy said, "This is so hard."

"I know."

"So unfair."

"What death isn't?"

She rose from her chair. "You won't let her die, will you, Oddie?"

"I'll do what I can."

We went outside, hoping to be gone before the promised police officer arrived and became curious about my involvement.

No cops on the Pico Mundo force understand my relationship with Chief Porter. They sense that something's different about me, but they don't realize what I see, what I know. The chief covers well for me.

Some think that I hang around Wyatt Porter because I'm a cop wannabe. They assume that I yearn for the glamour of the police life, but that I don't have quite the smarts or the guts to do the job.

Most of them believe that I regard the chief as a father figure because my real father is such a hopeless piece of work. This view contains some truth.

They are convinced that the chief took pity on me when at the age of sixteen I could no longer live with either my father or my mother, and found myself turned out into the world. Because Wyatt and Karla were never able to have children, people think that the chief has a fatherly affection for me and regards me as a surrogate son. I am deeply comforted by the fact that this seems to be true.

Being cops, however, the members of the Pico Mundo PD sense instinctively that they lack some crucial knowledge to be able to fully understand our relationship. Likewise, although I appear uncomplicated and even simple, they regard me as a puzzle with more than one missing piece.

When Stormy and I stepped out of Green Moon Lanes at ten o'clock, an hour after nightfall, the temperature in Pico Mundo remained over a hundred degrees. By midnight the air might cool below triple digits.

If Bob Robertson was intent on making Hell on Earth, we had the weather for it.

Walking toward Terri Stambaugh's Mustang, still thinking about the death-marked blond bartender, Stormy said, "Sometimes I don't know how you can live with all the things you see."

"Attitude," I told her.

"Attitude? How's that work?"

"Better some days than others."

She would have pressed me for a further explanation, but the patrol car arrived, pinning us in its headlights before we reached the Mustang. Certain that I would have been recognized, I waited hand-in-hand with Stormy for the cruiser to stop beside us.

The responding officer, Simon Varner, had been on the force only three or four months, which was longer than Bern Eckles, who had regarded me with suspicion at the chief's barbecue, but not long enough for the sharp edge to have been worn off his curiosity about me.

Officer Varner had a face as sweet as that of any

host of a children's TV program, with heavy-lidded eyes like those of the late actor Robert Mitchum. He leaned toward the open window, his burly arm resting on the door, looking like the model for a sleepy bear in some Disney cartoon.

"Odd, pleasure seeing you. Miss Llewellyn. What should I be looking for here?"

I was certain that the chief had not used my name when he had dispatched Officer Varner to the bowling center. When I was involved in a case, he made a point of keeping me as invisible as possible, never alluding to information acquired by preternatural means, the better not only to protect my secrets but also to ensure that no defense attorney could easily spring a murderer by claiming that the entire case against his client had been built upon the word of a flaky, self-proclaimed psychic.

On the other hand, because of my intrusion at the barbecue that resulted in the effort by the chief and Bern Eckles to put together a quick profile of Robertson, Eckles knew that I had some connection to the situation. If Eckles knew, then word would get around; it might already be on the police-department grapevine.

Still, it seemed best to play dumb. "What should you be looking for? Sir, I don't understand."

"I see you, I figure you told the chief something that makes him send me out here."

"We were just watching some friends bowl," I said. "I'm no good at it myself."

Stormy said, "He *owns* the gutter."

From the car seat beside him, Varner produced a computer-printed blow-up of Bob Robertson's driver's-license photograph. "You know this guy, right?"

I said, "I've seen him twice today. I don't really know him."

"You didn't tell the chief he might show up here?"

"Not me. How would I know where he'd show up?"

"Chief says if I see him coming but I can't see both his hands, don't figure he's just getting a breath mint from his pocket."

"I wouldn't second-guess the chief."

A Lincoln Navigator pulled in from the street and paused behind Varner's cruiser. He stuck his arm all the way out of the window and waved the SUV around him.

I could see two men in the Navigator. Neither was Robertson.

"How do you know this guy?" Varner asked.

"Before noon, he came in the Grille for lunch."

The lids lifted slightly from those sleepy-bear eyes. "That's all? You cooked his lunch? I thought . . . something went down between you and him."

"Something. Not much." I compressed the day, leaving out what Varner didn't need to know: "He was weird at the Grille. The chief was there at the time, saw him being weird. So then this afternoon, I'm off work, out and about, minding my own business, and this Robertson flips me off, gets aggressive with me."

Varner's heavy lids became hoods, narrowing his eyes to slits of suspicion. Instinct told him that I was withholding information. He wasn't as slow as he looked. "Aggressive how?"

Stormy saved me from a rough lie with a smooth one: "The creep made a crude pass at me, and Odd told him to back off."

Fungus Man didn't look like the kind of macho stud who thought every woman was panting for him.

Stormy, however, is so strikingly good-looking that Varner, already in a suspicious mood, seemed inclined to believe that even a schlump like Bob Robertson would work up enough hormones to try his luck with her.

He said, "Chief thinks this guy vandalized St. Bart's. You know about that, I guess."

Deflecting this dogged Sherlock, Stormy said, "Officer Varner, curiosity is killing me. Do you mind my asking—what's your tattoo mean?"

He wore a short-sleeve shirt, exposing his massive forearms. On his left arm, above his watch, were three block letters: POD.

"Miss Llewellyn, I'm sorry to say that as a teenager I was one screwed-up puppy. Got myself involved in gangs. Turned my life around before it was too late. I thank the Lord Jesus for that. This tattoo was a gang thing."

"What do the letters stand for?" she asked.

He seemed embarrassed. "It's a crude obscenity, miss. I'd rather not say."

"You could have it removed," she said. "They've gotten a lot better at that in recent years."

Varner said, "Thought about doing just that. But I keep it to remind me how far off the right path I once went and how easy it was to take that first wrong step."

"That's so fascinating and so admirable," she said, leaning closer to the window as if to get a better look at this paragon of virtue. "Lots of people rewrite their past rather than face up to it. I'm glad to know we've got men like you looking out for us."

She poured this verbal syrup so smoothly that it sounded sincere.

While Officer Varner was basking in her flattery as happily as a waffle in whipped butter, she turned to me and said, "Odd, I've *got* to get home. I have an early morning."

I wished Officer Varner good luck, and he made no attempt to continue grilling me. He seemed to have forgotten his suspicions.

In the car, I said to her, "I never realized you had such a talent for deceit."

"Oh, that's too serious a word for it. I just manipulated him a little."

"After we're married, I'm going to be on the lookout for that," I warned her as I started the car.

"What do you mean?"

"In case you ever try to manipulate *me* a little."

"Good heavens, odd one, I manipulate you every day. And fold and spindle you, as well."

I couldn't tell if she was serious. "You do?"

"Gently, of course. Gently and with great affection. And you always like it."

"I do?"

"You have numerous little tricks to get me to do it."

I put the car in gear but kept my foot on the brake. "You're saying I *invite* manipulation?"

"Some days I think you thrive on it."

"I can't tell if you're serious."

"I know. You're adorable."

"Puppies are adorable. I'm not a puppy."

"You and puppies. Totally adorable."

"You *are* serious."

"Am I?"

I studied her. "No. No, you're not."

"Aren't I?"

I sighed. "I can see the dead, but I can't see through you."

When we drove out of the parking lot, Officer Varner was parked near the front entrance to Green Moon Lanes.

Instead of running a quiet surveillance of the place with the hope of nabbing Robertson before violence could be committed, he was making himself highly visible, as a deterrent. This interpretation of his assignment was most likely not one the chief would have approved.

As we passed him, Officer Varner waved at us. He appeared to be eating a doughnut.

Granny Sugars always railed against negative thinking because she superstitiously believed that when we worry about being afflicted by one evil or another, we are in fact inviting in the very devil that we fear and are assuring the occurrence of the event we dread. Nevertheless, I could not help but think how easily Bob Robertson might approach the cruiser from behind and shoot Simon Varner in the head while he noshed on his Krispy Kremes.

CHAPTER 24

VIOLA PEABODY, THE WAITRESS WHO HAD served lunch to me and Terri at the Grille just eight eventful hours ago, lived only two blocks from Camp's End, but because of her tireless gardening and painting and carpentry, her home seemed to be a world away from those dreary streets.

Although small and simple, the house resembled a fairy-tale cottage in one of those romantic paintings by Thomas Kinkade. Under the gibbous moon, its walls glowed as softly as backlit alabaster, and a carriage lamp revealed the crimson petals of the flowers on the trumpet vine festooning the trellis that flanked and overhung the front door.

Without any apparent surprise that we arrived unannounced at this hour, Viola greeted Stormy and me graciously, with a smile and with an offer of coffee or ice tea, which we declined.

We sat in the small living room where Viola herself had stripped and refinished the wood floor. She had woven the rag rug. She had sewn the chintz curtains and the slipcovers that made old upholstered furniture look new.

Perched on the edge of an armchair, Viola was as slim as a girl. The travails and burdens of her life had left no mark on her. She did not look old enough or harried enough to be the single mother of the five- and six-year-old daughters who were asleep in a back room.

Her husband, Rafael, who'd left her and who'd contributed not one penny to his children's welfare, was a fool of such dimensions that he should have been required to dress like a jester, complete with silly hat and curled-toe shoes.

The house lacked air conditioning. The windows were open, and an electric fan sat on the floor, the oscillating blades imparting an illusion of coolness to the air.

Leaning forward with her hands braced on her knees, Viola traded her smile for a look of solemn expectation, for she knew why I must have come. "It's my dream, isn't it?" she said softly.

I spoke quietly, too, in respect of the sleeping children. "Tell me again."

"I saw myself, a hole in my forehead, my face . . . broken."

"You think you were shot."

"Shot dead," she confirmed, folding her hands together between her knees, as if in prayer. "My right eye bloodshot and swollen all ugly, half out of the socket."

"Anxiety dreams," Stormy said, meaning to reassure. "They don't have anything to do with the future."

"We've been over this territory," Viola told her. "Odd . . . he was of that same opinion this afternoon." She looked at me. "You must have changed your mind, or you wouldn't be here."

"Where were you in the dream?"

"No place. You know, a dream place . . . all fuzzy, fluid."

"Do you ever go bowling?"

"That takes money. I have two colleges to save for. My girls are going to be somebody."

"Have you ever been inside Green Moon Lanes?"

She shook her head. "No."

"Did anything in the dream suggest the place might have been a bowling alley?"

"No. Like I said, it wasn't *any* real place. Why do you say the bowling alley? You have a dream, too?"

"I did, yes."

"People dead?" Viola asked.

"Yes."

"You ever have dreams come true?"

"Sometimes," I admitted.

"I knew you'd understand. That's why I asked you to read me."

"Tell me more about your dream, Viola."

She closed her eyes, striving to remember. "I'm running from something. There are these shadows, some flashes of light, but none of it *is* anything."

My sixth sense is unique in its nature and its clarity. But I believe that many people have less dramatic and undiscovered supernatural perceptions that manifest from time to time throughout their lives: presentiments that come sometimes in the form of dreams, as well as other moments of uncanny awareness and insight.

They fail to explore these experiences in part because they believe that acknowledging the supernatural would be irrational. They are also frightened, often unconsciously, by the prospect of opening their minds and hearts to the truth of a universe far more complex and meaningful than the material world that their education tells them is the sum of all things.

I was not surprised, therefore, that Viola's nightmare, which earlier in the day had seemed likely to be of no consequence, had proved to be a matter of importance, after all. "Do your dreams have voices, sounds?" I asked her. "Some people's don't."

"Mine do. In the dream, I can hear myself breathing. And this crowd."

"Crowd?"

"A roaring crowd, like the sound in a stadium."

Baffled, I said, "Where would such a place be in Pico Mundo?"

"I don't know. Maybe a Little League game."

"Not such a big crowd at one of those," Stormy noted.

"Wasn't necessarily thousands of voices. Could've been a couple hundred," Viola said. "Just a crowd, all roaring."

I said, "And then, how is it that you see yourself shot?"

"Don't see it happen. The shadows, the flashes of light, I'm running, and I stumble, fall on my hands and knees . . ."

Viola's eyes twitched behind their lids as though she were asleep and experiencing the nightmare for the first time.

" . . . on my hands and knees," she repeated, "hands in something slippery. It's blood. Then shadows whirl away and light whirls in, and I'm looking down at my own dead face."

She shuddered and opened her eyes.

Tiny beads of sweat stippled her forehead and her upper lip.

In spite of the electric fan, the room was warm. But she hadn't been sweating before she began to recall the dream.

"Is there anything else, any other details?" I asked. "Even the smallest thing might help me.

What were you . . . I mean your dead body . . . what was it lying on? A floor of some kind? Grass? Blacktop?"

She thought for a moment, shook her head. "Can't say. The only other thing was the man, the dead man."

I sat up straighter on the sofa. "You mean another . . . corpse?"

"Next to me . . . next to my body. He was sort of tumbled on his side, one arm twisted behind his back."

"Were there other victims?" Stormy asked.

"Maybe. I didn't see any but him."

"Did you recognize him?"

"Didn't get a look at his face. It was turned away from me."

I said, "Viola, if you could try hard to remember—"

"Anyway, I wasn't interested in him. I was too scared to wonder who he was. I looked in my own dead face, and I tried to scream, but I couldn't, and I tried harder, and then I was sitting up in bed, the scream squeezing out of me but, you know, only just the wheeze of a scream."

The memory agitated Viola. She started to get up from the chair. Maybe her legs were weak. She sat down again.

As though she were reading my mind, Stormy asked, "What was he wearing?"

"What—him in the dream? One foot bent back, the shoe half off. A loafer."

We waited while Viola searched her memory. Dreams that are as rich as cream while they unfold are skim milk when we wake, and in time they wash out of our minds, leaving as little residue as water filtered through cheesecloth.

"His pants were splattered with blood," Viola said. "Khakis, I think. Tan pants, anyway."

The slowly swiveling fan stirred the leaves of a potted palm in one corner of the room, raising from its fronds a dry rustling that made me think of cockroaches scurrying, and rats, and nothing good.

Reading the last details of her dream that yet remained in the cheesecloth of memory, Viola said, "A polo shirt . . ."

I got up from the sofa. I needed to move. I realized that the room was too small for pacing, but I remained on my feet.

"Green," Viola said. "A green polo shirt."

I thought of the guy behind the shoe-rental counter at Green Moon Lanes, the blonde drawing beer behind the bar—both in their new work uniforms.

Her voice growing even quieter, Viola said, "Tell me the truth, Odd. Look at my face. Do you see death in me?"

I said, "Yes."

CHAPTER 25

ALTHOUGH I'M UNABLE TO READ FACES to discover either a person's future or the secrets of her heart, I could not look a moment longer at Viola Peabody's face, for I imagined what I couldn't truly read, and in my mind's eye saw her motherless daughters standing at her grave.

I went to one of the open windows. Beyond lay a side yard overhung by pepper trees. Out of the warm darkness came the sweet fragrance of jasmine that had been planted and tended by Viola's caring hands.

Ordinarily, I have no fear of the night. I feared this one, however, because the change from August 14 to August 15 was coming express-train fast, as if the rotation of the earth had drastically gained speed by the flicking of a godly finger.

I turned to Viola, who still sat on the edge of her armchair. Her eyes, always large, were owlish now, and her brown face seemed to have a gray undertone. I said, "Isn't tomorrow your day off?"

She nodded.

Because she had a sister who could baby-sit her daughters, Viola worked at the Grille six days a week.

Stormy said, "Do you have plans? What are you doing tomorrow?"

"I figured I'd work around the house in the morning. Always things to do here. In the afternoon . . . that's for the girls."

"You mean Nicolina and Levanna?" I asked, naming her daughters.

"Saturday—that's Levanna's birthday. She'll be seven. But the Grille is busy Saturdays, good tips. I can't miss work. So we were going to celebrate early."

"Celebrate how?"

"That new movie, it's a big hit with all the kids, the one with the dog. We were going to the four-o'clock show."

Before Stormy spoke, I knew the essence of what she would say. "Might be more of a crowd in a cool theater on a summer afternoon than at a Little League game."

I asked Viola, "What did you plan after the movie?"

"Terri said bring them to the Grille, dinner on her."

The Grille could be noisy when all the tables were filled, but I didn't think that the enthusiastic conversation of the patrons in our little restaurant could be mistaken for the roar of a crowd. In dreams, of course, everything can be distorted, including sounds.

With the open window at my back, I suddenly felt vulnerable to an extent that made the skin pucker on the nape of my neck.

I looked out into the side yard again. All appeared to be as it had been a minute ago.

The graceful branches of the peppers hung in the breathless, jasmine-scented night air. Shadows and shrubs plaited their different darknesses, but as far as I could tell, they didn't give cover to Bob Robertson or anyone else.

Nevertheless, I stepped away from the window, to the side of it, when I turned once more to Viola. "I think you ought to change your plans for tomorrow."

By saving Viola from this destiny, I might be sentencing someone else to die horribly in her place, just as might have been the case if I had warned off the blond bartender at the bowling alley. The only difference was that I didn't know the blonde . . . and Viola was a friend.

Sometimes complex and difficult moral choices are decided less by reason and by right than by sentiment. Perhaps such decisions are the paving stones on the road to Hell; if so, my route is well paved, and the welcoming committee already knows my name.

In my defense, I can only say that I sensed, even then, that saving Viola meant saving her daughters, too. Three lives, not one.

"Is there any hope . . ." Viola touched her face with the trembling fingers of one hand, tracing the bones of jaw and cheek and brow, as if discovering not her skull but instead Death's countenance in the process of replacing her own. ". . . any hope this can pass from me?"

"Fate isn't one straight road," I said, becoming the oracle that earlier in the day I had declined to be for her. "There are forks in it, many different routes to different ends. We have the free will to choose the path."

"Do whatever Oddie says," Stormy advised, "and you'll be all right."

"It's not that easy," I said quickly. "You can change the road you take, but sometimes it can bend back to lead you straight to that same stubborn fate."

Viola regarded me with too much respect, perhaps even awe. "I was just *sure* you knew about such things, Odd, about all that's Otherly and Beyond."

Uneasy with her admiration, I went to the other

open window. Terri's Mustang stood under a streetlamp in front of the house. All quiet. Nothing to be alarmed about. Nothing and everything.

We had taken steps to be sure we weren't being followed from the bowling center. I remained concerned, anyway, because Robertson's appearance at Little Ozzie's house and again in the churchyard had surprised me, and I could not afford to be surprised a third time.

"Viola," I said, turning to her once more, "changing all your plans for tomorrow isn't enough. You'll also need to remain vigilant, alert to anything that seems . . . wrong."

"I'm already as jumpy as a cricket."

"That's no good. Jumpy isn't the same as vigilant."

She nodded. "You're right."

"You need to be as calm as possible."

"I'll try. I'll do my best."

"Calm and observant, prepared to react fast to any threat but calm enough to see it coming."

Poised on the edge of the chair, she still appeared to be as ready to leap as any cricket.

"In the morning," Stormy said, "we'll bring you a photo of a man you ought to be on the lookout for." She glanced at me. "Can you get her a good picture of him, Oddie?"

I nodded. The chief would provide me with a computer-printed blow-up of the photo of Robertson that the DMV had released to him.

"What man?" Viola asked.

As vividly as possible, I described Fungus Man, who had been at the Grille during the first shift, before Viola had arrived for work. "If you see him, get away from him. You'll know the worst is coming. But I don't think anything will happen tonight. Not here. From all indications, he's intending to make headlines in a public place, lots of people . . . "

"Tomorrow, don't go to the movies," Stormy said.

"I won't," Viola assured her.

"And not out to dinner, either."

Although I didn't understand what could be gained from having a look at Nicolina and Levanna, I suddenly knew that I should not leave the house without checking on them. "Viola, may I see the girls?"

"Now? They're sleeping."

"I won't wake them. But it's . . . important."

She rose from the chair and led us to the room that the sisters shared: two lamps, two nightstands, two beds, and two angelic little girls sleeping in their skivvies, under sheets but without blankets.

One lamp had been set at the lowest intensity on its three-way switch. The apricot-colored shade cast a soft, inviting light.

Two windows were open to the hot night. As insubstantial as a spirit, a translucent white moth beat its wings insistently against one of the screens, with the desperation of a lost soul fluttering against the gates of Heaven.

Mounted on the inside of the windows, with an emergency-release handle that couldn't be reached from outside, were steel bars that would prevent a man like Harlo Landerson from getting at the girls.

Screens and bars could foil moths and maniacs, but neither could keep out bodachs. Five of them were in the room.

CHAPTER 26

TWO SINISTER SHAPES STOOD AT EACH bed, visitors from one hell or another, travelers out of the black room.

They hunched over the girls and appeared to be studying them with keen interest. Their hands, if they had hands, floated a few inches above the sheets, and seemed slowly to trace the shrouded contours of the children's bodies.

I couldn't know for sure what they were doing, but I imagined that they were drawn to the very life energy of Nicolina and Levanna—and were somehow basking in it.

These creatures seemed to be unaware that we had entered the room. They were enthralled if not half hypnotized by some radiance that the girls emitted, a radiance invisible to me but evidently dazzling to them.

The fifth beast crawled the bedroom floor, its movements as fluid and serpentine as those of any reptile. Under Levanna's bed it slithered, seemed to coil there, but a moment later emerged with a salamandrian wriggle, only to glide under Nicolina's bed and whip itself silently back and forth, like a thrashing snake in slomo.

Unable to repress a shudder, I sensed that this fifth intruder must be savoring some exquisite spoor, some ethereal residue left by the passage of the little girls' feet. And I imagined—or hope I did —that I saw this squirming bodach repeatedly lick the carpet with a cold thin tongue.

When I would not venture far past the doorway, Viola whispered, "It's all right. They're deep sleepers, both of them."

"They're beautiful," Stormy said.

Viola brightened with pride. "They're such good girls." Seeing in my face a faint reflection of the abhorrence that gripped my mind, she said, "What's wrong?"

Glancing at me as I summoned an unconvincing smile, Stormy at once suspected the truth. She squinted into the shadowy corners of the room—left, right, and toward the ceiling—hoping to catch at least a fleeting glimpse of whatever supernatural presence revealed itself to me.

At the beds, the four hunched bodachs might have been priests of a diabolic religion, Aztecs at the altar of human sacrifice, as their hands moved sinuously and ceaselessly in ritualistic pantomime over the sleeping girls.

When I failed to answer Viola's question at once, she thought that I'd seen something wrong with her daughters, and she took a step toward the bed.

Gently I gripped her arm and held her back. "I'm sorry, Viola. Nothing's wrong. I just wanted to be sure the girls were safe. And with those bars on the windows, they are."

"They know how to work the emergency release," she said.

One of the entities at Nicolina's bedside appeared to rise out of its swoon and recognize our presence.

Its hands slowed but did not entirely stop their eerie movements, and it raised its wolfish head to peer in our direction with disturbing, eyeless intensity.

I was loath to leave the girls alone with those five phantoms, but I could do nothing to banish them.

Besides, from everything that I have seen of bodachs, they can experience this world with some if not all of the usual five senses, but they don't seem to have any *effect* on things here. I have never heard them make a sound, have never seen them move an object or, by their passage, disturb so much as the dust motes floating in the air.

They are of less substance than an ectoplasmic wraith drifting above the table at a seance. They are dream creatures on the wrong side of sleep.

The girls would not be harmed. Not here. Not yet.

Or so I hoped.

I suspected that these spirit travelers, having come to Pico Mundo for ringside seats at a festival of blood, were entertaining themselves on the eve of the main event. Perhaps they took pleasure in studying the victims before the shots were fired; they might be amused and excited to watch innocent people progress all unknowing toward imminent death.

Pretending to be unaware of the nightmarish intruders, putting one finger to my lips as if suggesting to Viola and Stormy that we be careful not to wake the girls, I drew both women with me, out of the room. I pushed the door two-thirds shut, just as it had been when we'd arrived, leaving the bodachs to slither on the floor, to sniff and thrash, to weave their patterns of sinuous gesticulations with mysterious purpose.

I worried that one or more of them would follow us to the living room, but we reached the front door without a supernatural escort.

Speaking almost as quietly as in the girls' bedroom, I said to Viola, "One thing I better clarify. When I tell you not to go to the movies tomorrow, I mean the girls shouldn't go, either. Don't send them out with a relative. Not to the movies, not anywhere."

Viola's smooth satin brow became brown corduroy. "But my sweet babies . . . they weren't shot in the dream."

"No prophetic dream reveals everything that's coming. Just fragments."

Instead of merely sharpening her anxiety, the implications of my statement hardened her features with anger. Good. She needed fear *and* anger to stay sharp, to make wise decisions in the day ahead.

To stiffen her resolve, I said, "Even if you *had* seen your girls shot . . . God forbid, dead . . . you might've blocked it from your memory when you woke."

Stormy rested her hand on Viola's shoulder. "You wouldn't have wanted those images in your mind."

Tense with determination, Viola said, "We'll stay home, have a little party, just ourselves."

"I'm not sure that's wise, either," I said.

"Why not? I don't know what place that was in my dream, but I'm sure it wasn't this house."

"Remember . . . different roads can take you to the same stubborn fate."

I didn't want to tell her about the bodachs in her daughters' room, for then I would have to reveal all my secrets. Only Terri, the chief, Mrs. Porter, and Little Ozzie know most of the truth about me, and only Stormy knows all of it.

If too many people are brought into my innermost circle, my secret will leak out. I'll become a media sensation, a freak to many people, a guru to some. Simplicity and quiet hours will be forever beyond my reach. My life will be too complicated to be worth living.

I said to Viola, "In your dream, this house wasn't where you were gunned down. But if you were destined to be shot at the movies, and now you aren't going to the theater . . . then maybe Fate comes here to find you. Not likely. But not impossible."

"And in *your* dream, tomorrow is the day?"

"That's right. So I'd feel better if you were *two* steps removed from the future you saw in your nightmare."

I glanced toward the back of the house. Still no bodachs had ventured after us. I *think* they have no effect on this world.

Nevertheless, taking no chances with the girls' lives, I lowered my voice further. "Step one—don't go to the movies or the Grille tomorrow. Step two—don't stay here, either."

Stormy asked, "How far away does your sister live?"

"Two blocks. Over on Maricopa Lane."

I said, "I'll come by in the morning, between nine and ten o'clock, with the photo I promised. I'll take you and the girls to your sister's."

"You don't have to do that, Odd. We can get there ourselves."

"No. I want to take you. It's necessary."

I needed to be certain that no bodachs followed Viola and her daughters.

Lowering my voice to a whisper, I said, "Don't tell Levanna and Nicolina what you're going to do. And don't call your sister to say you're coming. You could be overheard."

Viola surveyed the living room, worried but also astonished. "Who could hear?"

By necessity, I was mysterious: "Certain . . . forces." If the bodachs overheard her planning to move the kids to her sister's house, Viola might not have taken two safe steps away from her dreamed-of fate, after all, but only one. "Do you really believe, like you said, that I know about all that's Otherly and Beyond?"

She nodded. "Yes. I believe that."

Her eyes were so wide with wonder that they scared me, for they reminded me of the staring eyes of corpses.

"Then trust me on this, Viola. Get some sleep if you can. I'll come around in the morning. By tomorrow night, this'll have been all just a nightmare, nothing prophetic about it."

I didn't feel as confident as I sounded, but I smiled and kissed her on the cheek.

She hugged me and then hugged Stormy. "I don't feel so alone anymore."

Lacking an oscillating fan, the night outside was hotter than the warm air in the little house.

The moon had slowly ascended toward the higher stars, shedding its yellow veils to reveal its true silver face. A face as hard as a clock, and merciless.

CHAPTER 27

LITTLE MORE THAN AN HOUR BEFORE MIDnight, worried about a new day that might bring children in the line of gunfire, I parked the Mustang behind the Pico Mundo Grille.

When I doused the headlights and switched off the engine, Stormy said, "Will you ever leave this town?"

"I sure hope I'm not one of those who insists on hanging around after he's dead, like poor Tom Jedd out there at Tire World."

"I meant will you ever leave it while you're alive."

"Just the idea gives me hives on the brain."

"Why?"

"It's big out there."

"Not all of it is big. Lots of towns are smaller and quieter than Pico Mundo."

"I guess what I mean is . . . everything out there would be *new*. I like what I know. Considering everything else I have to deal with . . . I can't at the same time handle a lot of new stuff. New street names, new architecture, new smells, all new people . . . "

"I've always thought it would be nice to live in the mountains."

"New weather." I shook my head. "I don't need new weather."

"Anyway," she said, "I didn't mean leave town permanently. Just for a day or two. We could drive to Vegas."

"That's your idea of a smaller, quieter place? I'll bet that's a place with *thousands* of dead people who won't move on."

"Why?"

"People who lost everything they owned at the craps tables, the roulette wheels, then went back to their rooms and blew their brains out." I shivered. "Suicides always hang around after they're dead. They're afraid to move on."

"You have a melodramatic view of Las Vegas, odd one. The average hotel maid doesn't turn up a dozen suicides every morning."

"Bunch of guys murdered by the mob, their bodies dumped in the fresh concrete footings of new hotels. You can bet your ass *they* have unfinished business and plenty of postmortem rage. Besides, I don't gamble."

"That doesn't sound like the grandson of Pearl Sugars."

"She did her best to turn me into a card hustler, but I'm afraid I disappointed her."

"She taught you poker, didn't she?"

"Yeah. We used to play for pennies."

"Even just for pennies is gambling."

"Not when I played with Granny Sugars."

"She let you win? That's sweet."

"She wanted me to travel the Southwest poker circuit with her. Grandma said, 'Odd, I'm going to grow old on the road, not in a rocking chair on some damn retirement-home porch with a gaggle of farting old ladies, and I'm going to die facedown in my cards in the middle of a game, not of boredom at a tea dance for toothless retirees trying to cha-cha in their walkers.'"

"On the road," Stormy said, "would have been too much new."

"Every day, new and more new." I sighed. "But we sure would have had fun. She wanted me along to share the laughs . . . and if she died in the middle of a particularly rough game, she wanted me to be sure the other players didn't split her bankroll and leave her carcass in the desert as a coyote buffet."

"I understand why you didn't go on the road, but why don't you gamble?"

"Because even if Granny Sugars didn't play sloppy to give me an edge, I almost always won anyway."

"You mean because of your . . . gift?"

"Yeah."

"You could see what cards were coming?"

"No. Nothing that dramatic. I just have a feeling for when my hand is stronger than those of other players and when it's not. The feeling proves to be right nine times out of ten."

"That's a *huge* advantage at cards."

"It's the same with blackjack, any card game."

"So it's not really gambling."

"Not really. It's just . . . harvesting cash."

Stormy understood at once why I'd given up cards. "It would be pretty much the same as stealing."

"I don't need money that bad," I said. "And I never will as long as people want to eat what's been fried on a griddle."

"Or as long as they have feet."

"Yeah. Assuming I make the move into shoe retailing."

"I said Vegas not because I want to gamble," she explained.

"It's a long way to go for an all-you-can-eat buffet."

"I said Vegas because we could be there in maybe three hours, and the wedding chapels are open around the clock. No blood tests required. We could be married by dawn."

My heart did one of those funny gyrations that only Stormy can make it do. "Wow. That's almost enough to give me the nerve to travel."

"Only almost, huh?"

"We can have our blood tests tomorrow morning, get a marriage license Thursday, get hitched by Saturday. And our friends can be there. I want our friends there, don't you?"

"Yes. But I want married more."

I kissed her and said, "After all the hesitation, why the sudden rush?"

Because we had sat for a while in that unlighted alley, our eyes were thoroughly dark-adapted. Otherwise I would not have fully recognized the depth of concern in her face, her eyes; in fact, she seemed to be gripped not by mere anxiety but by a quiet terror.

"Hey, hey," I assured her, "everything's going to be all right."

Her voice didn't quaver. She's too tough for easy tears. But in the softness of her speech, I could hear a haunted woman: "Ever since we were sitting on the edge of the koi pond and that man came along the promenade . . ."

When her voice trailed away, I said, "Fungus Man."

"Yeah. That creepy sonofabitch. Ever since I saw him . . . I've been scared for you. I mean, I'm always scared for you, Oddie, but I don't usually make anything of it because the last thing you need, on top of everything else on your mind, is a weepy dame always nagging you to be careful."

"'Weepy dame'?"

"Sorry. I must've flashed back to a prior life in the 1930s. But it's true, the last thing you need is some hysterical bitch always on your case."

"I liked 'weepy dame' a lot better. Listen, I think this guy is maximum sick, he's ten megatons of blast power with a fast-ticking timer, but the chief and I are on his case, and we're going to pluck his fuse before he blows."

"Don't be so sure. Please, Oddie, don't be so sure. Being too sure with this guy will get you killed."

"I'm not going to be killed."

"I'm scared for you."

"By tomorrow night," I told her, "Bob Robertson, alias Fungus Man, is going to be wearing a jail-issued orange jumpsuit, and maybe he'll have hurt some people, or maybe we'll have stopped him right before he pulls a trigger, but whatever the situation, I'm going to be with you for dinner, and we'll be planning our wedding, and I'll still have both legs, both arms—"

"Oddie, stop, don't say any more—"

"—still have the same stupid head you're looking at now—"

"*Please* stop."

"—and I won't be blind, because I really *need* to see you, and I won't be deaf because how can we plan our wedding if I can't hear you, and I won't be—"

She punched me in the chest. "Don't tempt fate, dammit!"

In a sitting position, she couldn't get enough swing behind her fist to land a solid blow. I was hardly winded by the punch.

With as little wheeze as I could manage, I drew a breath and said, "I'm not worried about tempting fate. I'm not superstitious that way."

"Maybe I am."

"Well, get over it."

I kissed her. She kissed back.

How *right* the world was then.

I put an arm around her and said, "You silly, weepy dame. Bob Robertson might be so psychotic he wouldn't even qualify to manage the Bates Motel, but he's still just a mug. He has nothing going for him except sixteen wheels of craziness spinning in his head. I will come back to you with no punctures, no scrapes, no dents. And none of my federally mandated stuffing-identification tags will have been ripped off."

"My Pooh," she said, as sometimes she does.

Having somewhat calmed her nerves and partially settled her fears, I felt quite manly, like one of those stout-hearted and rock-ribbed sheriffs in old cowboy movies, who with a smile sets the minds of the lady-folk at ease and sweeps legions of gunfighters off the streets of Dodge City without smudging his white hat.

I was the worst kind of fool. When I look back on that August night, changed forever by all my wounds and all my suffering, that undamaged Odd Thomas seems like a different human being from me, immeasurably more confident than I am now, still able to hope, but not as wise, and I mourn for him.

I am told not to let the tone of this narrative become too dark. A certain 400-hundred-pound muse will park his 150-pound ass on me by way of editorial comment, and there is always the threat of his urine-filled cat.

CHAPTER 28

WHEN WE GOT OUT OF THE MUSTANG, the familiar alleyway dwindled north and south into deeper gloom than I recalled from other nights, little-revealed by moonlight, obscured by moonshadows.

Above the back entrance to the restaurant kitchen, a security lamp glowed. Yet the darkness seemed to press toward it rather than to shrink away.

Uncovered stairs led to a second-floor landing and the door to Terri Stambaugh's apartment. Light shone behind the curtains.

At the top of the steps, Stormy pointed at the northern sky. "Cassiopeia."

Star by star, I identified the points of the constellation.

In classic mythology, Cassiopeia was the mother of Andromeda. Andromeda was saved from a sea monster by the hero Perseus, who also slew the Gorgon Medusa.

No less than the fabled Andromeda, Stormy Llewellyn, daughter of another Cassiopeia, is stellar enough to deserve a constellation named for her. I have slain no Gorgons, however, and I am no Perseus.

Terri answered the door when I knocked, accepted

the car keys, and insisted that we come in for coffee or a nightcap.

Light from two candles throbbed pleasantly over the kitchen walls as cool drafts of conditioned air teased the flames. Terri had been sitting at the table when I knocked. A small glass of peach brandy stood on the red-and-white-checkered oilcloth.

As always, the background music of her life was Elvis: this time, "Wear My Ring Around Your Neck."

We had known that she would expect us to visit for a while, which is why Stormy hadn't waited at the bottom of the stairs.

Terri sometimes suffers from insomnia. Even if sleep slips upon her with ease, the nights are long.

When the CLOSED sign is hung on the front door of the Grille at nine o'clock and after the last customer leaves between nine and ten, whether Terri is drinking decaf coffee or something stronger, she opens as well a bottle of loneliness.

Her husband, Kelsey, her high-school sweetheart, has been dead for nine years. His cancer had been relentless, but being a fighter of uncommon determination, he had taken three years to die.

When his malignancy was diagnosed, he swore that he would not leave Terri alone. He possessed the will but not the power to keep that oath.

In his final years, because of the unfailing good humor and the quiet courage with which Kelsey waged his long mortal battle, Terri's love and respect for him, always deep, had grown profound.

In a way, Kelsey had kept his promise never to leave her. His ghost does not linger around the Grille or anywhere else in Pico Mundo. He lives vividly in her recollections, however, and his memory is etched on her soul.

After three or four years, her grief had matured into a settled sorrow. I think she has been surprised that even after arriving at an acceptance of her loss, she has had no desire to mend the tear in her heart. The hole that Kelsey left has become more comforting to her than any patch with which she could close it.

Her fascination with Elvis, his life and music, began nine years ago, when she was thirty-two, the same year that Kelsey died.

The reasons for her intense interest in Presley are numerous. Without a doubt, however, among them is this one: As long as she has an Elvis collection—music, memorabilia, biographical facts—to build and maintain, she has no time to be attracted to a living man and can remain emotionally true to her lost husband.

Elvis is the door that she closes in the face of romance. The architecture of his life is her mountain retreat, her high redoubt, her nunnery.

Stormy and I sat at the table. Terri subtly steered us away from the fourth chair, the one that Kelsey had always occupied when alive.

The subject of our impending wedding came up before we properly settled in our seats. With the peach brandy that she poured for us, Terri raised a toast to our enduring happiness.

Every autumn, she brews crocks full of peach skins into this elixir: ferments, strains, bottles it. The flavor is irresistible, and the brandy packs a punch best handled in small glasses.

Later, as Stormy and I were finishing our second servings, and as the King was singing "Love Me Tender," I told Terri about taking Elvis for a ride in her car. She was thrilled at first, but then saddened to hear that he had wept throughout our travels.

"I've seen him cry a few times before," I said. "Since

his death, he seems emotionally fragile. But this was the worst he's ever been in my experience."

"Of course," Terri said, "there's no mystery why he would be a total mess today of all days."

"Well, it's a mystery to me," I assured her.

"It's August fourteenth. At three-fourteen in the morning on August 14, 1958, his mama died. She was only forty-six."

"Gladys," Stormy said. "Her name was Gladys, wasn't it?"

There is movie-star fame like that enjoyed by Tom Cruise, rock-star fame like that of Mick Jagger, literary fame, political fame . . . But mere fame has grown into real legend when people of different generations remember your *mother's* name a quarter of a century after your death and nearly half a century after hers.

"Elvis was in the service," Terri recalled. "August twelfth, he flew home to Memphis on emergency leave and went to his mother's bedside in the hospital. But the sixteenth of August is a bad day for him, too."

"Why?"

"That's when he died," Terri said.

"Elvis himself?" Stormy asked.

"Yes. August 16, 1977."

I had finished the second peach brandy.

Terri offered the bottle.

I wanted more but didn't need it. I covered my empty glass with my hand and said, "Elvis seemed concerned about me."

"How do you mean?" Terri asked.

"He patted me on the arm. Like he felt sympathy for me. He had this . . . this melancholy look, as if he was taking pity on me for some reason."

This revelation alarmed Stormy. "You didn't tell me this. Why didn't you tell me?"

I shrugged. "It doesn't mean anything. It was just Elvis."

"So if it doesn't mean anything," Terri asked, "why did you mention it?"

"It means something to *me*," Stormy declared. "Gladys died on the fourteenth. Elvis died on the sixteenth. The fifteenth, smack between them—that's when this Robertson sonofabitch is going to go gunning for people. *Tomorrow*."

Terri frowned at me. "Robertson?"

"Fungus Man. The guy I borrowed your car to find."

"Did you find him?"

"Yeah. He lives in Camp's End."

"And?"

"The chief and I . . . we're on it."

"This Robertson is a toxic-waste mutant out of some psycho movie," Stormy told Terri. "He came after us at St. Bart's, and when we gave him the slip, he trashed some of the church."

Terri offered Stormy more peach brandy. "He's going to go gunning for people, you said?"

Stormy doesn't drink heavily, but she accepted another round. "Your fry cook's recurring dream is finally coming true."

Now Terri looked alarmed. "The dead bowling-alley employees?"

"Plus maybe a lot of people in a movie theater," Stormy said, and then she tossed back her peach brandy in one swallow.

"Does this also have something to do with Viola's dream?" Terri asked me.

"It's too long a story for now," I told her. "It's late. I'm whipped."

"It has everything to do with her dream," Stormy told Terri.

"I need some sleep," I pleaded. "I'll tell you tomorrow, Terri, after it's all over."

When I pushed my chair back, intending to get up, Stormy seized my arm and held me at the table. "And now I find out Elvis Presley himself has warned Oddie that he's going to die tomorrow."

I objected. "He did no such thing. He just patted me on the arm and then later, before he got out of the car, he squeezed my hand."

"Squeezed your hand?" Stormy asked in a tone implying that such a gesture could be interpreted only as an expression of the darkest foreboding.

"It's no big deal. All he did was just clasp my right hand in both of his and squeeze it twice—"

"Twice!"

"—and he gave me that look again."

"That look of *pity*?" Stormy demanded.

Terri picked up the bottle and offered to pour for Stormy.

I put my hand over the glass. "We've both had enough."

Grabbing my right hand and holding it in both of hers as Elvis had done, Stormy said insistently, "What he was trying to tell you, Mr. Macho Psychic Batman Wannabe, is that his mother died on August fourteenth, and he died on August sixteenth, and *you're* going to die on August fifteenth—the three of you like a hat trick of death—if you don't *watch your ass.*"

"That isn't what he was trying to tell me," I disagreed.

"What—you think he was just *hitting* on you?"

"He doesn't have a romantic life anymore. He's dead."

"Anyway," Terri said, "Elvis wasn't gay."

"I didn't claim he was gay. Stormy made the inference."

"I'd bet the Grille," Terri said, "and my left butt cheek that he wasn't gay."

I groaned. "This is the craziest conversation I've ever had."

Terri demurred: "Gimme a break—I've had a hundred conversations with you a *lot* crazier than this."

"Me too," Stormy agreed. "Odd Thomas, you're a fountain of crazy conversations."

"A geyser," Terri suggested.

"It's not me, it's just my *life*," I reminded them.

"You better stay out of this," Terri worried. "Let Wyatt Porter handle it."

"I *am* going to let him handle it. I'm not a cop, you know. I don't pack a gun. All I can do is advise him."

"Don't even advise this time," Stormy said. "Just this one time, stay out of it. Go to Vegas with me. Now."

I wanted to please her. Pleasing her pleases me, and then the birds sing sweeter than usual and the bees make better honey and the world is a place of rejoicing—or so it seems from my perspective.

What I *wanted* to do and the *right* thing to do were not one and the same. So I said, "The problem is that I was put here for this work, and if I walk away from the job, it will only follow me, one way or another."

I picked up my glass. I'd forgotten it was empty. I put it down again.

"When I've got a specific target, my psychic magnetism works in two directions. I can cruise at random and find who I need to find . . . in this case Robertson . . . or he'll be drawn to me if he wants to be, sometimes even if he doesn't. And in the second case, I have less control and I'm more likely to be . . . unpleasantly surprised."

"That's just a theory," Stormy said.

"It's nothing I can prove, but it's true. It's something I know in my gut."

"I've always figured you don't think with your head," Stormy said, her tone changing from one of insistent—and almost angry—persuasion to one of resignation and affection.

Terri said to me, "If I were your mother, I'd box your ears."

"If you were my mother, I wouldn't be here."

These were the two most important women in the world to me; I loved each of them in a different way, and declining to do what they wanted, even in the interest of doing the right thing, was difficult.

The candlelight burnished their faces to the same golden glow, and they regarded me with an identical anxiety, as though by virtue of their female intuition they knew things that I could not perceive even with my sixth sense.

From the CD player, Elvis crooned, "Are You Lonesome Tonight?"

I consulted my wristwatch. "It's August fifteenth."

When I tried to get to my feet, Stormy didn't restrain me as she had done previously. She, too, rose from her chair.

I said, "Terri, I guess you'll have to cover for me on the first shift—or get Poke to come in if he's willing."

"What—you can't cook and save the world at the same time?"

"Not unless you want the bacon burnt. Sorry to give you such short notice."

Terri accompanied us to the door. She hugged

Stormy, then me. She boxed one of my ears. "You be here day after tomorrow, on time, at the griddle, flippin' those cakes, or I'm going to demote you to fountain jockey."

CHAPTER 29

ACCORDING TO THE BIG DIGITAL SIGN AT the Bank of America, the temperature had fallen to a comparatively chilly ninety degrees here on the side of midnight when broomsticks are licensed to fly.

A lazy breeze stirred through town, repeatedly dying and rising again, as though rust inhibited the mechanisms of the wind gods. Hot and dry, it traveled in crisp and fitful whispers among ficuses, palms, and jacarandas.

The streets of Pico Mundo were quiet. When the breeze held its breath, I could hear the click of the switches in the traffic-signal control boxes as the lights changed from green to yellow to red at the intersections.

As we walked to Stormy's apartment, we remained alert, half expecting Bob Robertson to pop like a jack-in-the-box from behind a parked car, out of a doorway.

Other than the wind-licked leaves, the only movement was the dart-and-swoop of a swarm of bats pursuing a flurry of moths through the glow of a streetlamp, to the moon, and then out past Cassiopeia.

Stormy lives three blocks from the Pico Mundo Grille. We held hands and walked in silence.

My course was set irrevocably. In spite of her objections, she knew as well as I did that I had no choice but to do whatever I could to help Chief Porter stop Robertson before he committed the slaughter that had drenched my dreams for three years.

Anything that could be said on the subject now would be useless repetition. And here on the dark side of a threatening dawn, small talk had no charm.

The old, two-story Victorian house had been divided into four apartments. Stormy lives in the ground-floor unit on the right.

We didn't expect Robertson to be waiting there for us. Though he had somehow learned who I was, it didn't follow that he would easily discover Stormy's address.

If he was lying in wait for me, my apartment over Rosalia Sanchez's garage was a better bet than Stormy's place.

Prudence, however, made us cautious as we entered the foyer and then her apartment. Inside, the cool air had a faint peach scent. We left the Mojave far behind us when we closed the door.

She has three rooms, a bath, and a kitchen. Switching on lights, we went directly to her bedroom, where she keeps her 9-mm pistol.

She ejected the magazine, checked it to be sure that it was fully loaded, and snapped it back into the weapon.

I am wary of any gun, anywhere, anytime—except when it's in Stormy's hand. She could sit with her finger on the detonation button of a nuclear weapon, and I would feel safe enough to nap.

A quick check of the windows revealed that they were locked, as she had left them.

No boogeyman had taken up residence in any of the closets.

While Stormy brushed her teeth and changed for bed, I called Green Moon Lanes and listened to a recorded message regarding their hours, services, and prices. They opened for business at 11:00 A.M. Thursday through Sunday, and at 1:00 P.M. Monday through Wednesday.

The earliest that Robertson could walk into the bowling center with murder in mind was when they unlocked the doors at one o'clock.

Two multiplex cinemas with a total of twenty screens serve the greater Pico Mundo area. By phone, I learned that the movie to which Viola had intended to take her daughters was playing at two theaters in only one multiplex. I made a mental note of the show times, the earliest of which was 1:10 P.M.

In the bedroom, I turned down the bedclothes, took off my shoes, and stretched out atop the thin blanket, waiting for Stormy.

She has furnished her humble home with items from thrift shops run by Goodwill and the Salvation Army; however, the look is neither shabby nor without character. She has a talent for eclectic design and for discerning the magic in objects that others might see as merely old or peculiar, or even grotesque.

Floor lamps featuring silk shades with beaded fringes, chairs in the Stickley style paired with plump Victorian footstools upholstered in tapestries, Maxfield Parrish prints, colorful carnival-glass vases and bibelots: The mix should not work, but it does. Her rooms are the most welcoming that I have ever seen.

Time seems suspended in this place.

In these rooms I am at peace. I forget my worries. The problems of pancakes and poltergeists are lifted from me.

Here I cannot be harmed.

Here I know my destiny and am content with it.

Here Stormy lives, and where she lives, I flourish.

Above her bed, behind glass, in a frame, is the card from the fortune-telling machine: YOU ARE DESTINED TO BE TOGETHER FOREVER.

Four years ago, on the midway of the county fair, a gaudy contrivance called Gypsy Mummy had waited in a shadowy back corner of an arcade tent filled with unusual games and macabre attractions.

The machine had resembled an old-fashioned phone booth and had stood seven feet high. The lower three feet were entirely enclosed. The upper four feet featured glass on three sides.

In the glass portion sat a dwarfish female figure attired in a Gypsy costume complete with garish jewelry and colorful headscarf. Her gnarled, bony, withered hands rested on her thighs, and the green of her fingernails looked less like polish than like mold.

A plaque at her feet claimed that this was the mummified corpse of a Gypsy dwarf. In 18th-century Europe, she had been renowned for the accuracy of her prognostications and foretellings.

The mottled skin of her face stretched tight over the skull. The eyelids were stitched shut with black thread, as were her lips.

Most likely this was not the art of Death working in the medium of flesh, as claimed, but instead the product of an artist who had been clever with plaster, paper, and latex.

As Stormy and I arrived at Gypsy Mummy, another couple fed a quarter to the machine. The woman leaned toward a round grill in the glass and asked her question aloud: "Gypsy Mummy tell us, will Johnny and I have a long and happy marriage?"

The man, evidently Johnny, pushed the ANSWER button, and a card slid into a brass tray. He read it aloud: "A cold wind blows, and each night seems to last a thousand years."

Neither Johnny nor his bride-to-be regarded this as an answer to their question, so they tried again. He read the second card: "The fool leaps from the cliff, but the winter lake below is frozen."

The woman, believing that Gypsy Mummy had misheard the question, repeated it: "Will Johnny and I have a long and happy marriage?"

Johnny read the third card: "The orchard of blighted trees produces poisonous fruit."

And the fourth: "A stone can provide no nourishment, nor will sand slake your thirst."

With irrational persistence, the couple spent four more quarters in pursuit of an answer. They began bickering on receipt of the fifth card. By the time Johnny read number eight, the cold wind predicted by the first fortune was blowing at gale-force between them.

After Johnny and his love departed, Stormy and I took our turn with Gypsy Mummy. A single coin produced for us the assurance that we were destined to be together forever.

When Stormy tells this story, she claims that after granting to us what the other couple had wanted, the mummified dwarf winked.

I didn't see this wink. I don't understand how a sewn-shut eye could perform such a trick and yet fail to pop a single stitch. The image of a winking mummy resonates with me nonetheless.

Now, as I waited under the Gypsy Mummy's framed card, Stormy came to bed. She wore plain white cotton panties and a SpongeBob SquarePants T-shirt.

All the models in the Victoria's Secret catalogue, in thongs and skimpy teddies and peekaboo bras, collectively possess a fraction of the erotic allure of Stormy in schoolgirl briefs and SpongeBob top.

Lying on her side, cuddling against me, she put her head upon my chest to listen to my heart. She got an earful.

She often likes to be held in this way until she falls asleep. I am the boatman she trusts to row her into restful dreams.

After a silence, she said, "If you want me . . . I'm ready now."

I am no saint. I have used my driver's license to trespass in homes to which I've not been invited. I answer violence with violence and never turn the other cheek. I have had enough impure thoughts to destroy the ozone layer. I have often spoken ill of my mother.

Yet when Stormy offered herself to me, I thought of the orphaned girl, then known to the world as Bronwen, alone and afraid at the age of seven, adopted and given safe harbor, only to discover that her new father wanted not a daughter but a sex toy. Her confusion, her fear, her humiliation, her shame were too easy for me to imagine.

I thought also of Penny Kallisto and the seashell that she had handed to me. From the glossy pink throat of that shell had come the voice of a monster speaking the language of demented lust.

Though I didn't confuse my clean passion with Harlo Landerson's sick desire and savage selfishness, I could not purge from memory his rough breathing and bestial grunts. "Saturday is almost here," I told Stormy. "You've taught me the beauty of anticipation."

"What if Saturday never comes?"

"We'll have this Saturday and thousands more," I assured her.

"I need you," she said.

"Is that something new?"

"God, no."

"It's not new for me, either."

I held her. She listened to my heart. Her hair feathered like a raven's wing against her face, and my spirits soared.

Soon she murmured to someone she seemed pleased to see in her sleep. The boatman had done his job, and Stormy drifted on dreams.

I eased off the bed without waking her, drew the top sheet and thin blanket over her shoulders, and switched the bedside lamp to its lowest setting. She doesn't like to wake in darkness.

After slipping into my shoes, I kissed her forehead and left her with the 9-mm pistol on her nightstand.

I turned out the lights elsewhere in the apartment, stepped into the public hall, and locked her door with a key she'd given to me.

The front door of the apartment house featured a large oval of leaded glass. The beveled edges of the mosaic pieces presented a fragmented and distorted view of the porch.

I put one eye to a flat piece of glass to see things more clearly. An unmarked police van stood at the curb across the street.

Law-enforcement in Pico Mundo involves few clandestine operations. The police department owns only two unmarked units.

The average citizen wouldn't recognize either vehicle. Because of the assistance that I've provided to the chief on numerous cases, I have ridden in and am familiar with both.

Of the white van's identifying features, the stubby shortwave antenna spiking from the roof at the back was the clincher.

I had not asked the chief to grant protection to Stormy; she would have been angry at the implication that she couldn't take care of herself. She has her pistol, her certificate of graduation from a self-defense course, and her pride.

The danger to her, if any, would seem to exist only when I was with her. Bob Robertson had no beef with anyone but me.

This chain of logic brought me to the realization that Chief Porter might be providing protection not to Stormy but to me.

More likely, it wasn't protection but surveillance. Robertson had tracked me to Little Ozzie's place and had found me again later at St. Bart's. The chief might be keeping a watch on me in the hope that Robertson would sniff out my trail once more, whereupon he could be taken into custody for questioning about the vandalism at the church.

I understood his thinking, but I resented being used as bait without first being asked politely if I minded having a hook in my ass.

Besides, in the course of meeting the responsibilities of my supernatural gift, I sometimes resort to tactics frowned upon by the police. The chief knows this. Being subjected to police surveillance and protection would inhibit me and, if I acted in my usual impulsive fashion, would make Chief Porter's position even more difficult.

Instead of leaving by the main entrance, I walked to the end of the public hall and departed by the back door. A small moonlit yard led to a four-car garage, and a gate beside the garage opened into an alleyway.

The officer in the van thought that he was running surveillance on me, but now he served as Stormy's guardian. And she couldn't get angry with me because I had never asked that she be provided with protection.

I was tired but not ready to sleep. I went home anyway.

Maybe Robertson would be waiting for me and would try to kill me. Maybe I would survive, subdue him, call the chief, and thereby put an end to this.

I had high hopes of a violent encounter with a satisfactory conclusion.

CHAPTER 30

THE MOJAVE HAD STOPPED BREATHING. The dead lungs of the desert no longer exhaled the lazy breeze that had accompanied Stormy and me on our walk to her apartment.

By streets and alleyways, along a footpath bisecting a vacant lot, through a drainage culvert dry for months, and then to streets again, I made my way home at a brisk pace.

Bodachs were abroad.

First I saw them at a distance, a dozen or more, racing on all fours. When they passed through dark places, they were discernible only as a tumult of shadows, but streetlights and gatepost lamps revealed them for what they were. Their lithe motion and menacing posture brought to mind panthers in pursuit of prey.

A two-story Georgian house on Hampton Way was a bodach magnet. As I passed, staying to the far side of the street, I saw twenty or thirty inky forms, some arriving and others departing by cracks in window frames and chinks in door jambs.

Under the porch light, one of them thrashed and writhed as if in the throes of madness. Then it funneled itself through the keyhole in the front door.

Two others, exiting the residence, strained themselves through the screen that covered an attic vent. As comfortable on vertical surfaces as any spider, they crawled down the wall of the house to the porch roof, crossed the roof, and sprang to the front lawn.

This was the home of the Takuda family, Ken and Micali, and their three children. No lights brightened any windows. The Takudas were asleep, unaware that a swarm of malevolent spirits, quieter than cockroaches, crawled through their rooms and observed them in their dreaming.

I could only assume that one of the Takudas—or all of them—were destined to die this very day, in whatever violent incident had drawn the bodachs to Pico Mundo in great numbers.

Experience had taught me that these spirits often gathered at the site of forthcoming horror, as at the Buena Vista Nursing Home before the earthquake. In this case, however, I didn't believe that the Takudas would perish in their home any more than I expected that Viola and her daughters would die in their picturesque bungalow.

The bodachs were not concentrated in one place this time. They were all over town, and from their unusually wide disbursement and their behavior, I deduced that they were visiting the potential victims prior to gathering at the place where the bloodshed would occur. Call this the pregame show.

I hurried away from the Takuda house and didn't glance back, concerned that the slightest attention I paid to these creatures would alert them to the fact that I could see them.

On Eucalyptus Way, other bodachs had invaded the home of Morris and Rachel Melman.

Since Morrie had retired as the superintendent of

the Pico Mundo School District, he'd stopped resisting his circadian rhythms and had embraced the fact that he was a night lover by nature. He spent these quiet hours in the pursuit of various hobbies and interests. While Rachel slept in the dark upstairs, warm light brightened the lower floor.

The distinctive shadowy shapes of bodachs in their erect but hunch-shouldered posture were visible at every ground-floor window. They appeared to be in ceaseless, agitated movement through those rooms, as though the scent of impending death stirred in them a violent and delirious excitement.

To one degree or another, this silent frenzy marked their behavior wherever I had seen them since walking to work less than twenty-four hours ago. The intensity of their malignant ecstasy fueled my dread.

In this infested night, I found myself glancing warily at the sky, half expecting to see bodachs swarming across the stars. The moon wasn't veiled by spirit wings, however, and the stars blazed unobstructed from Andromeda to Vulpecula.

Because they have no apparent mass, the bodachs should not be affected by gravity. Yet I have never seen them fly. Although supernatural, they seem to be bound by many, though not all, of the laws of physics.

When I reached Marigold Lane, I was relieved that the street on which I lived appeared to be free of these beasts.

I passed the spot where I had stopped Harlo Landerson in his Pontiac Firebird 400. How easily, by comparison, the day had begun.

With her killer named and prevented from assaulting other girls, Penny Kallisto had made her peace with this world and moved on. This success gave me hope that I might prevent or minimize the pending carnage that had drawn legions of bodachs to our town.

No lights glowed at Rosalia Sanchez's house. She is always early to bed, for she rises in advance of the dawn, eager to hear if she remains visible.

I didn't approach her garage by the driveway. I crossed the side lawn from one oak tree to the next, stealthily scouting the territory.

When I determined that neither Robertson nor any other enemy had stationed himself in the yard, I circled the garage. Although I didn't find anyone lying in wait, I flushed a frightened rabbit from a lush bed of liriope, and when it shot past me, I achieved a personal best in the vertical-jump-and-gasp event.

Climbing the exterior stairs to my apartment, I watched the windows above, alert for the telltale movement of a blind.

The teeth of the key chattered faintly across the pin-tumblers in the lock. I turned the bolt and opened the door.

When I switched on the light, I saw the gun before anything else. A pistol.

With Chief Porter as my friend, with Stormy as my fiancee, I would know the difference between a pistol and a revolver even if my mother hadn't instructed me in various fine points of firearms on numerous harrowing occasions.

The pistol had not merely been dropped on the floor but appeared to have been arranged as surely as a diamond necklace on a jeweler's black-velvet display board, positioned to catch the lamplight in such a way that its contours had an almost erotic quality. Whoever left it there had hoped to entice me to pick it up.

CHAPTER 31

MY SALVAGE-YARD FURNITURE (TOO scarred and tacky to meet the standards of the thrift shops that sold to Stormy), my paperback books neatly arranged on shelves made of stacked bricks and boards, my framed posters of Quasimodo as played by Charles Laughton and Hamlet as played by Mel Gibson and ET from the movie of the same name (three fictional characters with whom I identify for different reasons), the cardboard Elvis perpetually smiling . . .

From the open doorway in which I stood, everything appeared to be as it had been when I'd left for work Tuesday morning.

The door had been locked and bore no signs of a forced entry. Circling the building, I had noticed no broken windows.

Now I was torn between leaving the door open to facilitate a hasty exit and locking it to prevent anyone from entering at my back. After too long a hesitation, I quietly closed the door and engaged the deadbolt.

Except for the occasional chirr-and-coo of a night bird that filtered through two screened windows I'd left open for ventilation, the hush was so profound that a drop of water, in the kitchenette, fell from faucet to sink pan with a *plonk* that quivered my eardrums.

Certain that I was meant to pick up the gun, easily resisting its allure, I stepped over the weapon.

One of the benefits of living in a single room—the armchair a few steps from the bed, the bed a few steps from the refrigerator—is that the search for an intruder takes less than a minute. Your blood pressure hasn't the time to rise to stroke-inducing levels when you need only look behind the sofa and in a single closet to clear all possible hiding places.

Only the bathroom remained to be searched.

That door was closed. I had left it open.

After a shower, I always leave it open because the bathroom has a single small window, hardly more than a porthole, and an exhaust fan that makes all the noise of—but stirs less air than—a drum set hammered by a heavy-metal musician. If I didn't leave the door open, the bath would be ruled by aggressive mutant molds with a taste for human flesh, and I would be forced henceforth to bathe in the kitchen sink.

Unclipping the phone from my belt, I considered calling the police to report an intruder.

If officers arrived and found no one in the bathroom, I would look foolish. And scenarios occurred to me in which I might appear worse than merely foolish.

I glanced at the gun on the floor. If it had been placed with careful calculation, with the intent that I should pick it up, why did someone want me to have possession of it?

After putting the phone on the breakfast counter, I stepped to one side of the bathroom door and listened intently. The only sounds were the periodic song of the night bird and, after a long pause, the *plonk* of another water drop in the kitchen sink.

The knob turned without resistance. The door opened inward.

Someone had left a light on.

I am diligent about conserving electricity. The cost may be only pennies, but a short-order cook who hopes to marry cannot afford to leave lights burning or music playing for the pleasure of the spiders and spirits that might visit his quarters in his absence.

With the door open wide, the small bathroom would offer nowhere for an intruder to hide except in the bathtub, behind the closed shower curtain.

I always close the curtain after taking a shower, because if I left it drawn to one side, it would not dry properly in that poorly vented space. Mildew would at once set up housekeeping in the damp folds.

Since I'd left Tuesday morning, someone had pulled the curtain aside. That person or another was at this moment facedown in the bathtub.

He appeared to have fallen into the tub or to have been tumbled there as a dead weight. No living person would lie in such an awkward position, face pressed to the drain, his right arm twisted behind his body at a torturous angle that suggested a dislocated shoulder or even a torn rotator cuff.

The fingers of the exposed, pale hand were curled into a rigid claw. They did not twitch; neither did they tremble.

Along the far rim of the tub, a thin smear of blood had dried on the porcelain.

When blood is spilled in quantity, you can smell it: This is not a foul odor when fresh, but subtle and crisp and terrifying. I couldn't detect the faintest scent of it here.

A glistening spill of liquid soap on the tile counter around the sink and thick soap scum in the bowl suggested that the killer had washed his hands vigorously after the deed, perhaps to scrub away blood or traces of incriminating gunpowder.

After drying, he had tossed the hand towel into the tub. It covered the back of the victim's head.

Without conscious intent, I had backed out of the bathroom. I stood just beyond the open door.

My heart played an inappropriate rhythm for the melody of the night bird.

I glanced toward the gun on the carpet, just inside the front door. My instinctive reluctance to touch the weapon had proven to be wise, although I still didn't grasp the full meaning of what had transpired here.

My cell phone lay on the breakfast counter, and the apartment phone was on the nightstand beside my bed. I considered those whom I *should* call and those I *could* call. None of my options appealed to me.

To better understand the situation, I needed to see the face of the corpse.

I returned to the bathroom. I bent over the tub. Avoiding the hooked and twisted fingers, I clutched handfuls of his clothing and, with some struggle, wrestled the dead man onto his side, and then onto his back.

The towel slid off his face.

Still a washed-out gray but devoid now of their characteristic eerie amusement, Bob Robertson's eyes were more sharply focused in death than in life. His gaze fixed intently on a distant vision, as though in the final instant of existence, he had glimpsed something more startling and far more terrifying than just the face of his killer.

CHAPTER 32

FOR A MOMENT I EXPECTED FUNGUS MAN to blink, to grin, to grab me and drag me into the tub with him, to savage me with those teeth that had served him so well during his gluttony at the counter in the Pico Mundo Grille.

His unexpected death left me with no immediate monster, with my plan derailed and my purpose in doubt. I had assumed that he was the maniacal gunman who shot the murdered people in my recurring dream, not merely another victim. With Robertson dead, this labyrinth had no Minotaur for me to track down and slay.

He had been shot once in the chest at such close range that the muzzle of the gun might have been pressed against him. His shirt bore the gray-brown flare of a scorch mark.

Because the heart had stopped functioning in an instant, little blood had escaped the body.

Again I retreated from the bathroom.

I almost pulled the door shut. Then I had the strange notion that behind the closed door, in spite of his torn heart, Robertson would rise quietly from the tub and stand in wait, taking me by surprise when I returned.

He was stone dead, and I *knew* that he was dead,

and yet such irrational worries tied knots in my nerves.

Leaving the bathroom door open, I stepped to the kitchen sink and washed my hands. After drying them on paper towels, I almost washed them again.

Although I had touched only Robertson's clothes, I imagined that my hands smelled of death.

Lifting the receiver from the wall phone, I unintentionally rattled it against the cradle, almost dropped it. My hands were shaking.

I listened to the dial tone.

I knew Chief Porter's number. I didn't need to look it up.

Finally I racked the phone again without entering a single digit on the keypad.

Circumstances had altered my cozy relationship with the chief. A dead man awaited discovery in my apartment. The gun that had killed him was here, as well.

Earlier I had reported an unsettling encounter with the victim at St. Bartholomew's. And the chief knew that I had illegally entered Robertson's house on Tuesday afternoon and had thereby given the man reason to confront me.

If this pistol was registered to Robertson, the most obvious assumption on the part of the police would be that he had come here to demand to know what I'd been doing in his house and perhaps to threaten me. They would assume that we had argued, that the argument had led to a struggle, and that I had shot him with his own gun in self-defense.

They wouldn't charge me with murder or with manslaughter. They probably wouldn't even take me into custody for questioning.

If the pistol *wasn't* registered to Robertson, however, I'd be as stuck as a rat on a glue-board trap.

Wyatt Porter knew me too well to believe that I could kill a man in cold blood, when my life was not at risk. As the chief, he set the policies for the department and made important procedural decisions, but he wasn't the only cop on the force. Others would not be so quick to declare me innocent under questionable circumstances, and if for no reason but appearances, the chief might have to park me in a cell for a day, until he could find a way to resolve matters in my favor.

In jail, I would be safe from whatever bloody catastrophe might be descending on Pico Mundo, but I would be in no position to use my gift to prevent the tragedy. I couldn't escort Viola Peabody and her daughters from their house to the safer refuge of her sister's home. I couldn't find a way to induce the Takuda family to change their Wednesday plans.

I had hoped to follow the bodachs to the site of the impending crime as Wednesday morning gave way to afternoon, when this event seemed destined to occur. Those malevolent spirits would gather in advance of the bloodshed, perhaps giving me enough time to change the fates of *all* those who were unwittingly approaching their deaths at that as yet unknown place.

Odysseus in chains, however, cannot lead the way back to Ithaca.

I include this literary allusion solely because I know Little Ozzie will be amused that I would have the audacity to compare myself to that great hero of the Trojan War.

"Give the narrative a lighter tone than you think it deserves, dear boy, lighter than you think that you can bear to give it," he instructed before I began to write, "because you won't find the truth of life in morbidity, only in hope."

My promise to obey this instruction has become more difficult to fulfill as my story progresses relentlessly toward the hour of the gun. The light recedes from me, and the darkness gathers. To please my massive, six-fingered muse, I must resort to tricks like the Odysseus bit.

Having determined that I couldn't turn to Chief Porter for help in these circumstances, I switched off all the lights except the one in the bathroom. I couldn't bear to be entirely in the dark with the corpse, for I sensed that, even though dead, he still had surprises in store for me.

In the gloom, I quickly found my way through the cluttered room with as much confidence as if I had been born sightless and raised here since birth. At one of the front windows, I twisted the control rod to open the Levolor.

To the right, I could see the moonlit stairs framed in slices by the slats of the blind. No one was ascending toward my door.

Directly ahead lay the street, but because of the intervening oaks, I didn't have an unobstructed view. Nevertheless, between the branches I could see enough of Marigold Lane to be certain that no suspicious vehicles had parked at the curb since my arrival.

Judging by the evidence, I wasn't under observation, but I felt certain that whoever had whacked Bob Robertson would be back. When they knew that I had come home and discovered the cadaver, they would either pop me, too, and make the double murder look like murder-suicide, or more likely place an anonymous call to the police and land me in the cell that I was determined to avoid.

I knew a set-up when I saw one.

CHAPTER 33

AFTER CLOSING THE LEVOLOR AT THE window, leaving the lights off, I went to the bureau, which was near the bed. In this one room, everything could be found near the bed, including the sofa and the microwave.

In the bottom drawer of the bureau I kept my only spare set of bed linens. Under the pillowcases, I found the neatly pressed and folded top sheet.

Although without a doubt the situation warranted the sacrifice of good bedclothes, I regretted having to give up that sheet. Well-made cotton bedding is not cheap, and I am mildly allergic to many of the synthetic fabrics commonly used for such items.

In the bathroom, I opened the sheet on the floor.

Being dead and therefore indifferent to my problems, Robertson could not be expected to make my job easier; however, I was surprised when he resisted being hauled out of the tub. This wasn't the active counterforce of conscious opposition, but the passive resistance of rigor mortis.

He proved to be as stiff and difficult to manage as a pile of boards nailed together at odd angles.

Reluctantly, I put a hand to his face. He felt colder than I'd expected that he would.

Perhaps adjustments needed to be made in my understanding of the events of the previous evening. Unthinkingly, I had made certain assumptions that Robertson's condition didn't support.

To learn the truth, I had to examine him further. Because he had been lying facedown in the tub when I'd found him, before I'd turned him over, I now unbuttoned his shirt.

This task filled me with loathing and repugnance, which I had anticipated, but I wasn't prepared for the abhorrent sense of intimacy that spawned a slithering nausea.

My fingers were damp with sweat. The pearlized buttons proved slippery.

I glanced at Robertson's face, certain that his gaze would have refocused from some otherworldly sight to my fumbling hands. Of course his expression of shock and terror had not changed, and he continued staring at something beyond the veil that separates this world and the next.

His lips were slightly parted, as though with his last breath he had greeted Death or had spoken an unanswered plea.

Looking at his face had only made my heebie-jeebies worse. When I lowered my head, I imagined that his eyes tracked the shifting of my attention to the stubborn buttons. If I had felt a fetid breath exhaled against my brow, I might have screamed, but I wouldn't have been surprised.

No corpse had ever creeped me out as badly as this one. For the most part, the deceased with whom I interact are apparitions, and I am spared too much familiarity with the messy biological aspect of death.

In this instance, I was troubled less by the scents and sights of early-stage corruption than by the physical peculiarities of the dead man, mostly that spongy fungoid quality that had marked him in life, but also by his extraordinary fascination—as revealed in his files—for torture, brutal murder, dismemberment, decapitation, and cannibalism.

I undid the final button. I folded back his shirt.

Because he wore no undershirt, I saw the advanced lividity at once. After death, blood settles through the tissues to the lowest points of the body, giving those areas a badly bruised appearance. Robertson's flabby chest and sagging belly were mottled, dark, and repulsive.

The coolness of his skin, the rigor mortis, and the advanced lividity suggested that he had not died within the past hour or two but much earlier. The warmth of my apartment would have accelerated the deterioration of the corpse, but not to this extent.

Very likely, in St. Bart's cemetery, when Robertson had given me the finger as I'd looked down on him from the bell tower, he had not been a living man but an apparition.

I tried to recall if Stormy had seen him. She had been stooping to retrieve the cheese and crackers from the picnic hamper. I had accidentally knocked them from her hands, spilling them across the catwalk . . .

No. She hadn't seen Robertson. By the time she got up and leaned against the parapet to look down at the graveyard, he had gone.

Moments later, when I opened the front door of the church and encountered Robertson ascending the steps, Stormy had been behind me. I had let the door fall shut and had hustled her out of the narthex, into the nave, toward the front of the church.

Before going to St. Bart's, I'd seen Robertson twice at Little Ozzie's place in Jack Flats. The first time, he had been standing on the public sidewalk in front of the house, later in the backyard.

In neither instance had Ozzie been in a position to confirm that this visitor was a real, live person.

From his perch on the windowsill, Terrible Chester had seen the man at the front fence and had strongly reacted to him. But this did not mean that Robertson had been there in the flesh.

On many occasions, I have witnessed dogs and cats responding to the presence of spirits—though they don't see bodachs. Usually animals do not react in any dramatic fashion, only subtly; they seem to be totally cool with ghosts.

Terrible Chester's hostility was probably a reaction not to the fact that Robertson was an apparition but to the man's abiding aura of evil, which characterized him both in life and death.

The evidence suggested that the last time I'd seen Robertson alive had been when he'd left his house in Camp's End, just before I had loided the lock, gone inside, and found the black room.

He had haunted me since, and angrily. As though he blamed me for his death.

Although he'd been murdered in my apartment, he must know that I hadn't pulled the trigger. Facing his killer, he'd been shot from a distance of no more than a few inches.

What he and his killer had been doing in my apartment, I could not imagine. I needed more time and calmer circumstances to think.

You might expect that his pissed-off spirit would have lurked in my bathroom or kitchenette, waiting for me to come home, eager to threaten and harass me as he had done at the church. You would be wrong because you forget that these restless souls who linger in this world do so because they cannot accept the truth of their deaths.

In my considerable experience, the *last* thing they want to do is hang around their dead bodies. Nothing is a more poignant reminder of one's demise than one's oozing carcass.

In the presence of their own lifeless flesh, the spirits feel more sharply the urge to be done with this world and to move on to the next, a compulsion that they are determined to resist. Robertson might visit the place of his death eventually, but not until his body had been removed and every smear of blood had been scrubbed away.

That suited me fine. I didn't need all the hullabaloo associated with a visitation by an angry spirit.

The vandalism in St. Bart's sacristy had not been the work of a living man. That destruction had been wrought by a malevolent and infuriated ghost in full poltergeist mode.

In the past, I'd lost a new music system, a lamp, a clock radio, a handsome bar stool, and several plates during a tantrum by such a one. A short-order cook can't afford to play host to their kind.

This is one reason why my furnishings are thrift-shop rejects. The less that I have, the less I can lose.

Anyway, I looked at the lividity in Robertson's flabby chest and sagging belly, quickly made the aforementioned deductions, and tried to button his shirt without looking directly at his bullet wound. Morbid interest got the best of me.

In the soft and livid chest, the hole was small but ragged, wet,—and strange in some way that I didn't immediately grasp and that I didn't want to contemplate further.

The nausea crawling the walls of my stomach

slithered faster, faster. I felt as if I were four years old again, with a dangerously virulent case of the flu, feverish and weak, staring down the barrel of my own mortality.

Because I had enough of a mess to clean up without reenacting Elvis's historic last spew, I clenched my teeth, repressed my gorge, and finished buttoning the shirt.

Although I surely know more than the average citizen about how to read the condition of a corpse, I am not a specialist in forensic medicine. I couldn't accurately determine, to the half hour, the exact time of Robertson's death.

Logic put it between 5:30 and 7:45. During that period, I had searched his Camp's End house and explored the black room, had driven Elvis to the chief's barbecue and subsequently to the Baptist church, and had cruised alone to Little Ozzie's house.

Chief Porter and his guests could verify my whereabouts for part of that time, but no court would look favorably on the claim that the ghost of Elvis could provide me with an alibi for another portion of it.

The extent of my vulnerability became clearer by the moment, and I knew that time was running out. When a knock at the door eventually came, it would most likely be the police, sent here by an anonymous tip.

CHAPTER 34

A SENSE OF URGENCY BORDERING ON panic gave me new strength. With much grunting and the invention of a few colorful obscenities, I hauled Robertson out of the bathtub and flopped him onto the sheet that I'd spread on the bathroom floor.

Remarkably little blood had spilled in the tub. I cranked on the shower and washed the stains off the porcelain with steaming-hot water.

I'd never be able to take a bath here again. I would either have to go unwashed for the rest of my life or find a new place to live.

When I turned out Robertson's pants pockets, I found a wad of cash in each: twenty crisp hundred-dollar bills in the left pocket, twenty-three in the right. Clearly, he hadn't been killed for money.

I returned those bankrolls to his pockets.

His billfold contained more cash. I stuffed that money in one of his pockets, as well, but kept the wallet with the hope that it might contain a clue to his murderous intentions when I had time to examine its remaining contents.

The corpse gurgled alarmingly as I wrapped it in the sheet. Bubbles of phlegm or blood popped in its throat, disturbingly like a belch.

I twisted the ends shut at the head and feet, and tied them as securely as possible with the white laces that I stripped out of a spare pair of shoes.

This package looked like an enormous doobie. I don't do drugs, not even pot, but that's what it looked like, anyway.

Or maybe a cocoon. A giant larva or pupa inside, changing into something new. I didn't want to dwell on what that might be.

Using a plastic shopping bag from a bookstore as a suitcase, I packed a change of clothes, shampoo, toothbrush, toothpaste, electric razor, cell phone, flashlight, scissors, a package of foil-wrapped moist towelettes—and a roll of antacids, which I was going to need to get through the rest of the night.

I dragged the body out of the bathroom, across my dark room, to the larger of the two south-facing windows. If I had lived in an ordinary apartment house, with neighbors below, the tenants' committee would have met first thing in the morning to draft a new rule forbidding corpse-hauling after 10:00 P.M.

The body weighed far too much for me to carry it. Tumbling it down the outside stairs would have been a noisy proposition—and a memorable spectacle if someone happened to be passing in the street at an inopportune moment.

A half-size dinette table and two chairs stood in front of the window. I moved them aside, raised the lower sash, removed the bug screen, and leaned out to be sure I correctly remembered that the backyard could not be seen from neighboring houses.

A board fence and mature cottonwood trees provided privacy. If a narrow line of sight between branches gave neighbors a sliver of a view, the moonlight alone didn't brighten the scene enough to lend credibility to their testimony in a courtroom.

I muscled the sheet-wrapped cadaver off the floor, into the open window. I shoved him out feetfirst because though he was inarguably dead, I felt squeamish about dropping him on his head. Halfway out the window, the sheet hung up on a protruding nail head, but with determination, I maneuvered him far enough to let gravity take over.

The drop from the windowsill to the ground measured twelve or thirteen feet. Not far. Yet the impact produced a brutal, sickening sound that seemed instantly identifiable as a dead body plummeting to hard earth from a height.

No dogs barked. No one said, *Did you hear something, Maude?* No one said, *Yes, Clem, I heard Odd Thomas drop a corpse out his window.* Pico Mundo slept on.

Using paper towels to avoid leaving fingerprints, I plucked the pistol off the carpet. I added the gun to the contents of the plastic shopping bag.

In the bathroom once more, I checked to be sure that I hadn't missed anything obvious during the cleanup. Later I would need to do a more thorough job than I had time for now: vacuum for incriminating hairs and fibers, wipe every surface to eliminate Bob Robertson's prints . . .

I wouldn't be helping the killer get away with the crime. By all indications, he was a cool professional who would have been too smart and too self-aware to have left fingerprints or any other evidence of his presence.

When I consulted my wristwatch, what I saw surprised me. One-thirty-eight A.M. The night had seemed to be *racing* toward dawn. I'd thought it must be two-thirty or later.

Nonetheless, time was running out for me. My watch was digital, but I could hear my opportunity for action tick-tick-ticking away.

After turning off the bathroom light, I went to the front window once more, cracked the blind, and studied the street. If anyone was standing vigil, I still couldn't spot him.

Carrying the shopping bag, I went outside and locked the front door behind me. Descending the steps, I felt as intently watched as a Miss America contestant during the swimsuit competition.

Although pretty much certain that no eyes were on me, I balanced a load of guilt that made me self-conscious. I nervously scanned the night, looking everywhere but at the steps in front of me; it's proof of miracles that I didn't fall and break my neck and leave a second body for the police to puzzle over.

You might wonder what I had to feel guilty about, considering that I hadn't killed Bob Robertson.

Well, I never need a good reason to embrace guilt. Sometimes I feel responsible for train wrecks in Georgia, terrorist bombs in distant cities, tornadoes in Kansas . . .

A part of me believes that if I worked more aggressively to explore my gift and to develop it, instead of merely *coping* with it on a day-by-day basis, I might be able to assist in the apprehension of more criminals and spare more lives from both bad men and brutal nature, even in places far removed from Pico Mundo. I know this is not the case. I know that to pursue much greater involvement with the supernatural would be to lose touch with reality, to spiral down into a genteel madness, whereafter I would be no good to anyone. Yet that chastising part of me weighs my character from time to time and judges me inadequate.

I understand why I am such an easy mark for guilt. The origins lie with my mother and her guns.

Recognizing the structure of your psychology doesn't mean that you can easily rebuild it. The Chamber of Unreasonable Guilt is part of my mental architecture, and I doubt that I will ever be able to renovate that particular room in this strange castle that is me.

When I reached the bottom of the steps without anyone rushing forward to shout *J'accuse!*, I started around the side of the garage—then stopped, struck by the sight of the nearby house and the thought of Rosalia Sanchez.

I intended to use her Chevy, which she herself seldom drives, to move Robertson's body, then return the vehicle to the garage without her being the wiser. I didn't need a key. As a high-school student, I may not have paid as much attention in math class as would have been advisable, but long ago I had learned to hot-wire a car.

My sudden concern about Rosalia had nothing to do with the possibility of her seeing me at this nefarious bit of work, and everything to do with her safety.

If another man, with murder on his mind, had gone with Robertson into my apartment between 5:30 and 7:45, they'd done so in daylight. Bright Mojave daylight.

I suspected that the two men had arrived as conspirators and that Robertson thought they were engaged on a bit of nasty business aimed at me. Perhaps he believed they were going to lie in wait for me. He must have been surprised when his companion drew a gun on him.

Once Robertson was dead and I'd been set up for murder, the killer would not have hung around to try on my underwear and sample the leftovers in my refrigerator. He would have left quickly, also in daylight.

Surely he had worried that someone in the nearby house might have seen him entering with his victim or departing alone.

Unwilling to risk a witness, he might have knocked on Rosalia's back door after he had dealt with Robertson. A gentle widow, living alone, would have been an easy kill.

In fact, if he were a thorough and cautious man, he probably would have visited her *before* bringing Bob Robertson here. He would have used the same pistol in both instances, framing me for two murders.

Judging by the swiftness and boldness with which he had acted to eliminate a compromised associate, this unknown man was thorough, cautious, and much more.

Rosalia's house stood silent. No lights shone at any of her windows, only a ghostly face that was, in fact, merely the reflection of the westering moon.

CHAPTER 35

I STARTED ACROSS THE DRIVEWAY TOWARD Rosalia's back porch before I realized that I had begun to move. After a few steps, I halted.

If she was dead, I could do nothing for her. And if Robertson's killer had visited her, he had surely *not* left her alive.

Until now I had thought of Robertson as a lone gunman, a mental and moral freak scheming toward his bloody moment in history, like so many of those infamous scum in his exquisitely maintained files.

He might have been exactly that at one time, but he had become that and more. He had met another who thrilled to the same fantasies of mindless slaughter, and together they had grown into a beast with two faces, two hateful hearts, and four busy hands to do the devil's work.

The clue had hung on the study wall in Robertson's house, but I had not understood it. Manson, McVeigh, and Atta. None of them had worked alone. They had conspired with others.

In the files were case histories of numerous serial killers and mass murderers who acted alone, but the three faces in his shrine were men who had found meaning in a brotherhood of evil.

My illegal visit to Robertson's residence in Camp's End had somehow become known to him. Maybe cameras were hidden in the house.

Sociopaths are frequently paranoids, as well. If he chose to do so, Robertson had financial resources large enough to equip his home with well-concealed, state-of-the-art videocams.

He must have told his murderous friend that I had prowled his rooms. His kill buddy might then have decided that he himself was at risk if his association with Robertson became known.

Or because of my nosing around, Robertson might have grown nervous about their plans for August 15. He might have wanted to postpone the slaughter that they had been prepared to commit.

Perhaps his psychotic friend had been too excited to accept a delay. Having for so long contemplated this delicious violence, he now had a hunger for it, a *need.*

I turned away from Rosalia's house.

If I went in there and discovered that she had been murdered as a consequence of my actions, I doubted that I would have the will to deal with Robertson's body. At the very thought of discovering her corpse—*Odd Thomas, can you see me? Odd Thomas, am I still visible?*— I felt a loosening occur in the hinges of my reason, and I knew that I was at risk of coming apart emotionally if not psychologically.

Viola Peabody and her daughters were depending on me.

Unknown numbers of people currently destined to die in Pico Mundo before the next sunset might be saved if I could stay out of jail, if I could learn the place and the time of the planned atrocity.

As if magic suddenly overruled physics, the moonlight seemed to acquire weight. I felt the burden of that lunar radiance with every step that I took to the back of the garage, where the corpse waited in its white wrapping.

The rear door of the garage was unlocked. That interior darkness smelled of tire rubber, motor oil, old grease, and a raw-wood aroma baked from the exposed rafters by the summer heat. I set my shopping bag inside.

Grimly aware that the day had taken both a mental and a physical toll from me, I dragged the body across the threshold and closed the door. Only then did I fumble for the light switch.

This detached garage contained two stalls, plus a home workshop where a third car might otherwise have been parked. Currently one stall was empty, and Rosalia's Chevy stood in the space nearest the house.

When I tried the car trunk, I found it locked.

The thought of loading the corpse in the rear seat and driving with it behind my back disturbed me.

In my twenty years, I have seen many strange things. One of the more bizarre was the ghost of President Lyndon Johnson disembarking from a Greyhound at the Pico Mundo bus terminal. He arrived from Portland, Oregon, by way of San Francisco and Sacramento, only to board at once an outbound Greyhound destined for Phoenix, Tucson, and points in Texas. Because he had died in a hospital, he wore pajamas, no slippers, and he looked forlorn. When he realized that I could see him, he glared angrily, then pulled down his pajamas and mooned me.

I have never seen a corpse restored to life, however, nor have I encountered any corpse animated by evil sorcery. Yet the thought of turning my back on Robertson's cadaver and chauffeuring it to a lonely corner of Pico Mundo filled me with dread.

On the other hand, I couldn't prop him, fully wrapped, on the front passenger's seat and drive around with what appeared to be a 250-pound doobie.

Getting the corpse into the back of the Chevy taxed both my strength and my stomach. In his cocoon, Robertson felt loose, soft . . . *ripe.*

Repeatedly, the vivid memory of the ragged, wet bullet hole in his chest rose in my mind: the flabby and livid flesh around it, the dark custardy ooze that had drooled from it. I had not peered closely at the wound, had quickly glanced away, yet that image kept rising like a dark sun in my mind.

By the time I loaded the corpse in the car and closed the back door, sweat streamed from me as though some giant had wrung me out like a washcloth. That's how I felt, too.

Outside, at two o'clock in the morning, the temperature had fallen to a brisk eighty-five. Here in the windowless garage, the climate was ten degrees more desperate.

Blinking the perspiration out of my eyes, I fumbled under the dashboard and found the wires that I needed. Shocking myself only once, I got the engine started.

Through all of this, the dead man on the backseat did not stir.

I turned out the garage light and put my plastic shopping bag on the passenger's seat. I got behind the wheel and used the remote control to raise the garage door.

Blotting my face on a handful of Kleenex plucked from the box in the console, I realized that I hadn't given a thought about where to unload my cargo. Neither the town dump nor a Goodwill Industries collection box seemed like a good idea.

If Robertson were found too soon, Chief Porter

would have hard questions for me that might interfere with my attempts to deflect whatever horror was soon to descend on Pico Mundo. Ideally, the body would lie quietly decomposing for at least twenty-four hours before someone found it and had a new love for Jesus scared into him.

Then I thought of the perfect hiding place: the Church of the Whispering Comet Topless Bar, Adult Bookstore, and Burger Heaven.

CHAPTER 36

THE CHURCH OF THE WHISPERING COMET had been erected more than twenty years ago, off the state highway and a few hundred yards past the town limits of Pico Mundo, on a tract of desert scrub.

Even when it had been a house of unusual worship, it had not resembled a church. Here in the clear and starry night, the main building—a two-hundred-foot-long, sixty-foot-wide, semicylindrical, corrugated-metal Quonset hut with porthole windows—looked like a spaceship, minus its nose cone, half buried in the earth.

Nestled among dead and dying trees, more than half concealed by a mottling camouflage of shadows and pale moonlight, smaller Quonsets ringed the perimeter of the property. These had been barracks for the true believers.

The founder of the church, Caesar Zedd Jr., preached that he received whispered messages, mostly in dreams but also sometimes when awake, from alien intelligences aboard a spacecraft traveling toward Earth inside a comet. These aliens claimed to be the gods who had created human beings and all species on the planet.

Most people in Pico Mundo had assumed that the

services at the Church of the Whispering Comet would one day culminate in a communion with poisoned Kool-Aid and hundreds of deaths. Instead, the sincerity of Zedd's religious faith came under question when he and his entire clergy were indicted and convicted of operating the largest Ecstasy production-and-distribution ring in the world.

After the church ceased to exist, an outfit calling itself the First Amendment Protection Society, Inc.—the largest operator of adult bookstores, topless bars, Internet porn sites, and karaoke cocktail lounges in the United States—intimidated Maravilla County into giving it a business license. They remade the property into a cheesy, sex-theme amusement park, converting the original church sign to neon and extending it to read CHURCH OF THE WHISPERING COMET TOPLESS BAR, ADULT BOOKSTORE, AND BURGER HEAVEN.

Rumor has it that the burgers and fries were excellent and that the promise of free soft-drink refills was generously honored. Yet this establishment never succeeded in winning over the family dining crowd or the upscale professional couples who are so essential to any restaurant operation.

The enterprise, known locally as the Whispering Burger, turned a handsome profit even after covering its food-service losses. The topless bar, the bookstore (which stocked no books, but offered thousands of videotapes), and the whorehouse (not mentioned in the original business-license application) brought oceans of money to this desert oasis.

Although the corporation's lawyers, courageous defenders of the Constitution, managed to keep the doors open through ten convictions for operation of a prostitution ring, the Whispering Burger imploded following the gunning down of three prostitutes by a naked customer strung out on PCP and excessive doses of Viagra.

In lieu of unpaid taxes and fines, the property had fallen into the hands of the county. During the past five years, cessation of all maintenance and the relentless repossession efforts of the desert had reduced a once-proud house of alien gods to rust and ruin.

The church grounds had been landscaped as a tropical paradise, with lush lawns, several varieties of palm trees, ferns, bamboo, and flowering vines. Without daily watering, the brief rainy season in the desert wasn't sufficient to preserve this Eden.

Having switched off my headlights when I turned in from the state highway, I drove through the shaggy moonshadows cast by dead palm trees. The cracked and potholed blacktop driveway led to the back of the main building, and then farther to the arc of smaller Quonset huts.

I was reluctant to leave the car with the engine running, but I wanted to be able to make a quick getaway. Without keys, I could not start the engine quickly enough in a crisis.

With the flashlight I'd packed in my shopping bag, I set out to find a suitable place to stash an inconvenient corpse.

The Mojave had recovered its breath again. A lazy exhalation blew out of the east, smelling of dry brush, hot sand, and the strange life of the desert.

Each of the ten Quonset huts used as barracks by the church had housed sixty cult members in the cramped fashion of opium-den bunks. When the church was replaced by a bordello with burgers, a few of these structures were gutted, partitioned, and redecorated to serve as cozy cribs for the hookers who delivered what the topless dancers in the bar only promised.

In the years since the property had been abandoned, morbidly curious people had explored and vandalized the main building and all the barracks. Doors had been broken open. Some had fallen off their corroded hinges.

At the third barracks that I inspected, the spring latch on the door still worked well enough to hold it closed.

I didn't want to leave the corpse in a space to which coyotes could easily gain access. Robertson had been a monster; I remained convinced of that; however, regardless of what he might have done or might have been capable of doing, I couldn't consign his remains to the indignity that Granny Sugars had feared might befall her if she dropped dead in a poker game with hardhearted players.

Maybe coyotes weren't carrion eaters. Maybe they would eat only meat they killed.

The desert, however, teemed with more life than could be seen at casual inspection. Much of it would be pleased to dine on a carcass as fleshy as Robertson's.

After pulling the Chevy as close to the chosen building as possible—about ten feet from the door—I required a minute to summon the nerve to deal with the corpse. I chewed two antacid tablets.

During the drive from town, Bob Robertson had not once asked, *Are we there yet?* Nevertheless, and against all reason, I didn't trust him to stay dead.

Hauling him out of the car proved easier than getting him into it, except that at one point, when his big gelatinous body quivered inside the bed-sheet shroud, I felt as if I were handling a bag full of live snakes.

After I dragged him to the door of the Quonset hut, which I had wedged open with the flashlight, I paused to wipe the sweat from my dripping brow—and saw the yellow eyes. Low to the ground, twenty or thirty feet away, they watched me with unmistakable hunger.

I snatched up the flashlight and focused the beam on the very thing I had feared: a coyote that had come in from the open range, exploring among the abandoned buildings. Big, sinewy, rough-hewn, sharp of brow and jaw, it was less wicked by nature than are many human beings, but at that moment it looked like a demon that had slipped through the gates of Hell.

The flashlight didn't frighten it off, which suggested that it had become dangerously certain of itself in the presence of people— and that it might not be alone. I swept the immediate night with the flashlight and discovered another slouching beast to the right of and behind the first.

Until recent years, coyotes rarely savaged children and never adults. As human settlements encroached on their hunting grounds, they had become bolder, more aggressive. Within the past five years, several adults in California had been stalked and even attacked.

These two didn't appear to find me in the least intimidating, only savory.

I searched the ground near my feet, seeking a stone, and settled for a chunk of concrete that had broken off the edge of the walkway. I hurled it at the nearest predator. The missile struck the blacktop six inches wide of the target and bounced away into the darkness.

The coyote shied from the point of impact but did not run. The second stalker took its cue from the first and stood its ground.

The wheeze and clatter of the idling car, which

didn't faze the coyotes, worried me. Whispering Burger was an isolated property; no one should have been near enough to have his curiosity pricked by the grumbling engine. If other intruders were already on the grounds, however, the noise would mask the sound of their movements.

I couldn't deal with two things at once. Getting the corpse out of sight took precedence over dealing with the coyotes.

By the time I returned, maybe the predators would have gone, led away by the scent of rabbits or other easy game.

I dragged the wrapped cadaver across the threshold, into the Quonset hut, and then closed the door securely behind me.

A hallway along one side of the building served a bath and four rooms. Each room had been the workplace of a prostitute.

My flashlight revealed dust, spider webs, two empty beer bottles, a litter of dead bees . . .

After all these years, the air was still thinly laced with the faded bouquet of scented candles, incense, perfume, fragrant oils. Underlying this faint but sweet melange was a fainter, acrid smell that might have been the stale urine of animals that had come and gone.

The furniture had been trucked away long ago. In two rooms, mirrors on the ceiling suggested where the beds had been positioned. The walls were painted hot-pink.

Each room featured two portholes. Most of the glass had been shot out by kids with air guns.

In the fourth room, both small windows were intact. Here, none of the larger carrion eaters could get at the corpse.

One of the securing shoelaces had snapped. An end of the shroud sagged loose, and Robertson's left foot became exposed.

I considered taking both laces and the sheet. They were possible connections to me, though they were such common brands, sold in so many stores, that they alone would not convict me.

As I bent to the task, into my mind came an image of the wound in Robertson's chest. And in memory I heard my mother's voice: *You want to pull the trigger for me? You want to pull the trigger?*

I'd had much practice turning my mind away from certain memories of my childhood. I could quickly dial her remembered voice from a whisper to a silence.

Casting from my mind the image of Robertson's wound was not as easy. That wet hole pulsed in memory as though his dead heart were beating under it.

In my bathroom, when I'd opened his shirt to check for lividity and had seen the entrance wound in his empurpled flesh, something had compelled me to look more closely. Disgusted by my own morbid impulse and, indeed, frightened by it, afraid that my fascination proved I'd been twisted by my mother in ways I hadn't realized, I had resisted looking closer and had at once turned away, rebuttoned his shirt.

Now, on one knee beside Robertson, fumbling with the knots in the remaining shoelace that secured the shroud, I tried to close the memory of that shirt over the memory of the oozing wound, but still it throbbed in my mind's eye.

In the bloating cadaver, gas swizzled up a series of chuckles culminating in what sounded like a sigh from the lips of the dead man, there behind his cotton veil.

Unable to spend another second with the corpse, I

shot to my feet, fled the hot-pink room with my flashlight, and was halfway along the hall before I realized that I had left the door open. I went back and closed it, further protecting the body from the desert's larger scavengers.

I used the tail of my T-shirt to wipe the door handles to all the rooms that I had investigated. Then, scuffing my feet through the prints I'd left earlier, I smeared the thick dust on the floor with the hope that I could avoid leaving clear shoe-tread impressions.

When I opened the outer door, my flashlight beam struck flares of eyeshine from three coyotes that waited between me and the idling Chevy.

CHAPTER 37

WITH THEIR SINEWY LEGS, LEAN FLANKS, and narrow muzzles, coyotes appear to be designed for speed and savage assault, and yet even as they face you down with a predatory gleam in their eyes, they have some of the appeal of dogs. Prairie wolves, some people call them, and although they lack most of the charm of wolves, they do have a puppylike quality because their feet are too big for their bodies and their ears are too big for their heads.

These three beasts appeared more quizzical than threatening—if you failed to read the right message in their tense posture and in the flare of their nostrils. Their large ears were pricked, and one of them cocked its head as if it found me to be deeply puzzling, an opinion of me that is not limited to coyotes.

Two stood in front of the Chevy, perhaps fourteen feet away. The third waited between me and the passenger's side of the car, where I had left the rear door open.

I let out a shout at the greatest volume I could muster, for common wisdom holds that sudden loud noises will frighten coyotes into flight. Two twitched, but none of them retreated so much as an inch.

Stewed in my own sweat, I must have smelled like a salty but delicious dinner.

When I stepped back from the threshold, they didn't spring at me, which meant their boldness had not yet matured into the absolute conviction that they could take me down. I let the door fall shut between us.

Another door at the farther end of the hall also opened to the outside, but if I slipped out by that exit, I would be at too great a distance from the Chevy. I couldn't hope to circle around behind the car and get in through the door that I'd left open. Long before I got there, the three brethren of Wile E. would have caught my scent and would be waiting, and none would need to rely on a Byzantine killing machine purchased by mail from Acme, Inc.

If I waited inside until dawn, I might escape them, for these were night hunters, and possibly too hungry to outwait me. The fuel gauge in Rosalia's car had shown a half-full tank, which might last long enough, but the engine would almost surely overheat before the fuel gave out, leaving the car unusable.

Besides, the batteries in my flashlight most likely wouldn't last an hour. For all my brave talk earlier about being unafraid of the unknown, I could not tolerate being trapped in the pitch-black Quonset hut in the company of a dead man.

With nothing to entertain my eyes, I'd obsess on the recollected image of his bullet wound. I'd be convinced that every breath of the night breeze, whispering at a broken window, was in fact the sound of Bob Robertson peeling out of his cocoon.

I went in search of something to throw at the coyotes. Unless I was prepared to strip the shoes off the corpse, I had nothing but the two empty beer bottles.

After returning to the door with the bottles, I switched off the flashlight, jammed it under the waistband of my jeans, and waited a few minutes, giving peace a chance, but also letting my eyes adapt to darkness.

When I opened the door, hoping the chow line had broken up and slouched away, I was disappointed. The three remained almost where they had been when I'd left them: two in front of the car, the third near the forward tire on the passenger's side.

In sunshine, their coats would be tan with reddish highlights and a peppering of black hairs. Here they were the patinated gray of old silver. Subtly their eyes glowed with a moony madness.

Solely because it appeared to be the boldest of the trio, I pegged the nearest coyote as the pack leader. It was the biggest specimen, as well, with a grizzled chin that suggested much experience in the hunt.

Experts advise that, when confronted by an angry dog, you should avoid eye contact. This constitutes a challenge to which the animal will respond aggressively.

If the canine in question is a coyote pondering your nutritional value, the experts will get you killed. Failure to make eye contact will be read as weakness, which indicates that you are suitable prey; you might as well offer yourself on a platter with double spuds twice in Hell and an order of midnight whistleberries.

Making eye contact with the pack leader, I tapped one of the bottles against the metal door frame, then tapped harder, breaking it. I was left holding the neck, jagged shards protruding from my fist.

This would be a less than ideal weapon with which to confront an adversary that had the stiletto-packed jaws of a dedicated carnivore, but it was marginally better than my bare hands.

I hoped to challenge them with such confidence

that they would have a momentary doubt about my vulnerability. All I might need to reach the open back door of the Chevy was a three- or four-second hesitation on their part.

Letting the door fall shut behind me, I moved toward the pack leader.

At once it bared a wicked clench of teeth. A low vibrous growl warned me to back off.

Ignoring the warning, I took another step, and with a sharp snap of my wrist, I threw the intact beer bottle. It struck the leader hard on the snout, bounced off, and shattered on the pavement at its feet.

Startled, the coyote stopped growling. It moved to the front of the car, not retreating from me, not drawing any closer, either, but merely repositioning itself to present a united front with its two companions.

This had the desirable effect of presenting me with a direct, unguarded route to the open back door of the Chevy. Unfortunately, a full-out run for cover would require that I take my attention off the pack.

The moment that I sprinted for the car, they would spring at me. The distance between them and me was not much greater than the distance between me and the open door—and they were far quicker than I was.

Holding the broken bottle in front of me, thrusting it at them in sharp, threatening jabs, I edged sideways toward the idling Chevy, counting every inch a triumph.

Two watched with obvious curiosity: their heads raised, mouths open, tongues lolling. Curious but also alert for any opportunity that I might give them, they stood with their weight shifted toward their hind legs, ready to launch forward with their powerful haunch muscles.

The leader's posture troubled me more than that of the other pack members. Head lowered, ears laid back against its skull, teeth bared but not its tongue, this individual stared at me intently from under its lowered brow.

Its forepaws were pressed so hard against the ground that even in the wan moonlight, its toes spread in clear definement. With the forward knuckles sharply bent, the beast seemed to be standing on the points of its claws.

Although I continued to face them, they weren't directly in front of me any longer, but to my right. The open car door was to my left.

Fierce snarling could not have frayed my nerves as effectively as their bated breath, their expectant silence.

Halfway to the Chevy, I figured that I could risk a rush to the backseat, throw myself into the car, and pull the door shut just in time to ward off their snapping jaws.

Then I heard a muted growl to my left.

The pack now numbered four, and the fourth had stolen up on me from the back of the Chevy. It stood between me and the open door.

Sensing movement to my right, I snapped my attention to the threesome again. During my brief distraction, they had slunk closer to me.

Moonlight silvered a ribbon of drool that slipped from the lips of the pack leader.

To my left, the fourth coyote's low growl grew louder, rivaling the grumble of the car. It was a living engine of death, idling right now but ready to shift into high gear, and at the periphery of my vision, I saw it creep toward me.

CHAPTER 38

THE DOOR OF THE QUONSET HUT LAY A daunting distance behind me. Before I reached it, the pack leader would be on my back, its teeth in my neck, and the others would be tearing at my legs, dragging me down.

In my hand, the broken beer bottle felt fragile, a woefully inadequate weapon, good for nothing more than slashing my own throat.

Judging by a sudden overwhelming pressure in my bladder, these predators would be getting marinated meat by the time they took a bite of me—

—but then the nasty customer to my left chewed up his growl and let out a submissive mewl.

The fearsome trio to the right of me, as one, traded menace for perplexity. They rose from their stalking posture, stood quite erect, ears pricked and cupped forward.

The change in the coyotes' demeanor, so abrupt and inexplicable, imparted to the moment a quality of enchantment, as though a guardian angel had cast a rapture of mercy over these creatures, granting me a reprieve from evisceration.

I stood stiff and stupefied, afraid that by moving I would break the spell. Then I realized that the coyotes' attention had shifted to something behind me.

Warily turning my head, I discovered that my guardian was a pretty but too thin young woman with tousled blond hair and delicate features. She stood behind and to the left of me, barefoot, naked but for a pair of skimpy, lace-trimmed panties, slender arms crossed over her breasts.

Her smooth pale skin seemed luminous in the moonlight. Beryl-blue eyes, lustrous pools, were windows to a melancholy so profound that I knew at once she belonged to the community of the restless dead.

The lone coyote on my left settled to the ground, all hungers forgotten, the fight gone out of it. The beast regarded her in the manner of a dog waiting for a word of affection from its adored master.

To my right, the first three coyotes were not as humbled as the fourth, but they, too, were transfixed by this vision. Although they hadn't exerted themselves, they panted, and they licked their lips incessantly—two signs of nervous stress in any canine. As the woman stepped past me and toward the Chevy, they shied from her, not in a fearful way but as if in deference.

When she reached the car, she turned to me. Her smile was an inverted crescent of sadness.

I stooped to put the broken bottle quietly on the ground, then rose with new respect for the perceptions and priorities of coyotes, which seemed to give greater importance to the experience of wonder than to the demands of appetite.

At the car, I closed the back door on the passenger's side, opened the front door.

The woman regarded me solemnly now, as though she was as deeply moved by being seen, years after her death, as I was moved by seeing her in this purgatory of her own creation.

As lovely as a rose half bloomed and still containing promise, she appeared to have been not much more than eighteen when she died, too young to have sentenced herself for so long to the chains of this world, to such an extended lonely suffering.

She must have been one of the three prostitutes who were shot by an unbalanced man five years earlier, in the event that had closed Whispering Burger forever. Her chosen work should have hardened her; but she seemed to be a tender and timid spirit.

Touched by her vulnerability and by the harsh self-judgment that kept her here, I held out a hand to her.

Instead of taking my hand, she bowed her head demurely. After a hesitation, she uncrossed her arms and lowered them to her sides, revealing her breasts—and the two dark bullet holes that marred her cleavage.

Because I doubted that she had any unfinished business in this desolate place, and because her life had evidently been so hard that she would have little reason to love this world too much to leave it, I assumed that her reluctance to move on arose from a fear of what came next, perhaps from a dread of punishment.

"Don't be afraid," I told her. "You weren't a monster in this life, were you? Just lonely, lost, confused, broken—like all of us who pass this way."

Slowly she raised her head.

"Maybe you were weak and foolish, but many are. So am I."

She met my eyes again. Her melancholy seemed deeper to me now, as acute as grief but as enduring as sorrow.

"So am I," I repeated. "But when I die, I will move on, and so should you, without fear."

She wore her wounds not as she would have worn divine stigmata, but as if they were the devil's brand, which they were not.

"I've no idea what it's like, but I know a better life awaits you, beyond the miseries you've known here, a place where you'll belong and where you'll be truly loved."

From her expression, I knew that the idea of being loved had been for her only a cherished hope that had never been realized in her short unhappy life. Terrible experience, perhaps from the cradle to the sound of the shot that killed her, had left her in a poverty of imagination, unable to envision a world beyond this one, where love was a promise fulfilled.

She raised her arms once more and crossed them over her chest, concealing both her breasts and her wounds.

"Don't be afraid," I said again.

Resumed, her smile seemed to be as melancholy as before, but also now enigmatic. I couldn't tell if what I'd said had been of comfort to her.

Wishing that I were more persuasive in my faith, and wondering why I wasn't, I got into the front passenger's seat of the car. I closed the door and slid behind the steering wheel.

I didn't want to leave her there among the dead palm trees and the corroded Quonset huts, with as little hope as she had physical substance.

Yet the night ticked on, the moon and all the constellations moving across the heavens as relentlessly as hands across the face of a clock. In too few hours, terror would descend on Pico Mundo, unless I could somehow stop it.

As I slowly drove away, I glanced repeatedly at the rearview mirror. There she stood in the moonlight, the charmed coyotes resting on the ground at her feet, as if she were the goddess Diana between one hunt and another, mistress of the moon and all its creatures, receding, dwindling, but not ready to go home to Olympus.

I drove from the Church of the Whispering Comet back into Pico Mundo, from the company of a gunshot stranger to the bad news about a gunshot friend.

CHAPTER 39

IF I HAD KNOWN THE NAME OR EVEN THE face of the one I should be seeking, I might have tried a session of psychic magnetism, cruising Pico Mundo until my sixth sense brought me in contact with him. The man who had killed Bob Robertson, and who craved to kill others in the coming day, remained nameless and faceless to me, however, and as long as I sought only a phantom, I would be wasting gasoline and time.

The town slept, but not its demons. Bodachs were in the streets, more numerous and more fearsome than packs of coyotes, racing through the night in what seemed to be an ecstasy of anticipation.

I passed houses where these living shadows gathered and swarmed with particular inquisitiveness. At first I tried to remember each of the haunted residences, for I still believed that the people who interested the bodachs were also those who would be murdered between the next dawn and the next sunset.

Although small by comparison to a city, our town is much larger than it once was, with all its new neighborhoods of upscale tract houses, encompassing more than forty thousand souls in a county of half a million. I have met only a tiny fraction of them.

Most of the bodach-infested houses belonged to people I didn't know. I had no time to meet them all, and no hope of gaining their confidence to the extent that they would take my advice and change their Wednesday plans, as Viola Peabody had done.

I considered stopping at the houses of those who were known to me, to ask them to list every place they expected to be the following afternoon. With luck, I might discover the single destination that would prove common to them all.

None were in my small inner circle of friends. They didn't know of my supernatural gift, but many regarded me as a sweet eccentric, to one degree or another, and therefore wouldn't be surprised by either my unscheduled visit or my questions.

By seeking this information in the presence of bodachs, however, I would earn their suspicion. Once alert to me, they would eventually discern my unique nature.

I remembered the six-year-old English boy who had spoken aloud of the bodachs—and had been crushed between a concrete-block wall and a runaway truck. The impact had been so powerful that numerous blocks had shattered into gravel and dust, exposing the ribs of steel rebar around which they had been mortared.

Although the driver, a young man of twenty-eight, had been in perfect health, his autopsy revealed that he suffered a massive, instantly fatal stroke while behind the wheel.

The stroke must have killed him at the precise moment when he crossed the crest of a hill—at the bottom of which stood the English boy. Accident-scene analysis by the police determined that the lateral angle of the slope, in relationship to the cross street below, should have carried the unpiloted truck away from the boy, impacting the wall thirty feet from where it actually came to a deadly stop. Evidently, during part of the descent, the dead body of the driver had been hung up on the steering wheel, countering the angle of the street that should have saved the child.

I know more about the mysteries of the universe than do those of you who cannot see the lingering dead, but I do not understand more than a tiny fraction of the truth of our existence. I have nevertheless reached at least one certain conclusion based on what I know: There are no coincidences.

On the macro scale, I perceive what physicists tell us is true on the micro: Even in chaos, there is order, purpose, and strange meaning that invites—but often thwarts—our investigation and our understanding.

Consequently, I didn't stop at any of those houses where the bodachs capered, didn't wake the sleeping to ask my urgent questions. Somewhere a healthy driver and a massive truck needed only a timely cerebral aneurysm and an expedient failure of brakes to bring it across my path in a sudden rush.

Instead, I drove to Chief Porter's house, trying to decide if I should wake him at the ungodly hour of three o'clock.

Over the years, I had only twice before interrupted his sleep. The first time, I had been wet and muddy, still wearing one of the shackles—and dragging a length of chain—that had bound me to the two corpses with which I had been dumped into Malo Suerte Lake by bad men of sour disposition. The second time that I'd awakened him, there had been a crisis needing his attention.

The current crisis hadn't quite reached us yet, but it loomed. I thought he needed to know that Bob Robertson was not a loner but a conspirator.

The trick would be to deliver this news convincingly but without revealing that I'd found Robertson dead in my bathroom and, breaking numerous laws without compunction, had bundled the cadaver to a less incriminating resting place.

When I turned the corner half a block from the Porter address, I was surprised to see lights on in several houses at that late hour. The chief's place blazed brighter than any other.

Four police cruisers stood in front of the house. All had been parked hastily, at angles to the curb. The roof-rack beacons of one car still flashed, revolved.

On the front lawn, across which rhythmic splashes of red light chased waves of blue, five officers gathered in conversation. Their posture suggested that they were consoling one another.

I had intended to park across the street from the chief's house. I would have called his private number only after concocting a story that avoided any mention of my recent exertions as a dead-man's taxi service.

Instead, with a helpless sinking of the heart, I abandoned the Chevy in the street, beside one of the patrol cars. I switched the headlights off but left the engine running, with the hope that none of the cops would get close enough to see that no keys were in the ignition.

The officers on the lawn were all known to me. They turned to face me as I ran to them.

Sonny Wexler, the tallest and toughest and softest-spoken of the group, extended one brawny arm as if to stop me from rushing past him to the house. "Hold on, stay back here, kid. We've got CSI working the place."

Until now I had not seen Izzy Maldanado on the front porch. He rose from some task that he'd been attending to on his knees, and stretched to get a kink out of his back.

Izzy works for the Maravilla County Sheriff's Department crime lab, which contracts its services to the Pico Mundo police. When the body of Bob Robertson was eventually found in that Quonset hut, Izzy would most likely be the technician meticulously sifting the scene for evidence.

Although I desperately wanted to know what had happened here, I couldn't speak. I couldn't swallow. Some gluey mass seemed to be obstructing my throat.

Trying unsuccessfully to choke down that phantom wad, which I knew to be only a choking emotion, I thought of Gunther Ulstein, a much-loved music teacher and director of the Pico Mundo High School band, who had experienced occasional difficulty swallowing. Over several weeks, the condition rapidly grew worse. Before he had it diagnosed, cancer of the esophagus spread all the way into his larynx.

Because he couldn't swallow, his weight plummeted. Doctors treated him first with radiation, intending subsequently to remove his entire esophagus and to fashion a new one from a length of his colon. Radiation therapy failed him. He died before surgery.

Thin and withered-looking, as he had been in his final days, Gunny Ulstein can usually be found in a rocking chair on the front porch of the house that he built himself. His wife of thirty years, Mary, still lives there.

During his last few weeks of life, he had lost his ability to speak. He'd had so much that he wanted to say to Mary—how she had always brought out the best in him, how he loved her—but he couldn't write down his feelings with the subtlety and the range of emotion that he could have expressed in speech. He lingers now, regretting what he failed to say, futilely hoping that as a ghost he will find a way to speak to her.

A muting cancer seemed almost to be a blessing if it would have kept me from asking Sonny Wexler, "What happened?"

"I thought you must've heard," he said. "I thought that's why you came. The chief's been shot."

Jesus Bustamante, another officer, said angrily, "Almost an hour ago now, some pusbag sonofabitch plugged the chief three times in the chest on his own front porch."

My stomach turned over, over, over, almost in time with the revolving beacons on the nearby cruiser, and the phantom obstruction in my esophagus became real when a bitter gorge rose into the back of my throat.

I must have paled, must have wobbled on suddenly loose knees, for Jesus put an arm against my back to support me, and Sonny Wexler said quickly, "Easy, kid, easy, the chief's alive. He's bad off, but he's alive, he's a fighter."

"The doctors are working on him right now," said Billy Munday, whose port-wine birthmark, over a third of his face, seemed to glow strangely in the night, lending him the aura of a painted shaman with warnings and portents and evils imminent to report. "He's going to be all right. He's got to be. I mean, what would happen without him?"

"He's a fighter," Sonny repeated.

"Which hospital?" I asked.

"County General."

I ran to the car that I'd left in the street.

CHAPTER 40

THESE DAYS, MOST NEW HOSPITALS IN southern California resemble medium-rent retail outlets selling discount carpet or business supplies in bulk. The bland architecture doesn't inspire confidence that healing can occur within those walls.

County General, the oldest hospital in the region, features an impressive porte-cochere with limestone columns and a dentil-molding cornice all the way around the building. At first sight of it, you know that nurses and doctors work inside, instead of sales clerks.

The main lobby has a travertine floor, not industrial carpet, and the travertine face of the information desk boasts an inlaid bronze caduceus.

Before I reached the desk, I was intercepted by Alice Norrie, a ten-year veteran of the PMPD, who was running interference to keep reporters and unauthorized visitors from advancing past the lobby.

"He's in surgery, Odd. He's going to be there awhile."

"Where's Mrs. Porter?"

"Karla's in the ICU waiting room. They'll be taking him there pretty much straight from the OR."

The intensive-care unit was on the fourth floor. In a tone meant to imply that she would have to arrest me to stop me, I said, "Ma'am, I'm going up there."

"You don't have to bust my badge to get there, Odd. You're on the short list Karla gave me."

I took the elevator to the second floor, where County General has its operating rooms.

Finding the right OR proved easy. Rafus Carter, in uniform and big enough to give pause to a rampaging bull, stood guard outside the door.

As I approached through the fluorescent glare, he rested his right hand on the butt of his holstered gun.

He saw me react to his suspicion, and he said, "No offense, Odd, but only Karla could come along this corridor and not get my back up."

"You think he was shot by somebody he knew?"

"Almost had to be, which means it's probably someone I know, too."

"How bad is he?"

"Bad."

"He's a fighter," I said, echoing Sonny Wexler's mantra.

Rafus Carter said, "He better be."

I returned to the elevator. Between the third and fourth floors, I pressed the STOP button.

Uncontrollable trembling shook the strength out of me. With my legs too weak to stand on, I slid down the wall of the cab and sat on the floor.

Life, Stormy says, is not about how fast you run or even with what degree of grace. It's about perseverance, about staying on your feet and slogging forward no matter what.

After all, in her cosmology, this life is boot camp. If you don't persevere through all its obstacles and all the wounds that it inflicts, you cannot move on to your next life of high adventure, which she calls "service," or eventually to your third life, which she assumes will be filled with pleasures and glories far greater even than a bowl of coconut cherry chocolate chunk.

Regardless of how hard the winds of chance might blow or how heavy the weight of experience might become, Stormy always stays on her feet, metaphorically speaking; unlike her, I find that sometimes I must pause if ultimately I am to persevere.

I wanted to be calm, collected, strong, and full of positive energy when I went to Karla. She needed support, not tears of either sympathy or grief.

After two or three minutes, I was calm and *half* collected, which I decided would have to be good enough. I rose to my feet, took the elevator off STOP, and continued to the fourth floor.

The dreary waiting room, just down the hall from the intensive-care unit, had pale-gray walls, a gray-and-black speckled vinyl-tile floor, gray and mud-brown chairs. The ambience said *death*. Someone needed to slap the hospital's decorator upside the head.

The chief's sister, Eileen Newfield, sat in a corner, red-eyed from crying, compulsively twisting an embroidered handkerchief in her hands.

Beside her sat Jake Hulquist, murmuring reassurances. He was the chief's best friend. They had joined the force the same year.

Jake was out of uniform, wearing khakis and an untucked T-shirt. The laces in his athletic shoes were untied. His hair bristled in weird twists and spikes, as if he hadn't taken the time to comb it after he'd gotten the call.

Karla looked like she always does: fresh, beautiful, and self-possessed.

Her eyes were clear; she hadn't been crying. She was a cop's wife first, a woman second; she wouldn't give in to tears as long as Wyatt was fighting for his life because she was fighting with him in spirit.

The moment I stepped through the open doorway, Karla came to me, hugged me, and said, "This blows, doesn't it, Oddie? Isn't that what young people your age would say about a situation like this?"

"It blows," I agreed. "Totally."

Sensitive to Eileen's fragile emotional condition, Karla led me into the hallway, where we could talk. "He got a call on his private night line, just before two o'clock in the morning."

"From who?"

"I don't know. The ringing only half woke me. He told me to go back to sleep, everything was fine."

"How many people have the night line?"

"Not many. He didn't go to the closet to dress. He left the bedroom in his pajamas, so I figured he wasn't going out, it was some problem he could handle from home, and I went back to sleep . . . until the gunshots woke me."

"When was that?"

"Not ten minutes after the call. Apparently he opened the front door for someone he was expecting—"

"Someone he knew."

"—and he was shot four times."

"Four? I heard three to the chest."

"Three to the chest," she confirmed, "and one to the head."

At the news of a head shot, I almost needed to slide down the wall and sit on the floor again.

Seeing how hard this information hit me, Karla quickly said, "No brain damage. The head shot was the least destructive of the four." She found a tremulous but genuine smile. "He'll make a joke out of that, don't you think?"

"He probably already has."

"I can hear him saying if you want to blow out Wyatt Porter's brains, you've got to shoot him in the ass."

"That's him, all right," I agreed.

"They think it was meant to be the coup de grace, after he was already down, but maybe the shooter lost his nerve or got distracted. The bullet only grazed Wyatt's scalp."

I was in denial: "Nobody would want to kill him."

Karla said, "By the time I dialed nine-one-one and managed to get downstairs with my pistol, the shooter was gone."

I pictured her coming fearlessly down the stairs with the gun in both hands, to the front door, ready to trade bullets with the man who had shot her husband. A lioness. Like Stormy.

"Wyatt was down, already unconscious when I found him."

Along the corridor, from the direction of the elevators, came a surgical nurse dressed in green scrubs. She had a please-don't-shoot-the-messenger expression.

CHAPTER 41

THE SURGICAL NURSE, JENNA SPINELLI, HAD been one year ahead of me in high school. Her calm gray eyes were flecked with blue, and her hands were made to play piano concertos.

The news that she brought was not as grim as I feared, not as good as I would have liked. The chief's vital signs were stable but not robust. He'd lost his spleen, but he could live without that. One lung had been punctured, but not beyond repair, and none of his vital organs had been irreparably damaged.

Complex vascular repairs were required, and the physician in charge of the surgical team estimated that the chief would be in the OR another hour and a half to two hours.

"We're pretty sure he'll come through surgery good enough," Jenna said. "Then the challenge will be to prevent postoperative complications."

Karla went into the ICU waiting room to share this report with the chief's sister and Jake Hulquist.

Alone in the hallway with Jenna, I said, "Have you swung both hammers, or are you holding one back?"

"It's just the way I said, Oddie. We don't soften bad news for the spouse. We tell it straight and all at once."

"This blows."

"Like a hurricane," she agreed. "You're close to him, I know."

"Yeah."

"I think he's eventually going to make it," Jenna said. "Not just out of surgery but all the way home on his own two feet."

"But no guarantees."

"When is there ever? He's a mess inside. But he's not half as bad as we thought he'd be when we first put him on the table, before we opened him up. It's a thousand to one odds that anyone can survive three chest wounds. He's incredibly lucky."

"If that's luck, he better never go to Vegas."

With a fingertip, she pulled down one of my lower eyelids and examined the bloodshot scenery: "You look wrecked, Oddie."

"It's been a long day. You know—breakfast starts early at the Grille."

"I was in with two friends the other day. You cooked our lunch."

"Really? Sometimes things are so frantic at the griddle, I don't get a chance to look around, see who's there."

"You've got a talent."

"Thanks," I said. "That's sweet."

"I hear your dad's selling the moon."

"Yeah, but it's not a great place for a vacation home. No air."

"You're nothing at all like your dad."

"Who would want to be?"

"Most guys."

"I think you're wrong about that."

"You know what? You ought to give cooking classes."

"Mostly what I do is fry."

"I'd still sign up."

"It's not exactly healthy cuisine," I said.

"We've all got to die of something. You still with Bronwen?"

"Stormy. Yeah. It's like destiny."

"How do you know?"

"We have matching birthmarks."

"You mean the one she got tattooed to match yours?"

"Tattooed? No. It's real enough. We're getting married."

"Oh. I didn't hear about that."

"It's breaking news."

"Wait'll the girls find out," Jenna said.

"What girls?"

"All of them."

This conversation wasn't always making perfect sense to me, so I said, "Listen, I'm walking grime, I need a bath, but I don't want to leave the hospital till Chief Porter comes out of surgery safe like you say. Is there anywhere here I can get a shower?"

"Let me talk to the head nurse on this floor. We should be able to find you a place."

"I've got a change of clothes in the car," I said.

"Go get them. Then ask at the nurse's station. I'll have arranged everything."

As she started to turn away, I said, "Jenna, did you take piano lessons?"

"Did I ever. Years of them. But why would you ask?"

"Your hands are so beautiful. I bet you play like a dream."

She gave me a long look that I couldn't interpret: mysteries in those blue-flecked gray eyes.

Then she said, "This wedding thing is true?"

"Saturday," I assured her, full of pride that Stormy would have me. "If I could leave town, we'd have gone to Vegas and been married by dawn."

"Some people are way lucky," Jenna Spinelli said. "Even luckier than Chief Porter still sucking wind after three chest wounds."

Assuming that she meant I was fortunate to have won Stormy, I said, "After the mother-father mess I was handed, fate owed me big."

Jenna had that inscrutable look down perfect. "Call me if you decide to give cooking lessons, after all. I'll bet you really know how to whisk."

Puzzled, I said, "Whisk? Well, sure, but that's mainly just for scrambled eggs. With pancakes and waffles, you've got to *fold* the batter, and otherwise almost everything is fry, fry, fry."

She smiled, shook her head, and walked away, leaving me with that perplexity I'd sometimes felt when, as the player with the best stats on our high-school baseball team, I had been served up what appeared to be a perfect strike-zone slow pitch and yet had swung above it, not even kissing the ball.

I hurried out to Rosalia's car in the parking lot. I took the gun from the shopping bag and tucked it under the driver's seat.

When I returned to the fourth-floor nurses' station with my bag, they were expecting me. Although tending to the sick and dying would seem to be grim work, all four nurses on the graveyard shift were smiling and clearly amused about something.

In addition to the usual range of private and semi-private rooms, the fourth floor offered a few fancier co-payment accommodations that could pass for hotel rooms. Carpeted and decorated in warm colors, they featured comfortable furniture, nicely framed bad art, and full bathrooms with under-the-counter refrigerators.

Ambulatory patients able to afford to augment their

insurance benefits can book such swank, escaping the dreary hospital ambience. This is said to speed recuperation, which I'm sure that it does, in spite of the paint-by-the-number sailing ships and the kittens in fields of daisies.

Provided with a set of towels, I was given the use of a bathroom in an unoccupied luxury unit. The paintings followed a circus theme: clowns with balloons, sad-eyed lions, a pretty high-wire walker with a pink parasol. I chewed two tablets of antacid.

After shaving, showering, shampooing, and changing into fresh clothes, I still felt as if I'd crawled out from under a steamroller, fully flattened.

I sat in an armchair and went through the contents of the wallet that I'd taken off Robertson's body. Credit cards, driver's license, a library card . . .

The only unusual item was a plain black plastic card featuring nothing but a line of blind-embossed dots that I could feel with my fingertips and see clearly in angled light. They looked like this:

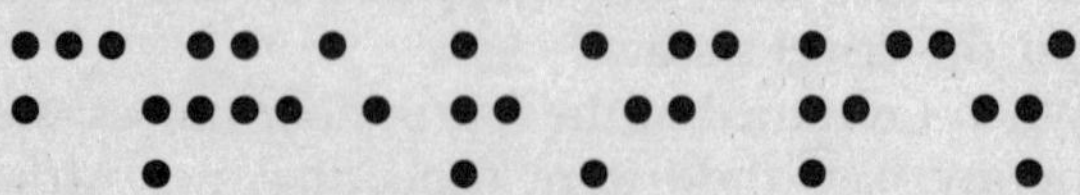

The dots were raised on one side of the card, depressed on the other. Although it might have been coded data that could be read by some kind of machine, I assumed that it was a line of tangible type, otherwise known as Braille.

Considering that he had not been blind, I couldn't imagine why Robertson would have carried a card bearing a statement in Braille.

Neither could I imagine why any blind person would have kept such an item in his wallet.

I sat in the armchair, slowly sliding a thumb across the dots, then the tip of a forefinger. They were only bumps in the plastic, unreadable to me, but the more that I traced their patterns, the more disquieted I became.

Tracing, tracing, I closed my eyes, playing at being blind and hoping that my sixth sense might suggest the purpose of the card if not the meaning of the words spelled by the dots.

The hour was late, the moon sinking beyond the windows, the darkness intensifying and marshaling itself for a futile resistance against the bloody dawn.

I must not sleep. I dared not sleep. I slept.

In my dreams, guns cracked, slow-motion bullets bored visible tunnels in the air, coyotes bared fierce black plastic teeth marked by cryptic patterns of dots that I could *almost* read with my nervous fingers. In Robertson's livid chest, the oozing wound opened before me as if it were a black hole and I were an astronaut in deep space, drawing me with irresistible gravity into its depths, to oblivion.

CHAPTER 42

I SLEPT ONLY AN HOUR UNTIL A NURSE WOKE me. Chief Porter was being moved from surgery to the intensive-care unit.

The window presented a view of black hills rising to a black sky full of Braille dots leafed with silver. The sun still lay an hour below the eastern horizon.

Carrying my shopping bag of dirty clothes, I returned to the hallway outside the ICU.

Jake Hulquist and the chief's sister were waiting there. Neither had seen anything like the black plastic card.

Within a minute, a nurse and an orderly entered the long hallway from the elevator alcove, one at the head and one at the foot of a gurney bearing the chief. Karla Porter walked at her husband's side, one hand on his arm.

When the gurney passed us, I saw that the chief was unconscious, with the prongs of an inhalator in his nose. His tan had turned to tin; his lips were more gray than pink.

The nurse pulled and the orderly pushed the gurney through the double doors of the ICU, and Karla followed them after telling us that her husband wasn't expected to regain consciousness for hours.

Whoever murdered Robertson had wounded the chief. I couldn't prove it; however, when you don't believe in coincidences, then two shootings with the intent to kill, hours apart, in a sleepy town as small as Pico Mundo, must be as indisputably connected as Siamese twins.

I wondered if the caller on the chief's private night line had attempted to imitate my voice, if he had identified himself as me, seeking counsel, asking to be met downstairs at the front door of the house. He might have hoped that the chief would not only be fooled by the deception but would mention my name to his wife before he left the bedroom.

If an effort had been made to frame me for one killing, why not for two?

Though I prayed that the chief would recover quickly, I worried about what he might say when he regained consciousness.

My alibi for the time of his shooting amounted to this: I had been hiding a corpse in a Quonset hut at the Church of the Whispering Comet. This explanation, complete with verifying cadaver, would not give heart to any defense attorney.

At the fourth-floor nurses' station, none of the women on duty recognized the item that I'd found in Robertson's wallet.

I had better luck on the third floor, where a pale and freckled nurse with a fey quality stood at the station counter, checking the contents of pill cups against a list of patients' names. She accepted the mysterious plastic rectangle, examined both sides of it, and said, "It's a meditation card."

"What's that?"

"Usually they come without the bumps. Instead they have little symbols printed on them. Like a series of crosses or images of the Holy Virgin."

"Not this one."

"You're supposed to say a repetitive prayer, like an Our Father or a Hail Mary, as you move your finger from symbol to symbol."

"So it's like a convenient form of a rosary you can carry in your wallet?"

"Yeah. Worry beads." Sliding her fingertips back and forth over the raised dots, she said, "But they're not only used by Christians. In fact, they began as a New Age thing."

"What're those like?"

"I've seen them with rows of bells, Buddhas, peace signs, dogs or cats if you want to direct your meditative energy toward the achievement of rights for animals, or rows of planet Earths so you can meditate for a better environment."

"Is this one for blind people?" I wondered.

"No. Not at all."

She held the card against her forehead for a moment, like a mentalist reading the contents of a note through a sealed envelope.

I don't know why she did this, and I decided not to ask.

Tracing the dots again, she said, "About a quarter of the cards are Braille like this. What you're supposed to do is press a finger to the dots and meditate on each letter."

"But what does it say?"

As she continued to finger the card, a frown took possession of her face as gradually as an image rising out of the murk on Polaroid film. "I don't read Braille. But they say different things, this and that, a few inspirational words. A mantra to focus your energy. It's printed on the package the card comes in."

"I don't have the package."

"Or you can also order a custom imprint, your personal mantra, anything you want. This is the first black one I've ever seen."

"What color are they usually?" I asked.

"White, gold, silver, the blue of the sky, lots of times green for the environmentalist mantras."

Her frown had fully developed.

She returned the card to me.

With evident distaste, she stared at the fingers with which she had traced the dots.

"Where'd you say you found this?" she asked.

"Downstairs in the lobby, on the floor," I lied.

From behind the counter, she picked up a bottle of Purell. She squirted a gob of the clear gel onto her left palm, put the bottle down, and vigorously rubbed her hands together, sanitizing them.

"If I were you, I'd get rid of that," she said as she rubbed. "And the sooner the better."

She had used so much Purell that I could smell the ethyl alcohol evaporating.

"Get rid of it—why?" I asked.

"It's got negative energy. Bad mojo. It'll bring wickedness down on you."

I wondered which school of nursing she had attended.

"I'll throw it in the trash," I promised.

The freckles on her face seemed to have grown brighter, burning like sprinkles of cayenne pepper. "Don't throw it away here."

"All right," I said, "I won't."

"Not anywhere in the hospital," she said. "Take a drive out in the desert, where there's nobody around, drive fast, throw it out the window, let the wind take it."

"That sounds like a good plan."

Her hands were dry and sanitized. Her frown had evaporated along with the alcohol gel. She smiled. "I hope I've been of some help."

"You've been great."

I took the meditation card out of the hospital, into the waning night, but not for a drive in the desert.

CHAPTER 43

THE STUDIOS OF KPMC RADIO, VOICE OF the Maravilla Valley, are on Main Street, in the heart of Pico Mundo, in a three-story brick Georgian townhouse, between two Victorian edifices housing the law offices of Knacker & Hisscus and the Good Day Bakery.

In this last hour of darkness, lights were on in the kitchen of the bakery. When I got out of the car, the street smelled of bread fresh from the oven, cinnamon buns, and lemon strudel.

No bodachs were in sight.

The lower floors of KPMC house the business offices. Broadcast studios are on the third level.

Stan "Spanky" Lufmunder was the engineer on duty. Harry Beamis, who managed to survive in the radio business without a nickname, was the producer of "All Night with Shamus Cocobolo."

I made faces at them through the triple-insulated view window between the third-floor hall and their electronic aerie.

After conveying by hand gestures that I should copulate with myself, they gave me the OK sign, and I continued along the hall to the door to the broadcast booth.

From the speaker in the hallway, at low volume, issued "String of Pearls," by the immortal Glenn Miller, the platter that Shamus was currently spinning on the air.

The music actually originated from a CD, but on his show, Shamus uses the slang of the 1930s and '40s.

Harry Beamis alerted him, so when I entered the booth, Shamus took off his headphones, tuned up the on-air feed just enough to stay on track with it, looked up from his stool, and said, "Hey, Wizard, welcome to *my* Pico Mundo."

To Shamus, I am the Wizard of Odd, or Wizard for short.

He said, "Why don't you smell like peach shampoo?"

"The only soap I had was unscented Neutrogena."

He frowned. "It's not over between you and the goddess, is it?"

"It's only just begun," I assured him.

"Glad to hear it."

The foam-cone walls mellowed our voices, smoothed rough edges.

The lenses of his dark glasses were the blue of old Milk of Magnesia bottles. His skin was so black that it, too, seemed to have a blue tint.

I reached in front of him and put down the meditation card, snapping it sharply against the countertop to intrigue him.

He played cool, didn't pick it up right away. "I plan to come by the Grille after the show, chow down on a heart-stopping pile of fried shaved ham, shoestring onions, and biscuits in gravy."

As I circled the microphone island, sat on a stool opposite him, and pushed the other mike aside on its flexible arm, I said, "I won't be cooking this morning. Got the day off."

"What do you do on a day off—go out there and moon around at the tire store?"

"I thought I might go bowling."

"You're one wild party animal, Wizard. I don't know how your lady keeps up with you."

The Miller tune wrapped. Shamus leaned into the mike and let ad-libbed patter dance off his tongue, cuing back-to-back cuts of Benny Goodman's "One O'Clock Jump" and Duke Ellington's "Take the A Train."

I like to listen to Shamus on the air and off. He has a voice that makes Barry White and James Earl Jones sound like carnival barkers with strep throat. To radio people, he's the Velvet Tongue.

From 1:00 A.M. to 6:00, every day but Sunday, Shamus spins what he calls "the music that won the big war," and recounts tales of the night life of that long-ago age.

The other nineteen hours of the day, KPMC eschews music in favor of talk radio. Management would prefer to shut down during those five least-listened hours, but their broadcast license requires them to serve the community 24/7.

This situation gives Shamus the freedom to do anything he wants, and what he wants is to immerse himself and his insomniac listeners in the glories of the Big Band era. In those days, he says, the music was *real*, and life was more grounded in truth, reason, and good will.

The first time I heard this rap, I expressed surprise that he would feel such affinity for an age of active segregation. His answer was, "I'm black, blind, seriously smart, and sensitive. *No* age would be easy for me. At least the culture had *culture* then, it had *style*."

Now he told his audience, "Close your eyes, picture

the Duke in his trademark white tux, and join me, Shamus Cocobolo, as I ride that A Train to Harlem."

His mother named him Shamus because she wanted her son to be a police detective. When he went blind at three, a law-enforcement career ceased to be an option. The "Cocobolo" came with his father, straight out of Jamaica.

Picking up the black plastic card, holding it by the top and bottom edges between the thumb and forefinger of his right hand, he said, "Some stupefyingly stupid bank give you a credit card?"

"I was hoping you could tell me what it says."

He slid one finger across the card, not really reading it, just determining its nature. "Oh, Wizard, surely you don't think I need meditation when I've got Count Basie and Satchmo and Artie Shaw."

"So you know what it is."

"The last couple years, people have given me maybe a dozen of these things, all different inspirational thoughts, as though blind people can't dance, so they meditate. No offense, Wizard, but you're entirely too cool to give me a plastic fantastic spiritual whizbang like this, and I'm a little embarrassed for you."

"You're welcome. But I'm not giving it to you. I'm just curious what it says in Braille."

"I'm relieved to hear that. But why curious?"

"I was born that way."

"I get the point. None of my business." He read the card with his fingertips and said, "'Father of Lies.'"

"'Father of flies'?"

"*Lies*. Untruths."

The phrase was familiar to me, but for some reason I couldn't make sense of it, perhaps because I didn't want to.

"The devil," Shamus said. "The Father of Lies,

Father of Evil, His Satanic Majesty. What's the story, Wizard? Is St. Bart's old-time religion just too boring these days, you need a whiff of sulfur to give your soul a thrill?"

"It's not my card."

"So whose card is it?"

"A nurse at County General told me to drive pedal-to-the-metal, into the desert, toss it out a window, let the wind take it."

"For a nice boy who makes an honest living with a fast spatula, you sure hang around with some seriously whacked people."

He slid the card toward me, across the microphone island.

I got up from my stool.

"Don't you leave that brimstone Braille here," he said.

"It's just a plastic fantastic spiritual whizbang, remember?"

My twin reflections watched me from the dark-blue lenses of his glasses.

Shamus said, "I knew a practicing Satanist once. The guy claimed he hated his mother, but he must've loved her. Cops found her severed head in his freezer, in a sealed plastic bag with rose petals to keep it fresh."

I picked up the meditation card. It felt cold.

"Thanks for your help, Shamus."

"You be careful, Wizard. Interestingly eccentric friends aren't easy to find. You were suddenly dead, I'd miss you."

CHAPTER 44

THE RED DAWN CAME, THE SUN LIKE AN executioner's blade slicing up from the dark horizon.

Elsewhere in Pico Mundo, a would-be mass murderer might have been looking at this sunrise while inserting cartridges in spare magazines for his assault rifle.

I parked in the driveway and turned off the engine. I could wait no longer to learn if the shooter who popped Bob Robertson had also murdered Rosalia Sanchez. Yet two or three minutes passed before I found sufficient courage to get out of the car.

The night birds had fallen silent. Usually active at first light, the morning crows had not yet appeared.

Climbing the back-porch steps, I saw that the screen door was closed but that the door stood open. The kitchen lights were off.

I peered through the screen. Rosalia sat at the table, her hands folded around a coffee mug. She appeared to be alive.

Appearances can be deceiving. Her dead body might be awaiting discovery in another room, and this might be her earthbound spirit with its hands around the mug that she had left when she'd gone to answer the killer's knock on her door the previous evening.

I could not smell freshly brewed coffee.

Always before, when she waited for me to arrive to tell her that she was visible, the lights had been on. I had never seen her sitting in the dark like this.

Rosalia looked up and smiled as I entered the kitchen.

I stared at her, afraid to speak, for fear that she was a lingering spirit and could not answer.

"Good morning, Odd Thomas."

Dread blew out of me with my pent-up breath. "You're alive."

"Of course I'm alive. I know I'm a long way down the road from the young girl I used to be, but I don't look dead, I hope."

"I meant—visible. You're visible."

"Yes, I know. The two policemen told me, so I didn't have to wait for you this morning."

"Policemen?"

"It was good knowing early. I turned out the lights and just enjoyed sitting here, watching the dawn develop." She raised her mug. "Would you like some apple juice, Odd Thomas?"

"No thank you, ma'am. Did you say two policemen?"

"They were nice boys."

"When was this?"

"Not forty minutes ago. They were worried about you."

"Worried—why?"

"They said someone reported hearing a gunshot come from your apartment. Isn't that ridiculous, Odd Thomas? I told them I hadn't heard anything."

I was sure that the call reporting the shot had been made anonymously, because the caller had likely been Robertson's killer.

Mrs. Sanchez said, "I asked them what on earth you'd be shooting at in your apartment. I told them you don't have mice." She raised her mug to take a sip of apple juice, but then said, "You don't have mice, do you?"

"No, ma'am."

"They wanted to look anyway. They were concerned about you. Nice boys. Careful to wipe their feet. They didn't touch a thing."

"You mean you showed them my apartment?"

After swallowing some apple juice, she said, "Well, they were policemen, and they were so worried about you, and they felt much better when they didn't find that you'd shot your foot or something."

I was glad I'd moved Robertson's body immediately upon finding it in my bathroom.

"Odd Thomas, you never came around last night to get the cookies I baked for you. Chocolate chip with walnuts. Your favorite."

A plate, heaped with cookies, covered with plastic wrap, stood on the table.

"Thank you, ma'am. Your cookies are the best." I picked up the plate. "I was wondering . . . do you think I could borrow your car for a little while?"

"But didn't you just drive up in it?"

My blush was redder than the spreading dawn beyond the windows. "Yes, ma'am."

"Well, then, you've already borrowed it," she said without the slightest trace of irony. "No need to ask twice."

I retrieved the keys from a pegboard by the refrigerator. "Thank you, Mrs. Sanchez. You're too good to me."

"You're a sweet boy, Odd Thomas. You remind me so much of my nephew Marco. Come September, he'll have been invisible three years."

Marco, with the rest of his family, had been aboard one of the planes that flew into the World Trade Center.

She said, "I keep thinking he'll turn visible again any day, but it's been so long now . . . Don't you ever go invisible, Odd Thomas."

She breaks my heart sometimes. "I won't," I assured her.

When I bent down and kissed her brow, she put a hand to my head, holding my face to hers. "Promise me you won't."

"I promise, ma'am. I swear to God."

CHAPTER 45

WHEN I PARKED IN FRONT OF STORMY'S apartment house, the undercover PD van was no longer across the street.

Obviously, when the police detail had been in place, it hadn't been providing security for her. As I'd suspected, they had been keeping a watch with the hope that Robertson would come looking for me. When I'd shown up at Chief Porter's house, after the shooting, they realized that I was no longer with Stormy, and evidently they pulled up stakes.

Robertson was embarked upon an endless sleep, watched over by the ghost of a young prostitute, but his murderer and former kill buddy remained at large. This second psychopath would have no reason to make a special target of Stormy; besides, she had her 9-mm pistol and the hard-nosed will to use it.

Yet into my mind came the image of Robertson's chest wound, and I could not turn away from it or close my eyes to it as I had done in my bathroom. Worse, my imagination transferred the mortal hole from the dead man's livid flesh to Stormy, and I thought also of the young woman who saved me from the coyotes, arms crossed modestly over her breasts and wounds.

On the front walkway, I broke into a run. Slammed up the stairs. Crashed across the porch. Threw open the door with the leaded glass.

I fumbled the key, dropped it, bent and snatched it from the air as it bounced off the hardwood floor, and let myself into her apartment.

From the living room, I saw Stormy in the kitchen, and I went to her side.

She stood at the cutting board, beside the sink, using a small grapefruit knife to section the prime Florida fruit. A small pile of extracted seeds glistened on the wood.

"What're you wired about?" she asked as she finished her task and set aside the knife.

"I thought you were dead."

"Since I'm not, do you want some breakfast?"

I almost told her that someone had shot the chief.

Instead, I said, "If I did drugs, I'd love an amphetamine omelet with three pots of black coffee. I didn't get much sleep. I need to stay awake, clarify my thinking."

"I've got chocolate-covered doughnuts."

"That's a start."

We sat at the kitchen table: she with her grapefruit, me with the box of doughnuts and with a Pepsi, full sugar, full caffeine.

"Why did you think I was dead?" she asked.

She was already worried about me. I didn't want to wind her anxiety spring to the breaking point.

If I told her about the chief, I'd wind up also telling her about Bob Robertson in my bathtub, about how he'd been a dead man already when I'd seen him in the churchyard, about the events at the Church of the Whispering Comet and the satanic meditation card.

She'd want to stay at my side for the duration. Ride

shotgun, give me cover. I couldn't allow her to endanger herself like that.

I sighed and shook my head. "I don't know. I'm seeing bodachs everywhere. Hordes of them. Whatever's coming, it's going to be big. I'm scared."

Warningly, she pointed her spoon at me. "Don't tell me to stay home today."

"I'd like you to stay home today."

"What'd I just say?"

"What'd *I* just say."

Chewing, silenced by grapefruit and by chocolate doughnut, we stared at each other.

"I'll stay home today," she said, "if you'll stay here all day with me."

"We've been through this. I can't let people die if there's a way to spare them."

"And I'm not going to live even one day in a cage just because there's a loose tiger out there somewhere."

I chugged Pepsi. I wished that I had some caffeine tablets. I wished that I had smelling salts to clear my head each time a fog of sleep began to creep upon me. I wished that I could be like other people, with no supernatural gift, with no weight to carry except whatever chocolate doughnuts might eventually put on me.

"He's worse than a tiger," I told her.

"I don't care if he's worse than a Tyrannosaurus Rex. I've got a life to live—and no time to waste if I'm going to have my own ice cream shop within four years."

"Get real. One day off work isn't going to destroy your chances of fulfilling the dream."

"Every day I work toward it *is* the dream. The process, not the final achievement, is what it's all about."

"Why do I even try to reason with you? I always lose."

"You're a fabulous man of action, sweetie. You don't need to be a good debater, too."

"I'm a fabulous man of action *and* a terrific short-order cook."

"The ideal husband."

"I'm going to have a second doughnut."

With full knowledge that she was offering a concession that I could not accept, she smiled and said, "Tell you what—I'll take a day off work and go with you, right at your side, everywhere you go."

Where I hoped to go, by the grace of psychic magnetism, was to the unknown man who'd killed Robertson and who might now be preparing himself to carry out the atrocity that they had planned together. Stormy wouldn't be safe at my side.

"No," I said. "You get on with your dream. Pack those cones, mix those milkshakes, and be the best damn purveyor of ice cream that you can be. Even little dreams can't come true unless you persevere."

"Did you think that up, odd one, or are you quoting?"

"Don't you recognize it? I'm quoting you."

She smiled affectionately. "You're smarter than you look."

"I'd have to be. Where are you going on your lunch break?"

"You know me—I pack my lunch. It's cheaper, and I can stay at work, on top of things."

"Don't change your mind. Don't go near a bowling alley, near a movie theater, near anything."

"Can I go near a golf course?"

"No."

"A miniature-golf course?"

"I'm serious about this."

"Can I go near a game arcade?"

"Remember that old movie, *Public Enemy*?" I asked.

"Can I go near an amusement park?"

"James Cagney's this gangster having breakfast with his moll—"

"I'm nobody's moll."

"—and when she irritates him, he shoves half a grapefruit in her face."

"And what does she do—castrate him? That's what I'd do, with my grapefruit knife."

"*Public Enemy* was made in 1931. You couldn't show castration on the screen back then."

"What an immature art form it was in those days. So enlightened now. You want half my grapefruit and I'll get my knife?"

"I'm just saying I love you and I'm worried about you."

"I love you, too, sweetie. So I'll promise not to eat lunch on a miniature-golf course. I'll have it right at Burke & Bailey's. If I spill salt, I'll immediately throw a pinch over my shoulder. Hell, I'll throw the entire shaker."

"Thanks. But I'm still considering the grapefruit-face smash."

CHAPTER 46

AT THE TAKUDA HOUSE ON HAMPTON Way, no bodachs were in sight. The previous night, they had been swarming over the residence.

As I parked in front of the place, the garage door rolled up. Ken Takuda backed out in his Lincoln Navigator.

When I walked to the driveway, he stopped the SUV and put down his window. "Good morning, Mr. Thomas."

He's the only person I know who addresses me so formally.

"Good morning, sir. It's a beautiful morning, isn't it?"

"A *glorious* morning," he declared. "A momentous day, like every day, full of possibilities."

Dr. Takuda is on the faculty of California State University at Pico Mundo. He teaches twentieth-century American literature.

Considering that the modern and contemporary literature taught in most universities is largely bleak, cynical, morbid, pessimistic, misanthropic dogmatism, often written by suicidal types who sooner or later kill themselves with alcohol or drugs, or shotguns, Professor Takuda was a remarkably cheerful man.

"I need some advice about my future," I lied. "I'm thinking of going to college, after all, eventually getting a doctorate, building an academic career, like you."

When his lustrous Asian complexion paled, he acquired a taupe tint. "Well, Mr. Thomas, while I'm in favor of education, I couldn't in good conscience recommend a university career in anything but the hard sciences. As a working environment, the rest of academia is a sewer of irrationality, hatemongering, envy, and self-interest. I'm getting out the moment I earn my twenty-five-year pension package, and then I'm going to write novels like Ozzie Boone."

"But, sir, you always seem so happy."

"In the belly of Leviathan, Mr. Thomas, one can either despair and perish, or be cheerful and persevere." He smiled brightly.

This wasn't the response I expected, but I pressed forward with my half-baked scheme to learn his schedule for the day and thereby perhaps pinpoint the place where Robertson's kill buddy would strike. "I'd still like to talk to you about it."

"The world has too few modest fry cooks and far too many self-important professors, but we'll chat about it if you like. Just call the university and ask for my office. My graduate assistant will set up an appointment."

"I was hoping we could talk this morning, sir."

"Now? What has caused this sudden urgent thirst for academic pursuits?"

"I need to think more seriously about the future. I'm getting married on Saturday."

"Would that be to Ms. Bronwen Llewellyn?"

"Yes, sir."

"Mr. Thomas, you have a rare opportunity for

perfect bliss, and you would be ill advised to poison your life with either academia or drug dealing. I have a class this morning, followed by two student conferences. Then I'm having lunch and seeing a movie with my family, so I'm afraid tomorrow is the absolute earliest we can discuss this self-destructive impulse of yours."

"Where are you having lunch, sir? At the Grille?"

"We're allowing the children to choose. It's their day."

"What movie are you seeing?"

"That thing about the dog and the alien."

"Don't," I said, though I hadn't seen the film. "It stinks."

"It's a big hit."

"It sucks."

"The critics like it," he said.

"Randall Jarrell said that art is long and critics are but the insects of a day."

"Give my office a call, Mr. Thomas. We'll talk tomorrow."

He put up his window, backed out of the driveway, and drove off toward the university and, later in the day, an appointment with Death.

CHAPTER 47

NICOLINA PEABODY, AGE FIVE, WORE PINK sneakers, pink shorts, and a pink T-shirt. Her wristwatch featured a pink plastic band and a pink pig's face on the dial.

"When I'm old enough to buy my own clothes," she told me, "I'll wear nothing but pink, pink, pink, every day, all year, forever."

Levanna Peabody, who would soon be seven, rolled her eyes and said, "Everybody'll think you're a whore."

Entering the living room with a birthday cake on a plate under a clear-glass lid, Viola said, "Levanna! That's an awful thing to say. That's just half a step from trash talk and two weeks with no allowance."

"What's a whore?" Nicolina asked.

"Someone who wears pink and kisses men for money," Levanna said in a tone of worldly sophistication.

When I took the cake from Viola, she said, "I'll just grab their box of activity books, and we'll be ready to go."

I had taken a quick tour of the house. No bodachs lurked in any corner.

Nicolina said, "If I kiss men for free, then I can wear pink and not be a whore."

"If you kiss lots of men for free, you're a slut," Levanna said.

"Levanna, enough!" Viola reprimanded.

"But Mom," Levanna said, "she's got to learn how the world works sooner or later."

Noticing my amusement and interpreting it with uncanny skill, Nicolina confronted her older sister: "You don't even know what a whore is, you only think you do."

"I know, all right," Levanna insisted smugly.

The girls preceded me down the front walk to Mrs. Sanchez's car, which was parked at the curb.

After locking the house, Viola followed us. She put the box of activity books in the backseat with the girls, and then she sat up front. I handed the cake to her and closed her door.

The morning was pure Mojave, blazing and breathless. The sky, an inverted blue ceramic cauldron, poured out a hot dry brew.

With the sun still in the east, all shadows slanted westward, as if yearning for that horizon over which the night had preceded them. And along the windless street, only my shadow moved.

If supernatural entities were present, they were not evident.

As I got in the car and started the engine, Nicolina said, "I'm never going to kiss any men, anyway. Just Mommy, Levanna, and Aunt Sharlene."

"You'll want to kiss men when you're older," Levanna predicted.

"I won't."

"You will."

"I won't," Nicolina firmly declared. "Just you, Mommy, Aunt Sharlene. Oh, and Cheevers."

"Cheevers is a boy," Levanna said as I pulled away

from the curb and set out for Sharlene's house.

Nicolina giggled. "Cheevers is a *bear*."

"He's a boy bear."

"He's *stuffed*."

"But he's still a boy," Levanna contended. "See, it's started already—you want to kiss men."

"I'm not a slut," Nicolina insisted. "I'm going to be a dog doctor."

"They're called veterinarians, and they don't wear pink, pink, pink, every day, all year, forever."

"I'll be the first."

"Well," Levanna said, "if I had a sick dog and you were a pink veterinarian, I guess I'd still bring him to you 'cause I know you'd make him well."

Following a circuitous route, checking the rearview mirror, I drove six blocks to wind up two blocks away on Maricopa Lane.

Using my cell phone en route, Viola called her sister to say that she was bringing the girls for a visit.

The tidy white clapboard house on Maricopa has periwinkle-blue shutters and blue porch posts. On the porch, a social center for the neighborhood, are four rocking chairs and a bench swing.

Sharlene rocked up from one of the chairs when we parked in her driveway. She is a large woman with a rapturous smile and a musical voice perfect for a gospel singer, which she is.

A golden retriever, Posey, rose from the porch floor to stand at her side, lashing a gorgeous plumed tail, excited by the sight of the girls, held in place not by a leash but by her master's softly spoken command.

I carried the cake into the kitchen, where I politely declined Sharlene's offer of ice-cold lemonade, an apple dumpling, three varieties of cookies, and homemade peanut brittle.

Lying on the floor with four legs in the air, forepaws bent in submission, Posey solicited a belly rub, which the girls were quick to provide.

I dropped to one knee and interrupted long enough to say happy birthday to Levanna. I gave each of the girls a hug.

They seemed terribly small and fragile. So little force would be required to shatter them, to rip them out of this world. Their vulnerability frightened me.

Viola accompanied me through the house to the front porch, where she said, "You were gonna bring me a picture of the man I'm supposed to be on the lookout for."

"You don't need it now. He's . . . out of the picture."

Her huge eyes were full of trust that I didn't deserve. "Odd, tell me honest-to-Jesus, do you still see death in me?"

I didn't know what might be coming, but though the desert day made a bright impression on my eyes, it seemed storm-dark to my sixth sense, with great thunder pending. Changing their plans, canceling the movie and dinner at the Grille—that would surely be enough to change their fate. Surely. "You're okay now. And the girls, too."

Her eyes searched mine, and I dared not look away. "What about you, Odd? Whatever's coming . . . is there a path for you to walk through it to someplace safe?"

I forced a smile. "I know about all that's Otherly and Beyond—remember?"

She locked eyes with me a moment longer, then put her arms around me. We held each other tight.

I didn't ask Viola if *she* saw death in *me*. She had never claimed to have a foretelling gift . . . but I was afraid nevertheless that she would say *yes*.

CHAPTER 48

LONG AFTER "ALL NIGHT WITH SHAMUS Cocobolo" had gone off the air and the strains of Glenn Miller had traveled out of the stratosphere toward distant stars, with no Elvis CDs to comfort me, I cruised the streets of Pico Mundo in the silence of the sun, wondering where all the bodachs had gone.

At a service station, I stopped to fuel the Chevy and to use the men's room. In the streaked mirror above the sink, my face suggested that I was a hunted man, haggard and hollow-eyed.

From the adjacent minimart, I bought a screw-top sixteen-ounce Pepsi and a small bottle of caffeine tablets.

With the chemical assistance of No-Doz, cola, and the sugar in the plate of cookies that Mrs. Sanchez had given me, I could remain awake. Whether I could think clearly enough on such a regimen would not be entirely evident until the bullets started flying.

Lacking a name or face to put to Robertson's collaborator, my psychic magnetism would not lead me to my quarry. Cruising randomly, I would arrive nowhere of consequence.

With clear intention, I drove to Camp's End.

The chief had ordered surveillance on Robertson's

house the previous evening, but that stakeout had apparently been withdrawn. With the chief shot and the entire police department in shock, someone had decided to shift resources elsewhere.

Suddenly I realized that the chief might not have been targeted solely to frame me for a second murder. Robertson's kill buddy might have wanted to eliminate Wyatt Porter in order to ensure that the Pico Mundo PD would be shaken, disoriented, and slow to respond to whatever crisis was coming.

Instead of parking across the street and down the block from the pale yellow casita with the faded blue door, I left the Chevy at the curb in front of the place. I walked boldly to the carport.

My driver's license still served its fundamental purpose. The door latch popped, and I entered the kitchen.

For a minute, I stood inside the threshold, listening. The hum of the refrigerator motor. Faint ticks and creaks marked the steady expansion of the old house's joints in the ascending heat of the new morning.

Instinct told me that I was alone.

I went directly to the neatly kept study. Currently, it didn't serve as a train station for incoming bodachs.

From the wall above the file cabinets, McVeigh, Manson, and Atta watched me as if with conscious awareness.

At the desk, I sifted through the contents of the drawers once more, seeking names. On my previous visit, I had considered the small address book to be of little value, but this time I paged through it with interest.

The book contained fewer than forty names and addresses. None resonated with me.

I didn't peruse the bank statements again, but I

stared at them, thinking about the $58,000 in cash that he'd withdrawn over the past two months. More than four thousand had been in his pants pockets when I found his body.

If you were a rich sociopath interested in funding well-planned acts of mass murder, how big a circus of blood could you purchase for approximately $54,000?

Even sleep-deprived, with a caffeine headache and a sugar buzz, I could answer that one without much consideration: big. You could buy a three-ring circus of death—bullets, explosives, poison gas, just about anything short of a nuclear bomb.

Elsewhere in the house, a door closed. Not with a bang. Quietly, with a soft thump and click.

Moving stealthily but quickly, I went to the open door of the study. I stepped into the hall.

No intruder in sight. Except me.

The bathroom and bedroom doors stood open, as they had been.

In the bedroom, the closet door was a slider. That couldn't have made the sound I heard.

Aware that death is frequently the reward for the reckless and the timid alike, I moved with cautious haste into the living room. Deserted.

The swinging door to the kitchen could not have been what I heard. The entry door to the house remained closed, as it had been.

In the front left corner of the living room, a closet. In the closet: two jackets, a few sealed cartons, an umbrella.

Into the kitchen. No one.

Maybe I had heard an intruder *leaving*. Which meant someone had been in the house when I arrived and had crept out when certain that I was distracted.

Perspiration prickled my brow. A single bead

quivered down the nape of my neck and traced my spine to the coccyx.

The morning heat was not the sole cause of my sweat.

I returned to the study and switched on the computer. I sampled Robertson's programs, surfed his directories, and found a library of sleaze that he had downloaded from the Internet. Files of sadistic porn. Child porn. Still others were about serial killers, ritualistic mutilation, and satanic ceremonies.

None of it seemed certain to lead me to his collaborator, at least not quickly enough to resolve the current crisis favorably. I switched the computer off.

If I'd had some Purell, the sanitizing gel that the nurse used at the hospital, I might have poured half a bottle on my hands.

During my first visit to this casita, I had conducted a quick search, which concluded when I'd made enough disturbing discoveries to take my case against Robertson to the chief. Although a countdown clock ticked in my head, this time I went through the house more thoroughly, grateful that it was small.

In the bedroom, in one drawer of a highboy, I found several knives of different sizes and curious design. Latin phrases were engraved in the blades of the first few weapons that I examined.

Although I don't read Latin, I sensed that the character of the words would prove, on translation, to be as wicked as the sharpness of each razor-edged blade.

Another knife featured hieroglyphics from the hilt to the point. These pictographs meant no more to me than did the Latin, although I recognized a few of the highly stylized images: flames, falcons, wolves, snakes, scorpions . . .

Searching a second drawer, I discovered a heavy

silver chalice. Engraved with obscenities. Polished. Cool in my hands.

This unholy chalice was a hateful mockery of the communion cup that held consecrated wine in a Catholic Mass. The ornate handles were inverted crucifixes: Christ turned on His head. Latin encircled the rim, and around the bowl of the cup were engraved images of naked men and women engaged in various acts of sodomy.

In the same drawer, I found a black-lacquered pyx likewise decorated with pornographic images. On the sides and the lid of this small box, colorful hand-painted scenes of lurid degradation depicted men and women copulating not with one another but with jackals, hyenas, goats, and serpents.

In an ordinary church, the pyx contains the Eucharist, communion wafers of unleavened bread. This box brimmed with coal-black crackers flecked with red.

Unleavened bread exudes a subtle, appealing aroma. The contents of this pyx had an equally faint but repellent odor. First whiff—herbal. Second whiff—burnt matches. Third whiff—vomit.

The highboy contained other satanic paraphernalia; but I'd seen enough.

I couldn't fathom how adults could take seriously the Hollywood trappings and hokey rituals of glamorized satanism. Certain fourteen-year-old boys, yes, because some of them were washed half loose from reason by shifting tides of hormones. But not adults. Even sociopaths like Bob Robertson and his unknown pal, as enthralled by violence and as crackbrained as they were, must have *some* clarity of perception, surely enough to see the absurdity of such Halloween games.

After replacing the items in the highboy, I closed the drawers.

A knocking startled me. The soft rap of knuckles.

I looked at the bedroom window, expecting to see a face at the glass, perhaps a neighbor tapping the pane. Only the hard desert light, tree shadows, and the brown backyard.

The knocking came again, as quiet as before. Not just three or four brisk raps. A stutter of small blows lasting fifteen or twenty seconds.

In the living room, I went to the window beside the front door and carefully parted the greasy drapes. No one waited on the stoop outside.

Mrs. Sanchez's Chevy was the only vehicle at the curb. The weary dog that had slouched along the street the day before now traveled it again, head held low, tail lower than its head.

Recalling the racket of the quarrelsome crows on the roof during my previous visit, I turned from the window and studied the ceiling, listening.

After a minute, when the knocking didn't come again, I stepped into the kitchen. In places, the ancient linoleum crackled underfoot.

Needing a name to put to Robertson's collaborator, I could think of no place in a kitchen likely to contain such information. I looked through all the drawers and cupboards, anyway. Most were empty: only a few dishes, half a dozen glasses, a small clatter of flatware.

I went to the refrigerator because eventually Stormy would ask if *this* time I had checked for severed heads. When I opened the door, I found beer, soft drinks, part of a canned ham on a platter, half a strawberry pie, as well as the usual staples and condiments.

Next to the strawberry pie, a clear plastic package held four black candles, eight-inch tapers. Maybe he kept them in the fridge because they would soften and distort if left in this summer heat, in a house without air conditioning.

Beside the candles stood a jar without a label, filled with what appeared to be loose teeth. A closer look confirmed the contents: dozens of molars, bicuspids, incisors, canines. Human teeth. Enough to fill at least five or six mouths.

I stared at the jar for a long moment, trying to imagine how he had obtained this strange collection. When I decided that I'd rather not think about it, I closed the door.

Had I found nothing unusual in the refrigerator, I would not have opened the freezer compartment. Now I felt obligated to explore further.

The freezer was a deep roll-out compartment under the fridge. The hot kitchen sucked a quick plume of cold fog from the drawer when I pulled it open.

Two bright pink-and-yellow containers were familiar: the Burke & Bailey's ice cream that Robertson had purchased the previous afternoon. Maple walnut and mandarin-orange chocolate.

In addition, the compartment held about ten opaque Rubbermaid containers with red lids, the shape and the size in which to store leftover deep-dish lasagna. I would not have opened these if the topmost containers hadn't featured freezer-proof hand-printed labels: HEATHER JOHNSON, JAMES DEERFIELD.

After all, I was looking specifically for names.

When I lifted aside the top containers, I saw more names on the lids under them: LISA BELMONT, ALYSSA RODRIQUEZ, BENJAMIN NADER . . .

I started with Heather Johnson. When I pried off the red lid, I found a woman's breasts.

CHAPTER 49

SOUVENIRS. TROPHIES. OBJECTS TO SPUR THE imagination and thrill the heart on lonely nights.

As though it had burned my hands, I dropped the container back in the freezer. I shot to my feet and kicked the drawer shut.

I must have turned away from the refrigerator, must have crossed the kitchen, but I was not aware of going to the sink until I found myself there. Leaning against the counter, bent forward, I struggled to repress the urge to surrender Mrs. Sanchez's cookies.

Throughout my life, I have seen terrible things. Some have been worse than the contents of the Rubbermaid container. Experience has not immunized me to horror, however, and human cruelty still has the power to devastate me, to loosen the locking pins in my knees.

Although I wanted to wash my hands and then splash cold water in my face, I preferred not to touch Robertson's faucets. I shrank from the thought of using his soap.

Nine more containers waited in the freezer. Someone else would have to open them. I had no curiosity about the rest of the grotesque collection.

In the file folder that bore his name, Robertson had

included nothing but the calendar page for August 15, suggesting that his own career as a murderer would begin on this date. Yet evidence in the freezer suggested that his file should already be thick.

Sweat sheathed me, hot on my face, cold along my spine. I might as well not have showered at the hospital.

I consulted my wristwatch—10:02.

The bowling alley didn't open for business until one o'clock. The first showing of the hot-ticket dog movie was also scheduled for one o'clock.

If my prophetic dream was about to be fulfilled, evidence suggested that I might have no more than three hours to find Robertson's collaborator and stop him.

I unclipped the cell phone from my belt. Flipped it open. Pulled out the antenna. Pressed the power button. Watched the maker's logo appear and listened to the electronic signature music.

Chief Porter might not yet have regained consciousness. Even if he surfaced, his thoughts would be muddled by the lingering effects of anesthetic, by morphine or its equivalent, and by pain. He would have neither the strength nor presence of mind to give instructions to his subordinates.

To one extent or another, I knew all the officers on the PMPD. None had been made aware of my paranormal gift, however, and none had ever been as good a friend to me as was Chief Porter.

If I brought the police to this house, revealed to them the contents of the freezer, and urged them to apply all their resources to learning the name of Robertson's kill buddy, they would need hours to wrap their minds around the situation. Because they did not share my sixth sense and would not easily be persuaded that it was real, they wouldn't share my urgency.

They would detain me here while they investigated the situation. In their eyes, I would be as suspect as Robertson, for I had entered his house illegally. Who was to say that I hadn't harvested these body parts myself and hadn't planted the ten Rubbermaid containers in his freezer to incriminate him?

If ever they found Bob Robertson's body, and if the chief—God forbid—succumbed to postoperative complications, I would surely be arrested and charged with murder.

I switched off the phone.

Without a name to focus my psychic magnetism, without anyone to turn to for assistance, I had hit a wall, and the impact rattled my teeth.

Something crashed to the floor in another room: not just the thump of a closing door this time, not merely a soft rapping, but a hard thud and the sound of breakage.

Driven by frustration so intense that it allowed no caution, I headed for the swinging door, trying to clip the phone to my belt. I dropped it, left it for later, and shoved through the swinging door, into the living room.

A lamp had been knocked to the floor. The ceramic base had shattered.

When I tore open the front door and saw no one on the stoop or on the lawn, I slammed it shut. Hard. The boom shook the house, and making noise greatly pleased me after so much pussyfooting. My anger felt good.

I rushed through the archway, into the narrow hall, seeking the perpetrator. Bedroom, closet, study, closet, bathroom. No one.

Crows on the roof hadn't knocked over the lamp. Nor a draft. Nor an earthquake.

When I returned to the kitchen to pick up my phone and get out of the house, Robertson was waiting there for me.

CHAPTER 50

FOR A DEAD MAN WHO NO LONGER HAD a stake in the schemes and games of this world, Robertson lingered with singular ferocity, as infuriated as he had been when I had watched him from the bell tower at St. Bart's. His mushroom-colony body now seemed powerful, even in its lumpiness. His soft face and blurry features hardened and sharpened with rage.

No bullet hole, scorch mark, or stain marred his shirt. Unlike Tom Jedd, who carried his severed arm and pretended to use it as a back scratcher out there at Tire World, Robertson was in denial of his death, and he chose not to sport his mortal wound, just as Penny Kallisto had initially manifested without evidence of strangulation, acquiring the ligature marks only in the company of Harlo Landerson, her killer.

In high agitation, Robertson circled the kitchen. He glared at me, his eyes wilder and more fevered than those of the coyotes at the Church of the Whispering Comet.

When I had begun to out him, I had unintentionally made him a liability to his collaborator, setting him up for murder, but I had not pulled the trigger. Evidently, his hatred for me nonetheless exceeded what he harbored for the man who had killed him;

otherwise, he would have done his haunting elsewhere.

Ovens to refrigerator, to sink, to ovens, he circled while I stooped and picked up the cell phone that I'd dropped earlier. Dead, he didn't worry me a fraction as much as he had when I had thought he'd been alive in the churchyard.

As I clipped the phone to my belt, Robertson came to me. Loomed before me. His eyes were the gray of dirty ice, yet they conveyed the heat of his fury.

I met his stare and didn't retreat from him. I've learned that it's not wise to show fear in these cases.

His heavy face indeed had the quality of a fungus, but a meaty variety. Very portobello. His bloodless lips drew back from teeth that had seen too little of a brush.

He reached past my face and cupped his right hand against the back of my neck.

Penny Kallisto's hand had been dry and warm. Robertson's felt damp, cold. This was not his real hand, of course, only part of an apparition, a spirit image, that only I could have felt; but the nature of such a touch reveals the character of the soul.

Although I refused to shy from this unearthly contact, I cringed inwardly at the thought of the creep playing with the ten souvenirs in his freezer. The visual stimulation of those frozen trophies might not always satisfy. Perhaps he thawed them now and then to increase his tactile pleasure and to conjure a more vivid memory of each kill—tweaking, pinching, petting, caressing, planting tender kisses upon those mementos.

No spirit, however evil, can harm a living person merely by touch. This is our world, not theirs. Their blows pass through us, and their bites draw no blood.

When he realized that he could not make me cower, Robertson lowered his hand from my neck. His fury doubled, trebled, wrenching his face into a gargoyle mask.

One way exists for certain spirits to harm the living. If their character is sufficiently pernicious, if they give their hearts to evil until malevolence ripens into incurable spiritual malignancy, they are able to summon the energy of their demonic rage and vent it upon the inanimate.

We call them poltergeists. I once lost a brand-new music system to such an entity, as well as the handsome award plaque for creative writing that I had won in that high-school competition judged by Little Ozzie.

As he had done in the sacristy at St. Bart's, Robertson's wrathful spirit stormed through the kitchen, and from his hands streamed pulses of energy that were visible to me. The air quivered with them, a sight similar to the concentric ripples that spread across water from the impact point of a stone.

Cabinet doors flew open, slammed shut, open, shut, banging even louder and with less meaning than the jaws of ranting politicians. Dishes erupted from shelves, each cutting through the air with the *whoosh* of a discus thrown by an Olympian.

I ducked a drinking glass, which exploded into an oven door, spraying sparkling shrapnel. Other glasses spun wide of me, shattered against walls, cabinets, countertops.

Poltergeists are all blind fury and thrashing torment, without aim or control. They can harm you only by indirection, a lucky blow. Even by indirection and chance, however, decapitation can ruin your day.

Accompanied by the hardwood applause of clapping cabinet doors, Robertson flung bolts of power from his hands. Two chairs danced in place at the dinette table, tapping on the linoleum, clattering against the table legs.

At the cooktop, untouched, four knobs turned. Four rings of gas flames shimmered eerie blue light into the otherwise gloomy kitchen.

Alert for deadly projectiles, I edged away from Robertson and toward the door by which I'd entered the house.

A drawer shot open, and a cacophony of flatware exploded out of it, glittering and clinking in a levitated frenzy, as if starving ghosts were carving-forking-spooning a dinner as invisible as they were themselves.

I saw those utensils coming—they passed *through* Robertson with no effect on his ectoplasmic form—and I turned aside, brought up my arms to shield my face. The flatware found me as iron will find a magnet, pummeled me. One fork speared past my defenses, stabbed my forehead, and raked back through my hair.

When this brittle rain of stainless steel rang to the floor behind me, I dared to lower my arms.

Like some great troll capering to a dark music that only he could hear, Robertson punched-clawed-twisted the air, appearing to howl and shout, but thrashing in the utter silence of the mute departed.

The upper compartment of the ancient Frigidaire sprang open, disgorging beer, soft drinks, the plate of ham, strawberry pie, a vomitous deluge that splashed and clattered across the floor. Ring tabs popped; beer and soda gouted from spinning cans.

The refrigerator itself began to vibrate, violently knocking side to side against the flanking cabinetry. Vegetable drawers chattered; wire shelves jangled.

Kicking aside rolling cans of beer and scattered flatware, I continued toward the door to the carport.

A juggernaut rumble alerted me to the fast approach of sliding death.

I dodged to my left, skidded on a foamy sludge of beer and a bent spoon.

With its grisly freight of frozen body parts still nestled in the freezer drawer, the Frigidaire slid past me and crashed into the wall hard enough to make the studs crack behind the plaster.

I plunged outside, into the shadows under the carport, and slammed the door behind me.

Inside, the tumult continued, the thump and crash, the rattle and bang.

I didn't expect Robertson's tortured spirit to follow me, at least not for a while. Once committed to a frenzy of destruction, a poltergeist will usually thrash out of control until it exhausts itself and wanders off in confusion to drift again in a purgatory zone between this world and the next.

CHAPTER 51

AT THE CONVENIENCE STORE WHERE I purchased the No-Doz and the Pepsi, I bought another cola, Bactine, and a package of large-patch Band-Aids.

The cashier, a man with a face made for astonishment, put aside the sports section of the *Los Angeles Times* and said, "Hey, you're bleeding."

Being polite is not only the right way to respond to people but also the easiest. Life is so filled with unavoidable conflict that I see no reason to promote more confrontations.

At that moment, however, I happened to be in a rare bad mood. Time was flushing away at a frightening rate, the hour of the gun rapidly drawing near, and I still had no name to hang on Robertson's collaborator.

"Do you know you're bleeding?" he asked.

"I had a suspicion."

"That looks nasty."

"My apologies."

"What happened to your forehead?"

"A fork."

"A fork?"

"Yes, sir. I wish I'd been eating with a spoon."

"You stabbed yourself with a fork?"

"It flipped."

"Flipped?"

"The fork."

"A flipped fork?"

"It flicked my forehead."

Pausing in the counting of my change, he gave me a narrow look.

"That's right," I said, "A flipped fork flicked my forehead."

He decided not to have any further involvement with me. He gave me my change, bagged the items, and returned to the sports pages.

In the men's room at the service station next door, I washed my bloody face, cleaned the wound, treated it with Bactine, and applied a compress of paper towels. The punctures and scratches were shallow, and the bleeding soon stopped.

This wasn't the first time—nor the last—that I wished my supernatural gift included the power to heal.

Band-Aid applied, I returned to the Chevy. Sitting behind the wheel, engine running, air-conditioning vents aimed at my face, I chugged cold Pepsi.

Only bad news on my wristwatch—10:48.

My muscles ached. My eyes were sore. I felt tired, weak. Maybe my wits hadn't shifted into low gear, as they seemed to have, but I didn't like my chances if I had to go one-on-one with Robertson's kill buddy, who must have enjoyed a better night's sleep than I had.

I'd taken two caffeine tablets no more than an hour ago, so I couldn't justify swilling down two more. Besides, already the acid in my stomach had soured into a corrosive strength sufficient to etch steel, and I had grown simultaneously exhausted and jumpy, which is not a condition conducive to survival.

Although I had no person—no name, no description—as a focus for my psychic magnetism, I drove at random through Pico Mundo, hoping to be brought to a place of enlightenment.

The brilliant Mojave day burned at white-hot ferocity. The air itself seemed to be on fire, as if the sun—by speed of light, less than eight and a half minutes from Earth—had gone nova eight minutes ago, giving us nothing more than this dazzling glare as a short warning of our impending bright death.

Each flare and flicker of light flashing off the windshield seemed to score my eyes. I hadn't brought my sunglasses. The searing glare soon spawned a headache that made a fork in the brow seem like a tickle by comparison.

Turning aimlessly from street to street, trusting intuition to guide me, I found myself in Shady Ranch, one of the newer residential developments on the Pico Mundo hills that a decade ago were home to nothing more dangerous than rattlesnakes. Now people lived here, and perhaps one of them was a sociopathic monster plotting mass murder in upper-middle-class suburban comfort.

Shady Ranch had never been a ranch of any kind; it wasn't one now, unless you counted houses as a crop. As for shade, these hills enjoyed less of it than most neighborhoods in the heart of town because the trees were far from maturity.

I parked in my father's driveway but didn't at once switch off the engine. I needed time to gather my nerve for this encounter.

Like those who lived in it, this Mediterranean-style house had little character. Below the red-tile roof, ornament-free planes of beige stucco and glass met at unsurprising angles arrived at less by architectural genius than by the dictates of lot size and shape.

Leaning closer to a dashboard vent, I closed my eyes against the rush of chilled air. Ghost lights drifted across the backs of my eyelids, retinal memories of the desert glare, strangely soothing for a moment—until the wound in Robertson's chest rose from deeper memory.

I switched off the engine, got out of the car, went to the house, and rang my father's doorbell.

At this hour in the morning, he was likely to be home. He had never worked a day in his life and seldom rose before nine or ten o'clock.

My father answered, surprised to see me. "Odd, you didn't call to say you were coming."

"No," I agreed. "Didn't call."

My father is forty-five, a handsome man with thick hair still more black than silver. He has a lean athletic body of which he is proud to the point of vanity.

Barefoot, he wore only khaki shorts slung low across his hips. His tan had been assiduously cultivated with oils, enhanced with toners, preserved with lotions.

"Why have you come?" he asked.

"I don't know."

"You don't look well."

He retreated one step from the door. He fears illness.

"I'm not sick," I assured him. "Just bone tired. No sleep. May I come in?"

"We weren't doing much, just finishing breakfast, getting ready to catch some rays."

Whether that was an invitation or not, I interpreted it as one, and I crossed the threshold, pulling the door shut behind me.

"Britney's in the kitchen," he said, and led me to the back of the house.

The blinds were drawn, the rooms layered with sumptuous shadows.

I've seen the place in better light. It's beautifully furnished. My father has style and loves comfort.

He inherited a substantial trust fund. A generous monthly check supports a lifestyle that many would envy.

Although he has much, he yearns for more. He desires to live far better than he does, and he chafes at terms of the trust that require him to live on its earnings and forbid him access to the principal.

His parents had been wise to settle their estate on him under those terms. If he had been able to get his hands on the principal, he would long ago have been destitute and homeless.

He is full of get-rich-quick schemes, the latest being the sale of land on the moon. Were he able to manage his own fortune, he would be impatient with a ten- or fifteen-percent return on investment and would plunge great sums on unlikely ventures in hopes of doubling and tripling his money overnight.

The kitchen is big, with restaurant-quality equipment and every imaginable culinary tool and gadget, though he eats out six or seven nights a week. Maple floor, ship's-style maple cabinets with rounded corners, granite counters, and stainless-steel appliances contribute to a sleek and yet inviting ambience.

Britney is sleek, as well, and inviting in a way that makes your skin crawl. When we entered the kitchen, she was standing hipshot at a window, sipping a morning champagne and staring out at sun serpents sinuously flexing across the surface of the swimming pool.

Her thong bikini was small enough to excite the jaded editors of *Hustler*, but she wore it well enough to make the cover of the *Sports Illustrated* swimsuit issue.

She was eighteen but looked younger. This is my father's basic criterion in women. They are never older than twenty, and they always look younger than they are.

Some years ago, he got in trouble for cohabiting with a sixteen-year-old. He claimed to be unaware of her true age. An expensive attorney plus payoffs to the girl and her parents spared him the indignity of a prison pallor and jail haircuts.

Instead of a greeting, Britney gave me a sullen, dismissive look. She returned her attention to the sun-dappled swimming pool.

She resents me because she thinks my father might give me money that would otherwise be spent on her. This concern has no validity. He would never offer me a buck, and I would never take it.

She would be better advised to worry about two facts: first, that she has been with my father for five months; second, that the average duration of one of his affairs is six to nine months. With a nineteenth birthday looming, she would soon seem old to him.

Fresh coffee had been brewed. I asked for a cup, poured it myself, and sat on a bar stool at the kitchen island.

Always restless in my company, my father moved around the room, rinsing out Britney's champagne glass when she finished with it, wiping a counter that didn't need to be wiped, straightening the chairs at the breakfast table.

"I'm getting married on Saturday," I said.

This surprised him. He'd been married to my mother only briefly and regretted it within hours of exchanging vows. Marriage doesn't suit him.

"To that Llewellyn girl?" he asked.

"Yes."

"Is that a good idea?"

"It's the best idea I've ever had."

Britney turned away from the window to study me with beady-eyed speculation. To her, a wedding meant a gift, a parental boon, and she was prepared to defend her interests.

She didn't stir in me the slightest anger. She saddened me, for I could see her deeply unhappy future without need of any sixth sense.

Admittedly, she scared me a little, too, because she was moody and quick to anger. Worse, the purity and the intensity of her self-esteem ensured that she would never doubt herself, that she could not conceive of suffering unpleasant consequences for any act that she might commit.

My father likes moody women in whom a perpetually simmering anger lies just beneath the surface. The more clearly that their moodiness indicates genuine psychological disorder, the more they excite him. Sex without danger does not appeal to him.

All of his lovers have fit this profile. He doesn't appear to spend much effort seeking them; as if sensing his need, drawn by vibes or pheromones, they find him with dependable regularity.

He once told me that the moodier a woman is, the hotter she will prove to be in bed. This was fatherly advice that I could have lived without.

Now, as I poured coffee into a gutful of Pepsi, he said, "Is this Llewellyn girl knocked up?"

"No."

"You're too young for marriage," he said. "My age—that's when it's time to settle down."

He said this for Britney's benefit. He would never

marry her. Later, she would remember this as a promise. When he ditched her, the fight would be more epic than *Godzilla vs. Mothra.*

Sooner or later, one of his hotties, during a bad mood swing, will maim or kill him. I believe that on some deep level, even if subconsciously, he knows this.

"What's that on your forehead?" Britney asked.

"Band-Aid."

"You fall down drunk or something?"

"Something."

"You in a fight?"

"No. It's an employment-related fork wound."

"A what?"

"A flipped fork flicked my forehead."

Alliteration seems to offend people. Her expression soured. "What kind of shit are you on?"

"I'm fully amped on caffeine," I admitted.

"Caffeine, my ass."

"Pepsi and coffee and No-Doz. And chocolate. Chocolate contains caffeine. I had some chocolate-chip cookies. Chocolate doughnuts."

My father said, "Saturday's not good. We can't make Saturday. We've got other plans we can't cancel."

"That's all right," I said. "I understand."

"I wish you'd have told us earlier."

"No problem. I didn't expect you'd be able to make it."

"What kind of dork," Britney wondered, "announces his wedding just three days before the ceremony?"

"Go easy," my father advised her.

Her psychological engine didn't have a go-easy gear. "Well, damn it, he's such a freak."

"That's really not helpful," my father admonished her, but in a honeyed tone.

"Well, it's true," she insisted. "Like we haven't talked about it maybe three dozen times. He doesn't have a car, he lives in a garage—"

"Above a garage," I corrected.

"—he wears the same thing every day, he's friends with every loser geek in town, he's a wannabe cop like a water boy hanging around a football team, and he's just a major freak—"

"You won't get an argument from me," I said.

"—such a major freak, the way he comes in here on some shit or other, talking about weddings and 'employment-related fork wounds.' Give me a break."

"I'm a freak," I said sincerely. "I acknowledge it, accept it. There's no reason to argue. Peace."

My father couldn't quite fake a convincing note of sincerity when he said, "Don't say that. You're not a freak."

He doesn't know about my supernatural gift. At the age of seven, when my previously weak and inconstant sixth sense grew in power and reliability, I didn't go to him for counsel.

I hid my difference from him in part because I expected him to harass me into picking winning lottery numbers, which I can't do. I figured he'd parade me before the media, parlay my gift into a TV show, or even sell shares in me to speculators willing to finance an infomercial and a psychic-by-the-minute 900 number.

Getting off the stool, I said, "I think now maybe I know why I came here."

As I started toward the kitchen door, my father followed me. "I really wish you'd picked another Saturday."

Turning to face him, I said, "I think I came here because I was afraid to go to my mother."

Britney stepped behind my father, pressing her nearly naked body against him. She put her arms around him, hands flat on his chest. He made no attempt to pull away from her.

"There's something I'm blocking on," I said, more to myself than to either of them. "Something I desperately need to know . . . or need to do. And somehow, some way, it's related to Mother. Somehow she has the answer."

"Answers?" he said incredulously. "You know perfectly well that your mother's about the last place to find answers."

Smiling wickedly at me over my father's left shoulder, Britney slid her hands slowly up and down his muscled chest and drum-flat belly.

"Sit down," my father said. "I'll pour you another coffee. If you have a problem you need to talk about, then let's talk."

Britney's right hand moved low on his belly, fingertips teasing under the waistband of his hip-slung shorts.

He wanted me to see the desire that he inspired in this lush young woman. He had a weak man's pride in his status as a stud, and this pride was so fierce that it filled his mind, leaving him quite incapable of recognizing his son's humiliation.

"Yesterday was the anniversary of Gladys Presley's death," I said. "Her son wept uncontrollably for days after losing her, and he grieved openly for a year."

A faint frown made the shallowest of furrows in my father's Botoxed forehead, but Britney was too engrossed in her game to be listening to me with full attention. Her eyes glittered with what might have been mockery or triumph as her right hand slowly slipped deeper in his khaki shorts.

"He loved his dad, too. Tomorrow is the anniversary of Elvis's own death. I think I'll try to look him up and tell him how lucky he was from the very day he was born."

I walked out of the kitchen, out of the house.

He didn't come after me. I hadn't expected that he would.

CHAPTER 52

MY MOTHER LIVES IN A LOVELY VICtorian house in the historical district of Pico Mundo. My father had inherited it from his parents.

In the divorce, she received this gracious residence, its contents, and substantial alimony with a cost-of-living adjustment. Because she has never remarried and most likely never will, her alimony will be a lifetime benefit.

Generosity is not my father's first or second—or last—impulse. He settled a comfortable lifestyle on her solely because he feared her. Although he resented having to share his monthly income from the trust, he didn't have the courage even to negotiate with her through attorneys. She received pretty much everything that she demanded.

He paid for his safety and for a new chance at happiness (as he defines it). And he left me behind when I was one year old.

Before I rang the doorbell, I brushed my hand across the porch swing to confirm that it was clean. She could sit on the swing, and I would sit on the porch railing while we talked.

We meet always in the open air. I had promised

myself that I would never enter that house again, even if I should outlive her.

After I'd rung the bell twice without a response, I went around the house to the backyard.

The property is deep. A pair of immense California live oaks stand immediately behind the house, together casting shade that is all but complete. Farther toward the back of the lot, sun falls unfiltered, allowing a rose garden.

My mother was at work among the roses. Like a lady of another era, she wore a yellow sundress and a matching sunbonnet.

Although the wide brim of the hat shaded her face, I could see that her exceptional beauty had not been tarnished during the four months since I last visited her.

She had married my father when she was nineteen and he was twenty-four. She is forty now, but she might pass for thirty.

Photographs taken on her wedding day reveal a nineteen-year-old who looked sixteen, breathtakingly lovely, shockingly tender to be a bride. None of my father's subsequent conquests have matched her beauty.

Even now, when she is forty, if she were in a room with Britney, she in her sundress and Britney in that thong bikini, most men would be drawn to her first. And if she were in a mood to rule the moment, she would enchant them such that they would think she was the only woman among them.

I drew near to her before she realized that she was no longer alone. She raised her attention from the flowers, stood taller, and for a moment blinked at me as though I were a heat mirage.

Then: "Odd, you sweet boy, you must have been a

cat in another life, to sneak across all that yard."

I could summon only the ghost of a smile. "Hello, Mom. You look wonderful."

She requires compliments; but in fact she never looks less than wonderful.

If she had been a stranger, I might have found her to be even lovelier. For me, our shared history diminishes her radiance.

"Come here, sweetie, look at these fabulous blooms."

I entered the gallery of roses, where a carpet of decomposed granite held down the dust and crunched underfoot.

Some flowers offered sun-pricked petals of blood in bursting sprays. Others were bowls of orange fire, bright cups of yellow onyx brimming with summer sunshine. Pink, purple, peach—the garden was perpetually decorated for a party.

My mother kissed me on the cheek. Her lips were not cold, as I always expect them to be.

Naming the variety, she said, "This is the John F. Kennedy rose. Isn't it exquisite?"

With one hand, she gently lifted a mature bloom so heavy that its head was bowed on its bent stem.

As Mojave-white as sun-bleached bone, with a faint undertone of green, these large petals weren't delicate but remarkably thick and smooth.

"They look as if they're molded from wax," I said.

"Exactly. They're perfection, aren't they, dear? I love all my roses, but these more than any other."

Not merely because this rose was her favorite, I liked it *less* than the others. Its perfection struck me as artificial. The sensuous folds of its labial petals promised mystery and satisfaction in its hidden center, but this seemed to be a false promise, for its wintry whiteness and waxy rigidity—and lack of fragrance—suggested neither purity nor passion, but death.

"This one's for you," she said, withdrawing a small pair of rose snips from a pocket of her sundress.

"No, don't cut it. Let it grow. It'll be wasted on me."

"Nonsense. You must give it to that girl of yours. If properly presented, a single rose can express a suitor's feelings more clearly than a bouquet."

She snipped off eight inches of stem with the bloom.

I held the flower not far below its receptacle, pinching the stem with thumb and forefinger, between the highest pair of thorns.

Glancing at my wristwatch, I saw that the lulling sun and the perfumed flowers only made time *seem* to pass lazily, when in fact it raced away. Robertson's kill buddy might even now be driving to his rendezvous with infamy.

Moving along the rosarium with a queenly grace and a smile of royal beneficence, admiring the nodding heads of her colorful subjects, my mother said, "I'm so glad you came to visit, dear. What is the occasion?"

At her side yet half a step behind her, I said, "I don't know exactly. I've got this problem—"

"We allow no problems here," she said in a tone of gentle remonstration. "From the front walk to the back fence, this house and its grounds are a worry-free zone."

Aware of the risks, I had nonetheless led us into dangerous territory. The decomposed granite under my feet might as well have been sucking quicksand.

I didn't know how else to proceed. I didn't have time to play our game by her rules.

"There's something I need to remember or something I should do," I told her, "but I'm blocked on it.

Intuition brought me here because . . . I think somehow you can help me figure out what I've overlooked."

To her, my words could have been barely more comprehensible than gibberish. Like my father, she knows nothing of my supernatural gift.

As a young child, I had realized that if I complicated her life with the truth of my condition, the strain of this knowledge would be the death of her. Or the death of me.

Always, she has sought a life utterly without stress, without contention. She acknowledges no duty to another, no responsibility for anyone but herself.

She would never call this selfishness. To her it's self-defense, for she finds the world enormously more demanding than she is able to tolerate.

If she fully embraced life with all its conflicts, she would suffer a breakdown. Consequently, she manages the world with all the cold calculation of a ruthless autocrat, and preserves her precarious sanity by spinning around herself a cocoon of indifference.

"Maybe if we could just talk for a while," I said. "Maybe then I could figure out why I came here, why I thought you could help me."

Her mood can shift in an instant. The lady of the roses was too frail to handle this challenge, and that sunny persona retreated to make way for an angry goddess.

My mother regarded me with pinched eyes, her lips compressed and bloodless, as if with only a fierce look she could send me away.

In ordinary circumstances, that look alone would indeed have dispatched me.

A sun of nuclear ferocity rose toward its apex, however, rapidly bringing us nearer to the hour of the gun. I dared not return to the hot streets of Pico Mundo without a name or a purpose that would focus my psychic magnetism.

When she realized that I would not immediately leave her to the comfort of her roses, she spoke in a voice as cold and brittle as ice: "He was shot in the head, you know."

This statement mystified me, yet it seemed to have an uncanny connection to the approaching atrocity that I hoped to prevent.

"Who?" I asked.

"John F. Kennedy." She indicated the namesake rose. "They shot him in the head and blew his brains out."

"Mother," I said, though I seldom use that word in conversation with her, "this is different. You've got to help me this time. People will die if you don't."

Perhaps that was the worst thing that I could have said. She didn't possess the emotional capacity to assume responsibility for the lives of others.

She seized the rose that she had cut for me, gripped it by the bloom and tore it out of my hand.

Because I failed to release the rose quickly enough, the stem ripped between my fingers, and a thorn pierced the pad of my thumb, broke off in the flesh.

She crushed the bloom and threw it on the ground. She turned away from me and strode toward the house.

I would not relent. I caught up with her, moved at her side, pleading for a few minutes of conversation that might clarify my thoughts and help me understand why I had come here, of all places, at this mortal hour.

She hurried, and I hurried with her. By the time she reached the steps to the back porch, she had broken into a run, the skirt of her sundress rustling like wings, one hand on her bonnet to hold it on her head.

The screen door slammed behind her as she disappeared into the house. I stopped on the porch, reluctant to go farther.

Although I regretted the need to harass her, I felt harassed myself, and desperate.

Calling to her through the screen, I said, "I'm not going away. I can't this time. I have nowhere to go."

She didn't answer me. Beyond the screen door, a curtained kitchen lay in shadows, too still to be harboring my tormented mother. She'd gone deeper into the house.

"I'll be here on the porch," I shouted. "I'll be waiting right here. All day if I have to."

Heart hammering, I sat on the porch floor, my feet on the top step, facing away from the kitchen door.

Later, I would realize that I must have come to her house with the subconscious intention of triggering precisely this response and driving her quickly to her ultimate defense against responsibility. The gun.

At that moment, however, confusion was my companion, and clarity seemed far beyond my reach.

CHAPTER 53

THE SHANK OF THE THORN PROTRUDED from my thumb. I plucked it free, but still the bleeding puncture burned as if contaminated by an acid.

To a shameful degree, sitting there on my mother's porch steps, I felt sorry for myself, as though it had been not a single thorn but a crown's worth.

As a child, when I had a toothache, I could expect no maternal pampering. My mother always called my father or a neighbor to take me to the dentist, while she retreated to her bedroom and locked her door. She sought refuge there for a day or two, until she felt certain I would have no lingering complaint that she might need to address.

The slightest fever or sore throat that troubled me was a crisis with which she could not deal. At seven, afflicted by appendicitis, I collapsed at school and was rushed from there to the hospital; had my condition deteriorated at home, she might have left me to die in my room, while she occupied herself with the soothing books and the music and the other genteel interests with which she determinedly fashioned her private *perfecto mundo*, her "perfect world."

My emotional needs, my fears and joys, my doubts and hopes, my miseries and anxieties were mine to explore or resolve without her counsel or sympathy. We spoke only of those things that did not disturb her or make her feel obliged to offer guidance.

For sixteen years we shared a house as though we lived not in the same world but in parallel dimensions that rarely intersected. The chief characteristics of my childhood were an aching loneliness and the daily struggle to avoid a bleakness of spirit that unrelieved loneliness can foment.

On those grim occasions when events had forced our parallel worlds to intersect in crises that my mother could not tolerate and from which she could not easily withdraw, she reliably resorted to the same instrument of control. The gun. The terror of those dark encounters and the subsequent guilt that racked me made loneliness preferable to any contact that distressed her.

Now, pressing thumb and forefinger tight together to stop the bleeding, I heard the twang of the spring on the screen door.

I couldn't bear to turn and look at her. The old ritual would play out soon enough.

Behind me, she said, "Just go."

Gazing into the complexity of shadows cast by the oaks, to the bright rose garden beyond, I said, "I can't. Not this time."

I checked my watch—11:32. My tension could not have wound any tighter, minute by minute, if this had been a bomb clock on my wrist.

Her voice had grown flat and strained under the weight of the burden that I'd placed upon her, the burden of simple human kindness and caring, which she could not carry. "I won't put up with this."

"I know. But there's something . . . I'm not sure what . . . something you can do to help me."

She sat beside me at the head of the porch steps. She held the pistol in both hands, aimed for the moment at the oak-shaded yard.

She engaged in no fakery. The pistol was loaded.

"I won't live this way," she said. "I won't. I can't. People always wanting things, sucking away my blood. All of you—wanting, wanting, greedy, insatiable. Your need . . . it's like a suit of iron to me, the weight, like being buried alive."

Not in years—perhaps never—had I pressed her as hard as I did on that fateful Wednesday: "The crazy thing is, Mother, after more than twenty years of this crap, down at the bottom of my heart, where it ought to be the darkest, I think there's still this spark of love for you. It may be pity, I'm not sure, but it hurts enough to be love."

She doesn't want love from me or anyone. She doesn't have it to give in return. She doesn't believe in love. She is *afraid* to believe in it and the demands that come with it. She wants only undemanding congeniality, only relationships that require less than lip service to be sustained. Her perfect world has a population of one, and if she does not love herself, she has at least the tenderest affection for herself and craves her own company when she must be with others.

My uncertain declaration of love inspired her to turn the gun upon herself. She pressed the muzzle against her throat, angling it slightly toward her chin, the better to blow out her brains.

With hard words and cold indifference, she can turn away anyone she chooses, but sometimes those weapons have not been sufficiently effective in our turbulent relationship. Even though she doesn't feel it, she recognizes the existence of a special bond between mother and child, and she knows that sometimes it won't be broken by any but the cruelest measures.

"You want to pull the trigger for me?" she asked.

As I always do, I looked away. As if I had inhaled the shade of the oaks along with the air, as if my lungs passed it into my blood, I felt a cold shadow arise in the chambers of my heart.

As she always does when I avert my eyes, she said, "Look at me, *look at me*, or I'll gut-shoot myself and die slow and screaming right here in front of you."

Sickened, trembling, I gave her the attention that she wanted.

"You might as well pull the trigger yourself, you little shit. It's no different than making me pull it."

I couldn't count—and didn't care to remember—how often I had heard this challenge before.

My mother is insane. Psychologists might use an array of more specific and less judgmental terms, but in the *Dictionary of Odd*, her behavior is the definition of insanity.

I have been told that she wasn't always like this. As a child, she had been sweet, playful, affectionate.

The terrible change occurred when she was sixteen. She began to experience sudden mood swings. The sweetness was supplanted by an unrelenting, simmering anger that she could best control when she was alone.

Therapy and a series of medications failed to restore her former good nature. When, at eighteen, she rejected further treatment, no one insisted that she continue with psychotherapy or drugs, because at that time she hadn't been as dysfunctional, as solipsistic, and as threatening as she became by her early twenties.

When my father met her, she was just moody enough and dangerous enough to infatuate him. As she grew worse, he bailed.

She has never been institutionalized because her self-control is excellent when she's not being challenged to interact with others beyond her capacity. She limits all threats of violence to suicide and occasionally to me, presenting a charming or at least rational face to the world.

Because she has a comfortable income without the need to work and because she prefers life as a recluse, her true condition is not widely recognized in Pico Mundo.

Her exceptional beauty also helps her to keep her secrets. Most people tend to think the best of those who are blessed with beauty; we have difficulty imagining that physical perfection can conceal twisted emotions or a damaged mind.

Her voice grew raw and more confrontational: "I curse the night I let your idiot father squirt you into me."

This didn't shock me. I'd heard it before, and worse.

She said, "I should've had you scraped out of me and thrown in the garbage. But what would I have gotten from the divorce then? You were the ticket."

When I look at my mother in this condition, I don't see hatred in her, but anguish and desperation and even terror. I can't imagine the pain and the horror of being her.

I take solace only in the knowledge that when she is alone, when she is not challenged to give anything of herself, she is content if not happy. I want her to be at least content.

She said, "Either stop sucking my blood or pull the trigger, you little shit."

One of my most vivid early memories is of a rainy night in January when I was five years old and suffering with influenza. When not coughing, I cried for attention and relief, and my mother was unable to find a corner of the house in which she could entirely escape the sound of my misery.

She came to my room and stretched out beside me on the bed, as any mother might lie down to comfort a stricken child, but she came with the gun. Her threats to kill herself always earned my silence, my obedience, my grant of absolution from her parental obligations.

That night, I swallowed my misery as best I could and stifled my tears, but I couldn't wish away my sore and inflamed throat. To her, my coughing was a demand for mothering, and its persistence brought her to an emotional precipice.

When the threat of suicide didn't silence my cough, she put the muzzle of the gun to my right eye. She encouraged me to try to see the shiny point of the bullet deep in that narrow dark passage.

We were a long time there together, with the rain beating on my bedroom windows. I have known much terror since, but none as pure as what I knew that night.

From the perspective of a twenty-year-old, I don't believe that she would have killed me then or that she ever will. Were she to harm me—or anyone—she would doom herself to exactly the interaction with other people that she most dreads. She knows that they would want answers and explanations from her. They would want truth and remorse and justice. They would want far too much, and they would never stop wanting.

I didn't know if here on the porch steps she would turn the gun on me again, and I didn't know exactly how I would react if she did. I had come seeking a confrontation that would enlighten me, though I didn't understand what it needed to be or what I could learn from it that would help me to find Robertson's collaborator.

Then she lowered the gun from her throat to her left breast, as she always does, for the symbolism of a bullet through the brain will not as powerfully affect any mother's son as will the symbolism of a shot through the heart.

"If you won't leave me alone, if you won't stop forever sucking and *sucking* on me, draining me like a leech, then for God's sake pull the trigger, give me some peace."

Into my mind's eye came the wound in Robertson's chest, as it had plagued me for nearly twelve hours.

I tried to drown that insistent image in the swamp of memory from which it had risen. It is a deep swamp, filled with much that stubbornly will not remain submerged.

Suddenly I realized that *this* was why I had come here: to force my mother to enact the hateful ritual of threatened suicide that was at the core of our relationship, to be confronted with the sight of a pistol pressed to her breast, to turn away as I always do, to hear her *command* my attention . . . and then, sickened and trembling, to find the nerve to look.

The previous night, in my bathroom, I hadn't been strong enough to examine Robertson's chest wound.

At the time, I'd sensed that something was strange about it, that something might be learned from it. Yet, nauseated, I had averted my eyes and rebuttoned his shirt.

Thrusting the pistol toward me, grip-first, my mother angrily insisted, "Come on, you ungrateful shit, take it, take it, shoot me and get it over with *or leave me alone*!"

Eleven-thirty-five, according to my wristwatch.

Her voice had grown as vicious and demented as ever it gets: "I dreamed and dreamed that you would be born dead."

Shakily, I rose to my feet and carefully descended the porch steps.

Behind me, she wielded the knife of alienation as only she can cut with it: "The whole time I carried you, I thought you were dead inside me, dead and rotting."

The sun, nurturing mother of the earth, poured a scalding milk upon the day, boiling some of the blue from the sky and leaving the heavens faded. Even the oak shadows now throbbed with heat, and as I walked away from my mother, I was so hot with shame that I would not have been surprised if the grass had burst into fire under my feet.

"Dead inside me," she repeated. "Month after unending month, I felt your rotting fetus festering in my belly, spreading poison through my body."

At the corner of the house I stopped, turned, and looked at her for what I suspected might be the last time.

She had descended the steps but had not followed me. Her right arm hung slackly at her side, the gun aimed at the ground.

I had not asked to be born. Only to be loved.

"I have nothing to give," she said. "Do you hear me? Nothing, nothing. You poisoned me, you filled me with pus and dead-baby rot, and I'm ruined now."

Turning my back on her for what felt like forever, I hurried along the side of the house toward the street.

Given my heritage and the ordeal of my childhood, I sometimes wonder why I myself am not insane. Maybe I am.

CHAPTER 54

DRIVING FASTER THAN THE LAW ALLOWED to the outskirts of Pico Mundo, I tried but failed to banish from my mind all thoughts of my mother's mother, Granny Sugars.

My mother and my grandmother exist in widely separated kingdoms of my mind, in sovereign nations of memory that have no trade with each other. Because I loved Pearl Sugars, I had always been loath to think of her in context with her demented daughter.

Considering them together raised terrible questions to which I had long resisted seeking answers.

Pearl Sugars knew that her daughter was mentally unstable, if not unbalanced, and that she had gone off medication at eighteen. She must have known, as well, that pregnancy and the responsibility of child-rearing would stress my fragile mother to the breaking point.

Yet she did not interfere on my behalf.

For one thing, she feared her daughter. I had seen evidence of this on numerous occasions. My mother's abrupt mood swings and hot temper cowed my grandmother even though she was not intimidated by anyone else and would not hesitate to take a swing at a threatening man twice her size.

Besides, Pearl Sugars liked her rootless life too much

to settle down and raise a grandchild. Wanderlust, the lure of rich card games in fabled cities—Las Vegas, Reno, Phoenix, Albuquerque, Dallas, San Antonio, New Orleans, Memphis—a need for adventure and excitement kept her away from Pico Mundo more than half the year.

In her defense, Granny Sugars could not have imagined either the intensity or the relentless nature of my mother's cruelty to me. She didn't know about the gun and the threats that shaped my childhood.

As I write this, no one knows except me and my mother. Although Stormy has been told all my other secrets, I withheld this one from even her. Only when Little Ozzie reads this manuscript, which I have written at his insistence, will I have shared entirely what my mother is to me and what I am to her.

Guilt and shame have, until now, kept me silent on this issue. I am old enough, even if just twenty, to know that I have no logical reason to feel either guilt or shame, that I was the victim, not the victimizer. Yet I've been so long marinated in both emotions that they will forever flavor me.

When I give this script to Ozzie, I will burn with humiliation. After he has read it, I will cover my face, abashed, when he speaks of these portions of the narrative.

Infected minds to their deaf pillows will discharge their secrets.

Shakespeare. *MacBeth*, Act 5, Scene 1.

That literary allusion is included here not merely to please you, Ozzie. There's bitter truth in it that resonates with me. My mother had infected my mind with such a potent virus that I had not been able to confess my shameful victimization even to my pillow, but carried it into sleep each night, unpurged.

As for Granny Sugars: I must now wonder whether her peripatetic lifestyle and her frequent absences, combined with her gambling and restless nature, contributed materially to my mother's psychological problems.

Worse, I cannot avoid considering that my mother's sickness might not be the result of inadequate nurturing, but might entirely be the consequence of genetics. Perhaps Pearl Sugars suffered from a milder form of the same psychosis, which expressed itself in more appealing ways than did my mother's.

Mother's hermetic impulse might have been an inversion of my grandmother's wanderlust. My mother's need for financial security, won at the expense of a pregnancy that repulsed her, might be my grandmother's gambling fever turned inside out.

This would suggest that much—though not all—of what I loved about Granny Sugars was but a different facet of the same mental condition that made my mother such a terror. This disturbs me for reasons I can understand but also for reasons that I suspect will not be clear to me until I've lived another twenty years, if I do.

When I was sixteen, Pearl Sugars asked me to come on the road with her. By then, I had become what I am: a seer of the dead with limitations, with responsibilities that I must fulfill. I had no choice but to decline her offer. If circumstances had allowed me to travel with her from game to game, adventure to adventure, the stresses of daily life and constant contact might have revealed a different and less appealing woman from the one I thought I knew.

I must believe that Granny Sugars had the capacity for genuine love that my mother lacks, and must believe that she did indeed love me. If these two things are not true, then my childhood will have been an unrelieved wasteland.

Having failed to banish these troubling thoughts on the drive out of Pico Mundo, I arrived at the Church of the Whispering Comet in a mood that matched the ambience of dead palm trees, sun-blasted landscape, and abandoned buildings on the slide to ruin.

I parked in front of the Quonset hut where the three coyotes had encircled me. They weren't in evidence.

They are generally night hunters. In the noonday heat, they shelter in cool dark dens.

The dead prostitute, charmer of coyotes, was not to be seen, either. I hoped that she had found her way out of this world, but I doubted that my fumbling counsel and platitudes had convinced her to move on.

From among the items in the bottom of the plastic shopping bag that served as my suitcase, I withdrew the flashlight, the scissors, and the package of foil-wrapped moist towelettes.

In my apartment, when I packed the bag, the towelettes had seemed to be a peculiar inclusion, the scissors even more peculiar. Yet subconsciously I must have known exactly why I would need them.

We are not strangers to ourselves; we only try to be.

When I got out of the car, the fierce heat of the Mojave was matched by its stillness, a nearly perfect silence found perhaps nowhere else but in a dioramic snow scene sealed in Lucite.

My watch revealed that time had not stood still—11:57.

Two desiccated brown phoenix palms cast frond shadows across the dusty ground in front of the Quonset hut, as if paving the way not for me but for an overdue messiah. I had not returned to raise the dead, only to examine him.

When I stepped inside, I felt as if I had cast my lot with Shadrach, Meshach, and Abednego in the furnace of Nebuchadnezzar, though this was a heat, laced with an unspeakable scent, from which even an angel could not spare me.

Alkaline-white desert light seared through the portal-style windows, but they were so small and set so wide apart that I still needed the flashlight.

I followed the littered hallway to the fourth door. I went into the pink room, once a den of profitable fornication, now a slow-cook crematorium.

CHAPTER 55

NO CURIOUS PEOPLE OR CARRION EATERS had been here in my absence. The corpse lay where I had left it, one end of the shroud open, one shod foot exposed, otherwise wrapped in the white bed-sheet.

The hot night and the blistering morning had facilitated and accelerated decomposition. The stench was much worse here than in the rest of the hut.

The suffocating heat and the stink had the power of two quick punches to the gut. I backed quickly out of the room, into the hall, simultaneously gasping for a cleaner breath and struggling to repress the urge to vomit.

Although I hadn't brought the foil-sealed towelettes for this purpose, I ripped open one of them and tore two strips from it. The moistened paper had a lemony fragrance. I rolled the saturated strips into dripping wads and plugged my nostrils with them.

Breathing through my mouth, I couldn't smell the decomposing corpse. When I reentered the room, I gagged again, anyway.

I could have cut the shoelace that secured the top of the shroud—the one at the foot had broken the previous night—and rolled the body out of its wrapping. The thought of the dead man tumbling across the floor, as if animated again, convinced me to approach the problem with a different solution.

Reluctantly, I knelt at the head of the corpse. I propped the flashlight against it in such a way as to best illuminate my work.

I snipped the shoelace and tossed it aside. The scissors were sharp enough to trim through all three layers of rolled sheeting at once. I cut with patience and care, repulsed by the possibility of gouging the dead man.

As the fabric fell away to both sides of the body, the face came into view first. I realized too late that if I had started from the bottom, I would have had to open the shroud only as far as the neck, to see his wound, and could have avoided this hideous sight.

Time and the ungodly heat had done their nasty work. The face—upside down to me—was bloated, darker than it had been when last I had seen it, and marbled with green. The mouth had sagged open. Thin cataracts of milky fluid had formed over both eyes, although I could still discern the delineation between the whites and irises.

As I reached across the dead man's face to cut the shroud away from his chest, he licked my wrist.

I cried out in shock and disgust, reared back, and dropped the scissors.

From the cadaver's sagging mouth exploded a squirming black mass, a creature so strange in this context that I didn't realize what it must be until it fully extracted itself. On Robertson's dead face, the thing reared up on its four back legs and raked the air with its forelegs. Tarantula.

Moving too quickly to give it a chance to bite, I backhanded the spider. It tumbled across the floor, sprang to its feet, and scurried into a far corner.

When I picked up the fallen scissors, my hand shook so badly that I gave the air a vigorous trimming before I was able to steady myself.

Concerned that more critters might have crawled into the bottom of the shroud to explore the fragrant contents, I resumed my work on the sheet with nervous care. I exposed the body to the waist without encountering another eight-legged forager.

In my startled reaction to the tarantula, I had blown the plug out of my right nostril. When the residue of lemony fluid evaporated, I could smell the body again, though not at full strength because I continued to breathe through my mouth.

Glancing toward the corner into which the spider had retreated, I discovered that it wasn't there anymore.

I searched anxiously for a moment. Then, in spite of the poor light, I saw the hairy beast just to the left of the corner, three feet off the floor, slowly ascending the pink wall.

Too shaky and too pressed for time to unbutton the dead man's shirt as I'd done in my apartment, I tore it open, popping buttons. One of them snapped off my face, and the others bounced across the floor.

When I pressed from my mind the inhibiting image of my mother with a pistol to her breast, I was able to focus the flashlight on the wound. Steeling myself to examine it closely, I saw why it had seemed strange to me.

I propped the flashlight against the body again and tore open three foil-wrapped towelettes. I sandwiched them into one thick pad and gently swabbed away the obscuring custardy ooze that had seeped from the wound.

The bullet had pierced a tattoo on Robertson's chest,

directly over his heart. This black rectangle was the same size and shape as the meditation card that I had found in his wallet. In the center of the rectangle were three red hieroglyphs.

Bleary-eyed, nervous, strung out on caffeine, I couldn't quickly make sense of the design when it was upside down.

As I shifted from behind Robertson's head to his side, those dead eyes seemed to move, tracking me under the semiopaque, milky cataracts.

When I checked on the tarantula, it had vanished from the farther wall. With the flashlight, I located it on the ceiling, working its way toward me. It froze in the direct light.

I turned the beam on the tattoo and discovered that the three red hieroglyphs were actually three letters of the alphabet in a script with flourishes. *F . . . O . . .* The third had been partially torn away by the bullet, but I was certain that it had been an *L*.

FOL. Not a word. An acronym. Thanks to Shamus Cocobolo, I knew what it meant: *Father of Lies*.

Robertson had worn the name of his dark lord over his heart.

Three letters: *FOL*. Three others, encountered elsewhere, and recently . . .

Suddenly I could see Officer Simon Varner vividly in memory: behind the wheel of the department cruiser in the parking lot at the bowling alley, leaning toward the open window, his face sweet enough to qualify him as the host of a children's TV program, his heavy-lidded eyes like those of a sleepy bear, his burly forearm resting on the driver's door, the "gang tattoo" that he claimed embarrassed him. Nothing as elaborate as Robertson's tattoo, no similarity of style whatsoever. No black rectangle inlaid with fancy red script. Just another acronym in black block letters: *D* . . . something. Maybe *DOP*.

Did Officer Simon Varner, of the Pico Mundo Police Department, wear the name of this same master on his left arm?

If Robertson's tattoo marked him with one of the devil's many names, then Simon Varner's put him in the same club.

Names for the devil raced through my mind: Satan, Lucifer, Old Scratch, Beelzebub, Father of Evil, His Satanic Majesty, Apollyon, Belial . . .

I couldn't think of the words that would explain the acronym on Varner's arm, but I had no doubt that I had identified Robertson's kill buddy.

At the bowling alley, there had been no bodachs around Varner as there had been, at times, around Robertson. If I'd seen him with bodachs in attendance, I might have realized what a monster he was.

Because they might take fingerprints, I hurriedly gathered the scraps of foil that had wrapped the towelettes and shoved them in a pocket of my jeans. I grabbed the scissors, stood, swept the ceiling with the flashlight, and found the tarantula directly overhead.

Tarantulas are timid. They do not stalk human beings.

I sprinted from the room, heard the spider drop to the floor with a soft but solid fleshy sound, slammed the door between us, and wiped prints off the knob with the tail of my T-shirt, then off the front door, too, as I left.

Because tarantulas are timid and because I believe there are no coincidences, I raced to the Chevy, threw the scissors and flashlight in the shopping bag, started the engine, and stomped the accelerator. I exited the grounds of the Church of the Whispering Comet with a shriek of tortured rubber, kicking up a spray of sand and crumbled blacktop, eager to reach the state highway before being surrounded by legions of tarantulas, an army of coyotes, and a slithering swarm of rattlesnakes all functioning in concert.

CHAPTER 56

NOT *DOP. POD.* PRINCE OF DARKNESS. THE source of Simon Varner's tattooed acronym, POD, occurred to me as I crossed the town line, returning to Pico Mundo.

Costumed satanists performing weird rituals with an obscenely decorated chalice would be regarded by most people as being less well intentioned but also markedly sillier than the elaborately fur-hatted members of a men's lodge called the Fraternal Order of Hedgehogs. Men who dress up to look *bad* are as suspect of being nerds as are those men with weed-whacker haircuts, tortoiseshell eyeglasses, pants worn five inches above the navel and three inches above the shoes, and bumper stickers that say JAR JAR BINKS RULES.

If I would have been inclined to dismiss them as nerds *playing* at evil, that inclination had not held past the moment when I found the Rubbermaid-boxed souvenirs in the freezer.

Now that I suspected the identity of Robertson's collaborator, I trusted my supernatural gift to lead me to him. Considering that in the grip of psychic magnetism—Stormy sometimes shortens it to PM syndrome or PMS—I occasionally make abrupt turns, I drove with as much speed as seemed prudent.

Under the influence of PMS, I zone out to some extent, and try to think only about the object of my interest—in this case, Varner—rather than about where I am at any moment or about where I might be going. I'll know where I'm going when I get there.

In this state, my conscious mind relaxes, and random thoughts pop into it almost as often as I make seemingly random turns in search of my quarry. This time, one of those thoughts involved my mother's older sister, Cymry, whom I have never met.

According to my mother, Cymry is married to a Czechoslovakian whose first name is Dobb. My father says Cymry has never married.

Neither of my parents has a history of reliability. In this case, however, I suspect that my father is telling the truth and that I have no uncle of either Czechoslovakian or any other heritage.

My father says that Cymry is a freak, but he will say no more. His assertion infuriates my mother, who denies Cymry's freakhood and calls her a gift from God.

This is an odd statement on my mother's part, considering that she lives her life as if with the firm conviction that God does not exist.

The first time that I asked Granny Sugars about her mysterious firstborn, she dissolved in tears. I had never seen her cry before. The next day, still red-eyed, she had hit the road again in pursuit of faraway poker games.

The second time I asked her about Cymry, she became angry with me for pursuing the issue. I had never before seen her angry. Then she became cold and distant. She had never previously been that way with me, and her behavior reminded me too much of my mother.

Thereafter, I never asked about Cymry.

I suspect that in an institution somewhere, managed with drugs and humane restraints, I have an aunt who is at least a little like me. I suspect that as a child she didn't conceal her special gift as I did.

This is probably why Granny Sugars, with all her poker winnings, left no estate of which I'm aware. I think she funded a trust to pay for Cymry's care.

Over the years, my father has let slip certain clues leading me to speculate that Cymry's sixth sense, whatever strange talents it may encompass, is accompanied by *physical* mutation. I think she scared people not just because of things that she said but also because of how she looked.

More often than not, a baby born with one mutation will, in fact, have two or more. Ozzie says—and apparently not in his role as a writer of fiction—that one in every eighty-eight thousand babies is born with a sixth finger on one hand, as he was. Hundreds if not thousands of them should be walking the streets of America, yet how many six-fingered hands have you seen on adults? You don't encounter them because most of those babies are born with other and more terrible deformities that cause them to die in early infancy.

Those six-fingered children fortunate enough to be robustly healthy will usually receive surgery if the superfluous digit can be removed without affecting the function of the hand. They walk among us, Little Ozzie says, passing for five-fingered "mundanes."

I think all this is true, because Ozzie is proud of his sixth finger and enjoys collecting lore on what he calls "the natural-born pickpockets who are members of my superior breed." He says that his second mutation is his ability to write well and swiftly, turning out enthusiastically received books at a prodigious pace.

I dream of Aunt Cymry from time to time. These are not prophetic dreams. They are full of yearning. And sadness.

Now, at 12:21, *day*dreaming about Cymry yet acutely and nervously aware of precious minutes passing, fully in the PMS zone, I expected to find Officer Simon Varner in the vicinity of either the bowling alley or the multiplex theater where the dog movie would unreel shortly after one o'clock. Instead, I was led unexpectedly to the Green Moon Mall.

What I saw was unusual for a Wednesday in summer: a packed parking lot. The giant banner reminded me that the mall merchants' annual summer sale had begun at ten o'clock this morning and would continue through the weekend.

What a crowd.

CHAPTER 57

A GALAXY OF SUNS BLAZED ON THE WINDshields of the serried cars and SUVs, a lightquake that shocked my bloodshot eyes and forced me to squint.

Three-story department stores anchored the north and south ends of the mall. Numerous specialty shops occupied the two levels between those leviathans.

PMS drew me to the department store at the north end. I drove around to the back and parked near a wide descending ramp that led to the subterranean loading docks where trucks delivered merchandise.

Three spaces away stood a black-and-white police cruiser. No cop in sight.

If this was Varner's car, he was already in the mall.

My hands shook. The buttons on my cell phone were small. To get it right, I had to key in the number of Burke & Bailey's twice.

I intended to tell Stormy to leave work immediately, to get out of the mall by the nearest door, to go quickly to her car and drive away fast, drive anywhere, just *drive*.

As the number was ringing, I hung up. She might not at this moment be destined to cross Varner's path, but if I persuaded her to get the hell out of there, she might cross his sights at the instant that he pulled his gun and opened fire.

Her destiny is to be with me forever. We have the card from the fortune-telling machine as proof. It hangs above her bed. Gypsy Mummy had given us, for a single quarter, what that other couple couldn't buy at any price.

Logic argued that if I did nothing, she would be safe. If she changed her plans at my urging, I might be thwarting her destiny and mine. Trust in fate.

My responsibility was not to warn off Stormy but to stop Simon Varner before he was ready to put his plan in action, before he killed *anyone*.

There you have your classic easier-said-than-done. He was a cop, and I wasn't. He carried at least one firearm, and I didn't. Taller than me, stronger than me, trained in every possible method to subdue an aggressive citizen, he enjoyed all the advantages—except a sixth sense.

The gun that had killed Robertson was stashed under the driver's seat. I had put it there the previous night, meaning to dispose of it later.

Leaning forward, I fumbled under my seat, found the weapon, and withdrew it. I felt as if I were holding hands with Death.

After more fumbling, I figured out how to eject the magazine. I counted nine rounds. Bright brass. Loaded nearly to capacity. The only round missing was the one that had put a hole in Robertson's heart.

I shoved the magazine back into the pistol. It clicked in place.

My mother's gun has a safety. A red dot is revealed when the safety is switched off.

This piece appeared to have no comparable feature. Perhaps the safety was built into the trigger, requiring a double pull.

No safety on my heart. It was booming.

I felt as though I were holding hands with death, all right—*my* death.

With the pistol in my lap, I picked up the phone and punched in Chief Porter's private cell number, not his police-department line. The keys seemed to be growing smaller, as if this were a phone Alice had gotten from a hookah-smoking caterpillar, but I entered the seven digits correctly on the first try, and pressed SEND.

Karla Porter answered on the third ring. She said that she was still in the ICU waiting room. She'd been allowed to see the chief on three occasions, for five-minute visits.

"He was awake the last time, but very weak. He knew who I was. He smiled for me. But he's not able to talk much, and not coherently. They're keeping him semisedated to facilitate healing. I don't think he'll be really talking much before tomorrow."

"But he's going to be all right?" I asked.

"That's what they say. And I'm beginning to believe it."

"I love him," I said, and heard my voice break.

"He knows that, Oddie. He loves you, too. You're a son to him."

"Tell him."

"I will."

"I'll call," I promised.

I pressed END and dropped the phone on the passenger's seat.

The chief could not help me. No one could help me. No sad, dead prostitute to quell the killing frenzy of this coyote. Just me.

Intuition told me not to take the pistol. I slid it under the seat again.

When I switched off the engine and got out of the car, the fiery sun was both a hammer and an anvil, forging the world between itself and its reflection.

Psychic magnetism works whether I'm rolling on wheels or afoot. I was drawn to the delivery ramp. I went down into the coolness of the subterranean loading docks.

CHAPTER 58

WITH A LOW CEILING AND ENDLESS GRAY concrete, the mall-employee underground parking garage and loading dock had the bleak and ominous atmosphere of an ancient tomb deep under Egyptian sands, the tomb of a hated pharaoh whose subjects had buried him on the cheap, without glittering gold vessels or ornamentation of any kind.

The elevated dock ran the length of the immense structure, and big trucks were backed up to it at various points. At the department store, two semis at a time could bypass the dock and pull directly into an enormous receiving room.

This place clattered and hummed with activity as the truck crews off-loaded late-arriving sales merchandise and the harried stockroom employees prepped it for delivery to the sales floors after the close of business.

I passed among racks, carts, carousels, bins, boxes, and drums of merchandise, everything from women's party dresses to culinary gadgets to sporting goods. Perfume, swimwear, gourmet chocolates.

Nobody challenged my right to be there, and when I plucked a hardwood baseball bat out of a drum full of them, no one ordered me to put it back.

Another drum contained hollow aluminum bats. They weren't what I wanted. I preferred a bat with heft. I required a certain balance to the instrument. You can better break an arm with a wooden club, more easily shatter a knee.

Maybe I would need the baseball bat, maybe I wouldn't. The fact that it was *there*—and that PMS brought me to it—seemed to suggest that if I didn't avail myself of it, then I would later regret my decision.

The only extracurricular activity I went out for in high school was baseball. As I wrote earlier, I had the best stats on the team, even though I could only play home games.

I'm not out of practice, either. The Pico Mundo Grille has a team. We play other businesses and civic organizations; we whup ass, year after year.

Repeatedly, loaded forklifts and electric carts announced their approach with soft beeps and musical toots. I stepped out of their way but kept moving, though I had no idea where I was going.

In my mind's eye: Simon Varner. Sweet face. Sleepy eyes. *POD* on his left forearm. Find the bastard.

A pair of extra-wide double doors swung into a corridor with a bare concrete floor and painted concrete walls. I hesitated, looked right, turned left.

My stomach churned. I needed antacids.

I needed a bigger bat, a bulletproof vest, and backup, too, but I didn't have them, either. I just kept moving.

Doors led to rooms off the right side of the corridor. Most were labeled. BATHROOMS. SHIPPING OFFICE. MAINTENANCE OFFICE.

Seeking Simon Varner. Sweet face. Prince of Darkness. Feel the pull of him, drawing me forward.

I passed two men, a woman, another man. We smiled and nodded. None of them seemed to wonder where the game was, what the score might be, whose team I was on.

Soon I came to a door marked SECURITY, I stopped. This didn't feel right . . . and yet it did.

When PMS works, I usually *know* that I've arrived. This time I *felt* that I'd arrived. I can't explain the difference, but it was real.

I put my hand on the knob but hesitated.

In my mind, I heard Lysette Rains as she'd spoken to me at the chief's recent barbecue: *I was just a nail technician, and now I'm a certified nail artist.*

For the life of me—and it really might *be* for the life of me, considering that I was about to plunge into a fire of one kind or another—I didn't know why I should recall Lysette at this juncture.

Her voice haunted me again: *It takes a while to realize what a lonely world it is, and when you do . . . then the future looks kinda scary.*

I took my hand off the knob.

I stepped to one side of the door.

Iron-shod hooves on hard-baked ground could have made no louder thunder than the internal booming of my galloping heart.

My instinct is a winning coach, and when it said *Batter up*, I didn't argue that I wasn't ready for the game. I gripped the bat in both hands, assumed the stance, and said a prayer to Mickey Mantle.

The door opened, and a guy stepped boldly into the corridor. He was dressed in black boots, a lightweight black jumpsuit with hood, a black ski mask, and black gloves.

He carried an assault rifle so big and wicked that it looked as unreal as the weaponry in an early Schwarzenegger movie. From a utility belt hung eight or ten spare magazines.

He looked to his left when he came out of the security room. I stood to his right, but he sensed me at once and in midstep turned his head toward me.

Never one who liked to bunt, I swung hard, high above the strike zone, and hit him in the face.

I would have been surprised if he hadn't gone down cold. I was not surprised.

The corridor was deserted. No one had seen. For the moment.

I needed to handle this as anonymously as possible, to avoid questions later if the chief remained unable to run interference for me.

After rolling the baseball bat into the security room and sliding the assault rifle after it, I grabbed the gunman by the jumpsuit and dragged him in there, too, out of the hallway, and shut the door.

Among overturned office chairs and spilled mugs of coffee, three unarmed security guards lay dead in this bunker. Apparently they had been killed with a silencer-fitted pistol, because the shots had not attracted attention. They looked surprised.

The sight of them tortured me. They were dead because I had been too slow on the uptake.

I know that I'm not responsible for every death I can't prevent. I understand that I can't carry the world on my back, like Atlas. But I *feel* that I should.

Twelve oversize TV monitors, each currently in quartered-screen format, featured forty-eight views provided by cameras positioned throughout the department store. Everywhere I looked, the aisles were busy; the sale had pulled in shoppers from all over Maravilla County.

I knelt beside the gunman and stripped off his ski mask. His nose was broken, bleeding; breath bubbled in the blood. His right eye would probably swell entirely shut. A welt had already begun to form on his forehead.

He wasn't Simon Varner. Before me lay Bern Eckles, the deputy who had been at the barbecue, who had been invited because the chief and Karla Porter had been trying to match him up with Lysette Rains.

CHAPTER 59

BOB ROBERTSON HAD NOT ONE COLLABO-rator but two. Maybe more. They probably called themselves a coven, unless that was only for witches. One more, and they could have a satanic combo, provide their own music for Black Mass, buy group health insurance, get a block discount at Disneyland.

At the chief's barbecue, I'd seen no bodachs around Bern Eckles. Their presence had tipped me to Robertson's nature but not to either of his co-conspirators—which now began to seem intentional. As if they had become aware of my gift. As if they had . . . manipulated me.

After turning Eckles on his side to ensure that he wouldn't choke on his own blood and saliva, I searched for something to tie his hands and feet.

I didn't expect him to regain consciousness within the next ten minutes. When he finally did come around, he would be crawling and puking and begging for painkillers, in no condition to snatch up the assault rifle and return to his mission.

Nevertheless, I disabled two security-room phones and quickly used their cords to bind his hands behind his back and to shackle his ankles. I yanked the knots tight and didn't worry unduly about inhibiting his circulation.

Eckles and Varner were the newest officers on the Pico Mundo Police Department. They had applied and signed up only a month or two apart.

Smart money would take the proposition that they had known each other before they arrived in Pico Mundo. Varner had been hired first and had paved the way for Eckles.

Robertson had moved to Pico Mundo from San Diego and purchased the house in Camp's End ahead of his two collaborators. If my memory could be trusted, Varner had previously been a police officer in the San Diego area if not in the city itself.

I didn't know in what jurisdiction Bern Eckles served before he had signed up with the PMPD. Greater San Diego would be a better bet than Juneau, Alaska.

The three of them had targeted Pico Mundo for reasons impossible to guess. They had planned long and carefully.

When I had gone to the barbecue, suggesting that a background profile on Bob Robertson might be a good idea, the chief had enlisted Eckles's assistance. At that instant, Robertson had been marked for death.

Indeed, he must have been murdered within half an hour. No doubt Eckles had telephoned Varner from the chief's house, and Varner had pulled the trigger on their mutual friend. Perhaps Simon Varner and Robertson had been together when Varner got Eckles's call.

With Eckles securely tied, I unzipped the front of his jumpsuit far enough to confirm that under it he wore his police uniform.

He had come into the security room in his blues and badge. The guards would have greeted him without suspicion.

Evidently he'd carried the assault rifle and the

jumpsuit in a suitcase. A two-suiter lay open and empty on the floor. Samsonite.

The plan had most likely been to go on a shooting spree in the department store and then, as the police arrived, to find a private place to strip out of the jumpsuit and the ski mask. Abandoning the assault rifle, Eckles could mingle with his fellow officers as though responding to the same call that they had received.

The *why* of it wasn't as easy to understand as the *how*.

Some people said that God talked to them. Others heard the devil whispering in their heads. Maybe one of these guys thought Satan had told him to shoot up Green Moon Mall.

Or maybe they were just doing it for fun. A lark. Their religion is tolerant of extreme forms of recreation. Boys will be boys, after all, and sociopathic boys will be sociopathic.

Simon Varner remained on the loose. Maybe he and Eckles had not come to the mall alone. I had no idea how many might be in a coven.

Using one of the working phones, I called 911, reported three murders, and without answering any questions, put the phone down, leaving it off the hook. The police would come, and a SWAT team. Three minutes, four. Maybe five.

That wouldn't be fast enough. Varner would be blasting away at shoppers before they arrived.

The baseball bat hadn't cracked. Good wood.

As effective as the bat had been with Eckles, I couldn't expect to be lucky enough to surprise Varner in the same way. Regardless of my fear of guns, I needed a better weapon than a Louisville Slugger.

On a counter in front of the security monitors lay the pistol that Eckles had used to kill the guards. On inspection, I found that four rounds remained in the ten-shot magazine.

As much as I wanted to avoid looking at them, the dead men on the floor commanded my attention. I hate violence. I hate injustice more. I just want to be a fry cook, but the world demands more from me than eggs and pancakes.

I unscrewed the silencer, tossed it aside. Pulled my T-shirt out of my jeans. Tucked the pistol under my waistband.

Without success, I tried not to think of my mother with the gun under her chin, against her breast. I tried not to remember what the muzzle of that pistol had felt like when she pressed it against my eye and told me to look for the brass of the bullet at the bottom of that narrow bore of darkness.

The T-shirt hid the weapon but not perfectly. Shoppers would be too preoccupied finding bargains and salesclerks would be too busy serving shoppers to notice the bulge.

Cautiously, I opened the door barely wide enough to slip out of the security room, and closed it behind me. A man was walking away from me, in the direction I needed to go, and I followed him, wishing that he would *hurry*.

He turned right, through the swinging doors to the receiving room, and I ran past elevators reserved for company employees to a door labeled STAIRS. I took them two at a time.

Somewhere ahead, Simon Varner. Sweet face. Sleepy eyes. *POD* on his left forearm.

At the first floor of the department store, I left the stairs and pushed through a door into a stockroom.

A pretty redhead was busy pulling small boxes off the packed shelves. She said, "Hey," in a friendly way.

"Hey," I said back at her, and I went out of the stockroom onto the sales floor.

The sporting-goods department. Bustling. Men, a few women, a lot of teenagers. The kids were checking out Rollerblades, skateboards.

Beyond the sporting goods were aisles of athletic shoes. Beyond the shoes, men's sportswear.

People, people everywhere. Too many people too tightly bunched. An almost festive atmosphere. So vulnerable.

If I hadn't waylaid him as he came out of the security room, Bern Eckles would have killed ten or twenty by now. Thirty.

Simon Varner. Big guy. Beefy arms. Prince of Darkness. Simon Varner.

Reliably guided by my supernatural gift as any bat is guided by echolocation, I crossed the first floor of the department store, heading toward the exit to the mall promenade.

I didn't expect to see another gunman here. Eckles and Varner would have chosen widely separated killing fields, the better to sow terror and chaos. Besides, they would want to avoid accidentally straying into each other's fire patterns.

Ten steps short of the promenade exit, I saw Viola Peabody, who was supposed to be at her sister's house on Maricopa Lane.

CHAPTER 60

THE BIRTHDAY GIRL, LEVANNA, AND HER pink-infatuated little sister, Nicolina, were not at their mother's side. I scanned the crowd of shoppers, but didn't see the girls.

When I hurried to Viola and seized her by the shoulder from behind, she reacted with a start and dropped her shopping bag.

"What're you doing here?" I demanded.

"Odd! You scared the salt off my crackers."

"Where are the girls?"

"With Sharlene."

"Why aren't *you* with them?"

Picking up the shopping bag, she said, "Hadn't done birthday shopping yet. Got to have a gift. Came here just quick for these Rollerblades."

"Your dream," I reminded her urgently. "This is your *dream*."

Her eyes widened. "But I'm just in and out quick, and I'm not at the movies."

"It's not going to be at the theater. It's happening *here*."

For an instant her breath caught in her throat as terror cocked the hammers of her heart.

"Get out of here," I said. "Get out of here *now*."

She exhaled explosively, looked wildly around as if any shopper might be a killer, or all of them, and she started toward the exit to the promenade.

"No!" I pulled her close to me. People were looking at us. What did it matter? "It's not safe that way."

"Where?" she asked.

I turned her around. "Go to the back of this floor, through the athletic shoes, through sporting goods. There's a stockroom not far from where you bought the Rollerblades. Go to the stockroom. Hide there."

She started away, stopped, looked at me. "Aren't you coming?"

"No."

"Where are you going?"

"Into it."

"Don't," she pleaded.

"Go now!"

As she moved toward the back of the department store, I hurried out into the mall promenade.

Here at the north end of the Green Moon Mall, the forty-foot waterfall tumbled over a cliff of man-made rocks, feeding the stream that ran the length of the public concourse. As I passed the base of the falls, the rumble and splash sounded uncannily like the roar of a crowd.

Patterns of darkness and light. Darkness and light as in Viola's dream. The shadows were cast by palm trees that rose alongside the stream.

Looking up into the queen palms, up toward the second floor of the promenade, I saw hundreds upon hundreds of bodachs gathered along the balustrade above, peering down into the open atrium. Pressed one against the other, excited, eager, twitching and swaying, squirming like agitated spiders.

A throng of bargain-hunting shoppers filled the first

floor of the promenade, browsing from store to store, unaware of the audience of malevolent spirits that was watching them with such anticipation.

My wonderful gift, my hateful gift, my terrifying gift led me along the promenade, farther south, faster, following the splash and tumble of the stream, in a frantic search for Simon Varner.

Not hundreds of bodachs. Thousands. I'd never seen such a horde as this, never imagined I ever would. They were like a celebratory Roman mob in the Colosseum, watching with delight as the Christians made unanswered prayers, waiting for the lions, for blood on the sand.

I had wondered why they had vanished from the streets. Here was the answer. Their hour had come.

As I passed a bed-and-bath store, the hard chatter of automatic gunfire erupted from the promenade ahead of me.

The first burst proved brief. For two seconds, three, after it ended, an impossible hush fell across the mall.

Hundreds of shoppers appeared to freeze as one. Although surely the water in the stream continued to move, it seemed to spill along its course without sound. I would not have been surprised if my watch had confirmed a miraculous stoppage of time.

One scream tore the silence, and at once a multitude answered it. The gun replied to the screamers with a longer death rattle than the first.

Recklessly, I pushed southward along the promenade. Progress wasn't easy because the panicked shoppers were running north away from the gunfire. People ricocheted off me, but I stayed on my feet, pressing toward a third burst of gunfire.

CHAPTER 61

I WILL NOT TELL EVERYTHING I SAW. I WILL not. Cannot. The dead deserve their dignity. The wounded, their privacy. Their loved ones, a little peace.

More to the point, I know why soldiers, home from war, seldom tell their families about their exploits in more than general terms. We who survive must go on in the names of those who fall, but if we dwell too much on the vivid details of what we've witnessed of man's inhumanity to man, we simply *can't* go on. Perseverance is impossible if we don't permit ourselves to hope.

The panicked throng surged past me, and I found myself among a scattering of victims, all on the ground, dead and wounded, fewer than I expected, but too many. I saw the blond bartender from Green Moon Lanes in her work uniform . . . and three others. Maybe they had come to the mall for lunch before work.

Whatever I am, I am not superhuman. I bleed. I suffer. This was more than I could handle. This was Malo Suerte Lake times ten.

Cruelty has a human heart . . . terror the human form divine.

Not Shakespeare. William Blake. Himself a piece of work.

Scores of bodachs had descended from the upper level of the mall. They were crawling among the dead and wounded.

Whether I could handle this or not, I had no choice but to make the effort. If I walked away, I might as well kill myself right here.

The koi pond lay not far ahead. The man-made jungle surrounded it. I saw the bench on which Stormy and I had sat to eat cones of coconut cherry chocolate chunk.

A man in a black jumpsuit, black ski mask. Big enough to be Simon Varner. Holding an assault rifle apparently modified for full—and illegal—automatic fire.

A few people were hiding among the palm trees, huddled in the koi pond; but most had fled the open promenade for the specialty shops, desperately taking cover there, perhaps hoping to escape by the back doors. Through the windows—jewelry store, gift shop, art gallery, culinary shop—I could see them crowding after one another, still too visible.

In this blood-jaded age that is as violent as video games, the cruel machine language increasingly in common use would refer to this as a target-rich environment.

His back to me, Varner sprayed the fronts of those businesses with bullets. The windows of Burke & Bailey's dissolved, cascaded into the shop in a glittering deluge.

We are destined to be together forever. We have a card that says so. We have matching birthmarks.

Sixty feet from the crazy bastard, then fifty feet and closing, I discovered that I was gripping the pistol. I didn't recall drawing it from my waistband.

My gun hand was shaking, so I held it with both hands.

I'd never used a firearm. I hated guns.

You might as well pull the trigger yourself, you little shit.

I'm trying, Mother. I'm trying.

Varner exhausted the assault rifle's extended magazine. Maybe it was already the second magazine. Like Eckles, he carried spares on a utility belt.

From forty feet, I fired a round. Missed.

Alerted by the crack of the shot, he turned toward me and ejected the depleted magazine.

I fired again, missed again. In the movies they never miss from this distance. Unless it's the hero being shot at, in which case they miss from five feet. Simon Varner was no hero. I didn't know what I was doing.

He did. He plucked a fresh magazine from the utility belt. He was practiced, swift, and calm.

With the pistol I had taken from him, Eckles had used six rounds on the security guards. I had expended two. Only two left.

From about thirty feet, I squeezed off a third shot.

Varner took the hit in his left shoulder, but it didn't drop him. He rocked, he recovered, he jammed the fresh magazine into the rifle.

Jittering, thrashing with excitement, scores of bodachs swarmed around me, around Varner. They were solid to me, invisible to him; they obstructed my view of him but not his view of me.

Earlier in the day, I had wondered if maybe I might be crazy. Issue settled. I am totally bugshit.

Running straight at him, through bodachs as opaque as black satin but as insubstantial as shadows, pistol held out stiff-armed in front of me, determined not to waste my final round, I saw the muzzle of the assault rifle coming up, and I knew that he would cut me down, but I waited one more step, and then one more, before I squeezed the trigger point-blank.

Whatever grotesque transformation occurred in his face, the ski mask concealed it, but the mask couldn't entirely contain the spray. He went down as hard as the Prince of Darkness himself had been cast out of Heaven, into Hell. The weapon clattered out of his hand.

I kicked the assault rifle a few feet away from him, out of his reach. When I stooped to examine him, there was no question that he was carrion. POD was DOA.

Nevertheless, I returned to the rifle and kicked it even farther from him. Then I followed it and kicked it farther still, and again.

The pistol in my hand was useless. I threw it aside.

As if I were suddenly standing on high ground, as if they were black water, the bodachs flowed away from me, seeking the spectacle of dead and dying victims.

I felt as if I might throw up. I went to the edge of the koi pond and dropped to my knees.

Although the motion of the colorful fish ought to have turned me inside out, the nausea passed in a moment. I didn't purge, but as I got to my feet, I started to cry.

Inside the stores, beyond the shot-out windows, people dared to raise their heads.

We are destined to be together forever. We have a card that says so. Gypsy Mummy is never wrong.

Trembling, sweating, wiping tears from my eyes with the backs of my hands, half sick with an expectation of unbearable loss, I started toward Burke & Bailey's.

People had risen to their feet from the ruination in the ice-cream shop. Some began to make their way cautiously across the broken glass, returning to the promenade.

I didn't see Stormy among them. She might have fled back to the storeroom, to her office, when the shooting started.

Suddenly I was overwhelmed by the need to move, move, move. I turned away from Burke & Bailey's and took several steps toward the department store at the south end of the mall. I stopped, confused. For a moment, I thought I must be in denial, that I was trying to run from what I might find in the ice-cream shop.

No. I felt the subtle but unmistakable pull. Psychic magnetism. Drawing me. I'd assumed that I had finished the job. Evidently not.

CHAPTER 62

THIS DEPARTMENT STORE STYLED ITSELF more upscale than the one in which Viola had bought the Rollerblades. The crap they sold here was of a more refined quality than the crap they sold in the store at the north end of the mall.

I passed through a perfume and makeup department with beveled-glass cabinets and glamorous displays that not so subtly implied the merchandise was as valuable as diamonds.

The jewelry department dazzled with black granite, stainless steel, and Starfire glass, as if it offered not common diamonds but baubles from God's own collection.

Although the gunfire had fallen silent, shoppers and employees still sheltered behind counters, behind marble-clad columns. They dared to peek at me as I strode among them, but many flinched and ducked out of sight again.

Even though I didn't have a gun, I must have appeared to be dangerous. Or maybe I only seemed to be in a state of shock. They weren't taking any chances. I didn't blame them for hiding from me.

Still crying, blotting my eyes with my hands, I was also talking aloud to myself. I couldn't *stop* talking to myself, and I wasn't even saying anything coherent.

I didn't know where psychic magnetism might be taking me next, didn't know if Stormy was alive or dead in Burke & Bailey's. I wanted to go back to find her, but I continued to be drawn urgently forward by my demanding gift. My body language was marked by tics, twitches, hesitations, and sudden rushes of new purpose. I must have looked not just spastic but psychotic.

Sweet-faced, sleepy-eyed Simon Varner didn't have such a sweet face anymore, or sleepy eyes. Dead in front of Burke & Bailey's.

So maybe I was tracking something *related* to Varner. I couldn't guess what that might be. This compulsion to keep moving without a clearly defined quarry was new to me.

Among racks of cocktail dresses, silk blouses, silk jackets, handbags, I hurried at last to a door marked EMPLOYEES ONLY. Beyond lay a storeroom. Directly across from the door by which I entered, another led to a concrete stairwell.

The layout was familiar from the department store at the north end of the mall. The stairs led down to a corridor where I passed employee-only elevators and came to oversize swinging doors marked RECEIVING.

This room reflected a thriving enterprise, though it didn't quite equal the size of the one at the north-end store. Merchandise on racks and carts awaited processing, prepping, and transfer to stockrooms and sales floors.

Numerous employees were present, but work appeared to have come to a halt. Most had gathered around a sobbing woman, and others were crossing the room toward her. Down here where no shots could have been heard, news of the horror in the mall had now arrived.

Only one truck stood in the receiving room: not a full semi, about an eighteen-footer, with no company name on the cab doors or the sides of the trailer. I moved toward it.

A burly guy with a shaved head and a handlebar mustache braced me as I reached the vehicle. "Are you with this truck?"

Without responding, I pulled open the driver's door and climbed into the cab. The keys weren't in the ignition.

"Where's your driver," he asked.

When I popped open the glove box, I found it empty. Not even the registration or proof of insurance required by California law.

"I'm the shift foreman here," the burly guy said. "Are you deaf or just difficult?"

Nothing on the seats. No trash container on the floor. No scrap of discarded candy wrapper. No air freshener or decorative geegaw hanging from the mirror.

This didn't have the feel of a truck that anyone drove for a living or in which anyone spent a significant amount of his day.

When I got out from behind the steering wheel, the foreman said, "Where's your driver? He didn't leave me a manifest, and the box is locked."

I went around to the back of the truck, which featured a roll-up door on the cargo trailer. A key lock in the base bar of the door secured it to a channel in the truck bed.

"I've got other shipments due," he said. "I can't let this just sit here."

"Do you have a power drill?" I asked.

"What're you going to do?"
"Drill out the lock."
"You're not the guy drove this in here. Are you his crew?"
"Police," I lied. "Off duty."
He was dubious.
Pointing to the sobbing woman around whom so many workers had now gathered, I said, "You hear what she's been saying?"
"I was on my way over there when I saw you."
"Two maniacs with machine guns shot up the mall."
His face drained of color so dramatically that even his blond mustache seemed to whiten.
"You hear they shot Chief Porter last night?" I asked. "That was prep for this."
With rapidly growing dread, I studied the ceiling of the immense receiving room. Three floors of the department store were stacked on top of it, supported by its massive columns.
Scared people were hiding from the gunmen up there. Hundreds and hundreds of people.
"Maybe," I said, "the bastards came here with something even worse than machine guns."
"Oh, shit. I'll get a drill." He sprinted for it.
After placing both hands flat against the roll-up door on the cargo box for a moment, I then leaned my forehead against it.
I don't know what I expected to feel. In fact, I felt nothing unusual. Psychic magnetism still pulled me, however. What I wanted wasn't the truck but what was *in* the truck.
The foreman returned with the drill and tossed me a pair of safety goggles. Electrical outlets were recessed in the concrete floor at convenient intervals across the

receiving room. He plugged the drill into the nearest of these, and the cord provided more than sufficient play.

The tool had heft. I liked the industrial look of the bit. The motor shrieked with satisfying power.

When I bored into the key channel, shavings of metal clicked off my goggles, stung my face. The bit itself deteriorated, but punched through the lock in mere seconds.

As I dropped the drill and stripped off the goggles, someone shouted from a distance. "Hey! Leave that alone!"

Along the elevated loading dock—no one. Then I saw him. Outside the receiving room, twenty feet beyond the foot of the long truck ramp.

"That's the driver," the foreman told me.

He was a stranger. He must have been watching, perhaps through binoculars, from out in the employee garage, past the three lanes that served the loading docks.

Seizing the two grips, I shoved up the door. Well-oiled and efficiently counterweighted, the panel rose smoothly and quickly out of the way.

The truck was packed with what appeared to be hundreds of kilos of plastic explosive.

A gun cracked twice, one slug cried off the truck frame, people in the receiving room screamed, and the foreman ran.

I glanced back. The driver hadn't come any closer to the foot of the ramp. He had a pistol, maybe not the best weapon for such a long shot.

On the truck bed in front of the explosives were a mechanical kitchen timer, two copper-top batteries, curious bits and pieces that I didn't recognize, and a nest of wires. Two of the wires ended in copper jacks that were plugged into that gray wall of death.

With a shrill kiss of metal on metal, a third shot ricocheted off the truck.

I heard the foreman fire up a nearby forklift.

The coven hadn't rigged the cargo to explode when the door was opened because they had set it on such a short countdown that they didn't think anyone could get at it fast enough to disable it. The timer had a thirty-minute dial, and the ticking indicator hand was three minutes from zero.

Click: two minutes

The fourth shot hit me in the back. I didn't at once feel pain, only the jolting impact, which drove me against the truck, my face inches from the timer.

Maybe it was the fifth shot, maybe the sixth, that slapped into one of the bricks of plastic explosive with a flat, wet sound.

A bullet wouldn't trigger it. Only an electrical charge.

The two detonation wires were set six or eight inches apart. Was one positive and the other negative? Or was one just a backup in case the first wire failed to carry the detonating pulse? I didn't know if I had to yank out just one or both.

Maybe it was the sixth shot, maybe the seventh, that again tore into my back. This time pain hammered me, plenty of it, excruciating.

As I sagged from the brutal impact of the bullet, I seized both wires, and as I fell backward, I jerked them out of the explosives, pulling the timer and the batteries and the entire detonator package with me.

Turning as I fell, I hit the floor on my side, facing the truck ramp. The shooter had ascended farther to get a better shot.

Though he could have finished me with one additional round, he turned away and sprinted down the ramp.

The foreman roared past me and descended the ramp in a forklift, somewhat protected from gunfire by the raised cargo tines and their armature.

I didn't believe that the shooter had fled from the forklift. He wanted to get out of there because he couldn't quite see what I had done to the detonator. He intended to escape the underground docks and the garage, and get as far away as luck allowed.

Worried people hurried to me.

The kitchen timer still functioned. It lay on the floor, inches from my face. *Click*: one minute.

Already my pain was subsiding; however, I was cold. Surprisingly cold. The underground loading docks and the receiving room relied on passive cooling, no air conditioning, yet I was positively chilly.

People were kneeling beside me, talking to me. They seemed to be speaking a host of foreign languages because I couldn't understand what they were saying.

Funny—to be so cold in the Mojave.

I never heard the kitchen timer click to zero.

CHAPTER 63

STORMY LLEWELLYN AND I HAD MOVED on from boot camp to our second of three lives. We were having great adventures together in the next world.

Most were lovely romantic journeys to exotic misty places, with amusing incidents full of eccentric characters, including Mr. Indiana Jones, who would not admit that he was really Harrison Ford, and Luke Skywalker, and even my Aunt Cymry, who greatly resembled Jabba the Hut but was wonderfully nice, and Elvis, of course.

Other experiences were stranger, darker, full of thunder and the smell of blood and slinking packs of bodachs with whom my mother sometimes ran on all fours.

From time to time I would be aware of God and His angels looking down upon me from the sky of this new world. They had huge, looming faces that were a cool, pleasant shade of green—occasionally white —though they had no features other than their eyes. With no mouths or noses, they should have been frightening, but they projected love and caring, and I always tried to smile at them before they dissolved back into the clouds.

Eventually I regained enough clarity of mind to

realize that I had come through surgery and was in a hospital bed in a cubicle in the intensive-care unit at County General.

I had not been promoted from boot camp, after all.

God and the angels had been doctors and nurses behind their masks. Cymry, wherever she might be, probably didn't resemble Jabba the Hut in the least.

When a nurse entered my cubicle in response to changes in the telemetry data from my heart monitor, she said, "Look who's awake. Do you know your name?"

I nodded.

"Can you tell me what it is?"

I didn't realize how weak I was until I tried to respond. My voice sounded thin and thready. "Odd Thomas."

As she fussed over me and told me that I was some kind of hero and assured me that I would be fine, I said, "Stormy," in a broken whisper.

I had been afraid to pronounce her name. Afraid of what terrible news I might be bringing down on myself. The name is so lovely to me, however, that immediately I liked the feel of it on my tongue once I had the nerve to speak it.

The nurse seemed to think that I'd complained of a sore throat, and as she suggested that I might be allowed to let a chip or two of ice melt in my mouth, I shook my head as adamantly as I could and said, "Stormy. I want to see Stormy Llewellyn."

My heart raced. I could hear the soft and rapid *beep-beep-beep* from the heart monitor.

The nurse brought a doctor to examine me. He appeared to be awestruck in my presence, a reaction to which no fry cook in the world is accustomed and with which none could be comfortable.

He used that word *hero* too much, and in my wheezy way, I asked him not to use it again.

I felt crushingly tired. I didn't want to fall asleep before I'd seen Stormy. I asked them to bring her to me.

Their lack of an immediate response to my request scared me again. When my heart thumped hard, my wounds throbbed in sympathy, in spite of any painkillers I was receiving.

They were worried that even a five-minute visit would put too much strain on me, but I pleaded, and they let her come into the ICU.

At the sight of her, I cried.

She cried, too. Those black Egyptian eyes.

I was too weak to reach out to her. She slipped a hand through the bed rail, pressed it atop mine. I found the strength to curl my fingers into hers, a love knot.

For hours, she had been sitting out in the ICU waiting room in the Burke & Bailey's uniform that she dislikes so much. Pink shoes, white socks, pink skirt, pink-and-white blouse.

I told her that this must be the most cheerful outfit ever seen in the ICU waiting room, and she informed me that Little Ozzie was out there right now, sitting on two chairs, wearing yellow pants and a Hawaiian shirt. Viola was out there, too. And Terri Stambaugh.

When I asked her why she wasn't wearing her perky pink cap, she put a hand to her head in surprise, for the first time realizing that she didn't have it. Lost in the chaos at the mall.

I closed my eyes and wept not with joy but with bitterness. Her hand tightened on mine, and she gave me the strength to sleep and to risk my dreams of demons.

Later she returned for another five-minute visit, and

when she said that we would need to postpone the wedding, I pushed to remain on schedule for Saturday. After what had happened, the city would surely cut all red tape, and if Stormy's uncle wouldn't bend church rules to marry us in a hospital room, there was always a judge.

I had hoped that our wedding day would be followed at once by our first night together. The marriage, however, had always been more important to me than the consummation of it—now more than ever. We have a long lifetime to get naked together.

Earlier she had kissed my hand. Now she leaned over the railing to kiss my lips. She is my strength. She is my destiny.

With no real sense of time, I slept on and off.

My next visitor, Karla Porter, arrived after a nurse had raised my bed and allowed me a few sips of water. Karla hugged me and kissed me on the cheek, on the brow, and we tried not to cry, but we did.

I had never seen Karla cry. She is tough. She needs to be. Now she seemed devastated.

I worried that the chief had taken a turn for the worse, but she said that wasn't it.

She brought the excellent news that the chief would be moved out of the ICU first thing in the morning. He was expected to make a full recovery.

After the horror at the Green Moon Mall, however, none of us will ever be as we had been. Pico Mundo, too, is forever changed.

Relieved to know the chief would be okay, I didn't think to ask anyone about my wounds. Stormy Llewellyn was alive; the promise of Gypsy Mummy would be fulfilled. Nothing else mattered.

CHAPTER 64

FRIDAY MORNING, JUST ONE DAY AFTER Chief Porter escaped the ICU, the doctor issued orders for me to be transferred to a private room.

They gave me one of their swanky accommodations decorated like a hotel suite. The same one in which they had let me take a shower when I'd been sitting vigil for the chief.

When I expressed concern about the cost and reminded them that I was a fry cook, the director of County General personally assured me that they would excuse all charges in excess of what the insurance company would be willing to pay.

This hero thing disturbed me, and I didn't want to use it to get any special treatment. Nevertheless, I graciously accepted their generosity because, while Stormy could only visit me in an ordinary hospital room, she could actually move right in here and be with me twenty-four hours a day.

The police department posted a guard in the corridor outside my room. No one posed any threat to me. The purpose was to keep the news media at bay.

Events at the Green Moon Mall had, I was told, made headlines worldwide. I didn't want to see a newspaper. I refused to turn on the TV.

Reliving it in nightmares was enough. Too much.

Under the circumstances, the Saturday wedding finally proved to be impractical. Reporters knew of our plans and would be all over the courthouse. That and other problems proved insurmountable, and we postponed for a month.

Friday and Saturday, friends poured in with flowers and gifts.

How I loved seeing Terri Stambaugh. My mentor, my lifeline when I'd been sixteen and determined to live on my own. Without her, I would have had no job and nowhere to go.

Viola Peabody came without her daughters, insisting that they would have been motherless if not for me. The next day she returned with the girls. As it turned out, Nicolina's love of pink had to do with her enthusiasm for Burke & Bailey's ice cream; Stormy's uniform had always enchanted her.

Little Ozzie visited without Terrible Chester. When I teased him about the yellow pants and the Hawaiian shirt that he'd worn to the ICU, he denied that he would ever "costume" himself in that fashion because such "flamboyant togs" would inevitably make him look even bigger than he was. He did, he said, have *some* vanity. As it turned out, Stormy had made up this colorful story to give me a smile in the ICU when I badly needed one.

My father brought Britney with him, full of plans to represent my story for books, movies, television, and product placements. I sent him away unsatisfied.

My mother did not visit.

Rosalia Sanchez, Bertie Orbic, Helen Arches, Poke Barnet, Shamus Cocobolo, Lysette Rains, the Takuda family, so many others . . .

From all these friends, I could not escape learning

some of the statistics that I preferred not to know. Forty-one people at the mall had been wounded. Nineteen had died.

Everyone said it was a miracle that only nineteen perished.

What has gone wrong with our world when nineteen dead can seem like any kind of miracle?

Local, state, and federal law-enforcement agencies had studied the quantity of plastic explosives in the truck and estimated that it would have brought down the entire department store plus a not insignificant portion of the south side of the mall.

Estimates are that between five hundred and a thousand would have been killed if the bomb had detonated.

Bern Eckles had been stopped before he killed more than the three security guards, but he'd been carrying enough ammunition to cut down scores of shoppers.

At night in my hotel-style hospital room, Stormy stretched out on the bed and held my hand. When I woke from nightmares, she pulled me against her, cradled me in her arms while I wept. She whispered reassurances to me; she gave me hope.

Sunday afternoon, Karla brought the chief in a wheelchair. He understood perfectly well that I would never want to talk to the media, let alone entertain offers for books, movies, and television miniseries. He had thought of many ways to foil them. He is a great man, the chief, even if he did break that Barney the dinosaur chair.

Although Bern Eckles refused interrogation, the investigation into the conspiracy had proceeded rapidly, thanks to the fact that a man named Kevin Gosset, having been run down by a forklift, was talking his hateful head off.

Gosset, Eckles, and Varner had been bent a long time. At the age of fourteen, they developed an interest in satanism. Maybe it was a game for a while. Quickly it grew serious.

On a mutual dare, they killed for the first time when they were fifteen. They enjoyed it. And satanism justified it. Gosset called it "just another way of believing."

When they were sixteen, they pledged to their god that they would go into law-enforcement because it would give them excellent cover and because one of the requirements of a devout satanist is to undermine the trusted institutions of society whenever possible.

Eckles and Varner eventually became cops, but Gosset became a schoolteacher. Corrupting the young was important work, too.

The three childhood pals had met Bob Robertson sixteen months previously through a satanic cult from which they cautiously sought out others with their interests. The cult had proved to be a gaggle of wannabes playing at Goth games, but Robertson had interested them because of his mother's wealth.

Their first intention had been to kill him and his mother for whatever valuables might be in their house—but when they discovered that Robertson was eager to bankroll what he called nasty news, they formed a partnership with him. They murdered his mother, made it appear that she'd died and been all but entirely consumed in an accidental fire—and gave Robertson her ears as a souvenir.

Indeed, the contents of the Rubbermaid containers in Robertson's freezer had come from the collections of Eckles, Varner, and Gosset. Robertson himself had never had the guts to waste anyone, but because of his generosity, they wanted to make him feel like a genuine part of their family.

With Robertson's money behind them, they were full of big plans. Gosset didn't recall who first proposed targeting a town and turning it into Hell on Earth with a series of well-planned horrors, with the cold intention of ultimately destroying it entirely. They checked out numerous communities and decided that Pico Mundo was ideal, neither too large to be beyond ruination nor too small to be uninteresting.

Green Moon Mall was their first target. They intended to murder the chief and parlay the mall disaster—and a list of other complex and Machiavellian moves—into firm control of the police department. Thereafter, the steady destruction of the town would be their sport and their form of worship.

Bob Robertson moved into Camp's End because the neighborhood offered him a low profile. Besides, he wanted to manage his money wisely, to ensure that he could buy as much fun as possible.

By the time Chief Porter got around to telling me and Stormy how he was going to protect me and help me to keep the secret of my sixth sense, his face had grown haggard, and I imagine I looked worse. Through Karla, I'd gotten word to him about Robertson's body out there at the Church of the Whispering Comet, so he'd been able to work that bizarre detail into his cover story. He'd always done well by me in the past, but *this* Porter-spun narrative left me in stunned admiration.

Stormy said it was a work of genius. Clearly, the chief had not been spending *all* his time recuperating.

CHAPTER 65

MY WOUNDS PROVED TO BE NOT AS BAD as I had feared in the ICU, and the doctor discharged me from County General the following Wednesday, one week to the day after the events at the mall.

To foil the media, they had been told that I'd be in the hospital another day. Chief Porter conspired to have me and Stormy conveyed secretly in the department's beige undercover van, the same one from which Eckles had watched Stormy's apartment that night.

If Eckles had seen me leaving, he would have arranged to have me caught in my apartment with the body of Bob Robertson. When I had slipped out the back, he had figured that I must be staying the night with my girl, and eventually he had given up the stakeout.

Leaving the hospital, I had no desire to return to my apartment above Mrs. Sanchez's garage. I'd never be able to use the bathroom there without remembering Robertson's corpse.

The chief and Karla didn't think it was wise to go to Stormy's place, either, because the reporters knew about her, too. Neither Stormy nor I was of a mind to accept the Porters' hospitality. We wanted to be alone, just us, at last. Reluctantly, they delivered us to her place through the alley.

Although we were besieged by the media, the next few days were bliss. They rang the doorbell, they knocked, but we didn't respond. They gathered in the street, a regular circus, and a few times we peeked at these vultures through the curtains, but we never revealed ourselves. We had each other, and that was enough to hold off not merely reporters but armies.

We ate food that wasn't healthy. We let dirty dishes stack up in the sink. We slept too much.

We talked about everything, everything but the slaughter at the mall. Our past, our future. We planned. We dreamed.

We talked about bodachs. Stormy is still of the opinion that they are demonic spirits and that the black room was the gate to Hell, opening in Robertson's study.

Because of my experiences of lost and gained time related to the black room, I have developed a more disturbing theory. Maybe in our future, time travel becomes possible. Maybe they can't journey to the past in the flesh but can return in *virtual* bodies in which their minds are embodied, virtual bodies that can be seen only by me. Me and one long-dead British child.

Perhaps the violence that sweeps our world daily into greater darkness has led to a future so brutal, so corrupt, that our twisted descendants return to watch us suffer, charmed by festivals of blood. The appearance of the bodachs might have nothing to do with what those travelers from the future really look like; they probably pretty much resemble you and me; instead, the bodachs may be the shape of their deformed and diseased souls.

Stormy insists they are demons on a three-day pass from Hell.

I find her explanation less frightening than mine. I wish that I could embrace it without doubt.

The dirty dishes stacked higher. We finished most of the truly unhealthy food and, not wanting to venture out, began to eat more sensible fare.

The phone had been ringing constantly. We'd never taken it off the answering machine. The calls were all from reporters and other media types. We turned the speaker volume off, so we wouldn't have to hear their voices. At the end of each day, I erased the messages without listening to them.

At night, in bed, we held each other, we cuddled, we kissed, but we went no further. Delayed gratification had never felt so good. I cherished every moment with her, and decided that we might have to delay the marriage only two weeks instead of a month.

On the morning of the fifth day, the reporters were rousted by the Pico Mundo Police Department, on the grounds that they were a public nuisance. They seemed ready to go, anyway. Maybe they had decided that Stormy and I weren't in residence, after all.

That evening, as we readied for bed, Stormy did something so beautiful that my heart soared, and I could believe that in time I might put the events at the mall behind me.

She came to me without her blouse, naked from the waist up. She took my right hand, turned it palm up, and traced my birthmark with her forefinger.

My mark is a crescent, half an inch wide, an inch and a half from point to point, as white as milk against the pink flush of my hand.

Her mark is identical to mine except that it is brown and on the sweet slope of her right breast. If I cup her breast in the most natural manner, our birthmarks perfectly align.

As we stood smiling at each other, I told her that I have always known hers is a tattoo. This doesn't trouble me. The fact that she wanted so much to prove that we share a destiny only deepens my love for her.

On the bed, under the card from the fortune-telling machine, we held each other chastely, but for my hand upon her breast.

For me, time always seems suspended in Stormy's apartment.

In these rooms I am at peace. I forget my worries. The problems of pancakes and poltergeists are lifted from me.

Here I cannot be harmed.

Here I know my destiny and am content with it.

Here Stormy lives, and where she lives, I flourish.

We slept.

The following morning, as we were having breakfast, someone knocked on the door. When we didn't answer, Terri Stambaugh called loudly from the hall. "It's me, Oddie. Open up. It's time to open up now."

I couldn't say no to Terri, my mentor, my lifeline. When I opened the door, I found that she hadn't come alone. The chief and Karla Porter were in the hall. And Little Ozzie. All the people who know my secret—that I see the dead—were here together.

"We've been calling you," Terri said.

"I figured it was reporters," I said. "They won't leave me and Stormy alone."

They came into the apartment, and Little Ozzie closed the door behind them.

"We were having breakfast," I said. "Can we get you something?"

The chief put one hand on my shoulder. That

hangdog face, those sad eyes. He said, "It's got to stop now, son."

Karla brought a gift of some kind. Bronze. An urn. She said, "Sweetheart, the coroner released her poor body. These are her ashes."

CHAPTER 66

FOR A WHILE I HAD GONE MAD. MADNESS runs in my family. We have a long history of retreating from reality.

A part of me had known from the moment Stormy came to me in the ICU that she had become one of the lingering dead. The truth hurt too much to accept. In my condition that Wednesday afternoon, her death would have been one wound too many, and I would have let go of this life.

The dead don't talk. I don't know why. So I spoke for Stormy in the conversations that she and I had shared during the past week. I said for her what I knew she wanted to say. I can almost read her mind. We are immeasurably closer than best friends, closer than mere lovers. Stormy Llewellyn and I are each other's destiny.

In spite of his bandaged wounds, the chief held me tightly and let me pour out my grief in his fatherly arms.

Later, Little Ozzie led me to the living-room sofa. He sat with me, tipping the furniture in his direction.

The chief pulled a chair close to us. Karla sat on the arm of the sofa, at my side. Terri settled on the floor in front of me, one hand on my knee.

My beautiful Stormy stood apart, watching. I have never seen on any human face a look more loving than the one with which she favored me in that terrible moment.

Taking my hand, Little Ozzie said, "You know you've got to let her go, dear boy."

I nodded, for I could not speak.

Long after the day of which I now write, Ozzie had told me to keep the tone of this manuscript as light as possible by being an unreliable narrator, like the lead character in Agatha Christie's *The Murder of Roger Ackroyd*. I have played tricks with certain verbs. Throughout, I have often written of Stormy and our future together in the present tense, as if we are still together in this life. No more.

Ozzie said, "She's here now, isn't she?"

"Yes."

"She hasn't left your side for a moment, has she?"

I shook my head.

"You don't want your love for her and hers for you to trap her here when she needs to move on."

"No."

"That's not fair to her, Oddie. Not fair to either of you."

I said, "She deserves . . . her next adventure."

"It's time, Oddie," said Terri, whose memory of Kelsey, her lost husband, is etched on her soul.

Trembling in fear of life without Stormy, I rose from the sofa and hesitantly went to her. She still wore her Burke & Bailey's uniform, of course, without the perky pink hat, yet she had never looked lovelier.

My friends had not known where she stood until I stepped before her and put one hand to her precious face. So warm to me.

The dead cannot speak, but Stormy spoke three

words silently, allowing me to read her lips. *I love you.*

I kissed her, my dead love, so tenderly, so chastely. I held her in my arms, my face buried in her hair, her throat.

After a while, she put a hand under my chin. I raised my head.

Three more words. *Be happy. Persevere.*

"I'll see you in service," I promised, which is what she calls the life that comes after boot camp.

Her eyes. Her smile. Now mine only in memory.

I let her go. She turned away and took three steps, fading. She looked over her shoulder, and I reached out to her, and she was gone.

CHAPTER 67

THESE DAYS I LIVE ALONE IN STORMY'S apartment with her eclectic mix of thrift-shop furniture. The old floor lamps with silk shades and beaded fringes. The Stickley-style chairs and the contrasting Victorian footstools. The Maxfield Parrish prints and the carnival-glass vases.

She never had much in this life, but with the simplest things, she made her corner of the world as beautiful as any king's palace. We may lack riches, but the greatest fortune is what lies in our hearts.

I still see dead people, and from time to time I am required to do something about it. As before, this proactive strategy often results in an unusual amount of laundry.

Sometimes, coming awake in the night, I think I hear her voice saying, *Loop me in, odd one*. I look for her, but she is never there. Yet she is always there. So I loop her in, telling her all that has happened to me recently.

Elvis hangs out with me more than he used to. He likes to watch me eat. I have purchased several of his CDs, and we sit together in the living room, in the low silken light, and listen to him when he was young and alive and knew where he belonged.

Stormy believed that we are in this boot camp to learn, that if we don't persevere through all this world's obstacles and all its wounds, we won't earn our next life of great adventure. To be with her again, I will have the perseverance of a bulldog, but it seems to me that the training is unnecessarily hard.

My name is Odd Thomas. I am a fry cook. I lead an unusual life, here in my pico mundo, my little world. I am at peace.